A shout echoes down the hall. I open my eyes. Two of the *Ranganathan*'s guards top the nearest stair and come charging toward us. I want to call out to them, but my voice isn't working.

The *ḍakait* glances over his shoulder, and then smiles down at me. "Lucky girl."

He pivots away, and in that split second, I see my chance. I can reach out and grab his ankle as he leaps over the twisted metal. I can trip him, cost him precious seconds, and the guards will be on him. I can stop him.

I see my chance, but my hand won't move. I can't make myself reach out. I can't stop him.

The *ḍakait* clears the rubble and is gone. The guards thunder after him. I'm left alone with the sound of the alarms and my own shallow breath.

ALEXANDRA DUNCAN

SOUND

GREENWILLOW BOOKS
An Imprint of HarperCollinsPublishers

Sound

Copyright © 2015 by Alexandra Duncan

All rights reserved. No part of this book may be used or reproduced in any manner whatsoever without written permission except in the case of brief quotations embodied in critical articles and reviews. Printed in the United States of America. For information address HarperCollins Children's Books, a division of HarperCollins Publishers, 195 Broadway, New York, NY 10007.

www.epicreads.com

The text of this book is set in Caslon 540.

Book design by Sylvie Le Floc'h

Library of Congress Cataloging-in-Publication Data
Duncan, Alexandra.
Sound / Alexandra Duncan.
pages cm
Companion to: Salvage.
Summary: "Ava's adopted sister Miyole is finally living her dream as a research assistant on her very first space voyage. But when her ship saves a rover that has been viciously attacked by looters and kidnappers, Miyole—along with a rescued rover girl named Cassia—embarks on a mission to rescue Cassia's abducted brother, and that changes the course of Miyole's life forever"—Provided by publisher.
ISBN 978-0-06-222017-2 (hardback)—ISBN 978-0-06-222018-9 (pbk ed.)
[1. Science fiction. 2. Scientists—Fiction. 3. Lesbians—Fiction.] I. Title.
PZ7.D8946So 2015 [Fic]—dc23 2015019327
16 17 18 19 20 CG/RRDH 10 9 8 7 6 5 4 3 2 1
First paperback edition, 2016

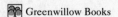 Greenwillow Books

To my mother

The butterflies keep dying. Their gossamer corpses line the back wall of Dr. Osmani's office—spotted swallowtails and dark-tinged bird-wings—all suspended in squat acrylic resin cylinders behind her desk.

"It has to be a genetic disorder." I hold the latest casualty, a common blue, out to Dr. Osmani in my gloved hand. "They can't handle the atmosphere."

She looks up from the clutter of broadscreens, holographic potted plants, and old teacups littering her desk, and prods it with the tip of her stylus. The blue lies lifeless on my palm.

Dr. Osmani presses her lips together, her version of a frown. "How do we know it isn't their caretaker's atmospheric algorithms that are the problem?"

I bunch my free hand inside the front pocket of my lab coat and raise my eyes to the rotating model of the doctor's prize show horse, Trafalgar, that occupies the top of the supply closet. Of course Dr. Osmani would blame me. Otherwise, her own genetic engineering would be at fault.

"The bees are healthy," I point out. I make myself unclench my hand and gingerly slide the blue back into its clear plastic carrying pouch.

"The bees aren't at issue here." Dr. Osmani shoots me a look that would have frozen me in the first months I was assigned to her. Even her high, sleek chignon looks as if it's glaring down at me.

"Do you want my charts?" I fight the urge to cross my arms. I never cared much for entomology before getting this assignment, but now I love all my pollinators— Lepidoptera and Anthophila alike. I spent my first few weeks aboard memorizing their names. *Brenthis daphne*, with wings like stained glass. *Euthalia nais*, black and gold like a tiger. *Bibasis sena*, all lavender gray except for a line of orange running along the edge of its wings like fire. The first time Dr. Osmani tried to blame me for the butterflies' failure to thrive, I thought she was right. My body filled up with shame so cold it burned. Could I really have caused them to die? I was so careful. But after I checked and double-checked my numbers, and the accusations kept coming, that shame curdled into indignation.

"I'm not treating them any less carefully than the bees." I say. "I can prove it."

"Let's see the charts, then." She holds out her hand.

I falter. In my hurry to show Dr. Osmani the blue, I left my handbook with my charts in the pollinators' simulation lab. "I . . . um . . . don't have them with me."

Her face goes hard as our ship's nacre. She sighs. "And where, pray tell, is your book?"

"In the sim lab?" I know exactly where it is, but when I'm nervous, everything I say tends to come out a question.

"Fine." She raises her hands in surrender and turns back to her array of screens. "Send me the charts. We'll see what's there."

I roll my eyes. It's not that I mean to, it's more that it happens without me thinking about it and I don't catch myself in time. My algorithms are solid.

"I saw that, Guiteau," Dr. Osmani says without looking up.

Chaila, I curse silently. When I get nervous, I tend to get "cheeky," as my foster mother, Soraya, says, which is a nicer way of saying "smart-ass." She's been trying to wean me off my eye-rolling habit ever since I came to live with her, but she hasn't been entirely successful. If I were back home, she would apologize for me, or my sister, Ava, would kick my shin to remind me to do it myself, but both of them are hundreds of thousands of kilometers away by now.

Dr. Osmani raises her cool glare at me. "How old are you, Specialist Guiteau?"

The old scars on my palms itch. Dr. Osmani has my records at her fingertips. She trots out questions like these only when she wants to make a point.

"Eighteen." The lie comes naturally now. Eighteen is the youngest you can be and still qualify to serve on a Deep Sound research and development vessel like ours, the R.S.S. *Ranganathan*. At times like these, I wish I had made myself older when I had my papers altered, but even as tall as I am, I doubt anyone would have believed that.

Dr. Osmani folds her arms and leans over her desk. "You're not some coddled preparatory school student anymore, Ms. Guiteau. Up here, you're a scientist. Do try to act the part."

Heat surges up my cheeks, and my eyes burn. Until now, Dr. Osmani has been one of the few crew members who hasn't said a word about my schooling. The flight crew especially likes to needle me for having attended Revati Academy, one of Mumbai's best private schools for girls, and even some of the other research assistants let out a low whistle when I tell them where I studied. No matter how hard I worked at Revati, how I gave up friendships, parties, and weekends to finish my secondary studies so early. No matter that the way I ended up going there in the first place was less than pretty. I'm automatically a spoiled brat for having gotten my education there.

"Right." I nod, fighting the raging fire under my cheeks. I am not going to cry in front of Dr. Osmani. I won't. "Okay."

Dr. Osmani seems done with me, so I stuff my hands in my coat pockets and slink for the door.

"Guiteau?"

I stop and turn on my heel.

She points to my bulging pocket.

"Oh." I double back and hold out the blue.

"Thank you." She takes the bag from me and then pulls a pair of long pincers from her desk drawer. "That will be all."

I hurry from the room, but not in time to avoid seeing Dr. Osmani lift the blue from its pouch and gently position it in a thermoplastic mold. Another specimen for her collection.

Outside her office, the corridor teems with people—

engineers, techs, and research assistants dodging through the crowd with handbooks held tight against their chests; flight crews snorting with laughter as they head back from their latest watch; and maintenance and operations workers trundling equipment carts along the moving sidewalks that ferry everyone along. Perfect conditions for disappearing.

I hurry onto the walkway. It whisks me forward, on trajectory for the heart of the ship. The *Ranganathan* is one of the largest research vessels in service, a kilometers-long conch shape spiraling through the depths of space. It's large enough to create its own gravity field as it rotates, and it docks its own fleet of smaller ships for short-range research missions and defense. Dr. Osmani's bioengineering project is only one of thousands inching toward completion in the *Ranganathan*'s laboratories. When she's done, we should have several hardy permutations of bees and other pollinators well suited to the harsh conditions down on the moons and planets we're terraforming for our colonists.

But not butterflies, apparently. Not unless we can figure out what's wrong with them.

I step to the right of the moving path, pull off my gloves, and scratch. A thick, pink-white scar cuts across each palm, obscuring my hands' natural lines and making it impossible for any of Mumbai's street-corner fortune-tellers to read my future. I close my eyes and lean against the handrail, letting the lights from the nature scenes glowing on the wall wash over me. No way am I running all the way to the simulation lab to fetch my handbook so I can play Dr. Osmani's scapegoat for the rest of the afternoon. She's probably forgotten about me anyway.

Not that I don't like my work; I do. Observing the pollinators' behavior, watching for patterns, trying to predict what will help them thrive—I love it all. Seeing a hypothesis come to life is electric. And this position is my path to my own research lab someday, my own experiments. But lately I've started to wonder if it's worth it. I thought I would fit in here better than I did at home in Mumbai. I thought I would be surrounded by people like me, people who understood me. But no. No matter where I go, there's something different about me. I'm too young. I don't look Indian. I can't take a joke.

"Have you had your potassium today?" My wrist coms pipe up in a friendly voice that reminds me of Shushri Advani, the horseback riding instructor back at Revati. *A proper electrolyte balance is vital for maintaining a healthy heart and musculature.*

"Not now, Advani-ji," I mutter, and switch her to

mute. Our coms and pressure suits link together to monitor our heart rate, neural patterns, and respiration for signs of distress. Which would be great, except Advani-ji can't always tell the difference between a potassium deficiency and annoyance.

Around me, the walls and ceiling cycle through scenes from home. A young wood, wet with dew and bathed in green-gold light, springs up alongside the moving path. Ivy rustles, birds sing, and parrot-bright shapes flash among the boughs. Every now and then, I catch a glimpse of a meadow between the leafy branches. You could almost imagine you were back on Earth, if it weren't for the slightly sterile smell. Some of my tension slides away.

"Hey, *memsahib*." Someone bumps me from behind. "Riding the path like the rest of us? Where's your horse?"

I stiffen and quickly shove my hands in my pockets. I don't have to turn around to know it's Hayden Rubio. The sharp, piney scent of his cologne gives him away. I should never have admitted to taking riding lessons at Revati, but that was before I knew the flight crew couldn't be trusted—especially pretty, green-eyed, tousle-haired Rubio.

I turn, groping in my pockets for my gloves, and give him my best imitation of Dr. Osmani's Penetrating Stare of Doom. "Rubio."

"Memsahib Guiteau." He presents me with an elaborate bow.

I raise my eyes to the false blue sky and sigh. The whole memsahib bit is something he picked up from one of those old movies about the British occupation of India, full of fainting, flushed white ladies decked out in neck-high lace and parasols. How he got from them to me, a dark-skinned girl with a sensible braid and a lab coat, I don't know.

"What?" He elbows me. "Is Our Lady of the Bees too good to talk to me?"

"Shut it, Rubio." I manage to wriggle into one glove.

"She speaks!" He clutches his chest. "My heart. It cannot withstand the magnificence. . . ."

I turn my back on him and try to tug on the other glove. I'm not letting Rubio get to me today. I'm just going to ride the path, and eventually he'll go away.

He bumps me again. "So, *memsahib*—"

My pinkie and ring finger catch in the same hole. "I swear, Rubio, call me that one more time and I'll make you wish you'd been born without a tongue."

The first time I met him, Rubio wouldn't believe I came from Mumbai. He and his flight squad were younger than my fellow research assistants, around the age my papers said I was, and less prone to reading through meals. I was tired of eating in silence, so I carried my tray to the far end of their table in the mess during our second week of flight.

He called down the table to me. "Hey, you. Lab girl."

I looked up and raised my eyebrows. "Me?"

"Yes, you."

I grimaced. "I have a name, you know."

"Yeah? Care to tell us what it is?"

"Miyole," I said.

"Miyole what?"

"Guiteau."

"Miyole Guiteau?" My name sounded flat and nasal the way he said it. He raised his eyebrows and popped a chunk of fried potato into his mouth. "What's that, French or something?"

"Haitian," I corrected. My mother's ancestral home may have been swallowed by the rising oceans, but she taught me where my name came from. That much I remembered about her, at least.

Rubio scoffed. "Yeah, right. And I boarded in Atlantis."

"What's that supposed to mean?"

"Haiti." Rubio took another bite and waved his fork at me. "Not real."

I stared at him, dumbfounded. "Are you serious?"

"He means not anymore," one of the other boys put

in. "What with it being drowned and all."

"That doesn't mean it's not real." I dropped my fork in my bowl of vegetable biryani, no longer hungry. This wasn't the first time I'd been told my mother's land didn't exist. It had happened at Revati. And at the stables. And even at the university. "That's where my mother's people were from. Originally, I mean."

"How'd you end up in Mumbai, then?" one of the girls—British, by the sound of her—asked.

"I—" I started to answer, but Rubio cut me off.

"You don't look Indian, either. Don't they mostly have lighter skin than you?"

I rolled my eyes. "No." How could this *badirchand* end up on an Indian research ship and not know the first thing about the country?

"Rubio, don't be such an ass," the British girl said.

"Sorry." Rubio held up his hands in mock apology.

I narrowed my eyes at him.

"I'm sorry, it's just you don't really sound Indian, either." Rubio shrugged. He turned to the others. "You know Sunita? From B Squad? She's from Mumbai, and she doesn't sound anything like that."

"Sunita's from Chennai," the first boy said.

I cleared my throat, drawing their attention back to

me. "I was going to say, I'm adopted." I glared at Rubio. "I've lived in Mumbai since I was eight. I'm as much a Mumbaikar as anyone."

"Well, pardon me, *memsahib*," Rubio said, soaking every word in sarcasm. Everyone laughed, and the name stuck.

After that, I went back to eating with the other research assistants and their handbooks. Better to be ignored than mocked.

The scene changes. The forest fades, and suddenly we're skimming a ridge above a series of rolling hills topped by windmills. A sun-bleached town nestles in the valley below. I finally work my hand into the glove.

Rubio leans on the walkway's handrail. "Not much of a sense of humor on you, is there, Guiteau?"

I stare down at the village. "I guess not."

"I'm going to figure you out one day." He tosses his soft brown hair and shakes a finger at me in mock admonition.

"Try not to strain yourself," I mutter, and push myself into the flow of people hurrying down the walkway to our left.

I stride along, scenes flipping rapidly on the walls around me—a cobbled street lined with wrought-iron lampposts, a summer garden bright with tinkling fountains, a quaint neighborhood catching the earliest sun in the solar arrays on its rooftops. Stupid Rubio. I look back to make sure he isn't following me.

What is it with boys like him? All they know how to do is cut you down. Back in Mumbai, I kept my head in my studies like Soraya said, skipped all the parties down in the Salt, and ignored the knot of boys and girls clustered outside Revati's gates after school—all so I could make my way here. And for what? So some swoop-haired *dhakkan* can haunt my every move, making smart-ass comments? This isn't what I signed up for.

Suddenly the arched walls give way, and the roof opens up to a high, vaulted view of the stars above. The walking path slows to a crawl as we approach a rolling, grassy expanse dotted with real wood park benches and topiary bushes cut in the shapes of ostriches, elephants, and jumping dolphins. The upper recreation gardens.

"Chaila," I curse. In my fog of pissed-offedness, I've ridden the path too far. The sim labs are back the way I came.

I turn around, find the right stop for the sim labs, and stalk through the observation areas, past anonymous researchers in white full-body anticontamination suits that cover everything but the small oval of their faces. The assistants in the outer labs raise their heads as I breeze past, but none of them waves or says hello. Maybe if we all weren't so socially awkward, we would have started greeting one another during our first week out of dock. But we didn't, and now it would be even more uncomfortable to start. Just as well. I head for the sanctuary of my lab. Well, really Dr. Osmani's lab, but she hasn't set foot in the place since our second week out of orbit, when she turned habitat maintenance over to me.

I key in my entry code and duck into the darkened room. The outer door slides into place behind me with a solid *click*. The world goes quiet. I lean against the door and close my eyes, breathe it in. This room is where everything makes sense, where everything follows a predictable pattern. It feels more like home than any other place on the ship, even the recreation gardens with their greenways and parks.

The lights flicker on. I blink and shrug out of my lab coat, drop it on the metal work desk next to my handbook, and pull off my gloves. The lights stagger on in the glass simulation chambers, too, illuminating two habitats Dr. Osmani and I have tweaked to perfectly replicate the conditions our specimens will face once they're delivered to the colonies. On the left, lush palms and hyacinths press against the sweating glass, and vines and moss have already begun to creep up the trees. The chamber on the right is mostly bare, the glass cold to the touch. Low-growing juniper bushes feather across the rocky soil, and the blue flax bobs as the bees come to rest on its blooms. Each chamber is its own slice of world, perfectly re-created.

I check the temperatures and gas balances—chamber two needs another 0.78 parts per million of nitrogen—and program the misters to deliver the evening dose of nutrient rain. Then I lock the outer door, push a desk chair against the wall, and climb up into my favorite spot in the whole ship.

Ships like the *Ranganathan* are grown, not built, which means the occasional imperfection. My lab is one such anomaly. The ceiling curves overhead on one side, cut by a ledge about two meters off the floor. If you shove a chair underneath and boost yourself up, you find an alcove hollowed out of the wall. At the far end of the alcove, a wedge-shaped viewport looks out on the endless expanse of space rushing by.

I crawl inside and scoot close to the window. I even sleep here sometimes, when my bunkmates bring boys or girls back to our room for the evening.

I pull off my standard-issue slippers, lean against the

pillow I borrowed from one of the crew lounges, and wrap my old sari around me like a blanket. It was one of the few keepsakes from home I was allowed to bring—the first sari Soraya ever bought for me. I only have to run my fingers over the threadbare blue silk and embroidered horses parading around the hem, and I'm back in that Mumbai shop with the old-fashioned wooden floors, twirling in my new clothes.

Soraya beams and claps for me. *Oh, we must get you that one. It's perfect on you. Isn't it perfect on her, Ava?*

And then the shop lady, holding up another shimmering swath of cloth next to my face.

Yes, yes, that one, too.

That feeling—so light, and everyone smiling, pleased and unworried for once. Even Ava, who was always fretting over money, smiled. And I wore my new sari home on the train.

"Feeling down?" Advani-ji asks kindly. "Vitamin D infusions can combat feelings of depression. . . ."

"Hush." I hit the mute button on my coms again.

I stare out at the distant glimmer of stars. This is the real reason I signed on. There is no thrill like this on Earth. The depths look so perfectly still, and yet I know they're alive with radiation, dust, and dark matter. Gravitational fields form tides around stars and pull their satellites along in the eddies. I can feel something moving out there, and moving in me, as if I am a bell sounding with some unseen resonance. I know that's scientifically inaccurate. There's not enough matter out there to transmit sound or sensation across the emptiness, but I feel its tug all the same.

Something gives, like an ice floe breaking free from a glacier, and I waver on the cusp of remembering. Images flicker and flee behind my eyes—a red kite, a black bantam hen strutting on a white-hot roof, a barefoot boy running before me. They're all there, waiting in a dark little box in my mind, spring-loaded. But do I want to let them out?

When I was little, Ava used to take me down to the *gaats* once a year to light a candle in a little paper boat for my mother. *To remember her,* Ava said. But to remember her means remembering what I lost—the kite, the hen, her. It means risking the quicksand that could suck me down if I'm not careful, if I remember too long, too much. It means risking the small, ungrateful thought that always comes gnawing: *Why didn't my mother stay in the pilot's seat when the wave came? Why didn't she send Ava down to rescue me instead? Why couldn't my mother have been the one to survive?*

I reach into my lab coat pocket and pull out my old handheld crow. It's next to useless here, away from Earth and its satellites, or any of the people I might want to message, but there is one thing it can still do. I pull up the recordings saved on it, and find the one I want. Maybe today will be the day. Maybe today I'll make it all the way through.

Ava's face appears on the screen, her dark hair swinging in a sharp, neat line at her chin. She wears the weather-worn jacket my mother gave to her before she died, and a stack of bangles on her wrist. Ava isn't my real sister, but my mother took her in when she was sick and had nowhere else to go. My chest aches at the sight of her. I shouldn't think those things. Ava loves me. She took care of me after the storm. If it weren't for her, I never would have met Soraya or grown up with everything I could possibly want. I wish I could talk to her now. She'd tell me what to do about Dr. Osmani, or at least agree with me about what a bloody *kuttiya* she's being, and she'd know exactly the right words to dispatch Rubio.

"Hey, Miyole." Ava tucks her hair behind her ears and leans closer to the camera. Behind her, her husband, Rushil, passes by in the kitchen, humming the tune to some old movie the two of them love. "Congratulations on getting into the DSRI. I know you've been aiming for it ever since you were a smallgirl, and Rushil and I, we're some proud of you."

Rushil sticks his head out of the kitchen to wave. "Hi, Miyole!"

Ava smiles over her shoulder at him, and then turns back to the camera. "Anyway, I know this means we won't see you again for a while, so I wanted you to have this." Her face goes serious. "It's a recording I found in my sloop's memory files earlier this year. I didn't know when to give it to you, exactly. I was thinking maybe when you turned eighteen, but with you going away, now seems like the right time."

She leans forward to switch off the camera's eye, and then pauses. "We love you, Miyole. I know if your mother were here, she'd be proud of you, too."

The screen goes black and silent, and then a rush of static kicks in, steady as monsoon rain. I know what's coming next, but something hard lodges in my throat anyway, and suddenly I'm less certain I can listen at all.

"Vector five, verified," a woman's voice reaches through the static. "Requesting landing coordinates."

My mother, Perpétue. When the hurricane came to our home in the Gyre, Ava spotted me and my friend Kai on our neighbor's widow's walk and held the sloop steady in the air while my mother climbed down to us. But then the waves came higher and harder. My mother saw the wall of water bearing down on us and pushed me up our ship's emergency ladder first, but not in time for everyone. The waves pulled her down, and Kai, too. All my nightmares end that way, with a rogue wave and someone or something I love sucked under.

Silence on the recording, and then: "Coordinates received. Sector B-point-294, field Delta. Assuming approach pattern."

We searched for my mother after the storm, but we couldn't find her. The whole Gyre had been swallowed by the waves. I used to think that meant my mother might still be alive somewhere, floating on a half-sunk pontoon or lying in some Pacific recovery ward, waiting for her memory to return. But I see those thoughts for what they are now—childish fantasies. The first time I heard my mother's voice on this recording, bits of memory I didn't know I had forgotten came surging up at me. My mother's uneven gait on the stairs, and an unmoored surge of joy and expectation. The buttery aroma of roast nuts in a paper bag. My mother cracking their shells with the flat of her knife. And I remembered what I knew all along—that if she was alive, she would have found me.

The lump in my throat expands, and I break out in a cold sweat. Something moves deep in my brain. I want to forget, but the feeling is there in my blood and bones, my long-untrodden neural pathways. I try to make myself breathe, but I can't. My palms burn where I cut them clinging to the emergency ladder. Panic swells in me, a great wall of dark water rising and rising until there is no sky. *It's not real*, I tell myself. But it is. It's inside me, always, guarding the passage back to my childhood and the Gyre, waiting to drown me if I stray too close.

I stop the recording, breathing hard.

I unclench my hands. My scars are still there, slick with sweat, not blood. It's too much. I bury my nose in the sari. It's better—easier—to be Soraya's daughter, the Mumbai private-school girl who rides horses for sport and spends her evenings studying for exams. Then I can remember Rushil teaching me how to swing a cricket bat at Shivaji Park and the sound of Soraya's old-fashioned teakettle, not my *manman* braiding my hair or rubbing lotion into her elbows before bed, not the bright and glassy sea after the storm.

THMP.

I jerk my head up. *That noise.* It takes a few breathless seconds for my mind to travel back to the present. *Something hit the viewport.*

My heart speeds to a steady pound. I lean forward. The viewport's glass is clear, triple-paned, and incredibly strong. Like the rest of the ship, it's made of a self-sealing nacre bioengineered to mimic the cellular structure of a mollusk shell. I don't see a scratch on it. In fact, I don't see anything but stars and the velvet emptiness of space. I crane my head down, trying for a different view. Nothing. I press my temple against the glass and strain my eyes up to check the vector above us.

And then I see it—a tangle of beacon lights and metal floating above us, and a fine, icy cloud pouring into the black. I can't process what it is at first.

Air, it comes to me. *That's a ship, venting air.*

For a few seconds I can't breathe, can't react. I can only watch the strange vessel hemorrhaging in the eerie silence.

The *Ranganathan's* alarm blares to life. The overhead lights cut out and emergency lamps snap on, yellow, in their place. I freeze, as though a deadly current has run through my body, locking my muscles in place. Some part of me is back on the ladder in the midst of the hurricane, my mother screaming for me to climb.

"ATTENTION, ATTENTION. CODE BLACK," a woman's calm voice carries over the insistent whine of the alarms. "ALL FIRST RESPONSE TEAMS TO STATIONS. ALL OTHER CREW MEMBERS,

PLEASE PROCEED TO INNER ZONES. REPEAT, CODE BLACK."

That's me. I'm supposed to be a first responder. But I can't peel myself away from the window. The wave is coming. Lights of one of our security squadrons rush into view as the fighters scramble around the venting hulk. Part of the wreck separates from itself, scattering debris like petals. I breathe in sharp. *That ship is breaking apart.* But then the detached half fires its engines, finally illuminating the scene enough so I can see what's truly happening.

The battered piece of silica and metal venting its precious air is a Rover ship, and the other, the one wheeling around to face our fighters, is a stripper ship, the kind that preys on smaller, unallied vessels. Two of its mates light up against the darkness and silently maneuver into place at its flanks. *Dakait.* Pirates.

CHAPTER • 2

I run through the echoing corridors, bare feet slapping, my lab coat and gloves forgotten, my med kit in my hands. For once, Advani-ji stays silent. Emergency lights flash yellow against the walls.

"CODE BLACK, CODE BLACK. PLEASE REMAIN CALM. PROCEED WITH CAUTION TO THE NEAREST SECURE LOCATION."

I fly down the path to the hangar bay. If the fighters can tow in the dying Rover ship, that's where they'll take it. How much air do they have left? I turn up the volume on my coms and select the first response frequency. "Casualties expected," a woman's voice intones. "All medical personnel required."

"The volume of a cylinder is equal to its height times radius squared times pi," I recite. Formulas sometimes help me keep my limbic system in check. If I can think about the volume of the Rover ship's air reserves, I don't have to think about—

The wall to the left of me explodes. The corridor crackles with bursts of light as the wall screens shatter. An avalanche of rubble tumbles down, chunks of the *Ranganathan*'s living skin ripped free. I don't recall falling, or even stopping, but I'm on the floor, shielding my face. And then the rumbling stops, and the only sound is the alarm blaring on behind the ringing in my ears. I raise my head. Dust hangs in the air. An enormous hunk of metal has pierced the ship's outer wall and driven itself through the screens. It takes me a moment to recognize it. One of our fighters.

"Breach, potential casualty, sim lab level, main corridor," I say into my coms, even though my voice is shaking and I'm not sure they're still working. Advani-ji emits a low, steady groaning noise that raises the hair on my arms.

I clamber up the hill of debris, slipping and nearly slicing my arm open on a shard of wallscreen, until I reach the cockpit. Powdered bits of the *Ranganathan*'s nacre cloud the windows. I hesitate. Someone could be in there. Rubio, maybe. I don't want to find him dead inside this fighter.

I rub at the dust with my sleeve and peer in through the cockpit window. Empty. The eject lever has been pulled, and the seat itself, with its temporary life-support systems, is gone. I let myself breathe and immediately cough. A fine powder still fills the air, giving the corridor the unreal air of a misty Mumbai night. All around me, a crinkling-crackling sound rises. Tiny fissures in the walls disappear, and then a shiny, translucent layer of nacre begins to creep out from the crash site and up from the floor, sealing the fighter and all the rubble beneath it. The *Ranganathan* has begun to scar over.

My coms babble with digital static. "Casualty report received," I make out. "Dispatching first response team."

"Cancel," I say back. My knees have begun to tremble. I want to sit down next to a clear stretch of wall, but I know if I do, I won't get up again. Some other responder will have to take care of me instead of doing her job. "No casualties found. Breach countermeasures in effect."

I check myself over. No major injuries, just smudges of ash on my clothes and dust in my hair. My feet are a mess of tiny cuts and powdered nacre caked with blood. I should have been wearing my lab slippers, but they would have been ripped to shreds all the same. If I had been in the same spot a mere second earlier, I would have been crushed beneath the ship.

The floor beneath me tremors, and the remaining lights flicker.

"SURFACE BREACH. CODE BLUE, UPPER RECREATION LEVEL." The calm warning voice returns. "CAUTION. PRESSURE SUIT USE ADVISED."

Surface breach. For a moment, I think that's my report, scrambled in the relay, but no. *Code blue.* That means critical damage, affecting respiration systems. It's a different breach altogether. I turn in place. My pressure suit and helmet are back in the lab, equidistant from the hangar. If I turn back, I might not make it to my post.

During my last year at Revati, a crack formed in the seawall above East Mumbai and flooded the transit lines. Twenty-nine people died in lev train crashes. Another fifteen drowned. Hundreds more ended up in makeshift field hospitals on roofs and train platforms. I wanted to help. I wanted to give blood, but the emergency relief volunteers wouldn't let me, because I was a kid. And Soraya wouldn't let me go down to the field hospitals, even though she went herself. All I could do was sit at home watching the feeds, wishing I could seal up that crack in the wall and staunch the world's hurt with my own blood.

I know what I have to do now.

The wreckage blocks my way, so I double back, find the nearest stair, and hurry up it to one of the sublevel access passages we use to transfer volatile or delicate materials we don't want to risk taking through the main corridor. The floor is cold on my bare feet. The alarm still sounds, but the lights hold steady, illuminating the curve of the shell-gray walls. Ahead, I spot something blocking part of the hall.

I slow. Another piece of the crashed fighter? It's metal, but too mangled to identify. The nacre scarring is further along, coalescing into something slick and pearlescent. Behind me, a footstep scuffs the floor. I turn just in time to duck the butt of a slug gun. Adrenaline floods my system, flowing like hot iron through my limbs. I drop to the deck and crawl backward on my elbows until I hit the wreckage. A man stands over me, tall and thickset in patchwork body armor, his straight blond hair pulled back in a topknot. A *dakait*.

He raises the gun like a bludgeon. There's not time to think, nowhere to dodge with my back against the fighter's remains. I turn my face to the wall. *Force equals mass times acceleration. Force equals mass times acceleration. . . .*

A shout echoes down the hall. I open my eyes. Two of the *Ranganathan*'s guards top the nearest stair and come

ALEXANDRA DUNCAN

charging toward us. I want to call out to them, but my voice isn't working.

The *dakait* glances over his shoulder, and then smiles down at me. "Lucky girl."

He pivots away, and in that split second, I see my chance. I can reach out and grab his ankle as he leaps over the twisted metal. I can trip him, cost him precious seconds, and the guards will be on him. I can stop him.

I see my chance, but my hand won't move. I can't make myself reach out. I can't stop him.

The *dakait* clears the rubble and is gone. The guards thunder after him. I'm left alone with the sound of the alarms and my own shallow breath.

I hyperventilate. I shake. And then I get to my feet again, because I'm still needed.

I meet one of the guards running back to me, empty-handed.

"You all right, Specialist?" he asks.

I nod. My mouth is dry. "He got away?" I ask, even though I already know the answer.

The guard shakes his head. "They're brazen. Trying to board us . . ." He looks over his shoulder, wide-eyed. He's skinny, with close-cut black hair, barely older than I am.

"They had a bore ship. Drove it into the ceiling above the upper recreation gardens."

"*Chaila,*" I whisper. The *dakait* have to be mad, thinking they can take a DSRI ship. But even as I think that, I remember reading a news story back in Mumbai about a group of *dakait* taking control of a government supply ship for several hours before security forces regained control. The threat is real enough that we have our own fighters and guards.

"You sure you're all right?" the guard asks.

"Yes." I try to swallow. "I'm okay."

The guard straightens his back. "We'll rout them, Specialist. Don't worry. Find yourself a pressure suit and stay out of sight. It won't be long now."

I nod, but as soon as he's out of sight, I tuck my med kit under my arm and make my way forward through the access passage. If what I've seen is any clue, they'll need all the medics they can get in the hangar bay.

The hangar is chaos. Emergency crews teem across the floor, lugging chemical dousers and running gurneys. The Rover ship hunkers in the middle of the dock, leaking smoke from the gashes in its skin. A trio in maintenance jumpsuits leans a whining metal saw into the ship's damaged hatch, trying to pry it open and release any survivors. White-hot sparks spout up and scatter embers across the floor. The thick chemical stink of smoldering metal and plastic burns in my nose.

I adjust my grip on my med kit and scan the crowd for the first response captain's red-and-yellow vest, but all I see are standard-issue white suits. I should jump in and help, but where? Do I grab one of the chemical dousers and help suffocate the flames? Join the medics hurriedly prepping burn salves and oxygen tanks? Elbow through the crowd to one of the guards standing shell-shocked with bloodstains all over his uniform?

The saw changes pitch and grinds to a halt. A shout goes up from the cluster of workers around the Rover's door. I finally spot the deck captain.

"Move back!" She waves her arms at us. "Everyone, move back! Fire crews only!"

The hatch tips to the floor with a heavy clang, and an avalanche of gray smoke pours from the ragged opening, up into the dock's rafters. The fire crew races to the ship. The responders with the dousing tanks don't stop, but the rest of us freeze, holding our breath and waiting for the fire crew to reemerge. Seconds pass. Thirty. Sixty. Ninety.

Then we see them. First, a thin young man in a too-large shirt and vest. For a moment, I think his hair is gray, but then I realize it's soot. It covers every inch of him. The medics nearest the hatch reach up to help him down, and he stares out at us, disoriented, eyes red in his gray face. Next a woman clutching a screaming baby, then an older, bearded man leaning heavily on one of the fire crew and cradling his left eye. Last, a girl my age spills out, carrying a limp toddler in her arms.

"Help her!" she shouts as the nearest medics rush to them. "She's not breathing."

I hurry forward. I don't know how exactly my med kit full of fast-compression bandages and I are planning to help, but I'll figure that out when I get there. The other medics swarm around the survivors, holding breathing masks to their faces and ripping open packages of skinknit bandages to cover their burns. I've almost reached the girl when someone cries out in surprise. A small gray-and-black blur bolts from the ship and hits the deck, parting the crowd in front of me. It skitters straight between my boots and streaks away.

"Someone catch that animal!" the deck captain shouts.

No one moves. We haven't drilled for this.

"You." The deck captain locks eyes with me and points.

"Go after it. I want that thing quarantined."

"Me?" I glance over at the gurney where two other medics are fitting an oxygen mask over the toddler's small, soot-streaked face. One of them starts chest compressions.

"Yes, you!" the deck captain shouts. "Go. Now, before it gets loose in the ship!"

I cast one last look at the little Rover girl—small and fragile as one of my butterflies before it sheds its cocoon— and run back the way I came, down the corridor leading to the gardens. If I'm in luck, the entrance to the gardens will still be sealed off, and it will only be able to run so far.

I slow as the entrance to the corridor closes over me. Emergency lights still flash, flipping the walls and floor from yellow to gray. A small dark shape moves at the far end, creeping across the floor. It turns and freezes. Its eyes flash at me, an eerie phosphorescence in the near dark.

A chill runs up my spine. A cat? I've heard of ships keeping them as good-luck charms and rat catchers, a throwback to the time when we had only Earth's seas to explore. The *Ranganathan* doesn't keep cats. Its vents are seeded with rodent-repelling biomarkers, and a top-of-the-line research vessel doesn't need to rely on superstition to make a safe flight.

Get the cat. Get out, I tell myself. The less time I spend in this yellow twilight, the better. I keep thinking I see shadows in the corner of my eye.

"Here, cat." I crouch and move forward slowly with my hand out, feeling more than a little ridiculous. I signed up for first response duty to save lives, not chase down pets. And I don't even particularly like cats. I'm definitely not letting a *dakait* take me down for one.

The animal's eyes go wide, and it slinks off.

"Dammit," I mutter, and follow. I try not to frighten it, but any time I start to close the distance, it startles and bolts ahead. The *dakait*'s smile plays over in my head, and I squeeze my nails into the nerveless flesh of my palms. Ava would know what to do. She's good with animals in a way I've never been, except when it comes to horses. I try to picture her and Rushil calling the half-feral cats that skulk around their salvage and repair shipyard. I kneel in the middle of the corridor and clear my throat. The cat watches me warily from a distance.

"Heeere, cat," I trill in my highest voice, hoping this is not the last thing I say before being knocked unconscious. I swallow and purse my lips to make a kissing noise I've seen Rushil do to call the strays. "Here, kitty-kitty."

The cat holds perfectly still, sizing me up, no doubt, and then takes a hesitant step in my direction.

"That's right." I drum my fingers on the floor and make the kissing noise again. "Come here, you little *sidey* bastard."

It pads closer, still eyeing me warily. Soot cakes its body, and the fur of its low-dragging tail is singed. It lets out a soft, hoarse *mew*.

Guilt softens my voice. I would bolt, too, if I had almost burned to death and some strange giant was chasing me. "Here, little guy." I hold out my hand again, and it bumps my palm with its head.

"Okay, very good." I coax it closer until it rubs against my leg, leaving a sooty streak on my uniform. "Nice cat."

I pick it and hold it against my chest. It hooks its claws into my shirt and presses its small body against me. Its heart beats out a rapid *thump-thump*, and a slight wheeze accompanies its every breath. It won't stop trembling.

"Hey, it's okay." I stroke the cat awkwardly. "Don't be scared. Everything's okay." The last thing I need is this thing developing supraventricular tachycardia and dying on me. Then I'd be stuck in quarantine until one of the senior medics got around to doing an autopsy.

I make my way back to the dock, the cat clinging to me the whole time. The crowd has thinned, and the only sign of the fire is a blue haze hanging in the air. The cat mewls hoarsely at me.

The girl I saw earlier, the one carrying the toddler, stands facing the first response captain, her hands planted on her hips. She can't be more than my age—my real age, not the one on my records. Oily ash covers her clothes and streaks her skin. Soot weighs down her hair.

"What do you mean, you're not going after them?" The smoke has left her voice low and hoarse, and something about it hits me dead in the chest. The glassy sea. Ava skimming the sloop over the water after the storm, when we still thought we might find survivors. When I was hanging on to a thread of hope that we might still find my manman.

"They have my brother. You have to go after them. You have to get him back." The girl's voice cracks, and she falls into a coughing fit.

The deck captain waits until she can breathe again. "Miss." She sounds weary. "This is a 128,000-acre research ship. Even if we could spare the fuel to change course, we could never outpace a *dakait* ship. They're designed for one thing we're not, and that's speed."

The girl wipes soot from her eyes. "You have those fighters. They could take them down."

The deck captain shakes her head. "They're short-range only. They gave chase as long as they could."

"Some help they were." The girl hugs her arms to

herself. "They let them get away. You couldn't catch a single one?"

The deck captain presses her lips into a line.

I hold the cat tighter. They didn't catch any of the *dakait*? A whole DSRI research ship kitted out with fighters and guards, and they still got away? The image of the *dakait*'s boot slipping away flashes through my mind, followed by a wave of shame. *They* didn't let them get away; *we* did. I did.

"Let me talk to your captain," the girl says.

"Commander," the deck captain corrects.

"Captain, commander, I don't care." Her voice trembles. "Don't you know what they'll do to him?"

The deck captain shifts her feet, weary. "I truly am sorry, miss. You can speak to the commander if you wish, of course." She waves over one of the medics stowing empty oxygen tanks in a cart. "But first we have to check you over. You've been through quite an ordeal—high carbon dioxide exposure, dermal burns . . ."

"I'm fine," the girl growls as the medic presses a stethoscopic meter to her chest.

"Please, miss," the medic says. "We're trying to help you."

The deck captain turns away and nearly walks into me.

"Oh." Relief flashes across her face. "You caught it."

"Yes." Behind her, the medics lead the girl to one of the gurneys.

"Very good, crew member . . . ?" She trails off, unsure of my name.

"Specialist Guiteau. I'm one of Dr. Osmani's assistants," I say.

"Dr. Osmani? You're in biology, then?"

"Sort of." I look past her to the girl, lying on the gurney with her hands over her eyes. "My specialties are more in biomorphology and biomimesis, but . . ."

"No, that's perfect," she interrupts. "You're exactly the person to take care of this problem." She gestures at the cat.

My eyes go as wide as the cat's. "Me? But . . . no, I don't—"

She nods. "You've done well with it so far. And if that animal is carrying any diseases, you've probably already been exposed to them. I can't think of a better candidate to run the quarantine and decontamination procedures."

My face must go ashen, because she changes her tone and pats me on the arm. "Don't worry, Specialist. It's only protocol. I'm sure it's not carrying anything fatal. I'll notify Dr. Osmani you're temporarily on emergency response duty."

"Thank you," I hear myself say.

I turn to go, but something stops me. "Captain?"

"Yes?"

"That little girl, the one who wasn't breathing," I say. "Did she make it? Is she okay?"

The deck captain face softens. "She'll be fine. They've got her on oxygen for a little while. Lucky thing she's so young. She won't remember any of this."

"Right," I agree, but part of me doubts it. Even if she doesn't remember the specifics, even if she tries to forget, will it ever completely go away? Or will it creep back in her nightmares and rise up on her when she smells smoke? Will it meld with who she is, like something grafted on to her genetic code? I cast one last look at the soot-covered girl lying still as a stone effigy on the gurney, then clutch my new charge to me and carry it back to my lab.

CHAPTER . 3

The month before I applied to the Deep Sound Research Institute, I was still officially sixteen. So I went to see the only person I knew who could fix my papers, the person who had helped Ava and me when we first came to Mumbai—Rushil.

As I rode the lev trains down from my own quiet, green neighborhood to the Salt, where Ava and Rushil ran their ship docking yard, the trees shrank away. Old buildings with bright new windows and the ghosts of old hand-painted signs on their brickwork rose up in their place. The lev rails skipped over *tapris* and juice carts sheltering in their shade, and over a cluster of enormous evacuation pipes meant to pump water back out into the sea and keep the lower city from flooding. The only reason Mumbai didn't disappear along with so many other seaside cities all those centuries ago was our civil engineering corps. They built the towering levee along our coast and the complex drainage system we still use to this day.

Of course, it didn't always work perfectly. I stepped off the train into a squelching stretch of mud and thanked my stars I had remembered to wear my boots. In High Mumbai, we wore open-toed sandals and delicate, embroidered slippers, but down in the Salt, the handful of trash-sucking machines on the streets were losing their battle with the dust and refuse that blew down the open alleys and out into the thoroughfares. The horse dung didn't help, either.

I put on my don't-touch-me glare and started down the street, weaving through the flow of bicycles, other pedestrians, and men and women on horseback. Mumbai's ban on combustion engines inside the city never seemed strange to me, but the London girls at Revati always complained about it until they heard they got to ride horses through the city.

I passed the street vendors, shops, and hole-in-the-wall restaurants across from Old Dharavi Station.

"*Chhatri! Chhaata!* Brollies and parasols!" shouted a vendor hawking cheap umbrellas. He caught sight of me. "Don't be caught out in the rains, *ladki*. You'll ruin those pretty clothes."

I laughed. "*Ji nahi.* I've got plenty of brollies."

"What about *choodi*?" He held up a handful of round metal bracelets. "You can never have enough *choodi*."

I shook my head. If my best friend, Vishva, had been with me like usual, we would have stopped. She shared the vendor's philosophy on *choodi*. But Vishva wasn't with me. Since I had started taking classes at the university instead of Revati, we had seen each other less and less. A wave of loneliness pulled at me. If we still went to school together, she would have tagged along. "For moral support," she would have said, but really to moon over Rushil. It never fazed Vishva that Rushil was a) married, b) sort of my brother, and c) ten years older than she was. Or maybe that's why she liked mooning, because she knew it was hopeless.

I pushed on past the brolly vendor and the other street sellers with their blankets of used crows and tablet parts. Deeper into the Salt, the streets quieted and security fences rose on both sides of the road. A high wall of corrugated metal closed in Rushil and Ava's lot, with razor wire accordioned along the top.

I pressed the call button at the gate. "Rushil!"

"Little Mi?" His voice came back full of static.

"It's me. Can I come in?" I would have died if my

classmates had overheard him using my childhood nickname, but inside the lot, I didn't mind. It was one of those half-embarrassing, half-nice things he and Ava did that I was never sure if I liked or hated.

"Course." A buzzer sounded, and the gate's locking mechanism released.

Inside, a hodgepodge of vessels sat baking on the tarmac, some all streamlined white lines and pristine shield panels, others spilling out their rusted guts around their landing gear. On top of Ava and Rushil's trailer, one of the scrapyard cats yawned and stretched in the shade of a receiving dish.

"Rushil?" I called into the quiet.

"Back here," he answered. "I'm in the garden."

I circled their tiny home and stepped into the small green space wedged between the trailer's back wall and the corrugated fence. Rushil straightened and wiped his hands on his white, sleeveless shirt as I rounded the corner. Sweat stippled his brow.

"Hey, Mi." He hooked a thumb at a plastic bowl brimming with cucumbers on the table behind him. "Soraya want some of these? We've got extra."

"Nah. You know how weird she is about pickles." Soraya was probably the only person on the entire subcontinent who didn't like pickles or chutneys. I dropped into one of the folding chairs beside the table and leaned back in the shade. "I'll tell her you offered, though."

"Oof." Rushil sank into the other chair and wiped the sweat from his face with both hands. "I'm glad you showed up. I needed a break. To what do I owe the pleasure of madame's company?"

I chewed my lower lip, suddenly nervous. "I need a favor."

"A favor?" Rushil raised his eyebrows. "You know Ava's on a run, right? She won't be back until nightfall."

"Not from her," I said. "From you."

"From me?" He frowned.

I leaned forward in my chair so I was more or less sitting straight. "You remember how when Ava and I first got here, you fixed her up with papers?"

"Uh-huh." Rushil nodded, a worried look overtaking his frown.

"I need . . ." I took a deep breath and let it all out in a rush. "I need you to help me get my papers sorted so I can apply for a Deep Sound mission."

Rushil sat silent for a moment, and then rocked forward onto his feet. "This heat. I think I need something to drink. What about you? Tea? Water? Juice . . ."

"Rushil." I rose and gave him my best imitation of Soraya's I-am-disappointed stare.

"Miyole." He planted his hands on his hips and volleyed the look back. "Ava would kill me. *Soraya* would kill me."

"No, they wouldn't." I shook my head. "Not if they understood. It's not like I'm doing anything bad, really."

Rushil rolled his eyes. "It's not like you're doing anything good, either. You know what this would take, right? Scamming a bunch of government scientists, hacking the national records database—"

"It's not *scamming*," I interrupted.

"Whatever." Rushil dropped back into his chair and leaned forward with his head in his hands.

"Please, Rushil," I said, in the voice I used when I was in pigtails and wanted more sugar for my tea. "I'm so close already. You have to be eighteen for the mission, and I'll be seventeen by the time they launch. It's just a little tweak, that's all."

What I didn't say—what no one knew but me—was that the records Soraya had drawn up for me all those years ago were wrong. The doctor marked me down as nine when I first came to Mumbai, probably because of my height, and no one had ever questioned it. Not my teachers, not

Soraya, not even Ava. It was only a matter of months—half a year at most—but I was eight when we fled the hurricane, not nine.

By the time I figured out the doctor had gotten it wrong, I was afraid to say anything. Soraya and my teachers might decide I was too young for Revati, and I loved Revati. It was the only thing making me wake up each morning, the only thing that could help me forget about my mother long enough to make it to nightfall. And then, later, it had simply seemed too awkward to bring up. *Oh, by the way, I know I've been going along with this for half my life, but the papers that make me a subcontinental citizen are completely wrong.* All of which meant I would be sixteen when the *Ranganathan* left dock. Not eighteen, not seventeen. Sixteen.

"A little tweak." Rushil laughed and shook his head, but then his eyes took on a glossy look. He rubbed a hand over his chin, thinking. "You'd need a good, solid hack to stand up to a government review. All the bells and whistles."

I smiled. "You know I'm good for it."

"I know you are." He looked at me, and suddenly he seemed tired, older than his twenty-seven years. "You're sure this is what you want?"

The smiled drained from my face. I knew what it would cost Rushil to get back in contact with Mumbai's network of hackers and purveyors of false documents. He tried so hard to keep any kind of criminal element away from his business, away from Ava, which was next to impossible for a kid raised among the gangs of the Salt, and there I was asking him to put his toe back in their waters. I could have backed off then. Maybe I should have. But that meant I would have had to spend the next two years shuttling between the university and home, stagnating in the same air while another class of my friends flew off to London or Chennai or Baghdad to launch their own lives. Even Vishva would be really and truly gone next year.

I swallowed. "It's what I've always wanted."

And that, at least, was no lie.

"You are the very devil," I tell the cat.

We stand faced-off in the lab, me with a syringe, gloved hands, and a crisscross of dermal bandages on my arms, the cat backed up against the stainless-steel storage cabinets, with its ears flat against its head and its coat puffed out to double its size. It turned out to be a curry-colored tabby with a rice-white belly beneath the ash, but that makes it no less terrifying now. I managed to wash the soot from its coat at the price of several deep gashes down my forearm, but every time I move in with the needle, the cat lets out a low, dangerous sound, bares its fangs, and hisses at me like a goose.

"What's wrong with you?" I've been reduced to pleading with the cat. "I'm trying to help."

A high tone sounds throughout the lab. Someone at the door.

I point the needle at my charge. "You stay there."

It emits another throaty growl but stays in place.

I go up on tiptoe and peek out the porthole. The Rover girl peers back in at me. Without the coating of ash, her hair hangs in damp honey-brown curls to her shoulders. A dense field of freckles covers her pale face, as if someone has spilled a cinnamon pot across the bridge of her nose. She's holding the toddler. They both wear the loose-cut blue tunic and trousers the medical ward gives their patients. Thick bandages sleeve the older girl's arms, and toddler has an oxygen feed taped beneath her nose.

The Rover girl frowns when she sees me and tries to say something I can't hear through the door.

"Hold on," I shout back, even though I know she can't hear me, either. I duck down to click on the intercom and pop back up into view. "I couldn't hear you. Say again?"

"They said you had our cat." The roll in her voice is sharp, like a hill cut off by a cliff.

"That's right." I try to match the impatience in her voice. "I'm administering the standard quarantine tests." Behind me, the cat issues another warning yowl.

She shifts the toddler to her other hip. "They said you should be done by now."

"Well, I'm not." I try to tamp down the annoyance in my voice. *Be professional.* I'm a research assistant, a representative of the DSRI, and the Rovers have been through hell. "I mean, I'll be done shortly, so if you'll kindly wait—"

"Wheels of heaven!" She swivels away for a second, and when she turns back, her jaw is tight, making her sharp chin stick out even more. She looks down at the toddler. "Look, Milah's gone through a lot today. She only wants to see the cat, and then we'll go."

"I can't let you see the cat," I try to explain. "Not until I've finished the quarantine procedure."

"Then finish it," she snaps.

"I'm trying," I shoot back. "If people would stop interrupting me, and if your mangy beast would cooperate!" I clap my hand over my mouth. I didn't mean to say that last part out loud.

She closes her eyes, heaves a sigh, and swallows down whatever she was about to say. "If you let me in, I can calm him down, and then you can get whatever tests you need. He's probably scared, is all."

I chew my lip. It's against regulations to break quarantine until I've finished the tests, but she has been living with the cat this whole time, and she hasn't caught anything deadly. The med ward wouldn't have let her out unless she was pathogen- and parasite-free. What could it hurt?

"If I let you in, you won't be able to leave until we finish processing the test results," I warn.

"Fine." A flicker of impatience crosses her face again, and she bounces the toddler on her hip.

I deactivate the lock. "It's your skin."

"Thank you." She edges in while the door is still opening. "You don't know how much this means to Milah and me."

I shrug, not sure what to make of her.

"Hey now, Tibbet." The Rover girl kneels and speaks softly to the cat, perched atop the counter. "It's okay. I'm here now."

The beast stops its goose noises and lowers its back, but its eyes stay black and dilated. An uneasy growl reverberates in its throat.

Milah stares wide-eyed at the cat, frozen beside the older girl. "Bit?" she asks.

The older girl glances at her. "Yes, Tibbet's mad, isn't he? He doesn't like this place." She cuts her eyes at me as she says the last part.

I pick up the syringe. *Professional*, I remind myself. "I have a sedative whenever you're ready."

The Rover girl turns back to the cat. "Here, Tibbet. Everything's okay now. No one's going to hurt you."

The animal hesitates on the counter edge. We all hold our breath, but then it finally hops down and pads cautiously to the Rovers.

"That's it," the girl croons, stroking the cat's head. "That's right." She looks up at me and nods. *Now.*

I kneel beside her and slide the needle beneath the cat's skin. It stiffens for a moment as I push the tiny dose of ketaphine, and then slowly relaxes in her arms. Its tongue lolls out, an undignified little pink tab.

Milah looks up, alarmed. "Bit dead?"

"No, no." The Rover girl rubs Milah's arm. "He's only sleeping, see?" She pets its fur.

Milah frowns. "Like Mama?"

The Rover girl hesitates. "No, Little Pea." She reaches out and strokes Milah's hair. "Your mama isn't waking up, remember? But Tibbet will."

Milah raises a small hand to her chin and makes a series of signs with her fingers, looking intently at the older girl the whole time.

A bolt of pain flickers across the Rover girl's face. "No," she says calmly, and signs in return. "He's coming back. I promise."

It takes me a moment to piece together what their movements mean. I've seen it in movies, and once we had a unit about it in the biomedical history class I took at the university. Before there were genetic cures and implants for deafness, people who couldn't hear talked with their hands. But that was forever ago.

"Is she . . . she's deaf?" I blurt out.

The Rover girl glares at me. "No."

"But then—"

"Her father is," she interrupts. "My brother, Nethanel. The one they took."

The words thump against my chest. *Her father. My brother. The one they took.* All the pieces tumble into place. No wonder she's been frantic. No wonder she's been sharp. Guilt balloons in my chest again. If I hadn't been frozen with fear, if I had just reached out and stopped that *dakait* . . .

"Oh." I swallow. "What did she say?"

The Rover girl's throat works silently for a moment. "She asked if Nethanel had gone to be with her mama."

"Oh." What can I even say? *Sorry about your brother. I might have had the chance to stop the people who took him, but I guess we'll never know. On the plus side, someday your niece will forget about her father.*

I look away, busy myself with preparing the next syringe. Behind me, the two of them continue their talk in a flurry of hands and soft murmurs. I try to block them out, give them some privacy, and focus on something other than my guilt. Line up the diagnostic strips. Program the pathogen analyzer. Right the boxes of swabs and syringe heads the cat scattered across the counter.

I check over my shoulder. Milah has that look little kids get where their faces seem like they're about to crumple. It hits the small soft spot in the center of my chest, and before I know what I'm really doing, I'm reaching up into my alcove and pulling down my sari.

Milah goggles at me as if I've produced a bird from thin air, like a street magician.

I shake out the sari. "Here." I spread it out on the ground, picnic style, and scoop up the limp bundle of fur.

"You hold him, and I'll take some blood. We'll be out of here in no time."

The Rover girl shoots me a small, grateful smile, settles Milah on the worn fabric, and piles the cat in her lap. His mouth hangs open and his legs splay sideways, but Milah strokes his back and coos at him anyway.

"Good job," I say. "You're an excellent assistant."

I draw the cat's blood and pipe it onto the diagnostic strips. Milah babbles on behind me, murmuring soothing sounds that aren't quite words.

The older girl clears her throat. "Thank you."

I finish fitting the strips into the analyzer and push the loading door closed. "No trouble." I glance over my shoulder at her and heat fills my cheeks. *Professional.* "I mean, I'm happy to be of service."

The Rover girl stands, holds out a hand. "I'm Cassia."

I take it, even though I feel weird and formal—adult—doing so. "Miyole."

We drop hands and stand, awkward. Behind me, the analyzer whirrs softly.

"Thanks for letting her see Tibbet." She nods at Milah and smiles again, just a little bit.

I shrug. "It's nothing. I wasn't getting anywhere with him."

"It's only . . . she wanted something familiar, you know?"

"Yeah." I glance at my sari and then down at my gloves. My scars itch beneath the latex. "I get that." More than she knows.

Cassia looks at me, and her face softens. "Yeah?"

That one word taps my chest, and suddenly the words are coming out. "I lost my mother, too."

I haven't said it in years. Not to anyone aboard the *Ranganathan*. Not to any of my professors at the university. Not to anyone who hasn't known me since I was a child.

"Oh." Cassia leans against the counter beside me. "I'm sorry."

We stand in silence for a moment, side by side, not touching, but close enough that I can feel the warmth of her shoulder beside mine.

"Who raised you?" she asks. "Your father?"

I hesitate, another set of memories pulling at me like an undertow. Darkness. A steamer trunk. A flash and the very air torn apart. I push them away. If I follow them down, I'm not sure I'll come back up.

"No," I say. "Not him."

The pathogen analyzer winds to a halt and beeps out a quick, four-beat tone. I shake myself. There's no time for any of that in the present.

"It's done." I pull up the results on my handbook. Cassia peers over my shoulder.

"He's fine." I say, running a finger down the list of results. "A few minor pathogens and a case of *otodectes cynotis*, but nothing we can't treat."

"Oto-what?" Cassia throws a worried look at her niece, who has just planted a kiss on top of the cat's head.

"Ear mites." I dismiss it with a wave.

She makes a face, and I can't help it—I laugh. For one brief moment, the heaviness in me dissolves. Milah looks up at us, puzzled.

"Sorry." I pull back my smile. *Neutral. Professional.* I'm supposed to be helping her, not pouring out my own sad history or subjecting her to my mad cackling.

"No, it's fine. It's . . ." Cassia's mouth twists. She blinks and looks away, but not before I see tears running down her cheeks.

"Oh, no." I reach for her but stop short. "Please. I'm so sorry. I didn't mean . . ."

"No, it's not your fault." She wipes furiously at her cheeks. "I just . . . I forgot about all of it for a second." Her eyes have dried, but her skin is still red and blotchy.

Part of me wants to put an arm around her, make her

some tea, rub her back the way Soraya did when I woke up crying in the middle of the night. *But she's not a little kid*, I remind myself. *She's my age, and I barely know her.*

"Sorry." She sniffs. "Stupid, crying."

"It's not," I say. "I'd be shaken up, too, after everything you've been through. The attack, losing your brother—"

"I haven't lost him." Some of the fire surges back into her voice.

I frown. "But the *dakait* . . ."

"I'm not afraid of a few jackers." The implication is there. *Unlike your captain.*

Her words hit me too hard. I step back.

"No one wanted this to happen." I cross my arms. "We all did our best."

She snorts.

All the soft parts of me harden over. "You know we can't break trajectory. The whole terraforming process depends on us hitting our payload deliveries exactly right. Commander Dhar would say the same."

"I'll find a way to do it myself, then. No matter what your commander says, I'm going to get my brother back."

I shake my head. "You'll get yourself killed."

Her jaw tightens. "Maybe." Her red-rimmed eyes pierce me. "Don't you have something you'd die for?"

Faces skim across my memory—Ava, Soraya, the blurred shadow of my mother. Hands on the ladder. *Climb, Miyole!* The broken seawall filling the feeds and drowning in a well of my own uselessness.

"Of course I do," I say quietly. I don't know what that thing is, exactly, but I can feel the edges of it. If my mother had it in her to sacrifice herself for someone else, maybe I do, too. Maybe she gave that to me. Maybe she inscribed it on my DNA or passed it to me when the wave took her. I meet Cassia's eyes, and an electric crackle arcs between us.

"I do," I say.

CHAPTER • 4

I slink away to the women's residential quarters and close myself in the showers. All my bunkmates are still on duty, thankfully, and the place has a rare quiet, like a back garden surrounded by a sound-dampening net. Every time I close my eyes, I see the *dakait*'s foot slipping out of reach and the Rover ship burning against the stars. All of it happens again and again in cold, perfect silence. Is that what Cassia's brother hears? Not the peaceful patter of water and the hush of the air circulators, but an absolute absence of sound? A shiver passes through me, despite the warm water. I stand under the shower long after the soft chime warns me I've used up my daily allotment, staring at the wall tiles without really seeing them.

Afterward I pad out to the living quarters. My handbook lies faceup on my bunk, blinking with an update.

SCHEDULE CHANGE: 18:00 SPC. GUITEAU TO
MIDDLE-TIER OFFICERS' DINING ROOM

Officers' dining room? Middle tier? My eyes go wide.
That's where the commander eats. Why would they want
me, of all people? Dining with the commander is the kind of
honor you get for pulling survivors from flaming wreckage,
not for failing to stop a *Dakait* and serving as kebab-slicing
practice for a fifteen-pound tomcat. There must be some
mistake. Any minute now, the duty clerks will realize the
error and wipe it from my schedule.

I comb out my hair and try to wrangle it into something
other than the poufy bell shape it likes to take when it isn't
tied down in a braid. I could never understand why Ava always
wanted her hair cut short when she was able to grow it out so
long. I look down at my handbook. The message hasn't gone
away. I sigh and wrestle my hair into two tight French braids
that meet at the base of my skull, then pull my midnight-
blue dress uniform from my clothing locker and spread it flat
on my bunk. I haven't worn it this whole journey. I haven't
needed to, since I spend most of my days in my lab coat or my
everyday pressure suit. I run my hand over the brass buttons.
No point putting it on when I'll be pulling it right back off.

I check the message again. Still blinking. SCHEDULE
CHANGE.

I know I should be excited. This is my chance to shine in front of the senior officers. But what I really want is to find Cassia and Milah and take them to the mess hall for biryani and okra—comfort food—and then maybe show them the gardens. *Cassia.* Our conversation in the lab comes rushing back to me, and I wince. What made me tell her about my mother? I've been so careful to leave that behind, to be the Mumbai version of myself, and then I go spilling it to a person I've only just met. Even back home, the only person outside my family I told was Vishva. But Vishva was my best friend, almost family herself, at least until the months before I left.

I pull my crow from my pocket and check the clock: 20:34 SATURDAY, 7 APRIL. I still have it set to Mumbai time. Sometimes it's comforting to look at it and think, *Oh, it's lunchtime at Revati,* or imagine Soraya riding the trains home from an afternoon class at the university. I've managed not to think about Vishva for several months, but something about Cassia brought her back. *Where is she now?* I wonder. *What's she doing?*

Saturday evening. Vishva is likely at a dance club down in the Salt, sweating and swinging her long dark hair everywhere. Or else she's off with a boy, snogging on a rowboat in the shadow of the Great Levee. I don't really know. We were inseparable those first few years—always choosing each other as partners on school outings and running the biomimesis club together after school. President and vice president. First and second in our class.

And then we were fifteen, and I was leaving Revati for college, and everything changed. Vishva changed.

The month before I started classes at the university, I met Vishva and a gaggle of other girls from our class at the train stop near my house.

"Miyole!" Vishva threw up her hands and tottered over to me on silver stilettos. Her long hair coiled in a sleek black chignon at the side of her head, and her flowing orange shirt had been slashed perfectly to show her shoulders. She grabbed me in a hug. "You came!"

"Of course I came." I looked down at my flat shoes and plain lavender shirtdress. Even with Vishva in heels, our heads were still level. Only I looked like a freakishly tall ten-year-old hanging out with a group of actual teenagers. "Where are we going?"

"You tell me." Vishva grinned. "It's your farewell party."

I gave her a playful shove and rolled my eyes. "I told you, it's not *farewell*. I'll still be in the city, just over at the university. We'll see each other all the time."

I could have gone farther. I'd been accepted to colleges in Bangalore, Oxford, Zurich, Cairo, Kolkata, and Jaipur, too, but Soraya hadn't wanted me straying so far from home until I was at least eighteen. So Mumbai University it was.

"So, where are we going?" Vishva asked.

"Up to Malabar Hill?" I suggested.

Vishva wilted. "Again? Seriously? And do what, sneak into one of the cafés and hope we catch a glimpse of Liam Chowdhury?" She said his name like we hadn't both been obsessed with his movies and filled our feeds with nothing but pictures of him for the past two years.

I frowned. "What's wrong with Liam Chowdhury?"

"Nothing." Vishva flopped her hands against her sides. "It's just . . . *chaila*, Mi. Don't you want to do something different for a change?"

I scratched my ankle with the top of my shoe and glanced at the other girls. My second-closest friend, Aziza, was off visiting her father in Istanbul, so Vishva had brought along a group of girls I knew from class but didn't hang around with unless we had to do a project together or something. Most of them were busy with their crows or talking, but Siobhan Nguyen and Chandra Avninder, two of the wealthiest girls in our school, were clearly listening in.

I shifted from one foot to the other. "Like what?"

Vishva's eyes sparkled, and I realized she had been waiting for me to ask that all along. She glanced at Siobhan and Chandra. "Your sister lives down in the Salt, doesn't she?"

I eyed Vishva. What was she up to? She knew exactly where Ava and Rushil lived. She'd been to their house for tea a million times before. "Yes?"

Vishva hurried on. "So you know your way around, yeah?"

Siobhan and Chandra were definitely listening now. They weren't even pretending to scroll through the feeds on their crows. And Vishva was giving me a look that said she might spontaneously combust if I didn't go along with whatever she had planned.

"Yeah." I nodded. "I know my way around."

"Brilliant. There's this club called Pradeep's that just opened on the hill and Chandra says they don't check ID for girls, so we could definitely get in." Vishva threw a smile over her shoulder at our classmates, then turned back to me. "What do you think?"

I looked down at my dress. Definitely more iced fruit on Malabar Hill than club wear. And Pradeep's . . . I liked the Salt, but I didn't particularly like its clubs. Packed-in crowds, loud music, flashing lights, people screaming at one another over the bass, a miasma of smoke, sweat, spilled drinks, perfume, and cologne choking the air. I knew some people liked it—I knew Vishva liked it—but something about being trapped in a dark room where no one could hear me put me ill at ease.

"Can't we go down to the talkies instead?" I whispered.

"We go to the talkies every week." Vishva drooped over like a marionette with her strings cut. "Come oooonn, Miyole."

I sighed. Siobhan and Chandra had gone back to their crows, but they were obviously still listening. Maybe it would be more fun than it looked. Maybe I'd love it. I liked dancing, after all, even if I wasn't as coordinated as Vishva, and what were clubs for if not dancing?

"Okay," I said. "Let's go."

Vishva squealed. "I knew it! This is going to be so *jhakaas*! You're going to love it, Mi."

We rode the train down to the Salt, everyone gabbing the whole way. Vishva dug in her purse and found gold shimmer cream to paint on my eyelids, and Chandra's friend Drishti loaned me her belt so I'd look a little less like I was heading to a violin recital. Vishva tried to get me to undo my braids, but I slapped at her hands until she left me alone. I didn't like anyone touching my hair except Soraya.

We piled off the train at Sion Station and started up the hill. Vishva and the other girls huddled together, pointing and giggling at everything we passed and shrieking when they accidentally stepped in mud puddles. A chai vendor glared at them over his cart, and farther down the street, a twentysomething guy nudged his friend and ogled Siobhan as she stopped to take a picture of one of the street-sweeper bots someone had graffitied to look like a turtle shell.

Unease fluttered in my stomach. Normally when I came to the Salt, I dressed in plain clothes and boots. I tried not to draw attention to myself. But my Revati friends were so obviously tourists, rich girls acting out every stereotype imaginable of the spoiled private-school girl slumming it on a weekend night.

I walked a little slower, put another meter of distance between myself and the group.

"Miyole!" Vishva shouted back down the street. "Hurry up! We don't know where we're going."

My heart fell. Not them. *Us.* I was one of them.

We arrived at Pradeep's as the sun disappeared behind the levee wall. Bass thumped through the red-painted cinder block walls, and the wind picked up, plastering my skirt against my legs and peppering us with grit from the streets.

"Bleh." Vishva turned her back to the wind and shuffled closer to me. "This is going to be so *jhakaas*, Miyole. You'll see."

A big man with close-cropped hair and a tight black shirt stood at the entrance, eyeing each person as they passed and occasionally cracking his stony face to wink at one of the girls.

Vishva and the others giggled as he whistled at them and waved them through, but when I stepped up, he held out a hand.

"Wait a second." He looked me up and down, and suddenly I wished I had let Vishva do something with my hair after all. "How old are you, kid?"

I glanced at Vishva, standing openmouthed just inside the door.

"Nineteen?" My voice squeaked.

The doorman shook his head. "I don't think so. Let's see some ID."

"She's with me." Vishva stepped back into the entryway. "She's my friend."

The doorman looked between the two of us and cocked an eyebrow at Vishva. "You nineteen, too?"

She stepped back. "No. Um...eighteen. I'm eighteen."

He grunted. "Well, you can stay or you can go, but

your friend doesn't get in without ID."

I looked helplessly at Vishva. *Don't leave me out here alone.* Fake IDs were expensive, and I'd never needed one before. Vishva had said I wouldn't need one.

She glanced over her shoulder at Siobhan and Chandra standing under the pulsing lights of the dance floor, and then back at me. "Sorry, Mi." She backed up another step.

A small, sharp pain shot through my chest. "Vishva . . ."

"I'll find you later, okay?" She angled her way into the crowd and shouted over the music. "We'll go up to the hill, like you wanted. Keep your crow on."

My eyes burned, but I wasn't about to cry in front of a bouncer and a whole line of people. That would be later, alone on the train, when I started to wonder whether they'd turned me away because I truly looked so young or if my being too dark and foreign had something to do with it. Instead I stared dumbfounded as my best friend disappeared into the darkness and thrash of bodies without so much as a backward look.

Another alarm chimes, warning me it's time to get dressed if I'm going to make it to the officers' tier on time. I can't keep dwelling on some dumb high school slight. Besides, my failed attempt to get into Pradeep's was what gave me the idea to tweak my records and get myself here. If Vishva hadn't dumped me for her new friends that night, I might still be knocking around Mumbai, waiting for my life to begin. Someone else would have had to rescue the universe's traumatized cats.

I stand and shake out my dress uniform, brush invisible flecks of lint from the sleeves, and hold it up against me before the full-length mirror on the back of the door.

"It'll be fine," I tell myself. If it was a mistake, surely they would have sorted it by now.

At that moment, the door slides open, and all three of my bunkmates walk in.

"Whoa-ho," Madlenka whoops as she shrugs out of her lab coat. "Fancy. Going somewhere special tonight, Miyole?"

Jyotsana and Lian grin when they see what I'm holding.

"Is it a boy?" Jyotsana's eyes light up. "It's a boy, isn't it? Is it that security pilot who's always following you around?"

For a split second, I think spontaneous human combustion might be possible after all. "Rubio?" I say faintly.

"That's him," Jyotsana agrees. "The one with the hair, right?"

"No," I choke out. "Definitely not. No."

"Come on, Jyotsana, not everyone's into boys." Madlenka rolls her eyes at me sympathetically. Her girlfriend works in propulsion maintenance, and once, when we were playing Truth or Dare during our first week aboard, she got me to admit to having a debilitating and unrequited crush on a girl from my biochem class at the university. Her name was Karishma, and she had hair all the way down to her waist. She was also six years older than I was and secretly engaged to our teaching assistant, but I didn't know that at the time.

"No," I say again, more forcefully than I mean to. "It's no one, okay?" I don't have time in my life for crushes anymore.

"All right." Jyotsana holds up her hands in surrender but shoots Madlenka a look that says she doesn't believe me for a second. They're all in their early twenties, which means they think they have some kind of sixth sense when it comes to my love life.

"So where *are* you going?" Lian folds her lab coat neatly and drops it in the laundry chute.

"I . . . um . . . the mid-tier officers' dining room?"

"The middle tier?" Madlenka gasps, and the three of them dissolve in excited shrieks.

"*Aiyo*, really?"

"So exciting!"

"How did you get an invite?"

"Is that what you're wearing?" Madlenka nods at the dress uniform still dangling in my hand.

"Y . . . yes?"

Madlenka shakes her head. "You have to dress up more than that."

Jyotsana agrees. "This is *mid-tier*, Miyole. This is your chance. You have to make them notice you."

My stomach flutters. "I . . . I don't know if I want that." I just want everyone to leave me alone and let me figure out what's wrong with the pollinators. If they notice me, I want it to be for my work, not my outfit.

"Of course you do." Madlenka pulls her hair back, all business. "These are the first officers. Make a good impression, and they can get you any assignment you want."

She's right; this is my way to my own lab, my own experiments. No more Dr. Osmani. All of us who signed on as research assistants know the way it works. On the outbound journey, all that matters is preparing for the terraforming drops, but on the way back, some of us will get the chance to take over the unused labs, run our own experiments. And the first officers are the ones who choose.

"Don't worry." Lian takes my arm. "We'll help you."

Jyotsana has already opened my locker and pushed my uniforms aside to look at the clothes I brought from home.

"Ooh." She pulls out a gold- and red-stamped sari with a startlingly blue *choli* and skirt to wear underneath.

"No way." The *choli* shows my arms and stops at the bottom of my rib cage, leaving most of my stomach bare, which is exactly what you want on a humid Mumbai afternoon, but not at an officers' dinner. Our prep instructions for the *Ranganathan* told us we could bring one item of civilian formal wear, but the moment I stepped on board and saw everyone in their long sleeves and high collars, I stuffed my sari at the back of my locker.

"But it's so pretty." Jyotsana holds the outfit up to me. "You look way better in bright colors anyway."

Madlenka nods. "And a lot of the first officers are from India, so it can't hurt to let them know you are, too."

I make a face. "I don't know. Isn't that kind of . . . what's the word? Nepotism? Favoritism?"

Madlenka rolls her eyes and shrugs. "It's called 'how the world works.'"

Jyotsana laughs. "You're so serious, Miyole."

"Here." Lian takes the sari and drapes it over the shoulder of my dress uniform. "What if you wear it over your blues like this?"

"I . . . I guess." Something about the uniform makes the gold cloth slightly more sober and elegant.

"Excellent!" Jyotsana claps her hands. "Put it on! Put it on!"

I change into my blues and let Jyotsana help me drape the sari, while Lian attacks my hair with her expert fingers. If I close my eyes, I'm back in the Gyre, my mother gently tugging my hair into braids. Another regret—forgetting how to replicate the intricate styles she did for us both on Seventh Market days. Soraya and Ava both tried to fix it the way I described, but their own hair was so different from my own. It was never the same.

Giggling bubbles up around me. I open my eyes. Madlenka is coming after me with her lipstick.

"Oh, no." I lean back, pulling out the neat tuck Jyotsana has just finished at my waist and making Lian yank my hair.

Madlenka sighs and raises her eyes to the ceiling. "Will you trust us? God, you're exactly like my fifteen-year-old cousin. You'd think you'd never gone to a dinner before."

I shut my mouth and let Madlenka go to work. That's

far closer to home than I want anyone to know.

When they're finished, they push me in front of the door mirror. I stop short, disoriented. The girl staring back looks nothing like me. The sari gives me hips I never have in my regular uniform, and the gold brings out the honey-brown tint in my eyes. Lian has even managed to braid my hair into an elegant spiral at the top of my head—I guess it's true what they say about needing nimble fingers to work in robotics. But it's the lips that put a hitch in my breath. That red . . . the fullness—my mother's face flashes before me, her hair a halo of free-floating curls, her lips painted the color of a crimson sunbird, the blurred memory snapping into perfect focus.

I steady myself against the wall. In my memories, my mother is always beautiful, perfect. But now I remember the scar slicing through the left side of her mouth, the stiffness when she smiled. It never stopped her from picking out the brightest colors to paint her lips. It's her. I look so much like her.

"Miyole?" Lian touches my shoulder. "Are you okay?"

In the mirror, my face has gone gray. I look like I might throw up.

"I'm fine." I turn away from the mirror and clear my throat. "Thanks for this. Really."

"Any time." Lian exchanges a worried look with Jyotsana and Madlenka. "You're sure you're okay?"

"Never better." I remember to make myself smile this time. Smiling always used to throw Ava and Soraya off my case when either of them went all mother hen on me.

"You'd better go," Madlenka says. "You don't want to be late to your first officers' dinner."

I escape into the corridors and wipe at the lipstick with the back of my hand. Normally I take the emergency stairwells to move from deck to deck—I run into fewer people that way—but I don't want to show up in the mid-tier dining room looking like I've come straight from a three-kilometer sim run, so I head for the lifts instead.

I find a spot near the back of the car, next to the window that overlooks the decks as we pass. A crowd of maintenance and repair technicians push in after me, several of them eyeing my outfit. The doors begin to slide shut, but a shout from the other side stops them short.

"Wait! Hold the door."

A carefully tousled brown head joins the crowd at the front of the lift. "Thanks."

I press myself against the window and sink down. Rubio. Perfect. Not for the first time, I curse my bad luck at being one of the tallest girls aboard the *Ranganathan*. Maybe he'll step off in a tier or two and never even notice I'm in the same car. I catch myself rubbing the smooth scar on my left palm, and clasp my hands to make myself stop.

The lift drops in a smooth descent. The upper recreation gardens spread out below us, green and orderly, dotted with crew members cleaning up debris from the attack. Its domed ceiling has already scarred over where the *dakait* breached the *Ranganathan*'s skin. Part of the hedge maze has burned down to blackened twigs, but I can still make out its design—a central hub and twenty-four spokes closed inside a circle, the wheel of life. The sign graces my adopted country's flag, but more than that, it means dharma, duty—the keystone of ship life. We each have a role in bringing life out to the Deep, to the shadowed worlds at the sun's farthest reach, even if that role occasionally feels ridiculous or pointless, like, say, chasing down a tomcat or putting on a sari to go to dinner with the first officers.

The lift stops even with the green lawns of the recreation garden. The maintenance techs pile out, but Rubio only steps aside to let them pass.

Don't let him see me. Don't let him see me, I beg. But it's no

ALEXANDRA DUNCAN

use. Rubio glances over and catches sight of me as the door slides closed.

His eyes light up. "Hey, memsahib!"

Dammit.

"Rubio." I straighten my spine and let my tone frost over with formality.

He makes his way to the back of the lift as it drops below the recreation level. The windows go black.

"Nice." His eyes flick over my sari and then home in on my breasts. *Charming.* "Where're you headed so dressed up?"

I stiffen. "First officers' dining room."

"No way." He jostles my shoulder in a far too friendly manner and grins. "Me, too."

"You?" For the first time, I notice he's dressed in his blues as well.

My face must offer up a clear diagram of my feelings on the subject, because Rubio laughs. "Yes, me. My squadron helped chase off those *dakait*." He arches an eyebrow. "What'd you do to get invited?"

"Nothing," I mutter, and stare past him at the dark window. Unless you count bathing a half-feral cat, which would be the most embarrassing reason to be invited to dinner ever. So it can't be that.

"Come on, memsahib, you can tell me," he says. "It

must have been something pretty good to get you invited down there." He nods to the floor below us, the first officers' tier at the heart of the ship.

"Really. It was nothing."

"You're on the first response team, right?" His eyes go wide. "Did you rescue one of those Rovers? Did you, like, bring them back from the brink of death or something?"

I almost laugh, but he looks so earnest. "Hardly."

"Tell me, Guiteau." He's reached the point of begging, which would be immensely satisfying if I were really holding a tidbit of information out of his reach.

But I'm not. And for once, he's dropped his stupid nickname for me.

"Honestly, I don't have any clue why they invited me. I got stuck behind some wreckage and was almost last on the scene. All I did was . . . um . . . ." I trail off.

"What?" He smiles, a flicker of mischief reigniting in his eyes.

Let one of the dakait *get away. Fail at everything I was supposed to do.*

"Tie up some loose ends," I finish.

"Hmph." He shoots me an unsatisfied look but doesn't say anything else.

The lift drops back into the open air above the middle

recreation level, and the glass brightens again to let in the artificial sunlight streaming down from the rafters. The gardens are eerily empty, though. Usually, someone has a pickup game of cricket going on the pitch, or off-duty couples are lounging on the grass. Everyone must be on extra duty or too shaken up to go out. A slimy finger of guilt creeps back into my stomach. I should be with them, not clean and pressed and going to a dinner.

The lift slows to a stop with a soft *bong.*

"That's us." Rubio inspects his hair in the metal doors. "You ready for this, memsahib?"

I sigh. Rubio can't fight his true nature forever. Or even for a handful of minutes, apparently. The moment the doors slide open, I speed out of the lift and stalk down the rolling walkway at brisk clip, trying to get away from myself as much as him.

I arrive at the officers' quarters first, Rubio jogging up behind me. The doors whisk open on a spacious sitting room, with white synthetic-leather couches and false windows flooded with ultraviolet light perfectly simulating late afternoon on the subcontinent. The ceiling plays an image of a hanging garden, hibiscus swaying gently in the breeze. On the far side of the parlor, an old-fashioned set of hinged doors opens onto the dining room.

"Name?"

I jump. A clerk at an antique wooden desk with claw feet sits immediately inside the door. She stands and rounds the desk, tablet at the ready.

"Um . . ." I'd heard the first officers liked their pomp and ceremony, but this was more than I'd expected. The ship's security system could do the same job and spare the clerk's labor for something more useful.

She smiles and taps her stylus against the screen, waiting.

"Science Specialist Miyole Guiteau?" I cringe. Ugh. *It's not a question.*

"Here you are. Have a pleasant evening, miss." She waves me ahead and turns to Rubio. "And you? Name?"

A burst of laughter spills out of the dining quarters. I hang back in the sitting room, watching. A long table laid with linen napkins, china, and crystal fills most of the inner room. Near the back, a group of officers in dress blues cluster around the bar, sipping some kind of cherry-red spirit from glass tumblers. I spot Dr. Osmani, wrapped in white raw silk from neck to toe. She smiles, more with her mouth than with her eyes, as the officer beside her says something.

At least I'm not the only one overdressed.

One of the officers, a handsome older man with a smooth brown face and white hair combed up into a subtle pompadour, spots me. "Ah, our guests have arrived." He waves me closer. "Come in, come in. Can I offer you a drink? Wine? Sherry?"

"Um . . ." Soraya never drinks, though she keeps wine and beer in the house in case she has guests to dinner. I've mostly fallen in with her, not out of any religious feeling like hers, but because the few times I tried it, the alcohol muffled up my head and blunted my thoughts. I didn't like the screen it lowered between me and the world.

"I don't—" I begin.

"We'd both love a sherry." Rubio sidles up beside me. "Thank you, sir."

"Good lad." The old man winks at Rubio and turns away.

"What are you doing?" I hiss. "I don't want a drink."

"You do when the head of telemetry offers." He keeps his eyes on the old man splashing red liquid into two more tumblers.

"But I—"

"You don't have to drink it. You just have to let him fix it for you." Rubio rolls his eyes. "Honestly, memsahib, an upper cruster like you, I'd have thought you've been to your share of these things."

"I keep telling you, I'm not—" But the telemetry officer and his pompadour return with our drinks.

"Thank you." Rubio smiles and raises his glass to take a sip.

"Thanks," I mumble after him.

"What a lovely sari." The officer smiles as he hands over my drink. "Miss . . . ?"

"Guiteau," I say. "Science Specialist."

"Guiteau." His smile spreads like butter. He gestures at my sari. "My colleagues and I are honored by your knowledge of our homeland. You must have gone to quite a lot of effort to procure such a fine piece."

His words hit me before I have a chance to brace myself. I stare at him, fighting to keep my face blank. *Senior officers make the lab assignments.* I've come to expect this sort of thing from Rubio, but the senior officers? Even the ones from my own country? Surely they can see I'm one of them, not an outsider trying to weasel my way into their good graces.

I shift from one foot to the other. "Not really." The sari came from a big, airy shop across the street from the one in South Mumbai where Soraya bought my school uniforms. It was only a twenty-minute lev train ride from our house. "Not much trouble at all."

"Guiteau's from India herself." Rubio volunteers. "Chennai, yeah?"

I scowl down into my sherry. "Mumbai."

"Ah, yes?" The officer blinks and looks me over more closely. "I would never have imagined."

I raise my eyebrows at him, the words lashing out before I can stop them. "What does that mean?"

An awkward silence follows. *Stupid, stupid, Guiteau.* I should have kept my tongue, taken a drink, anything other than biting the head off one of the officers. I grip the slick sides of my glass.

"Nothing." The head of telemetry gives me a tight little smile. "Nothing at all. If you'll excuse me . . ." He backs away with a little bow and melts into the crowd.

"Smooth," Rubio mutters.

"I didn't ask for your help," I snap back. I don't know why everything is coming out angry when all I feel is hurt, those million little scratches adding up to a deeper wound.

"Heaven forbid anyone should try to help the great Memsahib Guiteau." He swirls what's left of his sherry around in the bottom of his glass and throws it back in one gulp.

"I told you." I grit my teeth. "Stop calling me—"

Suddenly the officers' laughter fizzles out behind us, and silence slices through the room. Something acrid curdles the air. Rubio's mouth opens, his gaze fixed on something behind me. I turn. Cassia stands on the threshold, stinking of smoke and dressed in the same soot-stained clothes she wore when she carried Milah from the smoldering ship. I hadn't taken much notice of them before, in all the chaos. She wears a dark gray quilted jacket and a kilt with knife-sharp pleats over black trousers and boots. Her hair fans out in wild curls, her freckles have almost disappeared in the dangerous red flush creeping up from her neck, and the look in her eyes says that if she could, she would burn this whole room, this whole ship, and everyone in it, to cinders.

A man with Cassia's same honey hair—the lanky one who was first out of their burning vessel—waits behind her, in clean blue scrubs from the medical ward.

"Mr. Kaldero." Commander Dhar emerges from the knot of officers near the bar. She smiles in welcome "Ms. Kaldero. We're so glad you've accepted our invitation."

"Thank you." The man takes her proffered hand. "Please, call me Ezar."

"It's captain." Cassia corrects him with a harsh look. "Captain Kaldero. Not Ezar."

"For now." Ezar offers an apologetic smile. "Only until our father's well again."

"Of course," our commander agrees without missing a beat.

All the other officers and guests exchange the same pitying look. *Captain of what?*

"Won't you please have a seat?" Commander Dhar gestures to the dining table. "Now we're all here, we can begin."

Cassia drops into the nearest chair and scowls down the table while the rest of us find our seats. The officer to her left shifts his chair ever so slightly away from her. There's no escaping the odor that follows her, even on my side of the table, but apparently we're all going to follow the commander's lead and ignore it. Cassia stares at each of us in turn, as if daring us to comment on the state of her clothes. Her brows lift slightly when she comes to me—suddenly more hurt than angry—and then batten down again.

I swallow down the knot in my throat. How must this scene look to her, all of us laughing and drinking while the *dakait* fly her brother farther and farther into the Deep? She frowns down at the porcelain plate in front of her. My insides churn. Here I am moping around, feeling sorry for myself about the head of telemetry mistaking me for a foreigner, when she's the one who's truly lost something.

Look at me, I think. *Please, look at me.* If she would only look my way, she could at least see the apology in my eyes. *I'm not part of this. I didn't ask to be here.* But she doesn't.

The food comes in waves, served by the officers' stewards. Crispy paratha bread stuffed with spiced potatoes. Chickpea-encrusted pakoras, sweet, minty yogurt raita, green chutneys, mango chutneys, and platters of saffron-scented rice. Fried paneer cheese, for the vegetarians among us, and lamb vindaloo for the rest. Then stewed tamarinds and cardamom-laced kulfi, sweet and cold. The rest of our shipmates are eating plain chickpea chole or lentil stew with naan in the mess halls tonight, but part of me wishes I was there instead. I can hardly bring myself to raise a fork to my mouth.

I lean over to Rubio, seated beside me. "Do they eat like this every day?"

He shrugs. "What do you care? Just make the most of it." He forks a tender bit of lamb into his mouth and closes his eyes. "Augh. Heaven."

"Specialist Guiteau." Commander Dhar pushes aside her near-empty plate and leans forward, apparently still intent on maintaining the illusion that everything is normal. "I heard you went out of your way to help welcome our guests today."

I glance down the table at Cassia. Our eyes lock for a brief second.

"I didn't do much, ma'am." I lower my fork, suddenly

queasy. Is that really why I'm here, after everything that happened? The *chirkut* cat? "I'm sure Mr. Rubio's contribution was much more important."

"Never." Rubio leans forward on his elbows, eyes glinting, and aims one of his charming smiles at the commander. "We pilots get more than our fair share of glory."

Commander Dhar smiles, pleased. "Specialist Guiteau was instrumental in apprehending one of the more wayward members of Captain Kaldero's crew." Her voice lifts with humor.

A laugh makes the rounds among the senior officers. I look up, mortified. Never mind how Rubio is going to find out about my cat-wrangling skills; I doubt Cassia and her family are going to find any part of today's ordeal funny. What is the commander thinking? Now would be an excellent time for a minor hull breach or a ventilation systems failure. Something small, but enough to send everyone scurrying to security stations.

"Really?" Rubio turns to me, one eyebrow quirked. "Who?"

"Tibbet," I mutter, sinking down in my chair.

"Who?" he frowns.

"Tibbet." I clear my throat. "The . . . um . . . the ship's cat."

"The cat?" Rubio looks like someone has handed him a million *rupaye* and a medal for Interstellar Gossip Hunter Laureate.

My face goes hot as a Mumbai sidewalk. If he and the commander weren't both staring at me, I would crawl under the table and die.

"Do tell us about it, Specialist." Commander Dhar smiles. "I'm sure everyone could use a little levity after today's drama."

"I . . . um . . ." I shoot a miserable look at Cassia. *This wasn't my idea.* Behind her, Dr. Osmani titters as the head of telemetry whispers something in her ear.

Cassia slams her fork down on the table and pushes back her chair. "Commander Dhar. We didn't come here for *levity*. We came to figure out what we're going to do about my brother." She plants her hands on the table and leans forward. "Are you going to help us, or are you going to drink yourself into a stupor, like everyone else here?"

A shocked silence runs down the table. Dr. Osmani presses a napkin to her lips and raises an eyebrow. I know that look. *Uncouth*, she's thinking. My discomfort vaporizes into hot, white anger. Suddenly, I don't give a damn about what that woman thinks anymore, world-renowned bioengineer or no. Why did I ever care about pleasing her in the first place?

Captain Ezar clears his throat and steps into the silence. "What my sister means is, while we appreciate your hospitality, Commander, we have problems a meal won't solve."

"Yes, of course." Commander Dhar sobers. "Forgive me. We'll be approaching Ceres Station in a few days. We can spare a shuttle to take you there and help you book passage to your home station."

Cassia's eyes go wide, as if she's choked on a chicken bone. I cringe. I don't know much about Rovers, but the one thing I do know is that they skip from planet to station, picking up small jobs as they go. Surely someone should have briefed the commander about that.

Ezar shakes his head. "Thank you, but our ship was our home."

"Then you're welcome to stay aboard with us and try to repair it," the commander says without blinking. "You'll have whatever help we can give. Techs, engineers, equipment—"

"But what about our brother?" Cassia cuts in again.

The commander's face softens. "We're truly sorry for your loss. We can hold a memorial service once your father has recovered, of course, or sooner, if you prefer. If there was anything more we could do—"

"He's not lost." Cassia's clutches the edge of the table. "He was taken. And there is something you could do."

Commander Dhar stiffens. "Changing this ship's course isn't as small a matter as you seem to think, Ms. Kaldero." Her careful diplomacy is slipping.

"I'm not asking that," Cassia says. "But you have fighters. Couldn't you spare some of them to track the *dakait* down and bring him back?"

The senior security chief at the opposite end of the table clears his throat. "I wouldn't advise that, Commander. Without a full complement of fighters, you leave the ship vulnerable to attack. That's twelve thousand lives at stake, for the sake of one boy."

Rubio nods in agreement.

Cassia glowers at them. "He's not just one boy, he's my brother. He's Milah's father. " Her voice breaks on the last word.

"Cassia," Ezar says, low and warning. He reaches for her wrist.

"No." She pulls away from him. "I won't stand by and let them take him. I'm not a coward, like some people. I'll find a way." She rakes her eyes over each of us, stopping half a second on me, and then whirls on her heel and storms from the room.

A moment of stunned silence follows.

Finally Ezar clears his throat and glances apologetically at Commander Dhar. "Forgive us, Commander. My sister, she's young. Nethanel wasn't just her brother; he was her best friend. This whole experience has . . ." He pauses, searching for the right word. "It's shaken her."

"No apologies, Captain, please." Commander Dhar waves his concern away, and with that, the room lets out its breath. Dr. Osmani takes a thin sip of her sherry, and the murmur of conversation begins to grow around the room's edges.

"We've all been that young," the commander says. "I can have one of the ship's mental health counselors look in on her, if you like."

Captain Ezar blanches, as if she's offered him a rotten fish. "That won't be necessary. Thank you."

I look from him, to the commander, to the door. No one else is going to say it. "What if . . . ," I begin in a small voice, and then stop.

Everyone turns their heads to me. *Chaila.*

I clear my throat. I don't want to be the one do this, but I can't stay silent, not when I'm as much to blame as anyone for the *dakait* getting away.

"What if we gave her one of the shuttles?" I say. "If we can spare it long enough to drop her at Ceres Station, couldn't she take it and go looking for her brother herself?"

Rubio shakes his head. "Those shuttles aren't outfitted for long-range travel."

"But they could be," I insist, the idea clicking together in my head as I speak. "We could modify one. . . ."

"Even if we did," Commander Dhar interrupts, "what would happen if she found him? We'd be sending her to her death, or at least into slavery, if the *dakait* didn't kill her outright. This girl is under our protection now. Her safety is our concern."

"Then she could find them, and report back—"

"To who?" Rubio snorts. "We're not the law. We can't police the whole system."

"Someone should." I lean forward, digging my nails into my scarred palms. "We're the ones who know about it. We can't stand by and let this happen."

Dr. Osmani clears her throat and stares at me with her cold fish eyes. "Specialist Guiteau, may I remind you we are a research ship, not a paramilitary vessel?"

"But we can still stop them." I turn to Commander Dhar, my heart drumming. I have to make this right. "Please. One shuttle. You were going to give it up anyway."

For a moment, she hesitates, and I think she might say yes. But then she drops her eyes and shakes her head. "We can't let Ms. Kaldero throw away her life for someone who's good as dead."

For a split second, I am both in the officers' dining room and clinging to the iron railing of a widow's walk in the midst of the Gyre's first and only typhoon. Rain lashes my face and my hands burn. A high, whining sound fills my ears. I try to push down the memory, but it throbs through me, radiating out from my bones. What if my mother and Ava hadn't come after me that day? What if they'd seen the storm and given me up as dead? What if they'd done that same math and decided my one life wasn't worth risking the two of theirs?

"But it's her choice." My chest constricts. I always cry when I'm angry, but I'm not going to do it now. "She knows what she's asking. It's her life."

"She thinks she does." Commander Dhar meets my gaze with a sad, even look, and I know at once she isn't talking only about Cassia. "But she's just a girl. She doesn't see it's not that simple. If she goes after them and gets herself killed, she won't be the only one that suffers. When she's older, when she has a command of her own and people's lives depend on her, then she'll understand. We have to do what's best for the greatest number of people."

It's as if someone has pitched a tuning fork to the exact frequency of my memories. My palms burn. I can't get enough air. "But—"

"I think the commander has given sufficient consideration to your request, Specialist." Dr. Osmani says.

The whine sharpens and then drops. My pulse comes roaring back into my ears.

"Of course." I stand and shove my chair back, trying not to let the shaking I feel starting at my core spread out to my limbs. I stop before Commander Dhar. "Thank you for the lesson in moral relativity, Commander." My voice shakes only on the last word.

Utter silence swallows the room.

"Memsahib . . . ," Rubio mutters under his breath.

I ignore him. I ignore all of them. Part of me knows I'm making a terrible mistake, insulting the commander herself, but most of me doesn't care. I make for the door, hands and bones on fire, storming by the stunned officers and the clerk on my way out.

My whole life, I've wanted to work on a Deep Sound research ship. When I was a little girl in the Gyre, I would sit up on our roof and watch the distant lights of the ships and satellites orbiting overhead while the chickens clucked softly around my feet. I never lost that scrap of memory, maybe because it was safe, or maybe because that wanting was an indelible part of me. Then, in my first year at Revati Academy, the instructors arranged for us to tour a research ship docked in orbit, one of the *Ranganathan*'s smaller, older sisters. We walked the ship's pristine hallways two by two, Vishva and I holding hands, goggling at the researchers and techs in their smart white jumpsuits and soft-soled slippers. I couldn't have put into words what I felt then. Every person aboard carried a measured, peaceful industry with them down the corridors, smoothly interlocking their duties, as if they all knew their own small part was vital to the vessel's perfect clockwork.

I had never seen people work this way before, not in the frenetic pace of Mumbai, where everyone crushed up against his neighbor in competition for customers, time, profit, or in the Gyre, where one steady, monotonous day collecting trash on the waste plain bled into another. All I knew then, a wide-eyed girl aboard her first Deep Sound ship, was that this was what I wanted. This was the closest human beings got to perfection.

All of that crumples behind me as I stalk away from the dining quarters. The lift doors close—for once it's empty, thankfully—and my breath fills the small space, harsh and loud, as if I have been running. I cover my face with my hands and slide down against the corner. Did I imagine that shipside harmony all those years ago? Was I so young I couldn't see past the surface? Or have research ships changed? I thought I would be happy here. I thought I would be with people like me. But they aren't. They're exactly like Vishva, thinking only of themselves, ready to cast off anyone who's no longer of use.

The lift opens near the upper recreation gardens, and a crowd of techs and research assistants pile in, laughing. I struggle to my feet and push my way out.

"Feeling stressed?" Advani-ji asks. "Exercise can reduce anxiety. Why not try taking a walk in the recreation gardens?"

"Fine," I say, even though I feel more like crushing the grass and snapping branches from the hedge maze than taking a stroll along the gardens' designated walking paths.

I tramp through the neatly trimmed foliage into the Ashoka wheel. The maze isn't really so much a maze as it is a meditation path that swallows you in green and spits you out near the same place you entered. Normally, the solitude of the wheel brings my heart rate down, helps me troubleshoot whatever's gone wrong with the pollinators or figure out a way to avoid the crowds in the mess hall, but tonight it doesn't help. This is bigger than my own petty anxieties.

I leave the hedges behind and keep walking, past the gardens and down the moving sidewalks. The arched walls and ceiling play a lavender twilight dotted with fireflies, and then a stark mesa at sunset, the clouds striating the darkening sky with pink and gold. It's all fake, nothing more than electrical impulses skittering across a screen. This whole place is an illusion, even down to our supposed mission. Who cares if there are only bees and no butterflies on the colonies? If a human life isn't worth fighting for, why are theirs?

The corridor opens onto the hangar where we brought in the Rover ship. The pathway rolls to a stop, emptying me into the wide, darkened bay. On the far end, the blackened wreck of the Rover ship hunches beneath a fire-dampening tarp. All my thoughts snuff out, and then my pulse comes back, shuddering through my veins. *The ship, the ship, the ship.*

I approach, my footsteps amplified by the cavernous latticework of metal girders far above my head. Outside the wreck, I pause. A burned, oily smell lingers in the air; more than a smell—I can taste it. It takes on mass in my lungs. The *Ranganathan*'s microbionic air scrubbers must still be hard at their invisible work, cleaning the air, but they haven't managed to erase all traces of tragedy yet.

I lift the edge of the tarp and duck inside. My slippers stir the ash. I blink, willing my eyes to hurry up and dilate, but when they finally do, there isn't much to see. Only the curved metal frame remains overhead, most of the fuselage burned away around it. A line of storage lockers back against one of the partially intact sides, metal faces either punched in or coated with ash, and chunks of plating and insulation litter the floor. The hull on the far side bows out, its tattered edges twisted like tinfoil. Explosive decompression. It doesn't take much to destroy a ship, especially a small one without as many built-in fail-safes as the *Ranganathan*. One small, hull-penetrating round, and the whole vessel can burst open to space like a flower blooming in fast motion.

On the one remaining inner wall, someone has swiped away the ash, revealing a muted red-and-yellow design— thick lines radiating out against a field of shadow blue, a wreath of flowers with stars in place of pistils all around.

A muffled sob echoes through the gutted ship.

I start. "Hello?"

The crying stops. "Who's there? What do you want?"

Cassia's voice reaches out of the shadows, tremulous and defiant.

"It's me." I squint into the darkness. Cassia sits in the entrance to one of the ship's gangways. "Miyole."

She doesn't answer, only rubs her eyes on her sleeve.

"You shouldn't be in here." I step closer. "The air's still full of carcinogens."

I expect her to come back at me with some comment about the rain calling the ocean wet, but she doesn't. Instead she drops her head into her hands and kneads her scalp.

"Cassia?" Her silence is far worse than the crying.

"Your commander says we can rebuild this." She brings up her head. Red rims her eyes. "Do you think she's even been to see what's left?"

"I don't know." I don't know if Commander Dhar truly hasn't seen the extent of the Rover ship's damage, or if she was simply giving Cassia and her family an excuse to stay aboard. One look at their vessel, and even those of us in bioscience would know it was beyond repair.

Cassia drops her head back against the door frame. She looks up at the expanse of tarp where the ceiling should be. "Milah learned to walk here. We used to play Sparks and Kettles. That was Nethanel's favorite when we were little."

I don't know what to say. Soraya would know. She always knew when I needed soothing words and when I needed to be left alone up in the branches of the Japanese maple in the corner of our back garden. But she isn't here. It's just clumsy, awkward me. I finger the hem of my sari and stare down into the ash. I wish I was wearing my work clothes and not this costume. It feels even more out of place in the midst of the Rover ship's destruction. I hesitate for a moment, then sit down next to Cassia on the blackened floor.

"Do you think she'll remember him?" Cassia asks, almost too quiet for me to hear.

I look up. "Your brother?"

"Her father," she corrects, though the words sound as if they're shredding her throat. "Nethanel's not just my brother. He's her father, too."

I rub a spot on the floor. The soot smudges my fingers, oily and opaque, but the floor isn't any cleaner, either. It's as if it's spreading, staining everything it touches. Cassia's palms are thick with it.

I look up at the red-and-yellow design on the wall facing us and then back at her hands. "That drawing," I say. "What is it?"

Cassia glances up and scowls. "The Wheel of Heaven."

"Does it mean something?"

"It's supposed to protect us. You know, keep misfortune out of our path." She pulls at a loose thread on her trouser cuff. "Some help it's been. First Milah's mother, and now this. Nethanel . . ."

Guilt rolls over me again. If I had stopped that *dakait*, his ship might have been caught waiting for him instead of bolting. We might have had time to stage a rescue or negotiate a trade—him for Nethanel. Cassia might still have her brother. Milah might still have her father.

"I'm sorry." I look at her. "I wish I could have stopped it."

Cassia scoffs. "You say it like it's over." She scowls at the wheel, and then at me. "It isn't over until we have him back."

Helplessness wells up in my chest. That feeling of watching disaster unfold and not being able to do anything but watch the feeds. "If I could go back . . . ," I start to say, and then stop. What good would it do Cassia to know I had a chance to save her brother and failed?

I change tactics. "Maybe the commander will change her mind." Even as I say it, I hear how ridiculous it sounds.

Cassia gives a short, bitter laugh. "Right. The commander."

"I want to help." I reach for her sleeve, but stop short

and let my hand fall to the floor between us. "I just . . . I don't know what else to do."

Cassia looks down at my hand, then up at me. Our eyes meet. Dark circles hang beneath hers, like bruises. Something raw and charged passes between us—it's as if my whole body is holding its breath. This feels different from hanging out with Vishva or any of the girls I knew back home. Different even than my crush on Karishma. The hairs on my arms rise.

"If I could get to Ceres," she says cautiously. "I know someone who could help."

My throat goes dry. I know what she's asking. Part of me has known where this was going since the moment I stormed out of the officers' dining hall. I close my eyes.

"We have scouting shuttles," I say in a low voice. "The ones Commander Dhar was talking about. They're short-range, but they could be modded."

I open them again. Cassia is watching me with the silent intensity of a starving animal about to be fed.

"It wouldn't hurt the mission if one went missing," I go on. "The commander almost said as much."

Cassia stares at me, her brows knit, her lips pressed together. "And one of those . . . It could reach Ceres Station?"

I nod. "Not much farther, but if someone could find the right parts on Ceres . . ."

"And this person," Cassia says slowly, careful to keep her face neutral. "She could do this alone?"

"As long as she can fly a ship." I nod.

Her face falls. "And if she can't?"

I falter. I assumed all the Rovers knew how to fly. It would be like living on a boat and never learning how to swim. *Except that happened all the time,* I suddenly remember. Most of our neighbors in the Gyre thought my mother was crazy for taking me in the water. *You want your girl to be shark bait, Miss Captain, you?*

I bite my lip. "Not even a little bit?"

Cassia shakes her head. "I worked on the water recycling system. Kept up the air filters."

I swallow. Things just got several magnitudes more complex. "In that case, she would need someone to fly for her."

Cassia stifles a groan and grinds her palms into her eyes. When she lowers her hands, a half-moon of soot marks her cheek. "Someone has to stay behind with Milah and the baby. Aunt Rebekah, probably. My father's injured too badly. And Ezar . . ." She shakes her head and looks up at me, helpless. "He's willing to think

Nethanel's dead. He wouldn't have the stomach for a rescue anyway."

Dead. A rescue.

Times stops. My whole body hums, as if the bees have built a hive inside me. *Skimming the water, searching for my mother's body. Milah holding Tibbet's limp frame. Cassia, full of righteous fire, staring down the commander.* When I was younger, Ava insisted on showing me how to pilot my mother's old sloop. Just in case, she said. I thought it was pointless. I could have used those dusty afternoons to finish my homework or go out riding with Vishva. I already knew I wanted to be a scientist, not a pilot.

But I learned the basics.

I learned enough.

Cassia has to do this thing, and if she can't fly herself, there is only one other way it can be done. I know what I have to do. I know how to make it right. All at once, the bees rise to an unbearable hum, and then stop.

"I could go," I say in the silence. "I could fly for you."

CHAPTER • 6

One of the first things the early Deep Sound pioneers figured out was that if you spend too much time with the same people day after day in an enclosed space, all the fake gardens in the universe wouldn't stop you from going truly and profoundly insane. The stress, the isolation, it gets to you, and you start doing things you would never think of doing under the open sky, like starting fistfights or stabbing one another with cutlery. Or screaming at your commander and storming out of an officers' dinner.

Which is why, the morning after my outburst at dinner, I find my schedule full of mindfulness training and appointments with the ship's counselors.

"It could be worse." Lian peeks over my shoulder at the handbook screen and shrugs.

And she's right. It could be far worse. The *Ranganathan*'s

administration could have recorded the incident as a disciplinary misdemeanor, rather than a case of stress-induced emotional reactivity. Still.

"You won't tell anyone, will you?" I glance at my other suitemates' empty bunks.

Lian hesitates and gives me a sideways look. "I'm pretty sure they already know."

My stomach sinks.

Lian looks guilty. "Actually, I'm pretty sure everyone knows."

I stare at her for half a second before it hits me. *Oh, no.* "Rubio."

Lian nods. "Rubio."

"*Chaila.*" I drop back on my bunk and pull my pillow over my face. "At least tell me the thing with the officers made him forget about the cat."

Lian stays silent a beat too long. I peek out from under the pillow at her.

"I heard about that, too." Lian grimaces. "At the mess this morning."

I groan and roll over. What did I ever do to deserve Hayden Rubio? *It's not for much longer,* I remind myself. Two more days, and we'll be near enough for the shuttle to reach Ceres Station. Then Rubio will be the least of my problems.

I hurry through my morning duties—check the pollinator habitats, program the nutrient rain timer, and tweak the atmospheric mix. By some small, anomalous grace, none of the butterflies have died overnight. A blue-black sparrowtail perches on a mossy branch above me, gently folding and unfolding its wings. *Graphium cloanthus*, a glassy bluebottle.

Guilt twists in my chest. These fragile creatures—the bees and butterflies—their lives have been my responsibility since I came on board. I've watched them and their ancestors inch through their larval stages, cocoon themselves beneath leaves, burst forth in a flurry of wings, mate, lay their eggs, and die. I've stolen their eggs for Dr. Osmani's genetic alterations and sneaked them back into place afterward. I've charted every iteration's effect on their life span.

But now there's something more important to be done, something I can't ignore. Help Cassia. Rescue Nethanel. Make sure Milah grows up with at least one of her parents. I know it's the right thing to do, but I still feel seasick whenever I think about it. It isn't only the prospect of stealing a shuttle and the mountain of trouble that goes along with that. Or the knowledge that I'm giving up the years of work it took to make it to the DSRI. Or the thought of how disappointed Soraya will be when she finds out what I've done, because she'll never, ever understand. Maybe it's all of those things. Or maybe it's all the unknown factors in between. "Rescue Nethanel" is just a hypothesis. The outcome could just as easily be that we get caught stealing the shuttle, or we make it to Ceres Station, but we lose the trail. Nethanel disappears into the unending night of space.

I shake off the thought. "They'll assign you someone else," I say to the glass. "Someone good." Maybe Dr. Osmani herself will spend some time with the pollinators and see that I wasn't the one killing them after all.

I send off my morning report and race downstairs to the wellness level, avoiding the crowds on the lift. I don't want to see loads of people on a good day, and if Lian is right about Rubio's gossip reaching everyone, I especially want to stay hidden today.

The walls of the wellness level glow with a soft, lunar blue. Calm settles over me as I navigate the corridors. I know the ship is subtly manipulating my emotions, bathing me in shades empirically proven to exert a soothing influence, but my amygdala doesn't care that it's being had. My shoulders start to relax. A hologram of interlaced tree branches overhangs the ceiling, a blue sky sparkling beyond them. Only the smell gives away the lie—crisp, sterilized air where there should be leaves and damp earth.

I stop and double-check the schedule on my handbook. SEMINAR ROOM 12A—MINDFUL FOCUS WORKSHOP. I hug the screen to my chest and slip down the hall, checking the display on each glass doorway I pass until I find the one that matches my schedule.

The counselor sits at a table with his back to me, talking to a young man in a pale gray flight uniform. I know the pilot. Alan Hwang. A few weeks ago, he took one of the fighters out into the black and tried to sit in it until he ran out of oxygen. I can't be as bad off as he is, can I? I didn't try to off myself, after all. Maybe that's why I'm still on partial duty rotation and Alan has been confined to the wellness level for almost a month straight. I guess preadmission psych tests don't catch everything.

My forehead bumps the glass with a light *thump*. The counselor turns, smiles beatifically, and waves me in.

I square my shoulders. The sooner I get this over with, the sooner I can concentrate on socking away supplies and using Jyotsana's security clearance to hack the *Ranganathan's* logs. The *dakait* ship's call signature, the shuttle's security override codes, it's all there, waiting for me to download to my crow. But for now, I have to act normal, or as normal as someone undergoing a psych evaluation can be. I activate the door.

"Mindfulness increases accuracy and precision," Advani-ji reminds me. "Daily practice can reduce overall anxiety."

Alan looks up at me as I walk in. He seems healthy enough—maybe even a little pudgy—but his gaze is dull and subdued, like he doesn't have the energy to meet my eyes. No wonder. He's nineteen and his career as a pilot is over before it started, on top of whatever took him out into the emptiness in the first place.

I sit down across from him at the broad table in the center of the room. Stacks of pastel origami paper sit between us.

"Specialist Guiteau, right?" our instructor says. "So glad you could join us. Today we're learning how to make cranes."

If I have one good thing to say about origami, it's that it keeps me from worrying that I've made a horrible mistake, that I'll get caught and end up like Alan, everything over before it's begun. I go over the plan in my head as I fold, check it for glitches. Tomorrow, during ship's night, we'll pass within a short flight of Ceres Station. Three hours into third shift, when the flight and deck crews have retired to their bunks, I'll meet Cassia on the hangar floor. We'll sneak aboard a shuttle together, and the rest depends on speed and surprise. And Commander Dhar's distaste for altering the *Ranganathan*'s course simply to chase one tiny ship. I fold my koi paper in half so it forms a triangle and crease it with my thumb.

"How's it coming, Miyole?"

I jump. David, the counselor, smiles warmly and leans over my shoulder to inspect my work. Everyone else on the ship goes by his or her title and surname, but for some reason, the counselors are always simply David or Yumiko or Stjepan. I guess so we'll feel comfortable opening up about our innermost fears and anxieties to them or something.

"Fine." I gesture at the growing pile of therapy cranes I've managed to finish folding over the last hour. I tried doing them with my gloves on at first, but that didn't turn out so well. At least Alan and David don't seem like the gossiping types. So far, they either haven't noticed my scarred hands, or they don't care.

David plucks a bird out of the pile and examines it. He straightens out its beak, which, if I'm honest, I wasn't the most careful about folding.

"You're rushing." David gently places the crane back down on the table in front of me.

"I'm not trying to," I lie.

He takes a seat next to me and pulls a fresh piece of paper from the top of the stack. "It doesn't matter how many you make, you know."

"I know." I sigh and flick the lopsided bird back into the pile with its flock.

David folds his paper in half and creases it in one smooth, practiced motion. "Can I ask you something?"

I shrug.

"Do you like taking walks?"

I frown. "I guess." Back in Mumbai, I liked swimming and riding better, but water's too scarce for that out here, and we don't have any use for horses.

He opens up the paper and folds it in the opposite direction, so the creases cross each other. "This isn't a race. Think of it more as a walk. A stroll. Something you do simply for the pleasure of doing it." The square slip of paper becomes a diamond.

I nod and look down to pick at a hangnail. "I get it."

I don't mention how I never walk for fun, only when my coms remind me I'm falling behind on my weekly exercise quota or I'm too worked up to think straight. Or when I want to avoid the crowds in the lifts. I don't have room in my life for things without a purpose.

David finishes with a flourish and hands me a perfect paper crane with movable wings. "Be where you are, Miyole. If you're stuck up here"—he taps his head—"you'll only make yourself anxious over things you can't change. You'll miss everything out here." He spreads his hands to indicate this room, the ship, the universe.

And I know he's right, in a way. I should appreciate what I have. Out of all the billions of people on Earth, only a million or so have the education to qualify for a Deep Sound research mission, and out of those, only a few thousand actually end up selected to serve. I could have been born in the Siberian wastes, far from the center of the world. I could have grown up poor and been forced to take a factory job before I finished school, or worse. I could have died in that hurricane. Instead, all my dreams have come true. My pollinators will bring life and food to a newly terraformed colony. Someday people will live there and ease the overcrowding on Earth.

But all of that is so far away, so abstract. Cassia and Milah need me now. And there is something I can change. I have the chance to do for Milah what no one could ever do for me—give her back one of her parents. What good is all my luck and education if I can't do that? What good is my being here if I can't at least try to right this one wrong?

After the workshop, I'm supposed to spend an hour walking in the gardens. Instead, I wander wellness, keeping an eye out for Cassia. She's bound to be here somewhere. Her father has been getting skin grafts to cover his burns, and today bionics is replacing his injured eye. I know I probably should be avoiding her, but my stomach feels like it's percolating. My whole body quivers with nerves, as if I've downed an entire pot of tea in one sitting. I'll feel calmer when I see her.

"Wellness tip," Advani-ji chirps. "Have you had enough liquid today? Drinking water can reduce an elevated heart rate."

"Stuff it," I mutter, and switch her to silent.

I find Cassia in one of the visitation anterooms, watching her father sleep in a hospital bed on the other side of a glass partition. White gauze covers his left eye, and a tube snakes down his throat, parting his lips. His chest rises and falls regularly, but patches of sickly pale tissue show through the red, flaking skin along his shoulder and neck, where the medics haven't finished applying their dermal grafts yet. Cassia sits in the dark, eyes wide and back straight, almost swallowed by the white expanse of couch filling most of the room.

I sink down next to her. For a moment, neither of us says anything.

Then she speaks, raw and throaty, without breaking her gaze from her father's bed. "We shouldn't be seen together."

"I know." I stare straight ahead beside her. "I just . . ."

I needed to see you, I want to say. *I need you to remind me why I'm doing this.* For a fleeting moment, an impulse to reach out and squeeze her hand flitters through me. But Cassia holds herself so stiff, as if moving might cause her pain.

"How is he?" I nod at her father.

"Better." She finally turns to look at me and scratches unconsciously at her own bandages. "Your people fitted him with an eye."

"His body's accepting it?"

She nods and half laughs. "It's even the same color as the one he lost."

"That's . . . good." I don't know what else to say.

"Right." Bitterness seeps into her voice and she looks away again. "It's great. Everything's perfect now. He can go right back to bidding out on repair jobs, like nothing ever happened."

My anger flares up like a shield. "You know that's not what I meant."

Cassia clenches her jaw. She glares at me, and I glare right back.

Cassia looks away first. "I'm sorry." She lowers her voice, but her words tremble with the effort. "It's not that I'm not grateful. It's just . . . I know my father would give up that new matching eye if it would bring Nethanel back."

"I know." Before I realize what I'm doing, I lay my hand over hers. Her fingers rest cold and still beneath mine. Whatever fire was in her moments ago has burned out, making her touchable.

She looks down at our hands, and suddenly my body flashes hot with embarrassment. What am I doing? I don't want another incident like the one my final year at Revati, when we played the kissing-bottle game and my spin landed on Kiran. She had long brown arms, skin almost as dark as mine, and a funny dent in one of her knees that sealed my crush, for some reason. She had been smiling at me across the circle—shy, from underneath her long dark lashes, and I had been wondering if there was an algorithm that would help you control where the bottle stopped. When we kissed, it was chaste and slow, and an electric ripple shot through my nervous system. If I'd had feathers, that kiss would have ruffled them. But when Kiran pulled back, she scrunched up her face and made a big show of wiping off her lips, then trying to wipe her hands on all the other guys and girls around the circle. Since then, I've tried to be more cautious, more private. Not make assumptions.

"I'm sorry." I start to draw back, but Cassia's fingers twitch as if she's suddenly come awake, and she folds them up in mine.

"Don't." Her voice is dry. "Don't go yet. Stay with me."

Cardiac output equals heart rate times stroke volume.

I swallow so my throat won't stick together. "Okay."

The backs of her fingers brush my palm. I can't feel anything along the tracks of my scars, where the nerve endings are damaged, but everywhere else, her skin is warm on mine. Her hand freezes. I tense. She's felt the lines of waxy scar tissue, and now I know what comes next. Revulsion, or worse, a sick curiosity.

She turns my hand over and sucks in a breath. "What happened?"

I wince. But seconds pass, and she doesn't pull away.

"It was a long time ago," I say. "I didn't get to a medic in time to stop the scarring."

She nods, and I remember that access to medics is far less common out here than in the midst of modern Mumbai.

Maybe I'm less of a freak to Cassia than I would be to any of my crewmates aboard the *Ranganathan*.

"I'm sorry," she says.

"It's okay," I say. "It doesn't hurt anymore."

She doesn't say anything else, but she doesn't let go of my hand, either. She holds on to it, tight but not too tight, as she stares at the long glass window between her father and us. My skin warms against hers. The warmth travels up my arm, quieting the nervous hum inside me. She doesn't care about my scars. She doesn't need me to prove I belong. She only needs me. I've been looking all my life for a way to make the world a little bit right, and now that I have my chance, I'm not letting go.

CHAPTER 7

I lie in my bunk, fully clothed, the privacy shroud pulled closed to shutter the light from my handbook. In an hour and a half, I'm supposed to meet Cassia outside the hangar. Will I be able to fly the shuttle out of dock like I promised? Ava always said flying isn't something you forget, but it's been months since the last time we practiced together.

I roll over and plant my face in the pillow. There are way too many variables, so many ways for everything to go wrong. What if someone finds our supplies hidden aboard the shuttle before we get there? What if someone saw us holding hands? What if someone overheard Cassia and me whispering in the burned-out wreck from the very beginning, and Commander Dhar is only waiting to catch us in the act? Cassia hasn't exactly been quiet about wanting to go after her brother. Maybe they're watching her. I stifle a groan. I should have stayed up in the common room this evening. I should have talked to my bunkmates like everything was normal and I wasn't about to commit the kind of theft that could end with me brought before the DSRI's correctional board and banned from any future Deep Sound expeditions. Or worse, sent to a detention camp.

Every cold, logical part of me knows this is the stupidest thing I could ever do. I know what Soraya would say. Her voice circles in my head, disappointed, concerned. *You worked so hard for this. You're throwing away your future.*

She was so proud when I told her the DSRI had made an age exemption for me, the first ever. I even gave her fake forms to sign. Why shouldn't she believe it? I had been taking advanced classes at Revati since I was eight. I was accepted to the university when I was fifteen. Why shouldn't the DSRI let me in early, too?

Maybe they wouldn't have cared. Maybe they really would have made the first age exemption ever. But I couldn't risk it. I couldn't bring myself to their attention that way. Because if they said no, I was stuck on Earth until the next DSRI mission, taking courses just to have something to do, bumping into Vishva on the trains, always being the youngest, the darkest, the exotic outlier in my class. I would have been swimming in circles.

Ava was the one who saved me from that.

Ava was the one who got me here.

A few weeks after I dropped in on Rushil to plead my case for an identity hack, he and Ava invited me down to their place for dinner. I kept waiting for him to say something all through the meal, and then afterward as we sat around the orange glow of a citronella lamp in the back garden. But then it was long after dark and Rushil begged off to go sleep.

"I guess I should head back," I said.

"Stay a little." Something about the way Ava said it brought a charge into the air. She had a funny look on her face, as if she were trying to hide a frown.

I lowered myself back into my chair. The lamp cast sharp shadows on Ava's features.

"Rushil told me," she said.

"Ava—"

"Why would you do that, Miyole?" She leaned forward and looked down at her feet. "Don't you get what you're asking?"

"I do get it," I said quietly.

"But you did it anyway." She looks up. "What's your

rush, Mi? It's not like this is the last DSRI mission ever. There's going to be another in, what, three years?"

"Yeah, but I'll be *twenty* by then," I said.

Ava raised an eyebrow.

I knew how silly it sounded, but it wasn't only another two years studying, it was another two years waiting to do something useful, waiting for my life to begin.

"But if I can go now," I pressed on, frustrated, "I would turn eighteen only a few months into the voyage. Seventeen and a half? Eighteen? Does it really make that much of a difference?"

"Maybe not." Ava shrugged. She looked away at her ship, the *Perpétue*, named after my mother. We both knew what she had been doing at my age. Running for her life. Flying a ship all on her own. Taking care of me.

"I'm ready," I said. "All my friends at Revati are gone and the people I know at university are setting up their practicals and internships. What am I supposed to do, hang around for another couple of years and take more organic chemistry classes?"

"You like organic chemistry," Ava reminded me.

"That's not the point," I said.

Ava sighed. "You really want this, don't you?"

"I haven't ever wanted anything else." We both knew it

was true. Ava was there the first time I announced at dinner that I wanted to be a Deep Sound engineer. She read me science articles at bedtime when I was younger. She saw me studying late all those nights in my room.

Ava stood. "Come on."

My nerves picked up, half excited, half frightened. "Where are we going?"

Ava didn't answer at first. She picked up the lamp. "You have money?"

"Two thousand rupaye," I answered.

She nodded. "If I do this for you, you have to promise me something."

I tried to keep my voice from squeaking. Was she saying what I thought she was saying? "Anything."

"You never ask Rushil to do anything illegal ever again." Her features were hard in the lamp glow. "Not even jaywalking."

I laughed.

"I'm serious, Mi," Ava said. "He's worked too hard to get out. I love you to death, but you're not putting him in danger again."

I looked Ava over. She was shorter than me now, and had been since my thirteenth birthday, but I still hadn't gotten used to looking down at her instead of up. She was half a mother to me. Or maybe that's just what older sisters are.

"I promise." I put one hand over my heart and held the other up. "No more bothering Rushil."

"Good," she said, and blew out the lantern.

Rōrī Island stood in the middle of a soggy wetland to the east of the city proper, a warren of buildings made from modified metal shipping containers surrounded by banyan and mulberry trees. The skeleton of an abandoned high-rise jutted from the middle like an exposed spine.

Ava and I rented a skiff and poled across to solid ground. A boxy container with its outer doors sawed off served as the island's entrance, full of buzzing, flickering lights, but otherwise empty. Our footsteps clanged and echoed ahead through the tunnel. My skin prickled.

"We can go back," Ava said quietly. "If you've changed your mind . . ."

"No," I said, and swallowed my nerves. Only another hour or two, and then everything standing between me and my future would be gone. I glanced up at the tiny black bulbs bulging from the ceiling above us—spider-eye cameras. Walking this tunnel in the pitch-dark would have been less terrifying. At least then I wouldn't have been able to see the walls and ceiling closing in around us.

A drunk came shuffling the opposite way through the tunnel, muttering under his breath. I moved closer to Ava, who was wearing her jacket open to display the knife at her belt. He passed us with only a dirty look.

Soon we were out in the open air again, rattling up a metal staircase and across a footbridge to the main floor of the skyscraper. Purple and yellow lights, and electronic bhangra so loud its bass drowned out my own heartbeat, pulsed from the open spaces where the building's walls and windows used to be. The bottom floor was packed. A bar backed by a wall of glass bottles stood like an island in the center, surrounded by people dancing or grouped around tables in smoky corners. Somewhere in the darkened floors above us, someone whooped, and a beer bottle shattered on the promenade behind us.

"What is this place?" I shouted over the music. "You're taking me to a club?"

Ava didn't seem to have heard me. "You have to promise never to come here alone," she shouted as we threaded through the crowd and took a seat at the bar. "And don't tell Vishva about it, either. She's not as street smart as she thinks."

"Okay." I nodded. That wouldn't be a problem, seeing as I hadn't so much as talked to Vishva in at least half a year.

Ava leaned in close to my ear. "Put your crow on the counter and hold on to it."

"What?"

"Just do it," she said. "You'll see."

I took my handheld out of my pocket and placed it carefully on the bar in front of me. Almost at once, a man with a thin shirt and ridiculously defined pectoral muscles appeared in front of us, wearing a smile that had an awful lot to do with his eyebrows.

"What can I get you, ladies?" He reached for my crow with one hand and brought up two empty glasses with the other.

I snatched my crow back and looked at Ava.

"We don't want a drink." She placed one hand flat over her glass's empty mouth. "We need a chat."

He stood up straight. His smile disappeared. "About what?"

"Papers." Ava tilted her head at me. "For her."

He nodded. "Let me make you that drink."

I frowned. "We don't need—"

Ava put a hand on my arm. "Just wait."

My hands were sweating. The bartender filled my glass

with a violently blue liquid, then added a layer of something oily and orange to it, and topped it off by dropping in a whole gherkin on a white neon cocktail spear.

"Take the lift down two floors and turn left. Last door on the right," the bartender said as he slid the drink across to me.

I looked at Ava again. "Got it," she said.

"And, kid," the bartender called as I began to walk away. "I wouldn't drink that if I were you."

A man Ava's age answered the last door on the right. He took one look at the drink in my hand and beckoned me forward.

Ava moved to follow, but he held out a hand to stop her. "One drink, one visitor."

"We come as a pair," Ava said. "Auntie Rajni knows me."

He stared at her, his expression flat. "I said, one drink, one visitor."

Ava rested her hands on her hips, drawing back her jacket to reveal her knife. "And I said we come as a pair."

"What's all this fuss?" A woman's throaty voice called from inside. "Is that a drink for me?"

The man sighed and turned to reveal a stout woman in an electronic wheelchair positioned near a bank of screens in the corner of the room. "Yes, Auntie."

"You stop harassing these nice young ladies and bring it here, then." She rolled toward us and held out her hand. She wore sunglasses, even in the dimness of the room, and a system of interwoven braids piled on top of her head, with a shock of gray-white hair running through the construction.

"Auntie Rajni." Ava stepped forward. "Thank you for seeing us. This is my foster sister, Mi—"

"Yes, yes." Auntie Rajni stopped her chair beside me and looked meaningfully at the concoction in my hand. I held it out to her. "We drink first, then we talk."

"Of course." Ava smoothed her hands over her jacket. I knew that gesture. Ava calming herself, getting herself even keel for some difficult business.

Auntie Rajni fished out the pickle with her thumb and forefinger, then tilted the glass back. No one spoke as she gulped down the whole thing, then popped the pickle in her mouth and crunched it with relish.

"Now," she said, gesturing to a purple satin sofa. "We sit, like civilized people."

We sat. The guard took up his position next to the door and pretended not to listen.

"Auntie, as I was saying—" Ava started.

The woman shook a finger in Ava's face. "Not you." She turned to me. "Her. She's the one with the drink. She's the one wanting something."

I swallowed. I had been hoping Ava would do the talking for me, and all I would have to do was fork over the funds. I rubbed my palms together and wished I had brought a pair of gloves. I had a dozen pairs in blue velvet, faux yellow leather, and plain black smart cotton, but I hadn't expected to need them for a night at Ava and Rushil's.

"Speak up," Auntie Rajni said. "I have other business tonight."

"I, um . . . need some identification work," I said to the floor.

Auntie Rajni rubbed her chin. "Someone after you, child?"

I looked up, startled. "No. No, it's not that. Nothing like that."

"No?" Auntie Rajni raised an eyebrow over her glasses and turned to Ava. "This one's not like the girls you usually bring. What are you playing here, Parastrata?"

I darted a look at Ava. Sometimes she would get a message about a runaway girl—a girl like her, who had grown up with the merchant crewes that trawled the Deep—and she would disappear for hours or days. Some of those girls had even stayed with us while Ava tried to find a place for them. Was she bringing them to this Auntie Rajni for fake papers? Rushil did the same for her when we first landed in Mumbai—got her a work permit so we could get by. But why hadn't she told me what she was up to? I could have helped. I always helped her, especially at first, when it was just the two of us. Weren't we a team? Sisters? Didn't she trust me to keep quiet?

I push the sting to the back of my mind. "I need to be older," I said. "Eighteen. I need to be eighteen by this spring."

I held my breath. That had been far more awkward than it sounded in my head, but at least the words were out.

Auntie Rajni paused, then pulled off her sunglasses. One of her eyes was a cloudy blue—blind—but the other shone like mercury. A bionic eye. I tried not to stare and bit down my impulse to ask how it worked. I loved biomimetics and prosthetic grafts, but the problem was, they usually came attached to a person who didn't want to talk about the horrific injury or illness that had made them part machine. Something bad, something violent, must have happened to Auntie Rajni. We could cure most genetic disorders or malformations, but if there was some kind of trauma and the whole body part needed to be replaced . . .

She turned her quicksilver eye on Ava. "You're bringing me prep-school children who want a beer and *sutta* now?" She glared. "Is that what you think I'm about? There are plenty of simpletons running that business down in your Salt. *Rundi ki bachi . . .*"

My face burned. "That's not why."

"Oh?" Auntie Rajni's eye swiveled to me. "Why would a nice little rich girl like you be needing something like that, then? Hmm?"

"Does it really matter why she needs it, Auntie?" Ava cut in. "It's not so she can sneak out at night. I promise."

"*Kripayā,*" I leaned toward Auntie Rajni. This couldn't end here. I'd come too far. "This isn't for show. I need the real thing. Altered immigration papers, my school records, everything."

The old woman harrumphed and fumbled her glasses back over her nose. "These things are always a risk. Always. I like to know my customers aren't going to go pointing fingers if Mummy finds out." She gave me an acid look. At least she wasn't calling Ava names anymore.

"She won't," Ava said.

"Let's hear it from her, then."

"I won't," I promised.

And I meant it. I wouldn't. Getting aboard that DSRI ship meant everything to me, and I would say anything to get there.

I bury my face in my hands. Ava will go mental when she finds out what I've done. I'm fairly sure hacking into the ship's communication and security logs and abusing my security clearance—or rather, Jyotsana's security clearance—to steal a research shuttle counts as doing something illegal. And after the risks she took for me, the promises I made to her . . . once they find out I'm gone, they'll scour my records for whatever warning signs they missed, and they're sure to find evidence of the hack then. The only thing keeping me from rubbing holes in my palms is the thought that if anyone understands desperate measures, it's Ava.

I check the time. An hour until I'm supposed to meet Cassia. I can't lie still another moment longer. I power down the handbook, push the bed shroud aside, find my boots, and lace them up as quietly as I can.

Lian stirs as I creep for the door. "Miyole? What are you doing?"

"Nothing," I whisper. "Checking on the pollination lab. I think I set the nitrogen levels too high."

"Oh." She rolls back over and drops her head on the pillow.

I stop in the lab to check on my pollinators one last time. The butterflies' wings tremor as the lights flicker on inside their biomes. I stand staring at them for a moment, and then step into the air lock that separates them from the rest of the ship. I seal the door, alter the atmospheric pressure to match the enclosure, and let myself in.

The humid air swallows me. My nose prickles at the hint of rot beneath the bright smell of vegetation. More than the well-kept grounds of the recreation gardens, this place reminds me of Mumbai—its parks after monsoon season and the thick, wet heat of the greenhouses at school. I kneel down slowly beside a young kapok tree rooted in the center of the biome. The butterflies flutter nervously at first, but I take a seat on the damp peat, and within seconds, they've forgotten my existence. I check the time again. Three-quarters of an hour to go.

I lean back against the bark and close my eyes. An hour from now, I'll either be slicing through the utter darkness of space or sitting in the brig. Either way, I won't be smelling anything but recycled air for a long time, and I won't be touching anything as real as damp leaves and dirt.

Something tickles my hand. I open my eyes. A mangrove skipper, all dusky blue except for a cobalt pattern dappled across its back, balances on my knuckles. I stop breathing. Normally, when I come into the biome, I'm all efficiency and motion, trying to get in and out with the least disturbance to the pollinators. The idea that one of my subjects might alight on me, given enough stillness and time, has never crossed my mind.

The butterfly flexes its wings. I let out a breath, shaky and soft, trying not to disturb it. Will this creature survive after I'm gone? Will it live long enough to lay its eggs? Or will it end up in one of Dr. Osmani's acrylic displays? What about me? Out in the Deep, I'll be as vulnerable as the mangrove skipper. How long will I survive without the *Ranganathan* to protect me from hull-piercing asteroids and slavers?

I hug my knees to my chest. I could go back to bed, untie my boots, and sleep until ship's morning. Pretend none of this happened. Couldn't I? But Cassia will be waiting for me in the darkness of the dock. Could I live with myself if I knew I had the chance to help her get her brother back, to give Milah her father back, and didn't take it because I got cold feet at the last moment? Because I let fear get the best of me again? Will I be able to sleep at night, or will I see the *dakait*'s foot slipping my grasp every time I close my eyes?

I check my coms again. Fifteen minutes until I'm supposed to be on the dock. My sleep haze evaporates. Time to go. I don't know what will happen, or if anyone here will understand. Commander Dhar won't. Dr. Osmani won't. Rubio will hold court on how he always knew I was mad, and a liar. But that doesn't change what I have to do. It doesn't change what's right. I push myself to my feet. The mangrove skipper flits away, back to its cousins in the tree.

CHAPTER • 8

I exit the pollinator air lock and go up on tiptoe to reach the messenger bag I stashed in my alcove. I unstrap my coms from my wrist, zip a simple black jacket over my pressure suit, and power up my crow. Thank the stars Ava uploaded her good-bye message to it. I never would have thought to bring along a device that ran separate from the *Ranganathan*'s systems otherwise.

Ten minutes.

The lights shut off as I seal the lab's outer door behind me, leaving my coms bracelet blinking red in the dark. In several minutes, Advani-ji will notify security she hasn't been receiving life signs from my suit, but in the meantime, the ship won't be tracking me. I start down the dim corridor, night playing above me.

Five minutes.

The dock slides into view, quiet and dark. I step off the walkway and into the shadow of some supply crates stacked near the entrance. If the security rotation schedule I accessed with Jyotsana's clearance is accurate, Cassia and I have a seven-minute window to steal the shuttle after the guard on duty clears the area.

I catch sight of him on the opposite end of the dock, near the phalanx of fighters primed for duty. His black-gray uniform nearly disappears in the low light, but his coms bracelet gives off a regular blue flash every ten seconds. I count between the flashes. *One, two, three, four, five, six, seven, eight, nine . . .*

Three minutes to go.

"Clear." His voice carries across the silence. "Proceeding to sim labs."

Sim labs. My brain takes a moment to catch up. I just came from the sim labs.

The guard turns in my direction and starts walking.

"*Chaila*," I whisper, and shrink back behind the crates, as far as I can go. I didn't factor this in when I hacked the security roster. I'm wearing black over my pressure suit and I don't have my com bracelet to give me away, but the shadows aren't all that deep. One careful look in my direction, and the guard will spot me. I close my eyes and hold my breath, as if my own blindness will help me stay hidden.

His footsteps approach, strong and even. I press my back against the crates. *Degree of pupil dilation corresponds to ambient light or lack thereof....* He comes up beside me—*please don't stop*—and then passes out into the corridor and down the moving walkway.

I step out from the shadows and wait for my eyes to adjust. After a moment, Cassia emerges from behind her own wrecked ship, two satchels slung across her shoulders and another tucked under her arm. I raise my hand silently and start across the empty floor. She waves back and hurries to me as quickly as she can under the weight of the bags.

"You made it." She offers me a fragile smile. Her hair hangs in loose waves, and she's slightly out of breath. "You came."

"I told you I would." At the sight of her, my fear fades. *This is right. I can fix this.*

The corner of her mouth twists up. "I thought maybe I scared you off."

"Not yet." I grin and hold out a hand for one of the bags. "Here."

Cassia clutches them tighter to her chest. "No, it's okay."

"You're sure?" I frown.

"I've got them," she says, at the exact moment a low, almost inaudible growl escapes the bag under her arm.

My eyes widen. "What is that?"

"Nothing." Cassia pushes past me and starts for the row of shuttles docked on the left side of the bay.

"Hey!" I hiss. I hurry to catch up to her and grab her arm. We're wasting precious seconds. Any moment now, someone is going to notice us on one of the hundreds of fish-eyed cameras built into the walls and rafters. "Be serious. What do you have in there?"

She lifts her eyes to the ceiling and sighs, then slowly pulls back the bag's zipper. I know I'm not going to like whatever is inside, but I peer in anyway, and come face-to-face with a supremely pissed Tibbet. He glowers at me, his eyes black and dilated, and lets out another low growl that raises the hairs on the back of my neck.

I look up at Cassia in disbelief. "You brought the cat?"

She zips the bag partially closed again, leaving enough space to let in air. "I knew you wouldn't understand." She turns on her heel and storms away.

"You're right." I wrestle my voice back to a whisper and jog to keep pace with her. "Do you want to tell me why we need your pet to help us steal a shuttle?"

"He's not a *pet*." She ducks beneath the nose of the shuttle we've chosen and wheels around on me. In a split second, her expression flips from annoyance to shock.

"Miyole . . . ," she chokes out, before something cold and hard presses against the back of my neck.

"Don't move, memsahib."

I freeze. *Rubio.*

Rubio circles around, keeping his stunner trained on my chest. He looks from me to Cassia. "Either of you care to repeat that part about stealing a shuttle?"

"Rubio, listen . . ." My mouth has gone dry. I glance at Cassia, who is slowly pulling open the zipper on Tibbet's bag now. I shake my head. What is she playing at? "I don't think you heard us right. You must have misunderstood."

"Oh, I'm sure I heard right." He glances at Cassia, who stops unzipping, then back at me. "You're not as sly as you think, memsahib."

"Rubio, please." I'm pleading now, even though it kills me to grovel in front of him. Flashes of my own ruined future play in my head—Cassia and me in the brig; the inevitable investigation; "Who changed your records for you?"; returning to Earth empty-handed, Cassia's brother as lost as a grain of sand on a beach.

"You don't understand," I say. "Commander Dhar didn't leave us any choice. We had to."

"The only thing any of us *has* to do is call this in." Rubio raises his wrist com.

"Wait!" I say, in the same moment Cassia chucks Tibbet's bag forward, straight at Rubio's chest.

The cat springs from the satchel and lands on Rubio. Rubio lets out a yelp and steps back, his face registering more surprise than pain, even though a fine hatchwork of red lines has sprung up on his neck and face where Tibbet's claws have raked him. Cassia swings her other bag at his head.

Rubio's eyes pop wide. He falls like lead, smacking his head on the floor with a sickening thud.

Not good. Very, very not good.

We both stand over him in stunned silence.

Cassia covers her hand with her mouth. "Is he dead?"

I kneel beside Rubio and press my fingers against his neck. His pulse flutters. "No. Concussed, maybe."

She lets out a breath. "Good." She lunges for his legs and pulls him few steps, his jacket bunching up under his head. "Help me."

"Cassia—what are we doing?" I ask, lifting his arms and shuffling after her. Rubio hangs limp between us.

"We can't leave him here."

I glance up at the cameras. Maybe no one is watching now, but they'll play it all back once we're gone and see what we did. "I think we can."

"We don't know how much he overheard," Cassia says. "He could tell them where we're going."

"You don't mean . . ." I glance at the shuttle. "We can't take him with us."

Cassia grunts and repositions her grip on Rubio's ankle. "I don't see how we have much choice. He's going to wake up and raise the alarm."

Rubio moans. His head lolls back.

"And us overriding the security doors on a research shuttle won't?" I say.

"I guess we could hit him over the head again, if that's what you want."

"No!" I say, louder than I mean to. The word echoes across the hangar. I frown at Cassia. We've lost too much time already. We can't afford to argue anymore. "You're right, okay?"

She drops Rubio's feet as I gently lower his injured head to the floor. I slide my crow from my pocket, thumb through to the right screen, and connect my small device to the shuttle's hatch controls. The latches give way with a muted *thunk*, the hydraulics whine softly, and the hatch unfolds.

Cassia grabs Rubio's feet again and starts pulling him up the loading ramp. "I'll take care of him and Tibbet. You go power up."

"You're sure?" I hesitate. "You can do it alone?"

"Go," Cassia almost shouts. "That guard's going to be back any minute now."

I nod and race up the ramp, through the shuttle's small storage and maintenance access compartment, the cramped living quarters not meant for more than a few nights away from the *Ranganathan*, and up the short ladder to the cockpit. I crawl into the pilot's seat, plug my crow into the controls' line-in, and flip on the auxiliary power. The ship's panels flare to life, candy bright and new beneath my hands. A hint of fresh-soldered metal hangs in the air. I doubt if anyone has ever flown this shuttle before. It would have been made special for the research mission.

Jyotsana's codes cut through the ship's security wall like butter. One by one, the systems come online—environmentals, telemetry, navigation, repulsion shields, gravity. The sound of clanging metal and a grunt from Cassia echo up from the shuttle's berth. I slide back the blinders on the viewport and gaze out over the hangar.

On the far side, the silhouette of a guard passes under the entryway and stops dead.

Vaat lag gayii.

"Cassia!" I shout. "Time to go!"

She appears at the bottom of the ladder to the cockpit. "But Tibbet . . ."

"Will you forget about the *chirkut* cat?" I snap.

She scowls at me. "That . . ." She struggles with the word. "*Chirkut* cat saved us both."

I unlock the propulsion controls and feed power to the engines. A low thrum pulses through the ship's frame and a roar of wind licks in through the open hatch as the engines wind up.

"We can't!" I yell over the throbbing air. "We have to go!"

"I'm not leaving him!" she shouts back, and disappears.

I grip the propulsion bars and force myself to stay still. I may have the controls, but I can't leave without her. Across the hangar, the guard strides in our direction, stunner out, coms raised. This whole thing is going sideways, fast.

"Cassia!" My voice rattles in warning.

In answer, the hatch's hydraulics whine again, and the rushing chaos outside falls silent.

"Got him!" She appears again, breathless, at the base of the ladder. Tibbet stares up at me, moon-eyed and ruffled.

"Strap in," I call, and open up the thrusters without waiting. The shuttle lurches forward at an uneven pitch. Its nose dips and scrapes along the dock with a tooth-turning screech. *Chaila.* I strain against the push bars, trying to keep us level. Flying under gravity is always the trickiest part, and this ship is heavier than my mother's old sloop, the one Ava inherited. It's the difference between riding a horse and an elephant. I wrestle the ship's nose up and edge us out over the hangar floor, the wind from our thrusters buffeting the guard below. He shouts soundlessly into his coms and points his stunner at our shuttle's belly.

I engage the shuttle's communications line and transmit the command to unseal the air lock. The immense bay doors on the outer end of the hangar jolt and begin to unwind in a slow rotation. The warning system lights flare to life, washing the dock in red. The shuttle muffles all the outside sound, but our communication line relays the warning claxon and the calm voice intoning instructions.

"ALL PERSONNEL, CLEAR HANGAR Q-17 FOR TAKEOFF. WARNING: AIR LOCK DEPRESSURIZATION IMMINENT."

Below, the guard runs for the exit. A pinhole opens in the center of the inner air lock doors, then widens enough to admit our ship. I guide us forward, hands shaking, until we reach the opening. The hull scrapes against the aperture, sending a tremor down the length of the shuttle, but then we're through, into the darkness of the air lock.

For a blind second, I wonder if we're trapped, our override codes revoked.

The voice comes back: "DEPRESSURIZING." Our ship judders in the current as the pneumatics suck all the air from the chamber, but I grip the push bars and hold us steady.

"Miyole?" Cassia calls from below, and I remember she's blind down there with Rubio and the cat.

"Hold on," I shout back. "We're almost through."

The outer air lock door whirls open on a glittering bank of stars and the stark, pale expanse of the *Ranganathan*'s spiraling hull. Vertigo takes me. The sky pitches, and my eyes fight to track its path. I lean against the push bars, dizzy, and the shuttle dives down, smacks against the air lock's outer rim, and then skips forward, out into the emptiness.

The *Ranganathan*'s gravitational pull breaks, and my stomach flies up to meet my heart. In the small, endless stretch of time it takes the shuttle's own weaker gravitational field to flip on, I remember the time I went jumping from one of the lower levels of the Mumbai levee with Vishva and some other girls from Revati. We had heard some of the older girls at school talking about a place where you could jump down into a retention pool and climb back out again. It didn't look so bad from below, but when I stood on the ledge, bare toes gripping the hot metal, the fall seemed bottomless. But I had to jump, because I had teased Miranda Jae about being scared. Until this moment, I had never known anything could match the terror of momentarily freeing yourself from the universe's grip, only to have it reclaim you at terminal velocity.

Pressure on my shoulder. "Miyole."

I start. The universe's swing slows. I follow Cassia's furrowed gaze to the viewport.

"We have to move." She squeezes into the copilot's seat beside me.

Right. I blink, trying to will away the last of my vertigo. We can't linger around like a drowsy peacock. We have to move before the *Ranganathan* sends its fighters to haul us back in.

Movement in the rear relay screens. As if I've summoned them, the air lock dilates again, and a trio of matte black birds darts from the hangar behind us.

"Vaat!" I curse, and slam the push bars forward. The shuttle shoots off, jerking Cassia and me back against our seats and leaving the *Ranganathan* a shrinking shell in our rear viewport relays. Unhobbled by gravity and atmospheric resistance, the engines sing and the bars respond to my fingers' lightest touch.

Cassia glances over at me, half terrified, half awed.

"Chaila," I whisper appreciatively. This is a ship made for the Deep.

A warning flare strafes over our bow.

The shuttle's com lines spit to life. "Research shuttle 49-Q. You are not authorized for departure. Return to dock immediately."

Cassia gives me a worried look. I raise our shields in answer and lock the push bars forward. We have nothing to hide behind this far out from Ceres Station—only a fine grit of asteroid dust and radiation. Our best hope is to push for speed and trust the *Ranganathan* won't authorize its fighters to fire on us.

Another flare explodes before our front viewport, blinding me.

"Research shuttle 49-Q," the coms repeat. "Desist from your present course or we will be forced to disable your craft."

Cassia presses her back against the copilot's chair. Her eyes pop wide.

"They won't," I say, half to her, half to myself. "They won't."

I press the bars to their limit. The shuttle surges forward, and the *Ranganathan* fades to a bright speck behind us, but the fighters keep pace. Blood pounds in my ears. *Energy equals mass times the speed of light squared.*

"Research shuttle 49-Q," the coms start again, and then, as abruptly, they stop. Their silence unnerves me more than the flares or warnings. The birds continue by our sides, black shadows flanking us through the perfect night.

Keep going, I tell myself. I swallow the bile creeping up the back of my throat. *Keep going.*

Silence stretches out around us, heavy and oblique as dark matter. Then, when my lungs feel as if they are about to burst, the fighters drop away. I watch them recede in the aft relays. They blend into the darkness, and the *Ranganathan* itself becomes only one among a million stars.

CHAPTER . 9

"You can't do this, memsahib." Cassia has Rubio tied to the shuttle's medical gurney. She and Tibbet watch him warily from the passenger lounge on the far side of the shuttle's berth.

I drop down the last rung of the access ladder. "I think you might want to stop calling me that now."

Rubio glares at me. "You're in deep. Don't you get that? There's no going back. . . ."

"Yeah, we had pretty much figured that out." I wave an arm at the stolen shuttle and start shuffling through the cabinets to find the medical kit.

"No." He shakes his head and winces. "Maybe you'd get off light for stealing a ship, but kidnapping? You're going to spend the rest of your lives in a prison camp once the DSRI catches up to you."

Cassia looks spooked. "Is that true?"

I shrug, even though Rubio's words make me queasy. "So he says."

"I'm not just saying it, I know it." Rubio twists on the cot to look at me. "And if the higher-ups don't get you, my flight crew will make it a personal job."

I make a show of rolling my eyes and pop open the medical kit. "I guess we'd better take care of you, then." I pull out a penlight and click it on.

He shrinks back on the bed, pulling the nylon strapping Cassia used to tie him taut. "What are you doing?"

"Checking you for a concussion, *badirchand*." I reach for his head, but he jerks away again. "Hold still, would you?"

"Only if you untie me."

I raise my eyes to the ceiling. "We both know that's not happening. Now, would you like to let me look at your head, or would you rather not know if your brain is hemorrhaging?"

Rubio gives his bonds one last tug and then leans back on the cot, sullen. "Fine."

I shine the light in one eye, then the other. His pupils shrink in their pools of blue. Good. "Are you feeling nauseous?"

Rubio laughs. "Are you kidding? No, I feel perfectly fine about being shanghaied and tied to a gurney."

I glare down at him. "Be serious. Are you dizzy at all? Do you feel like you're going to throw up?"

Rubio sighs. "No. My head hurts like hell, though, thanks to her." He glares at Cassia, who pretends she hasn't heard and goes on stroking Tibbet's head.

"Right. And we'll forget all about how you pulled a stunner on us, shall we?" I pocket my light, pop an anti-inflammatory from its foil pouch, and hold it up to Rubio's mouth. "Here, take this."

He narrows his eyes at me. "What is it?"

I let out a sigh. "It's a painkiller. What do you think it is?"

He raises his eyebrows in answer.

"Fine." I slap the pill down on the medical kit's lid, out of Rubio's reach. "Cassia?"

She looks up, and I nod at the cockpit. We need a place where Rubio can't overhear us.

"What, you're going to leave me here like this?" Rubio squirms on the gurney.

"Spot on, brain trust." I pull myself up onto the ladder. "You'd better rest if you're not planning on taking any medicine."

Cassia follows me into the cockpit and seals the door behind us.

"Was he serious?" Worry pinches the skin between her brows. "Are you sure no one's going to come after us?"

"He's bluffing," I say. I hope I'm right.

"And if he's not?" She hugs herself.

"Then it'll be me they're after. They won't do anything to you."

She frowns. "How do you know?"

"Because I won't let them."

Cassia smiles and sinks down into the copilot's seat. "Now who's bluffing?"

"I mean it." I say. But something is wrong. Cassia won't look at me. "Are you okay?"

"Sure." Her voice bobs up, too cheerful. "Everything's going according to plan."

I lean over the control panels, trying to ignore the false buoyancy in Cassia's voice so I can make sense of the flashing lights and readouts scrolling thick with numbers. The shield indicators flicker yellow to green as we plow through the fine dust of the outer asteroid belt.

"We're six hours from Ceres Station." I pull my crow from my pocket and hand it to Cassia. "I made a list of everything we'll need to retrofit the shuttle for deep travel. You think we can find it all?"

"Have you ever been there?" Cassia scrolls through the list. "Ceres?"

I shake my head. I've heard of the station, but beyond the fact that it's built on a dwarf planet in the middle of an asteroid belt, I don't know much. "I'd never been deeper than Bhutto Station before I signed up for this mission."

Cassia leans back. "If it's not welded down, you can sell it on Ceres."

"What are we going to sell? Rubio?" I joke.

She looks at me, solemn, and I realize how not funny that is. I drop my eyes. "Sorry."

She rubs a finger over the telemetry readouts. "Actually, I know someone who'll give us a fair deal on this ship."

I blink. "You want to sell the shuttle? But . . . I thought you said—"

"I said I needed to get to Ceres. We can get a junker that's fitted out for Deep travel there."

"A junker?" I make a face.

"Sure." Cassia says. "What, did you really think we were going to take the time to retrofit this thing? Your people will be looking for it anyway."

"Why not?" I glance around at the bright new controls,

the pristine seats in dove gray. It's not exactly spacious, but it has to be better than any junker.

"That'd take too much time." She scowls out the front viewport. "They already have several days' head start. The longer they have Nethanel, the less likely we are to find him."

I chew my bottom lip. "So, this person who'll trade us . . ."

Cassia nods. "Sweetie."

"What?" A complicated combination of embarrassment and pleasure tumbles through my stomach. *Why is she calling me that?*

Cassia flushes boiled lobster red. "No. Sweetie, he's . . . well, he's sort of my uncle." She looks sheepish.

"*Sort of* your uncle?" My face feels as hot as Cassia's looks.

"Well, not really." She hesitates, trying to find the words. "He and my father looked at each other like brothers, except they weren't really. But they'd do anything for each other."

I raise my eyebrows. "And that means he'd do anything for you, too?"

"Probably."

The way she says it doesn't exactly fill me with confidence. "Probably?"

Cassia meets my eyes. "You trust me, right?"

I hesitate. I do, don't I? I wouldn't be here otherwise. But then again, what was that whole business with the cat about? And why did she let me believe we were going to modify the shuttle when she wanted to trade it all along? Why not tell me?

"Right?" Cassia's mouth twists in a troubled line.

I sit across from her and balance my fingertips under hers. Her hands are warm and soft, her nails smooth, like water-worn shells.

"I do," I say. I look down at our hands, at my scars, and then up at her again. "You just . . . if we're going to do this, you can't keep secrets from me. Like about Tibbet, or the ship. You have to tell me things."

"I'm sorry." A strand of wavy hair falls across Cassia's face, and she looks up at me through it. "I thought you'd change your mind if I told you."

I frown. "Why?"

She shrugs and looks away.

"Cassia—"

She shakes her head. "Everything's gotten so complicated."

I scoff. "You think I'm afraid of *complicated*?"

"No. Yes," she huffs. "I wasn't sure."

"Well, I'm not," I say. "We're in this together, right?"

She hesitates.

I lean back, stung. "Don't *you* trust *me*?"

"I want to," she says. "You're here and everything. I know what that means. I . . . it's only that it's always been me and my brothers. Me and Nethanel, especially since his wife, Ume, died."

"Yeah," I say quietly. It was Ava and me for a while, before we found Soraya. Just the two of us. A team. I never stopped feeling that way, even when she married Rushil and I left for the DSRI.

Cassia presses her lips together, and I think for a second I see something glistening in her eye. "What you're doing for me, it's— "

"It's not only for you," I say. "That's not why I came."

She rubs her eye. One side of her mouth lifts in mischief. "I know. You just wanted more time to get to know Tibbet."

The tension breaks. I laugh. "Yep. He's my favorite member of this crew."

"Not Rubio?" She raises an eyebrow.

"He's a close second," I agree.

We burst into giggles. We may be royally screwed, but at least we're not alone.

Ceres Station rotates beneath us, spread out over the dwarf planet's surface like a copper grid shining through black lacquer. As we fly lower, the grid resolves itself into a million amber bulbs marking the corners of buildings and shining out from beneath the dusty, domed ceilings of the hyperbaric walkways that link the station together. Vast boreholes interrupt the neat pattern of lights, each gently glowing, as if the planet's core houses a colony of fireflies.

"It's pretty," I murmur, easing the controls forward.

"Only from up here," Cassia says.

We dock near one of the smaller boreholes. Cassia checks Rubio's bonds while I test my pressure suit for breaches. DSRI protocol requires that we wear one whenever we cross over to an unstable environment, and from everything Cassia has said, I'm pretty sure Ceres qualifies.

"You're going to be hot in that." She tugs at the strap around Rubio's left wrist.

I frown. "Don't they mine ice?"

"I'm just saying." She circles the bed and pulls at his other restraint. "At least don't wear your jacket on top of all that."

"She's right, you know," Rubio says. "All that dust. The air circulation systems don't work too well."

I stare at them. "Are you two agreeing about something?"

They glance at each other. Rubio snorts, and Cassia looks away.

A wave of thick, hot air rolls over me as soon as we open the air lock. Our ship is docked directly on the hangar floor, along with a dozen other small vessels loading and unloading supplies. A fine skin of dust coats everything—the floor, the exposed ductwork snaking along the ceiling, even the men and women guiding along lev trolleys weighed down by head-high corks of glistening ice. The air scrubbers grind and whirr above our heads, trying to keep pace with each breath of carbon dioxide the crowd exhales.

As we watch, one of the scrubbers overheats. It blares out a series of panicked beeps and winds to a stop. Two little boys in ragged coveralls dart up one of the access ladders bolted to the wall and race across the tops of the ductwork, sure-footed as rats on a wire. One of them reaches into the scrubber's intake vent and scoops out a handful of black gunk—probably hair, dust, and sloughed skin turned damp in the humid air. The other straddles the duct and pulls a small suction fan from his pocket. Within seconds, they have the scrubber going again. The crowd below claps, and a few people toss coins or scraps of food up to the boys.

"Come on." Cassia nudges my back. "They'll see you gawping."

By the time we make our way out of the dock and into a low-ceilinged market, I'm sincerely wishing I had left the pressure suit behind and dressed in short sleeves and trousers like Cassia. We have more people in Mumbai, but we've worked out ways to move around one another for the most part, and where we haven't, at least we have the open sky above us. Here, the rafters rise only a meter or so above the tallest men's heads, and vendors selling food or used ship components narrow the room's current to one teeming lane. Everyone presses shoulder to shoulder to keep out of the way of the trundling ice sledges on their way to buyers at the docks. The thick smell of synthetic vegetable oil and frying dough permeates the air, undercut with the subtle stink of mechanics' oil. Cassia reaches for my hand, and I grab it. If I let the crush of people separate us, I'll never find her again.

"Where are we going?" I call.

She answers, but I can't hear her over the thundering of the sledges.

"What?" I say.

"Underneath," she repeats.

My stomach drops.

We ride an open-sided freight lift down a black rock shaft. The only light comes from a single lamp hooked to the top of the car and the eerie stripes of phosphorous paint guiding our descent. I look up through the lift's metal grating and notice two rat boys riding above us, two small, silent silhouettes against our tiny pool of light.

The lift comes to a stop before a wide, carved passageway leading to a massive air lock. I move to get off the lift with the rest of the crowd, but Cassia pulls me back.

"Not yet," she says. "Unless you want to mine some ice."

One of the miners—a boy a few years younger than I am—glances back at us as Cassia latches the metal grate. Our eyes meet for only half a second before we drop out of view, but it's long enough for me to see the fear and alarm running over his face like wildfire. No one else has stayed behind on the lift with us.

"So, this place we're going . . ." I clear my throat. "You've been there before?"

Cassia peers out and down into the shaft. "Once or twice."

I look up. The rat boys are gone. "And your Uncle Sweetie's down in the bore pits . . . why?"

"He's Ceres's *shateigashira*," she says simply.

"Its what?"

"You know," she says. "Like, the boss."

I frown. "The station head?" But why wouldn't she come out and say that? And why would the lift to the station head's office be down at the bottom of a deserted bore shaft? My palms begin to sweat inside my gloves.

"No," Cassia shakes her head. "Not like that. You know how sometimes one person's in charge officially, but somebody else really runs things?"

"Yes," I say uneasily.

"Sweetie's like that." She tucks a few escaped curls behind her ears. "He's the one you see if you need something done."

"Wait, your uncle's a . . ." I scramble for the right word and finally hit on one I remember from one of Ava and Rushil's old movies. "A mobster?"

"He's not a mobster, he's the *shateigashira*."

Vaat. First the cat, then kidnapping, and now organized crime? *You can't be so quick to trust, Mi*. Ava said that after I told her about Kiran and the kissing bottle. *You have to be careful with yourself. You have to get to know the person*. I push her voice away. What did she know about it? I knew Vishva better than practically anyone, and she still stabbed me in the back for a night of dancing. Besides, we're already deep in Ceres Station, with a DSRI pilot trussed up in the hold of our stolen ship. The time for second thoughts is long gone.

Darkness greets us at the bottom of the shaft. We step off the lift into what looks like one of Mumbai's man-high drainage tunnels. Phosphorus paint coats the rounded concrete walls, and a slush of mud and ice melt gathers at the bottom, dragging a dark line through the glow. Something chitters and scrabbles in the shadows ahead.

"Hello!" Cassia calls into the emptiness. An echo quavers back at her. "It's Cassia, Kaldero's daughter."

Silence. Cassia wets her lips and tries again. "We need to see Sweetie."

A heartbeat. Two. Then a pair of human shapes melt out of the shadow beyond the bend in the tunnel. They wear rags and black-painted body armor. Oddly shaped stunners hang at their sides. No, not stunners, guns. Real guns.

We're surrounded by rock. I try to calm myself. *No risk of decompression.* But decompression isn't the only way a bullet can kill.

Cassia steps forward wordlessly and holds out her arms to let the guards pat her down. I follow suit, trying not to look at their guns or breathe in the sour sweat stink that clings to them. Behind them, a rat skitters through the slush and freezes, staring at us. One of its eyes glows bright, electric red.

The guards lead us down the glowing drainage ways, past an air lock set into the stone, and through a barely lit corridor lined with humming refrigeration containers and crates. More rats watch us from behind the crates and from inside crevices built into the rock. I've never been afraid of rats—spiders are what turn my stomach to liquid—but I shudder anyway. There are too many of them, too many red eyes darting in and out of view.

At last we come to a metal door on rollers. One of the guards bangs on it.

His coms hiss to life. "What is it?"

"Visitors for Sweetie," the guard answers, and I'm surprised by the tenor of the voice—high and feminine, almost sweet.

A few seconds of silence, and then, "He's not expecting anyone."

Cassia grabs the guard's hand and leans close to the coms. "Tell him it's Cassia Kaldero."

The guard jerks her hand away and reaches for her gun, but before she can drop Cassia to the floor, the door shrieks, and a crack of light splits the darkness as it begins to rumble open.

I blink and hold up a hand to shield my eyes. Rows of day lamps hang from the ceiling of the long room before us, illuminating walls red as a whale's gullet. The back wall is full of feeds—hundreds of them glowing infrared green. A small group of men and women stand examining an array of jet-black small arms spread out over a table. They tense as we enter, hands hovering over the weapons.

A muscular man with sallow skin and a close-cropped stubble of bleached hair steps away from the table. Black and green tattoos crawl up the back of his neck and cradle the base of his skull. His long-sleeved shirt must have been white once, but years of sweat and dust have dulled it to a watery gray. His eyes are quick and black, close set around a crooked nose that looks as if it's been broken more than once.

"Ah." He smiles easily, revealing a mouth of teeth the dead brown of beetle carapaces, and holds out his arms. "Cassia. The littlest Kaldero. How are you, my dear?" His sleeves slip back to expose more ink on the back of his hands.

"Uncle." Cassia allows him to draw her into a hug. The rest of the group around the table relaxes and goes back to examining the cache of weapons spread out before them.

"It's been too long." Sweetie steps back and looks her up and down in a decidedly *un*-uncle-like fashion. "Much too long."

Cassia stiffens but keeps the smile on her face. "It has."

Sweetie swings his lazy gaze to me. "And who's this?" He frowns and shakes an admonishing finger at Cassia as he meanders back to a cluster of white leather couches below the wall of feeds. "I thought your father taught you better than to bring guests unannounced."

"Miyole's good." Cassia spares a glance for me as we trail after him. "And my father's hurt, or else he'd be here himself."

Something flits across Sweetie's face—worry, maybe, or surprise—but just as quickly, it's gone, and his expression is smooth and heavy-lidded again. He drops down onto one of the couches and spreads his arms along its back. "You've run into some trouble then, little tinker?"

From afar, the furniture looked pristine, even strangely luxurious against the bare concrete floor, but up close, a thousand rips and cracks show in the stained leather. The feeds jerk and swing wildly—a floor-level view of the phosphorous tunnel, another from high above a refrigeration unit, some showing nothing but the ghostly gleam of animal eyes. *The rats*, I realize.

Cassia stands before her uncle, her back straight. "Some jackers caught us. Razed our ship, took Nethanel . . ."

Sweetie examines his nails. "That's a sad story."

"Not if I get him back," Cassia says.

Sweetie looks up at her, sharp, all his casual manner gone. "And you expect me to fix it? For old times' sake?"

"Not fix it," Cassia says. "Help *me* fix it. Isn't twenty years of trading worth one favor?"

Sweetie rubs his chin. "What are you asking?"

"Lend me a ship. A junker, anything, so I can go after them."

Sweetie cocks an eyebrow. "You know where they are, then?"

Cassia and I exchange a look. We know their signal, but we most definitely do not know where they are.

Sweetie sighs. "What ship was it?"

I pull out my crow and flip through to the *dakait* ship's signature. "The *Proioxis*," I say, and hold it out to him.

Sweetie acts as if I haven't spoken. He only has eyes for Cassia. "Little tinker, that's a Söner ship."

She flinches, but barely.

"You know what that means."

She nods.

Something cold slides down the inside of my chest.

I don't know what a Söner is, but if it's something that gives Sweetie pause, I don't think I want to find out. Mumbai has its share of Bad Men and Bad Women, Auntie Rajni among them. But Sweetie is a different genus altogether.

I try to catch Cassia's eye, but she won't look at me. My palms itch like mad.

Sweetie leans back on the couch. "Your father would kill me if he knew I let his youngest go after some Söner Neitibu all alone."

"I'm not alone." She finally looks at me. "I have Miyole."

Sweetie glances at me. "Forgive me if I'm not full of confidence."

"We're going after them either way. We have a shuttle we can retrofit—"

"A shuttle?" Sweetie straightens.

"Yes." Cassia hurries on. "But it'll be much faster with your help."

Sweetie rubs his chin in silence.

"Please, uncle," Cassia says. "I know you hate them, too."

A smile flashes across Sweetie's face. "The enemy of my enemy is my friend. Is that it, little tinker? But you know I don't do charity work. What you're asking—it's a lot, even for your father's sake."

"I know."

"So what are you going to do for me in exchange?" He cocks his head, exposing a skull with elongated teeth, inked on the side of his neck.

"Anything," Cassia says without hesitation.

Sweetie's smile spreads. "Right answer."

CHAPTER . 10

We follow Sweetie and his guards along a deeper set of tunnels cut straight through the asteroid's core. Somewhere above us, a distant growl penetrates the rock.

"The Söner?" I hiss at Cassia. "What's that?"

"A separatist group. 'Native Sons,'" Cassia murmurs. "They run parts of Enceladus."

I frown. "No, they don't. The Satellite Authority's in charge there." I should know. Enceladus is the moon where the *Ranganathan* and all her sisters' bones were grown.

"I told you." Cassia sounds tired. "There's what's official and what's really . . ." Sweetie turns to us, and she trails off.

"Here we are, then." He spreads his arms wide.

Behind him, the tunnel opens into a pressurized hangar with raw rock walls. A collection of ships in various states of disrepair sprawls over the floor; some sport pocked hulls and burn streaks; other are up on lifts, with coolant lines and wires dangling from their open bellies. Sweetie leads us to a blocky craft, twice the size of our shuttle and twenty times older, but more or less intact. Grime lies thick as silt on its front viewport.

"Hybrid. Twenty square meters of cargo hold and a sleeping berth big enough for twelve," Sweetie says. "Commons and the galley are all one room, but it's plenty big."

Cassia eyes it. "What's her name?"

"The *Mendicant*," Sweetie says.

She nods. "We can work with that."

"Good." Sweetie lifts his chin at one of the guards, who disappears back the way we came. "We'll load you up, then."

Sweetie activates the berth's loading ramp and waves forward a group of men rolling two-hundred-liter drums across the hangar floor. Part of the "anything" Cassia promised.

I pull Cassia aside. "'We can work with that?' Are you out of your mind?"

She shrugs. "Sweetie says it's solid."

"How do we know it even runs?" I shoot a look at our benefactor.

"If he says it runs, it runs," Cassia says. "He wouldn't trust a faulty ship with his merchandise."

"Oh, I'm glad he's so concerned about his *merchandise*." I roll my eyes.

"You know what I mean," Cassia says.

"I don't like it." I shake my head and eye the drums. "Did you even ask what he's having us transport? Or where exactly we're taking it?"

"You'll find out in plenty of time," Sweetie had told us, but that didn't exactly fill me with confidence.

"Does it matter?" Cassia crosses her arms. "What happened to all that stuff about trusting each other?"

I run a hand over my braid. "It's not that I don't trust you, it's only that I'm not too thrilled about doing business with crime lords."

"He's not a crime lord, he's—"

"The *shateigashira*." I realize I'm probably talking loud enough for Sweetie to hear and drop my voice to a whisper. "I know. I thought he would be a little more helpful since he's supposed to be your uncle and all."

"If he wasn't my uncle, he would have had us shot on sight."

"Ladies."

I nearly jump out of my skin.

"There's only one more matter to discuss before we conclude our business here," Sweetie says with a polite grin.

Cassia pales. "Yes?"

"I'm in need of some assurance you won't simply fly away with my little bird here." He makes a fluttering motion with his hands. "Let's talk collateral."

"Well . . . there's the shuttle," Cassia says, sneaking a guilty look at me.

I press my lips into a line. Just because I agreed to this doesn't mean I have to be happy about it.

"Ah, yes," Sweetie says.

"DSRI issue," Cassia forges on. "Brand-new, except for the flight over."

Sweetie raises an eyebrow, interested. "DSRI?" He looks at me as though seeing me for the first time, as if he's finally figured out the formula that explains my existence.

I lean in close to Cassia. "I can't believe you're going to trade a new DSRI shuttle for this piece of *tatti*," I say under my breath. "There has to be something better he can give us."

"It's not a trade, it's collateral," she hisses back, shooting a nervous look at Sweetie.

"It's coercion."

"I don't care what it is," Cassia says. "We're taking it."

"My dear," Sweetie interrupts, reaching for my hand. "What is your name again?"

I swallow. *Vaat.* I should have kept my complaining mouth shut. "Miyole Guiteau."

"Miyole." He rolls the word around in his mouth. He smells like sour milk. "Let me explain. You stole a DSRI shuttle and brought it here, to my operation."

I open my mouth to protest, but Sweetie waves me silent.

"Don't bother. You wouldn't have come to me if you weren't in some kind of trouble to begin with." He folds my hand tightly inside his. "And now you've brought that trouble to me."

Cassia looks stricken. "We didn't mean—"

"Of course you didn't." Sweetie tightens his grip on my hand. "But a stolen DSRI shuttle is useless to me, new or not. Do you see? I don't need government types scratching too deep around here. If I sold it, it would only be for parts, so be glad I'm even willing to consider it collateral. Now thank me for my generous assistance, and we won't say another word about it." Sweetie's smile stays in place as my finger bones crush together.

"Thank you," I say hoarsely.

"Don't mention it." Sweetie loosens his grip and pats my hand before letting go. He turns to Cassia and lifts the back of her hand to his lips. "My dear, a pleasure doing business with your family, as always." Then he sweeps away, over to the men loading barrels onto our new junker.

Cassia puts a hand on my arm, and I jump.

"We've got to turn it over," she says softly. There's an apology in her voice, but I pretend not to hear it.

"Right," I say, and stalk off to the tunnel. If I walk fast enough, no one will see me shaking. We don't know what we're transporting or who we're taking it to, and our only backup option is out of play. In my head, this all went differently. It made sense. It was a calculated risk. But now the variables are multiplying in a way I never factored for, and I can't go back and rerun the experiment. This is it. This is my life, spiraling into a textbook example of chaos theory.

Cassia follows, one of Sweetie's masked guards trailing a few meters behind. No need to keep us under close surveillance now that Sweetie has us where he wants us.

She catches up to me. "I didn't have any other choice." Her voice is smooth, coaxing, now that the deal is done. "This is the only way we can find Nethanel."

I double my pace. She may be right, but I don't have to like it.

We pass the door to Sweetie's lair and the hall lined with refrigeration containers in silence. Red eyes follow us. Neither of us speaks until we're back in the lift.

"Miyole," Cassia says, pleading.

I sigh. "I get it, okay? It's done." I've known from the beginning Cassia would do anything to find her brother. I just underestimated what *anything* would be.

We ride the lift back up to the main hangar. The shuttle is unharmed, except for a patch on the door where someone has scratched the word *busu* into the shielding. The moment the shuttle hatch slides open, though, I know something is wrong. The lights are all on, clean and bright. I hold out my hand and send Cassia a worried look—*careful.* The dock's bustle and roar fades as we creep up the loading ramp. The gurney comes into view. Empty.

I catch a flash of movement in the corner of my eye and turn just in time to see Rubio swinging an oxygen tank full force at the back of Cassia's head.

"No!" I shout.

Cassia flinches and ducks, but not fast enough to avoid the blow. The tank glances the side of her forehead with an ugly, thick *clank*. She crumples at the edge of the loading ramp, eyes rolled back in her head and a deep gash opened above her left eye.

Rubio down stares at her. She isn't moving. There is no breath in me, only my blood moving in slow motion. Rubio stumbles back, drops the blood-smeared tank, and looks at me. This can't be happening. Any second she's going to raise a hand to her head and pick herself up. But she doesn't. And she doesn't. The only thing moving is the blood pouring down her forehead and into her hair. Her eyes stare unseeing at the ceiling. Is she dead? She can't be. She can't be living one second and dead the next, right in front of me. That can't happen.

Rubio bolts. My heart kicks, and time comes rushing back.

"No!" I scream again. I leap over Cassia and race after him, down the ramp, into the teeming crowd. Rubio glances back and lunges into the tide of close-packed bodies, fighting against the current. I charge in, too, shoving and ducking. *She can't be dead. She can't be.*

An ice sledge rumbles toward us, cutting Rubio's path short. He skids to a halt, looks left, then right, and dodges left. I cut across the crowd and dart after him, but he's faster. He's not stuck in a steaming-hot pressure suit.

He's going to get away. *All that blood . . .*

"Stop!" I shoulder forward and point at his back. "Someone stop him!"

The woman closest to me glances up briefly and looks away, but otherwise the dock keeps up its chaotic rhythm. The rattle of the air scrubbers and the din of voices drown me out. If he gets away, he'll alert the DSRI. They'll lock me away as an accessory, and if Cassia's dead—*she can't be, she can't be, but there was so much blood, and her eyes*—no one will ever find Nethanel.

Think, Miyole.

I look up. One of the rat boys sits on the air duct above me, gnawing on what I hope is a chicken bone.

"Hey!" I call up. "You!"

He wipes grease from his face. "Whatcha want?"

"Help me stop him." I point after Rubio.

He narrows his eyes. "What's in it for me?"

My mind races. What would this kid want? What can we afford to give up? "Food," I say. "We've got food."

"How much food?" he asks.

"You'll never find out if you don't stop him, will you?" I snap.

"A' right, a' right." He tucks the bone in his pocket, hops up, and skitters off over the ductwork.

I follow as best I can on the ground, elbowing my way through the crowd. Above, the boy darts left on an intersecting duct and then leaps over the edge. A shout of surprise rises from the crowd as he drops. I put on a burst of speed. The boy has wrapped himself around Rubio's leg like a sloth. He bites his shin.

Rubio cries out and topples over, trying to shake the boy loose. But it's too late. I leap on top of him, knocking the air from his lungs and pinning him to the wet, filthy ground. *The blood, her eyes . . .* The rat boy scrambles out of the fray.

I swing a fist at Rubio's face. I've never hit anyone before. I've never needed to. My knuckles connect with his cheekbone and burst with pain, but I don't care. *So much blood, and her skull and her eyes. Lying there bleeding and she wasn't seeing anything.* Somewhere in the back of my mind is Soraya, warning me that violence never helps anything, and somewhere deeper is the sick, trembling feeling I get when I'm about to remember something. I push it all aside and swing again, vaguely aware of the crowd forming around us.

Rubio blocks my blow. He drives his knee into my side and flips me off him. My ribs flare with pain. I rake my fingernails down his cheek and across his neck.

"Putamadre!" He clutches his face, and I deliver a swift kick to his testicles. Rubio cries out and doubles over.

I pick myself up and kick him again, in the stomach this time. *The blood, her eyes. She can't be, but I think maybe she is.* My arms might not be as strong as his, but years of walking and horseback riding in Mumbai have given me calves like steel.

"She's dead!" My face is wet, and my limbs shake with cold fire. Soraya is gone. Civilization and all the good it ever did me is gone. I'm alone on an outpost with the boy who murdered the one person in a thousand light years who wanted me, who needed me. "You killed her!"

"Let 'im have it, girl!" Someone in the crowd whoops, and answering calls ripple all around me.

I pause, panting, and look up. Traffic has come to a standstill, and a ring of people has formed around us. The rat boys perch on the ducts above, looks of animal glee on their faces. I brush the hair ripped loose from my braid out of my eyes. On the floor at my feet, Rubio moans.

What am I doing? I step back and unclench my fists, all the blood draining out of my chest. My heart beats like a timpani against my sternum. Rubio isn't fighting back anymore. Am I really going to beat someone to death in front of a cheering crowd? I grab his arm and drag him to his feet.

"Come on," I mutter. Civilization might be millions of kilometers away, but there's still some left in me.

A groan of disappointment rises from the crowd. The knot of people around us begins to disperse.

I twist Rubio's arm behind his back and march him to the shuttle. I need time to think without adrenaline poisoning my judgment. I need time to figure out what to do with him. But in the meantime, he's going to face what he's done. He's going to look at her, and if there's any decency in him, he's going to feel all the guilt of it.

No one pays us any mind, let alone tries to stop us, as I push him back the way we came.

"How could you?" I speak through my teeth. "You could have run. You could have gotten away. Why did you . . ." I trail off, the words stopped up in my throat. I should never have gotten angry with Cassia, never grudged her anything in the service of finding her brother. *Her eyes, the blood . . .*

"I didn't have time. Besides, she did the same to me." Rubio reaches up to touch the tender spot at the back of his head. "I didn't mean to hurt her so bad."

"You killed her." My lungs constrict. The words hurt coming out. "She's dead."

"You don't know that," Rubio says.

I step close, blood welling up in my chest again. "You bashed her head in."

"'Ey, miss!" I feel a tug on my sleeve and look down. The rat boy scowls up at me. "You said you had food."

I sigh, suddenly tired. "We do. In the ship."

The rat boy eyes the hatch suspiciously. "I ain't going in there. There's blood, an' you said he was a murderer."

Rubio looks pale.

"Wait here," I tell the boy. I grab Rubio's arm and push him up the ramp. He doesn't resist, but when we reach the top, where Cassia's blood pools, he stops cold.

"What?" I say. "Afraid to look at what you've done?"

But then I move to step around him and see what he sees.

Cassia, sitting bloody-faced and dazed on the gurney. Alive.

"Cassia." I run to her. I want to throw my arms around her and crush her against my body. I want to touch her and make sure she's real. I want to kiss her. Kiss her with relief and fear and giddy tears, because here she is, alive. But she's hurt, and I don't know if it's what she'd want, so instead I hold her at arm's length.

"I'm okay." She nods, and then catches sight of Rubio standing openmouthed at the top of the hatch. The flesh below his eye has already begun to puff up and bruise, and my scratch marks look more like gouges now. "Can't say the same for you."

Rubio stares at her as if he's seen a ghost. "I didn't kill you." Relief suffuses his voice.

She touches the open wound on her head. Her fingers come away bloody. "You'll have to try harder." She grimaces and glares at him.

Out of nowhere, he giggles. I stare at him, horrified. I could slap him, except something about the noise he's making sounds so frightened.

"Let's get you cleaned up," I say to Cassia. "Rubio—"

He interrupts me with a bout of hysterical laughter.

"Rubio," I say more firmly. I don't have time for this. I point to one of Cassia's bags. "Look in there and find some rations for that boy."

He makes his way to the bag, laughing so hard tears stream down his face. I ignore him and pull a disinfecting cloth from our medical supply box.

"Aren't you afraid he'll get away?" Cassia murmurs as I wipe the blood from her brow, careful of the laceration.

The bleeding has slowed, but it hasn't stopped yet. She was lucky. *We* were lucky.

I glance at Rubio as he teeters down the gangway, still laughing to himself. "At this point, I don't care. I'd like to see him survive on Ceres Station."

I raise the cloth again, but Cassia catches my wrist. "Thank you."

I look down, away, my face growing hot.

Her hand gently grazes my jaw. She raises my chin so we're staring into each other's eyes. Hers are aquamarine like the Pacific on a sunny day, ringed by lashes as gold as her hair. Her face is pale from blood loss, making her freckles look darker.

"Thank you," she repeats.

I lean my forehead against hers and close my eyes. She works her fingers beneath what's left of my braid and traces my ear with her thumb. I hold her tight, tight, and a hot tear rolls down over my chin, onto my neck. I could have lost her today. My blood fizzes in my veins, and I know there's no going back.

CHAPTER •

The barrels that Sweetie's minions stacked in the junker's hold stand four across and fifteen deep. I tilt one up on its rim experimentally. It's heavy, more so than a simple liquid should be, and yet I can make out sloshing inside. I let the barrel fall back on its base with a heavy *boom*.

"What the hell is that?" Rubio stops behind me, his arms full of thermal suits and jackets, his face a purpling mess. He moves stiffly, favoring his right ribs.

I plant my hands on my hips and blow out a lungful of air. I shake my head. "No telling." I nod at his armload. "What about you?"

"Gifts from that man, the one with the tattoos."

"Sweetie," I say, and scowl.

"Right," Rubio agrees. "He says we'll stick out like rats at a tea party if we go around wearing our DSRI gear."

I nod. He's right about the clothes, but I have a feeling Sweetie isn't the gift-giving kind. We're only adding more favors to his ledger.

I turn back to the barrels and work the tips of my fingers underneath the closest one's stopper. The seal is too tight. I only end up lifting one side of the barrel, and then losing my grip. The metal base crashes back down, nearly crushing my toe.

"You want help?" Rubio asks.

I look over my shoulder at him, incredulous. "You're offering?"

He shrugs and drops the pile of thermal clothes, then climbs on top of the barrel and holds it down with his weight while I try again to pry out the stopper. My fingertips pale with the effort, but I feel it giving, millimeter by millimeter. Suddenly, the seal comes free with a wet, sucking pop that sends me stumbling back. A sharp chemical odor floods the berth.

"*Chaila.*" I shake the feeling back into my fingers and pull up my undershirt to cover my nose and mouth.

Rubio jumps down, and we both lean forward to peer inside.

"What is that?" I say through my shirt.

Rubio sticks his hand inside.

I try to catch his arm. "Don't!"

But it's too late. He draws up a runny handful of translucent yellow goop and sniffs it. "Cryatine." He slops the handful back into the barrel. It rolls off his fingers as if he never touched it. "Antifreeze."

"You've seen it before?" I make a face.

Rubio nods. "You probably have, too, but you didn't know it." He looks at the pile of thermal clothes. "They use it in everything. Buildings, pressure suits, ships, anything that needs to withstand the cold. Smells like cat piss, but it'll keep you warm."

I frown. "How do you know so much about it?" Mumbai is too warm to have any use for antifreeze, but I've been around ships my whole life and never heard of the stuff.

"My father." Rubio shrugs and focuses on shoving the stopper back into the barrel. "He was a foreman at an Apex Group factory that made the stuff. Back on Earth."

I study him. I never thought of Rubio having a father and mother before. I guess I thought he sprang fully formed from the ether to annoy me.

"Apex," I say. "Isn't that one of the company-states?"

Rubio nods, eyes still on the barrel, even though he's done replacing the seal.

"How'd you get out?" I've heard about the company-states before. Almost everyone born there ends up working for them their whole lives.

Rubio looks at me for the first time. "We had overages in my year. My mom knew someone on the board, and she convinced them Apex ought to be represented on DSRI missions."

We stand in silence for a moment. "I guess they're going to be pretty pissed when you don't come back, huh?" I finally say.

"Who knows?" He looks away, his face unreadable. "I'm sure DSRI will find a way to compensate them."

A shiver of pity moves through my stomach. Something about the way he says "compensate" makes me think he means exactly that. As if he's a commodity—a valuable one, but still something with a price.

"Wait . . . so this stuff, it's legal?" What's going on here? "Why are we transporting it all secretively, then? Why not contract with a licensed freight captain?" Unless the issue isn't so much what we're shipping as who we're shipping it to. That might explain why Sweetie doesn't want to give us port coordinates yet. If we're stopped along the way, we can't tell what we don't know.

Rubio raises his hands in surrender. "It's your boat. I'm only the hostage here."

I nod. But it's not my boat. It's Sweetie's, and the only one of us who knows enough about him to guess what's going on in his head is lying in a bunk, recovering from head trauma.

I make for the gangway leading out of the cargo hold.

"Hey," Rubio calls after me. "Don't you want your new gear?" He holds up one of the thermal jackets.

"I'll get it later," I shout over my shoulder. For now, I have some things to straighten out with Cassia. Like who the hell needs cryatine smuggled to them on Enceladus? And what else is Sweetie going to ask of us before he finally lets us go?

The junker's cargo hold stands on the opposite side of the ship from the sleeping berth, so I have to cross the sad common room with its stained set of couches splitting at the seams. The mechanical access doors clang under my feet as I pass down the corridors. I'm so twisted up in my thoughts, I don't notice the armored sentry outside the sleeping berth until I'm nearly on top of her. Warning flares spark in the back of my head. Something is wrong.

"You can't go in." The guard lowers her rifle.

Very wrong.

"Like hell I can't." I shove the rifle up, grab the door handle, and roll it aside.

Cassia is propped up on pillows in the widest bunk, her hair tied back in a braid. An osmotic bandage hugs her temples, slowly leeching painkillers into her system at the same time it heals the gash on her forehead. Sweetie sits beside her, one arm across her body, trapping her in the bed. His free hand cradles her wrist. Cassia sits pillar straight, every muscle in her body tense. Her eyes find mine as I enter the room.

". . . know it would be better for everyone." He strokes the back of her hand with his thumb. "I only want to make life a little easier on you and your family."

I bristle. Whatever it is he's offering Cassia, it's not sitting easy with her. A sickening mixture of anger and fear chokes me. I clear my throat.

Sweetie turns, his hand still clamped around Cassia's. "Ah, the government girl." He smiles. "Come in, my dear. Cassia and I were just discussing some business."

I clench my jaw. Sweetie still scares me more than anyone I've ever met, and I don't want him to see me shaking. I narrow my eyes at his hand.

Sweetie glances down, and then back and forth between us, confused. Suddenly he throws his head back and laughs.

"Oh, I *see*." He winks at me, but his smile doesn't reach

his eyes. "Don't like me moving in on your territory, do you, my dear?"

"Cassia's not territory." I ball my hands and dig my fingers into my palms. *Stress response in humans increases cortisol production and suppresses immune function.* "She doesn't belong to anyone."

"Then you won't mind if I steal a small kiss." He looks at Cassia. "Will she, little tinker?" His hand tightens around hers, and I remember the sensation of bones grinding together when he asked my name.

Cassia blanches. "I . . . no," she says quietly. Her eyes are too wide when she looks at me again. Her chest moves fast and shallow.

Sweetie raises one inked hand, gently brushes his knuckles against Cassia's cheek, and grabs her by the back of the neck.

"Ow!" Cassia winces and tries to jerk her head back, but he only tightens his grip. His lips close in on hers.

"Stop!" I shout.

Sweetie stops. He swivels his head toward me, a grin spread out over his lips.

My whole body vibrates. "Let her go."

"You see?" He points at me, that same cruel smile still in place. "Territory."

I don't answer. Sweetie stands and straightens his shirt. He laughs again, but there's something dark in it.

"Best of luck to you, girls. Try not to get yourselves killed. And little tinker . . ." He smiles at Cassia. "If you change your mind, you know where to find me." He saunters from the berth, letting the door roll closed behind him.

Relief floods Cassia's face. She pulls the hand Sweetie held up to her chest and closes it into a fist.

I hurry to her side. "Are you okay?"

She looks as if she's about to cry but draws a trembling breath and pulls herself together. "He wants to set me up as his go-to girl after we find Nethanel. He said he'd let my family keep this ship if I'll stay with him on Ceres."

"Stay with him?" I say. "Like his mistress?" My voice squeaks on the word. I don't know if Cassia has any idea how I feel about her, but I'm too shaken up to do a good job of hiding it.

Cassia nods, then closes her eyes and leans her head back against the wall. "Maybe I should have said yes. We need the ship."

I huff in exasperation. "Don't you think you're worth more than a *chirkut* junker?" I snap.

Cassia winces. "Don't yell, okay? I'm only talking it through."

"Sorry." I pick at the pilled woolen blanket covering Cassia's legs. "It's just . . . you don't want that either, do you?"

Cassia laughs, not bitter, simply tired. "I didn't *want* any of this. But here I am."

"What, you'd do it?" I give her a look that says I think she's crazy.

She shrugs. "I don't know. If it means my whole family can keep trading . . ."

"That's stupid," I say. "You act like you're some bargaining chip."

"Not a bargaining chip." She shakes her head. "I'm the queen."

"What?"

"The queen. Like in chess," Cassia says. "Do you play that where you're from?"

"I guess." I wobble my head from side to side. Some of Soraya's colleagues from the university used to come over to our house to play, but I only ever watched.

"The queen can move the farthest and the fastest, any direction she wants." Cassia draws a diagonal line across the blanket. "But if winning means giving her up, you give her up."

"I never got that," I say. "Why can't you end the game with the queen in charge?"

"That's just the rules, Miyole." Cassia sighs.

I poke her in the leg. "You know what I mean."

"Yeah," Cassia says. "But what's the point if you're all alone?"

I look away. This conversation is cutting too close. "Well, if you decide to take his offer, I'll have to get you a metric ton of breath mints for a wedding present."

Cassia cracks a smile and whaps me with one of the pillows. "Stop it."

"I'm serious. Have you seen his teeth? We could scrape some samples and use them as biological weapons."

"Shut up," Cassia says, but she doesn't stop smiling. "He'll hear you."

"Not if we get out of here," I say.

Cassia wrinkles her brow. "Are you sure you can fly this thing alone?"

"I was thinking Rubio could help me," I say, trying to keep my tone light and carefully studying the chevron pattern of the blanket.

"Rubio?" She narrows her eyes. "Doesn't he want to stay behind and get rescued?"

"I think he's not too impressed with the hospitality on Ceres." I remember the rat boy leaping on his back and smile to myself. Now I know Cassia's not dead, it's a little funny.

"Well, it's not my fault if he ends up getting himself killed." Cassia folds her arms and hunches her shoulders.

"I think as long as you two stop trying to give each other concussions, he'll be safe." I grin.

Cassia hits me with the pillow again.

"Rest," I tell her. "I'm pretty sure Rubio has a healthy fear of me now."

"You are terrifying," Cassia agrees.

It isn't until later, when I'm up in the cockpit testing the systems, that I realize I never asked her who would want so much cryatine.

Cassia sleeps through takeoff, so it's Rubio and me in the cockpit when Sweetie's air lock rumbles open onto the dwarf planet's hundreds of abandoned mine shafts. Past the rough-hewn rock, a circle of stars waits for us.

"Good luck, Miss Guiteau." Sweetie's voice crackles over the *Mendicant*'s failing coms. "Tell Cassia my offer still stands. And remember, bring my ship back or don't come back at all."

"Good riddance," I say to myself. If we make it that far, if we find Nethanel, Sweetie can have our shuttle. Cassia is never crossing his threshold again if I have anything to say about it.

The coms aren't the only shoddy thing about the ship Sweetie's saddled us with. It's slow as a snake in summer, and instead of self-healing nacre, a collection of overlapping composite tiles makes up its skin. If one of them breaks, we'll have to put on pressure suits and climb outside to complete the repairs. There's rust in the water recycling system and mildew in the air scrubbers, not to mention the holes in the inner walls. Half of them look like mods or repairs abandoned midway, and the other half are clearly the work of rats and rust. Tibbet finds them endlessly fascinating. He's already brought us the carcass of one of Sweetie's spy-eyed rats.

We edge out into the black. I push the ship into the vector Sweetie recommended for us, the path out of the asteroid field with the least debris, and wish for the millionth time I was back in the *Ranganathan*'s shuttle, or even Ava's tiny sloop.

"You sure you don't want me to fly?" Rubio glances over at me from the copilot's seat.

"No." I make a show of checking the readouts so I don't have to look at him. Rubio may have stopped trying to brain us with things, but that doesn't mean I trust him to control the ship. We've come so far. I don't want to wake up one day to find us en route back to the *Ranganathan*.

"You know flying's what I do, right?" Rubio says. "It's my job."

"It's only till we're past the debris field." I look at him. "Then we can set it to autopilot."

Rubio's eyes widen and lock on the viewport. "Memsahib—"

"What?" I snap, and follow his gaze.

A jagged piece of rock the size of a lev train car spirals toward us, its ice and mineral deposits glistening in the far, faint sun.

"*Vaat,*" I curse, and throw my whole weight behind the vector bars. The ship turns sluggishly, veering out of the asteroid's path with mere millimeters to spare.

To his credit, Rubio keeps his mouth shut as I maneuver our ship back into Sweetie's lane.

I clear my throat. "Right, then."

Rubio raises his eyebrows at me.

I fiddle with a strip of synthetic leather that's come loose from the bars. "Maybe you should have a go at it."

"Are you sure?" Rubio puts on his most earnest face. "Because if you need another chance to try and kill us—"

I punch him in the arm and stand to give him the pilot's seat. "Don't push it."

He laughs and rubs the spot where I hit him. "Good

thing you don't have a pack of mangy kids to hold me down this time."

"It was just one kid," I point out.

"Yeah, but he had the element of surprise on his side." Rubio sinks into the pilot's seat, flexes his fingers, and takes the bars. "Plus, he was part feral. So he was really more like a pack."

I snort. "Whatever you need to tell yourself."

As much as I hate to admit it, Rubio flies well. Better than well, actually. Our clunky ship skirts the drifting clumps of rock and trash with the grace and ease of a pack elephant navigating Mumbai's dense inner-city streets.

"Where'd you learn to fly?" I ask.

"Apex," he says, gently nudging the ship over a spray of spiky pebbles I didn't notice until we were almost on them. "I trained to be a crop duster."

"You're good," I say grudgingly.

Rubio smirks. "I know."

"Of course, not at everything." I lean forward and pretend to check the oxygen saturation levels. We're almost past the debris field. "I mean, I know loads of people on flight crew who haven't had their asses handed to them by a research assistant."

"You know, memsahib, if you really are intent on

suicide, I can recommend some more effective methods—"

I punch him in the arm again and check telemetry. "Field's clear," I say. "We're good to switch to auto."

Rubio gives over the pilot's seat again, and I program in the trajectory lane Sweetie gave us, then activate the autopilot system. I stand and point at him. "Don't mess with the vectors. I'll be right back."

"Where're you going?" Rubio asks.

"To check Cassia's bandages."

Rubio sobers. "Tell her I'm sorry, okay? I didn't mean to—"

"She knows." I start down the steps, but Rubio calls out behind me.

"Hey, memsahib!"

I turn.

"What you're doing . . . I get it."

I raise an eyebrow at him. *Seriously?*

"I mean it," Rubio says. "You know? I don't know anyone who'd do this kind of thing for me."

"What, beat down a DSRI pilot?"

Rubio flinches. Immediately I regret my words. He's saying something real for once.

"Give up the thing they're best at to help someone," he says. "The thing that matters most to them."

Milah flashes through my head, signing to Cassia with her tiny fingers, and Cassia holding herself together as she signs back.

"The DSRI isn't what matters most," I say.

"You know what I mean." Rubio waves my words away. "If I couldn't fly anymore, if I were grounded, I wouldn't know what else to do. I'd probably pull a Hwang and try to off myself."

I turn away. "Don't say that." I know my career with the DSRI is over, but I haven't really let myself think about everything that means. I've been living in increments of minutes and hours. There is no future, only the past and present, mistakes and the chance to make them right.

"Memsahib—"

"I said *don't*!" I shout. I don't want to talk about it. Not with Rubio, not with anyone. Not even with myself.

I find Cassia asleep again, the blankets twisted around her legs and her curls stuck to her cheeks. I stand in the doorway a moment, watching her breathe deep and even, Tibbet curled up at her feet. I hate to wake her. I want to sit beside her. I want to hold her like I can heal everything broken in her, inside and out. I want to bend down and press my lips against hers, like in those storybooks. . . .

I stop. I'm not going to kiss someone who's unconscious. Besides, Cassia needs me as a medic now, not a . . . A what? A girlfriend? An obsessive mooner? My face flames. For the first time since the *Ranganathan* took flight, I wish I was back in Mumbai and things were simpler. I don't want Cassia hurt and bleeding, scouring the Deep for her brother. I want us to be able to spend the afternoon lounging on the levee wall, buying fruit drinks from the vendors set up in its shade. I want to hear her laugh and hit me with pillows again. I want to get to know those parts of her that are her when she isn't scrapping in terror for her brother's life.

I kneel by the bed. *Maybe after.* But will there be an after? Or will Cassia immolate herself along the way?

Cassia cracks her eyes open. "Hey."

"Hey." I try to smile. "Can you sit up?"

She pushes herself upright and winces.

"Your head?"

"Yeah," she says. "It's hurting again. And everything's spinning."

"Here." I unwrap the old bandage and fish a new one from my med kit. "Do you know where you are?"

She sighs. "I keep telling you, I don't have brain damage."

"Maybe, but you do have a brain *injury*." I finish

wrapping the new osmotic bandage around her head. "Humor me."

Cassia closes her eyes. "I'm Cassia Kaldero, I'm aboard the *Mendicant*, and my brain is working fine."

"Excellent." I sit back. "Is it kicking in yet?"

Cassia slumps against the pillows and stares up at the ceiling. "I think so." She moves her head a degree side to side. "Oh. Yes, there it is."

"Good." I smile. "Maybe now you won't be so cranky."

Cassia fakes a glare. "I'm not cranky. I have a *brain injury*." She looks at me, and a moment of true worry flits across her face. "Miyole . . ."

"Yeah?"

"Am I going to be better in time?" Her eyes widen with anxiety. "If I'm not—"

"You'll be fine," I interrupt. It's not a lie, exactly. Injuries like Cassia's can take anywhere from a few days to a few months to heal. We have three weeks until we reach Enceladus. It might be enough time, but if it's not, Cassia doesn't need to know. Not now, anyway. "You need rest, that's all."

I stand and pick up my med kit.

"Miyole," Cassia says.

I stop.

"Stay with me," she says. "Just for a little."

My muscles freeze, but my heart skips faster. Beneath the surface, I'm all motion and biology. "Are you sure?"

Cassia starts to nod, and then winces and catches herself. "I'm sure."

I sit on the bunk next to her, gingerly, careful not to jostle her.

"Not there." Cassia holds out a hand. "I'm cold. Climb in with me."

My stomach fills with butterflies. "Yeah?"

"Yeah," Cassia says.

I climb over her and prop myself up on my side. Beneath the faint smell of my med supplies and the musty bed sheets, Cassia's scent holds sway. It's something soft and sharp together, like bread and light vinegar.

Cassia rolls close to me. "It's better when you're here. It's distracting."

I laugh. "Distracting?"

"Good distracting," she says. "It gives me something else to think about."

She shifts her head on the pillow, and her hair brushes my palm, soft and cool like a silk sari. A current runs through me, as if all my nerve endings are exposed. I know I shouldn't be feeling this way when Cassia's sick. I shouldn't be feeling this way when she's lost her brother. But her breath falls on my skin and her eyelashes are gold against her freckled cheek and she thinks I'm distracting.

"Are you awake?" I ask.

"Mmm." Her eyelids flutter open. "I want to be, but the medicine . . ."

"Talk to me," I say. "Teach me some of those signs you and Milah know."

"Okay." She resettles herself on her side. "We should do the alphabet to start." She forms her hand into a fist with her thumb free. "That's *A*."

A dizzying sense of déjà vu comes over me, and all of a sudden I'm back in the Gyre, only I'm the one showing Ava how to write her alphabet. In my memory, we have a glowing tablet screen between us, but can that be right? We were poor in the Gyre. How could we have had a tablet when we had to rummage through bins of thirdhand clothes to find a pair of matching shoes on market day?

Cassia swats me lazily. "Pay attention."

I shake myself back to the present and find my knees trembling. "Sorry," I say. "Go on." This is why I shouldn't try to remember. At least I'm lying down and don't need to put my head between my knees.

"Are you all right?" Cassia frowns.

I make myself smile. "I'm fine." I'm not the one with the missing brother or the head trauma.

"Are you sure?"

I close my eyes. Am I? My pains are such distant ones. They shouldn't still be bothering me. I've had such good luck, so many breaks. I shouldn't still be wrapped up in my own misfortune. It shouldn't still hurt this much.

"I was thinking about my *manman*," I admit.

"Oh." Cassia traces the line of my hair with one finger. Her pupils are dilated, and I think the medicine might be making her a little looser and softer than usual. "Do you look like her?"

"I think so," I say, remembering the odd, unmoored feeling I had facing myself in the mirror before the officers' dinner. "Sometimes I think I remember everything there is to know about her, and then another detail comes up out of nowhere and hits me when I'm not looking. You know?"

"Yeah." She drops her hand to the pillow. "Nethanel said the same about Ume after she died."

Her eyes take on a faraway, glazed look. I reach out and lay a hand on her arm through the sheets, but at my touch, her face crumples. She cries quietly, fat tears escaping from beneath her lashes, her body shaking with the effort of containing the sound.

"Oh, no," I say. "I didn't mean to . . ."

She waves me silent and takes a deep, hiccupping breath.

I swallow. "Teach me more signs," I say. "Teach me a word."

"Yeah." She wipes her eyes. "Okay."

"How do you say 'sorry'?" I ask.

She laughs and rubs her eyes again, then makes the *A* symbol and circles it around her heart. "Like that."

I copy her. "What about 'Don't cry'?"

Cassia shakes her head. "I have a better one."

"Yeah?" I shuffle closer to her. We are knee to knee beneath the covers.

She touches a finger to her temple, then drops her hand and clasps it with the other.

"What's that one?" I ask.

"Trust," Cassia says.

CHAPTER 12

Four days out of dock, Cassia is still sleeping half the day. And then Rubio brings up the birds for the first time. We're crammed into the crawl space beneath the storage berth and the drums of cryatine, trying to figure out how to dampen the ship's beacon so we don't broadcast our position to the *Ranganathan* or the nests of *dakait* lurking outside Enceladus's sister moons.

"Did you hear that?" Rubio pauses with a jack in his gloved hand and looks up. "It sounds like geese."

Half of the *Mendicant*'s heating elements have shorted out, so we're both wearing our thermal jackets zipped up to the neck. Our breath forms frosty clouds in the stark blue light of the magnetic torch clipped to the ceiling.

"Geese?" I follow his gaze.

"You know." He moves his hands in a flapping motion. "Geese."

I roll my eyes. "I know what geese are."

"But you don't hear them?" The intensity in his voice starts to make me think he isn't joking.

"No," I say cautiously. I look up again. We've been trying to keep as quiet as possible so Cassia can rest. "I don't hear anything."

Rubio narrows his eyes as if he thinks I might be lying.

"Maybe it's Tibbet," I say. That cat makes some extraordinarily weird noises, especially when he catches one of the ship's seemingly endless supplies of mice. "Or some old pneumatics or something."

Rubio relaxes a fraction. "Maybe." He turns back to the coms access panel and concentrates on threading the jack into the line-in. It seals with a *click*. "Got it."

At that moment, the gravity fails.

My stomach lurches, and an eerie prickling sensation courses over my skin as all the hair on my body rises of its own accord. Above us, the barrels of cryatine rebound against one another with a series of odd metallic echoes. Cassia cries out, startled from sleep, and Tibbet mewls in distress.

My back hits the top of the access shaft with a soft thump. *"Vaat,"* I curse.

"*Mierda*," Rubio adds.

We claw our way out of the shaft and float up into the ship's main cabin. Cassia hovers outside the sleeping berth, her eyes wide and hair wild. She hugs another of the thermal jackets tight around her body.

"What happened?" Her lips have gone bloodless and blue in the cold.

"I don't know." I look at Rubio. "We were in there fixing the signal beacon when it went down."

"Is it down for good?" Cassia shivers. A few hours or days in zero G won't hurt us, but longer than that and our muscles will start to atrophy. By the time we reach Enceladus, we'll be too weak to walk under the moon's gravity, much less do any rescuing.

"Only one way to find out." Rubio flips a multitool in the air.

I make my way along the wall to Cassia. "You should go back to bed. It won't take us long to fix." At least that's what I hope.

Cassia hugs her coat tighter and scowls. "I'm tired of sleeping. I feel useless."

Rubio keeps his head down, trying to pry up the access panel for the gravity controls and pretending not to hear us.

"You're not useless." I put my arm around her. "You're hurt. It's not your fault you—"

She pushes away. "Stop coddling me. I'm not your baby."

"Of course you're not. What does that even—"

"Aha!" Rubio interrupts.

Cassia and I both stop short and look down at him.

Rubio smiles sheepishly and holds up two halves of an insulated wire. "Loose coupling, that's all."

I blink at him, momentarily disoriented. "Oh. Is it fixable?"

"Sure," Rubio says, and brings the halves together. Instantly, the gravity snaps back on. Cassia and I tumble to the floor, and a deafening series of crashes echo from the storage room. The cryatine barrels. Tibbet howls from somewhere down the corridor.

"What the hell, Rubio?" I struggle to my feet as the last of the barrels clangs to a stop.

"Would you make up your mind?" Cassia huffs.

"Sorry. Sorry." Rubio casts a worried look at Cassia, as if she might break, and waves us away. "You two go . . . talk, or whatever. I can fix this."

Cassia and I exchange a look. Despite his ramblings about geese, I've found myself trusting Rubio more and more over the past few days. Even if he isn't the best company, he's an excellent pilot and a competent mechanic. But then again, I'm not the one he tried to kill.

I look at Cassia. "Your call."

She sighs. "Fine." She spins and disappears down the hall to the sleeping berth. "Thank you," I mouth at Rubio, and hurry after her.

Cassia stands with her back to the door, struggling to tie her loose hair in a braid with clumsy, gloved fingers. After the third try, she utters a frustrated growl, pulls the gloves loose with her teeth, and hurls them at the bed.

"Here," I say. "Let me."

She sits on the bunk. I climb up behind her, unfasten the bandage, and comb through her curly locks with my fingers. I pause over the small area we had to cut short in order to patch up her head.

"How does it look?" she asks over her shoulder.

"Better," I say. The skin is still shiny pink and tender, but there's no sign of infection. "How does it feel?"

Cassia grimaces. "Less . . . open, I guess." But worry overlays her words. "I'm still getting the headaches."

"They'll pass," I promise, coaxing the knots out of her hair.

Tibbet stalks in with his ears pointed back and hops up

beside her. She rubs one of them between her thumb and forefinger.

"Talk to me," I say. I need to do my job and distract her. "Tell me something good. Like what you're going to do when we get Nethanel back."

"I don't know." She ducks her head and rubs her hands over her face. "I don't want to think about it."

Neither of us says anything, but the unspoken hangs in the air. *What if we don't get him back? What if we're too late?*

"A memory, then." I smooth Cassia's hair back behind her ears and begin to weave it into a French braid along the side of her head, where it will hide the shorn portion. "Tell me something good you remember."

She draws a steadying breath. "Okay." Her eyes fall on Tibbet, who has contorted himself into an uncomfortable-looking shape and is furiously grooming his back legs. "You want to hear how we got him?"

"Sure." I go on braiding.

A ghost of a smile creeps onto her face. "Nethanel and me, we stole him."

I pause. "You stole him?" I glance at Tibbet, who yawns through a mouth of needle-sharp teeth. With all the strays slinking around Mumbai, I sometimes forget how valuable an animal like a cat can be out in the Deep.

Cassia nods. "Our old tabby died when I was maybe eight and Nethanel was twelve. Our dad didn't want anyone to know, but we could tell he was broken up about it. He loved that thing. So me and Nethanel are out walking one day when we've stopped at a way station, and we see this old woman with a litter of kittens in a birdcage, right?"

I nod, urging her on.

"And Nethanel comes up with this plan where I'll cry and pretend I'm lost, and he'll sneak up behind and lift one of the kittens out of the cage." She smiles at the empty air. "Except when I start crying, the old lady doesn't care. And I have to keep crying louder and louder until she finally comes out from her stall to shoo me off, because I'm chasing her customers away."

"Bloody *kuttiya*," I mutter.

Cassia shrugs and smiles slyly over her shoulder. "Well, I mean, we *were* trying to steal from her."

"So what happened?" I tie off her braid and sit back on the bed.

"Right. So she was trying to push me away, and I bit her."

"You *bit* her?" I snort.

Cassia nods and shifts so she faces me. "Yup. Right on

the calf. So then she was running after me all through the station and screaming, and I thought for sure I was going to end up in one of those mystery stews you always find that far out."

"No!" I make a face. "Gross."

"Yes." Her eyebrows arch up in a wicked grin.

This is the Cassia I want, the one buried beneath all her grief. This is the Cassia that makes me want to grab her hand and swing it between us. I trace a small circle on the bedspread. "So did you get away?"

Cassia tilts her head side to side. "Well, I'm not soup, am I?"

I laugh. "No, you're more of a stew, I guess."

"Here." She moves closer to me. "My turn."

I put my hands over my hair. "No, that's okay."

"Come on." She pokes me in the ribs. "You did mine. Besides, I know all kinds of styles. I do my mother and Milah's all the time."

"It's gross," I say. I haven't washed my hair since before we left the *Ranganathan*, and I didn't bring along any of the oils or creams I normally use to keep it under control.

Cassia frowns. "No, it isn't."

I snort and roll my eyes.

"I'm serious," Cassia says. "I love your hair. It's so pretty when it gets out of your braid like that." She reaches out and fingers a curl that has escaped along the side of my neck.

I stop breathing. Our eyes meet, and we both freeze, her fingertips barely touching my skin, my lips slightly parted, as if some galvanic force has passed through us.

I swallow. "Okay."

I turn around on the bed. Somehow, with my back to Cassia, I feel even more aware of her. The rustle of her clothes, the gentle tug of her pulling the tie from my hair, the brush of her fingertips against my scalp as she finger-combs my curls. She hums a tune I don't recognize as she undoes my braid, something pretty in a minor key, and for some reason it stirs up a brief memory of my mother—*combing my hair, twisting it into two springy braids.*

I glance at Tibbet again, who has curled up in a crescent at the foot of the bed and draped his feathery tail over his nose to keep out the cold. Suddenly I understand why she wanted to bring him, why she wouldn't leave him alone on the dock.

"So . . . he was worth it?" I say.

I can hear the smile in Cassia's voice. "You should've seen our father. He tried to pretend like he was mad, but before we left dock, he was mixing up nutrient milk and trying out names on the kitten."

"Who named him?" I ask.

"I did, mostly." She laughs. "Nethanel wanted to name him Fangmelion, but my father . . ." She stops suddenly, and her hands drop away from my hair. I turn in time to see all the mirth run out of her face. The present is back. Her father is half blind. Her brother has been taken.

"I'm sorry." I should have known any memory would bring her back around to this; that the price of memory is remembering.

"It's fine." She shakes herself and forces a smile, but the sallow, pained look has already crept back into the space around her eyes. She looks at her pillow. "Maybe I should lie down again."

"Of course." I rise to go. This is all my fault, leading her thoughts back to her brother. "I'll just go check on—"

"No." She catches me. "Stay. Talk to me. I don't want to be alone right now."

I sit down. "What do you want to talk about?"

"Anything." She eases her head down onto the pillow, pulls her coat tight against the cold, and closes her eyes. "Tell me about you. Do you have any brothers or sisters?"

I draw my knees up to my chest. "A foster sister. Ava. She's much older than me, though."

Cassia opens her eyes. "You're adopted?"

I frown. "Is that so weird?"

"No, of course not," she says. "I mean, I know you lost your mother, but I thought maybe an aunt or uncle raised you or something. Did you know your family at all?"

I shift uncomfortably on the bed. "I don't remember much. I was eight when my mother died, and she didn't have any family around. I don't think I ever knew my father."

"Really?" Cassia cocks her head at me. "Eight's pretty old. You must remember something."

"Well, I don't," I snap.

Cassia recoils.

"I'm sorry." I look down. "I didn't mean . . ."

"I know," she says. "We're both tired. And cold."

I nod, staring at the empty bunk across the room.

"Come lie back down." Cassia holds out a hand to me. "Keep me warm."

I climb wordlessly into her bunk, coat and all, and pile up the blankets until we have a warm cocoon around us. Cassia drapes an arm over my hip bone and shifts closer so she can nestle her head against my clavicle.

I run my hand up and down the quilted lines of her sleeve. "I don't think I'm doing a very good job."

"Of what?"

"Being a distraction," I say.

"You're fine." Cassia's lashes flutter against my neck as she closes her eyes, and an electric thrill trips through me, melting away the last of my annoyance.

"I'm sorry I got mad," I whisper into her hair. It smells like her, like skin and faint oil.

"It doesn't matter." She tightens her grip on my waist and shivers. "I'm sorry for pushing you about your family."

"It doesn't matter," I echo. I wonder if I have my own smell, too, if it loosens all her muscles the way hers does mine.

Cassia raises her head so our lips almost brush. She slips her hand under the hem of my coat and trails her fingers down over my hip to the small of my back. Heat blooms through me. This is not how friends touch each other. I shiver and flex my toes.

"How could I stay mad when you're so good at keeping me warm?" she murmurs. She finds my hand beneath the covers and brings it up to her mouth. Her lips are warm on my fingertips when she kisses them.

I utter a soft "Oh." My eyes flutter closed.

Her mouth moves down my palm. I tense as she reaches my scar, but she doesn't stop. She presses her lips against it, too, and then against my wrist, lingering on the tender skin there. I push her hair back, my breath rising, and press my body against hers. She raises her lips to mine, and for a moment, our eyes catch.

"Yeah?" I breathe.

"Yeah."

All of me melts. This is nothing like the kissing bottle game. Kissing Cassia is like lying down in the still-warm evening sand. It is slow and sweet and full.

Cassia fumbles for my coat's zipper and pulls it down off my shoulders. I shrug one arm out of it, ignoring the goose bumps rising, prickling my skin, and reach for Cassia's coat in turn.

At that moment, a soft weight lands on my leg and pads its way up along my body, accompanied by a low rumbling sound.

"What . . . ?" I lift my head.

Tibbet pokes his face over the edge of the covers and stares down at us with his owlish yellow-green eyes, a choppy purr vibrating in his throat. Cassia and I catch each other's eyes and burst out laughing.

"Tibbet." Cassia groans and mock-glares at him. "You're interrupting."

He blinks lazily at her and hops onto her pillow, where he spends a few seconds purring like a corn diesel generator and kneading the stuffing, then flops down across the crown of Cassia's head and commences to give himself another bath.

Cassia sighs. "He's worse than my mother."

"Should I put him out?" I ask. The moment is gone, but I'm fairly sure we could build it back up if we didn't have company.

"No. I should rest anyway." She glowers at Tibbet and then reaches up and scratches him behind the ears. "You're a good heater, but you have terrible timing. You know that?"

The cat redoubles his generator noises in response.

I sit up and reluctantly throw the blankets from my legs. The cold is worse now that I've been so warm. "I should check on Rubio. Are you okay here?"

Cassia nods. "Tibbet'll keep me company."

I zip up my coat and shake a finger at the cat. "Not appreciated, sir. Not appreciated."

I find Rubio righting the cryatine barrels. I should help him, I know, or at least thank him. After all, it wasn't his fault the gravity failed. But our talk of my parents has left me feeling as though a chasm has opened between me and the rest of the human race. Hanging around Rubio will only remind me of it.

I slip my hand into my pocket and palm my crow,

smooth and cool as a river stone. I could listen to my mother's voice. My palms itch at the thought. If I want to remember more—if I push deeper—will I? Cassia's right. I see it in the flashes of my mother's face that surface in my mirror and the way smells spark my memory. I love Soraya and Ava, but what would it be like to know which parts of myself were born into me, and which I pieced together from my friends and teachers? Did my mother's temper flare like mine? Did she hum to herself when she worked? Were her hands my hands? Were her bones my bones? Did we have secret jokes and stories all our own? And if I go looking, can I bring them to life again?

I climb into the *Mendicant*'s cockpit, curl up in the pilot's seat, and flip open my crow. I thumb through to the recording Ava sent me and sit staring at it for a full minute, the screen pulsing where I should touch play. When I was little, Ava used to try to talk to me about the parts of my past she knew. *Do you remember Ms. Miko and the squid? What about your kite, the red one? You and Kai would take it flying.* And then, *I heard on the news people are coming back to the Gyre. Maybe we could go visit. Don't you want to see the place you came from?*

I didn't want to know then. I didn't want to remember. I wanted a fresh, clean start, full of bright, soft clothes like the ones Soraya wore. I wanted trigonometry and calculus to fill the vacant rooms in my head and dampen my memories. I wanted the comfort of order.

But now? My thumb hovers over the screen. I wish Ava was here. I wish I could call her and ask her to tell me everything she remembers. It would be safer that way, easier than having to do the remembering myself. She could catch me if I fell in too deep and the memories started pulling me down. She could distract me with funny stories about her customers or Rushil's pickling experiments. But Ava's not here. She's millions of miles away in the Mumbai sunshine.

I let my thumb fall, and Ava's face fills the screen, smiling softly. "Hey, Miyole . . ."

I listen, trying to breathe evenly, until my mother's voice starts amid the static rain.

Vector five, verified . . .

My throat constricts. *It's okay,* I tell myself. *It's not really her. It's only sound waves.* But the trembling starts in my stomach nonetheless, as if some geological force were rocking my whole being. The wave is coming, breaking up the frozen sea. I dig my nails into my palm and hold on.

Suddenly, my mother is singing—softly, to herself. A jolt of recognition runs through me.

Dodo ti ti-tit manman
Si li pa dodo
Krab la va manjé.
Papa li pa la
L'ale la rivyè . . .

The lullaby fades, almost lost in the background roar, and then returns. I couldn't have sung the words moments before, but some part of me remembers the cadence. I know when her voice will rise and when it will linger on a note. My eyes prickle and burn, and I let them. Another piece of memory surfaces. My mother—my *manman*—pinching my toes playfully when she got to the part in the song about the crab. *Go to sleep,* ma chère, *or Mr. Crab will get you.*

And suddenly, like an aftershock, my mother's smell comes back to me. It floods up around me as I strain to separate her voice from the static—the tang of sea salt, sweat, and grease from her little ship's hydraulics, mixed with the soft, full comfort of cooking spices and the oil she used in her hair. I grab on to it, tight as I can, even though I might as well be clinging to barbed wire. It's too much. Too much. My lungs constrict. I stop the recording.

I lean forward, limp and speckled in sweat, despite the cold.

"You okay, memsahib?"

I snap my head up. Rubio stands balanced uncertainly on the top rung of the ladder, eyeing me like I'm an injured bird.

"I'm fine." I swipe at the moisture gathered on my cheeks and forehead and dry my hands on my parka. I eye him in return. "How long have you been standing there?"

He shrugs. Long enough. "What was that you were listening to? Was it another ship?" He glances at the coms readout, which sits silent and blank among the other controls.

I narrow my eyes at him. "What do you think?"

He looks at me evenly, not a trace of mockery in his voice. "Was that your mother?"

"What?"

"Your mother." His eyes dart around the cockpit, looking for anyplace to land except on me. "I thought . . . she was singing a lullaby, so . . ."

We stare at each other. Seconds move like glaciers.

Rubio clears his throat and lowers his voice. "So, is she?"

I open my mouth to snap something at him, but at that moment, all the fight drains out of me. He's being sincere for once. "Yes. She is." I look out at the star-stippled darkness on the other side of the viewport. "Or she was."

"She's dead?" Rubio asks.

I nod.

"I'm sorry." Rubio pushes himself up the last rung and slides into the copilot's seat.

I shrug. "I don't remember her much."

"You were pretty little when she died, huh?" Rubio says.

"I was eight," I say.

"Was she sick?" he asks.

I shake my head. "You remember that freak storm that hit the Pacific Gyre all those years ago?"

Rubio nods. "That was a monster."

I nod along with him. "That's where we lived."

Rubio's eyes go wide. "You survived that?"

"I did," I say. "My mother didn't."

"*Vaya*," he says. "I'm sorry, memsahib. I never knew. . . ."

I sigh. "Well, now that you do, maybe you could quit it with the whole memsahib *bhankas*."

"You really don't like it?" He sounds genuinely surprised.

I raise both eyebrows. "Um, no. Haven't I said that a million times?"

"Yeah, but . . ." Rubio frowns. "I thought we were just, you know . . ."

I cock my head to the side, waiting.

"Playing," he finishes.

I stare at him. Even if I live to be five hundred, I don't think I'll ever understand what makes boys run the way they do. They are unfathomable creatures.

Suddenly Rubio's face shifts from earnest to puzzled. "Wait, you said you were eight when the storm hit the Gyre."

"That's right," I say cautiously. *What is he on about?*

"But that was . . ." He pauses, thinking. "Eight years ago. That would make you sixteen."

My mouth goes dry. *Stupid, stupid.* This is exactly why I stayed away from other people aboard the *Ranganathan*, so I wouldn't slip up like this.

Rubio must see the look on my face, because his eyes widen. "You *are* sixteen, aren't you?" He pushes back his hair. *"Chingame."*

"It doesn't really matter," I say quickly. "I did my job well, didn't I? I had all the qualifications except the age thing."

"No, it's not that." Rubio drops his head into a shake. "It's only . . . it explains a lot." He looks up at me.

I raise an eyebrow. "What does that mean?"

"Well, you're so touchy all the time. You can't take a joke. And this whole crazy kidnapping, ship-jacking thing . . ." Rubio stops. He looks as if he's realized he just stepped on a land mine.

I raise a single eyebrow. "You think it was crazy to help Cassia?"

"No. It took balls, is all." Rubio leans forward on his knees and folds his hands together. "I guess I might have done the same a few years ago, but I never would have done it now."

I cock my head to the side. "Why?"

"I guess . . ." He sighs and raises his eyes to the ceiling. "You start seeing so much wrong everywhere you go, and you know you can't fix all of it, so you start to think you can't fix any of it."

I shake my head. "I don't know if I get that."

Rubio wears a sad smile I've never seen on him before. He lays a hand awkwardly on my arm. "That's probably a good thing."

I give him a crooked grin. "Don't go getting all mushy on me. You're supposed to be my nemesis, remember?"

"Right." He straightens up. "We now return to our regularly scheduled banter."

I roll my eyes. "I take it that means you're going back to being annoying now?"

But Rubio doesn't answer. His eyes stay fixed on a spot above my left shoulder.

I turn. Nothing there. At least, nothing besides a wall

panel and an ancient foam-spray fire extinguisher with a rusted nozzle.

"Rubio?" I say cautiously, and when he doesn't answer, I snap my fingers beneath his nose. "Hey!"

He blinks out of his trance. "What? Yeah?"

I wrinkle my brow. "Everything okay?"

"Yeah. No, everything's fine." He nods, maybe a little too vigorously. "I just thought I . . . It was nothing. Never mind."

"You're sure?" I frown.

"Yup. Nothing to worry about. I got lost in thought for a second there." He stands and squares his shoulders. "I'd better go finish strapping down those cryatine barrels. Don't want to go through that if we lose gravity again."

"I thought you had that sorted," I say.

Rubio pauses in the doorway. "Yeah, but with this raggedy-ass heap? No telling what's about to happen."

CHAPTER 13

The next night, I wake to a crash. I sit bolt upright beside Cassia.

She moans and covers her eyes with both palms. "Miyole?" She's been up half the night vomiting into the chemical toilet across the hall. This does not bode well for her whole head injury thing.

"I'm here." I squeeze her elbow and scan the room. Tibbet blinks at me sleepily from the foot of the bed. Rubio's bunk is empty. "Don't worry. I'm on it."

My own head throbs as I pull on my boots and creep down the dim, narrow corridor, past the common room, and up the stairs to the cockpit. Rubio stands in the doorway, his eyes and hair wild. Every one of the access panels in the cockpit hangs open, exposing circuit boards and arrays of microscopic processing chips. Loose wires dangle from the panel in front of him.

"Rubio, what the hell—"

"They're in the walls, Miyole." His stare goes straight through me. "They're in the walls."

"What are?"

"The birds," he says, as if this should be obvious, and rips out a fistful of fiberoptic cables. "That cat is good for nothing."

Vaat.

"Rubio." I take a cautious step toward him.

"We have to find out how they're getting in," Rubio mutters, tugging on a second bundle of wires. "They'll build nests. They'll build nests and ruin all our hard work."

"Rubio." What happened to the calm, big-brotherly Rubio from yesterday? I edge closer and hold out a hand. "Let's talk about this."

"There's no time!" He whirls on me, wild-eyed. "We have to plug up the holes."

It takes every bit of my willpower not to flinch, but I don't. "Okay," I say calmly. "I understand. But you don't want to wake Cassia, do you?"

"Cassia?" He stares off into the middle distance for a moment, confused, and then he's back. "No, I don't. Her head . . . she needs rest."

"Good," I say, and gently take his elbow. "Let's go down to the common room and pull up some schematics. I bet we can figure out how they're getting in, and then we can fix it together." *And I can figure out what the hell is wrong with you.*

"Right." He runs a hand through his hair, visibly calmer. "We make a good team. You can help me get rid of them."

I could almost laugh, except that Cassia's already sick. I don't need Rubio out of commission, too. I lead him to the common room, deposit him on one of the couches, and unfold a smartscreen on the low, round table before him. I call up the ship's schematics.

"Start looking," I say. "I'll be right back."

"Where are you going?" he asks, suddenly suspicious.

"To check on Cassia," I say. "You get started without me."

He stares at me for a moment, as if he thinks I might betray him to the birds.

"It'll only take a minute." I force a smile. "And then we can take care of your bird problem."

"Our bird problem," he corrects.

"Right," I agree.

Rubio nods, satisfied, and hunches over the schematics.

I hurry from the room, up to the sleeping quarters, and kneel beside my bunk, rifling through my med kit.

"Miyole?" Cassia sits up in bed, hair mussed. "What's going on?"

"Nothing," I whisper. "Go back to sleep."

Cassia drops back against the pillows. I find what I need and palm it, then stand and walk back to the common room. *Kilograms of weight times dosage per kilogram equals desired dosage.*

I find Rubio watching the door when I enter.

"Is she okay?" he asks.

I nod. "She's fine. Sleeping." I drop down next to him. "So, what do we have?"

Rubio leans forward over the plan. "Possible entry points here and here." He taps his finger on an air-cycling vent and then moves it over to what I think is probably the ship's waste conversion system.

"How do you think they're getting in?" I move closer, assessing Rubio's body for the best access point. *His neck*, I decide. Some nice veins there. Besides, the rest of him is covered up by a parka and thermal jumpsuit.

Rubio looks at me as if I've asked what the weather's like out in space. "I don't think they're *getting in*," he says. "They probably roosted in here while this junker was in dock, and now we're disturbing them."

I frown. This is a far saner explanation than I was

expecting. "Are you sure it's not the rats you're hearing?" There are definitely rats aboard. I woke a few nights earlier to find Tibbet purring proudly beside me and another dead rat deposited on the blanket over my chest.

"Yes." Rubio draws out the word in exasperation. "Have you ever heard a rat sing like that?" He cocks his head and points up, listening.

I pause and hold my breath, straining to hear what Rubio does. Far away inside the ship, something gurgles, but otherwise, a complete, humming silence reigns over us.

"Okay," I say. "Medicine time." In one swift movement, I jab the tiny syringe hidden in my palm into his neck and depress the injector.

"What—" Rubio's eyes go wide and he flails, trying to bat me away.

Three, two, one, I count to myself, and Rubio goes limp. He slumps back against the couch, his eyes still wide and hurt.

"I'm sorry," I say, and mean it. "You're hallucinating."

Rubio slumps down farther on the couch. His eyelids droop.

"Might as well get comfortable." I pat his leg and stand.

I position Rubio so he lies flat on his back across the couch. Then I find several pillows and prop up his head, careful to turn his chin to the side so he won't aspirate his own vomit if the sedative doesn't sit well with him. Last, I carry down an armload of thermal blankets from the bunks and layer them over him. His fingers are already ice-cold from the drop in his blood pressure. I tuck the blankets tight around him.

"I hear them," he says plaintively, almost in a whisper.

I start. He should be out cold by now.

"I know you do," I say, gently as I can. "Get some sleep. They'll be gone when you wake up."

I wait with Rubio until his pulse slows and he stops struggling with his eyelids. Something thumps deep within the *Mendicant*, and suddenly it strikes me how quiet everything is. This ship was made to house a dozen people or more, not a skeleton crew of three.

Chaila. I hunch forward and chew on the inside of my lip. The pain in my head pulses with my heartbeat. I need a plan. I can fly the vessel on my own, more or less, but how am I going to sleep if I'm the only one on watch? And with the constant repairs this thing needs, how am I going to keep it from deteriorating into a chill, airless hunk of metal floating through the Deep with our corpses inside?

A questioning chirrup noise behind me interrupts the silence. I swivel in place and find Tibbet watching me with big, solemn eyes from the doorway.

"It's just me and you now," I say. "Are you any good with a cold fuser?"

Tibbet hunches over and starts to make a wet, choking noise I've learned means he's about to vomit.

"Gross," I tell him. I don't think any of the cats in Ava and Rushil's shipyard used to throw up nearly as much as Tibbet. There's something deeply wrong with this animal.

He finishes and sniffs the air. His pupils expand, and he bobs his head around the side of the door and darts back into the hallway, sure signs he's spotted a rat. At least we won't have vermin chewing on the wires and walls much longer. If I can keep the ship in one piece long enough for it to matter, that is.

I rise and run my hands through my hair. I haven't bothered to braid it again. I'm warmer with it covering my neck anyway, and pulling it tight doesn't help with the headaches I've been fighting. I rub my temples. First things first. I have to undo whatever damage Rubio's done to the cockpit wiring. I look down at him. If I've measured the dose right, he should be out for a solid eight hours.

Vaat, I curse again, and head up to the cockpit.

I lean my head against the cockpit wall and groan. Even with the small mercy that the wires Rubio ripped out are color coded, it has taken me forever to figure out how they match up. I rub a hand over my eyes and check the time on my crow. Three and a half hours, to be exact. Three and a half hours, and I'm only halfway there.

I slap a magnetic glow lamp on the side of the access panel alcove and kill the power to the cockpit. The last thing we need is for me to get electrocuted. The diagnostic displays that survived Rubio's attack wink out, one by one, taking their minute electronic hum with them. In the same moment, the overhead lights flicker and go dark. The glow lamp does little more than cast deep shadows across the cockpit.

I push my hair out of my eyes and lean into the alcove to begin the painstaking job of reconnecting the wires. The silence filling the room is so complete, it almost feels as if it's taking on mass. A high, nearly subaudible whine rings deep in my ears. I work my jaw in an attempt to pop them, and the tinny ring softens enough so I can think around it.

I bite my lip and twist two ragged ends of a wire together. What the hell could be wrong with Rubio? Sleep deprivation? But none of us have been sleeping well, and he's the only one hearing birds. Not isolation-induced psychosis, either.

We all had to attend a seminar on the early warning signs and symptoms before we boarded the *Ranganathan*. He's not exhibiting uncontrollable rage or paranoia or other antisocial behaviors. Well, maybe a little bit of paranoia. But he's not cutting himself or holing up in his bunk, refusing to come out, either. It doesn't make sense. He's just . . . hallucinating. I can set a broken bone and bandage a wound, but the brain is trickier territory. If a few hours of forced sleep don't fix him, I'm out of my depth.

I shake a cramp out of my hand and reach for a roll of insulating tape. Suddenly the ringing in my head spikes. I clamp my hands over my ears and double over, body pulsing with adrenaline. *Fight or flight.* Except there's nowhere to go, and nothing to fight. The sound is inside my head. In that moment, the high, even tone breaks into the melodic chaos of digital static.

". . . h . . . p us . . . radius . . . . ire . . ."

A broadcast? I glance at the control panels. That's impossible. We can't receive anything with power out in the cockpit and all our telemetry instruments down. I look to the coms console. It stays dark, hibernating with the rest of our functions.

The signal comes back, stronger this time. "Repeat . . . ny ships w . . . . radius, please help u . . ."

A distress call. I rush to the coms and press my ear against the speaker, even though common sense tells me I won't hear anything that way.

"... major functions down. Fire is eating up our oxygen reserves. Please ..." A woman's voice begs. "If anyone can hear us ..."

Fire. My palms break out in a clammy sweat. There are few things worse than a fire aboard a ship this far out in the Deep, especially if it reaches your oxygen reserves. You're going to die—fast, if you can't put out the flames; slow, if you do manage to douse them.

I jump up and flip the power breaker to the cockpit. No matter if all our systems aren't online. We have oxygen, and that's more than I can say for the other ship.

I race back to the coms and flip them to transmit. "Unidentified vessel, this is the *Mendicant*—vector 248, D245M. Responding to distress call. What is your position?"

The speaker beneath the controls stays silent, receiving nothing but static.

I press the transmit button again. "Unidentified vessel, this is the—"

"Miyole?" The woman's voice disintegrates and re-forms. "*Ma chère*, we're all alone out here. You have to save me."

My skin turns to ice. *My mother.* It hits me like a wall

of frigid water. *That's my mother's voice.* My hand falls away from the transmitter. That's not possible.

"Manman?" I whisper.

"Save me," she pleads. "*Ma chère*, don't leave me alone."

"Manman, how . . ." She's dead. I know she's dead, but she's speaking to me. There has to be an explanation. Someone, somewhere must have made a mistake. Maybe Ava and Soraya were wrong. Maybe my dreams of her drifting to safety were true after all. Maybe she's been waiting out here for me all along.

"Where are you?" I try to wrestle my voice under control, but it breaks anyway, full of want and loneliness.

"*Ma chère, ma chère,*" my mother begs, and then I see it. A ship glides into view, locked in an achingly slow death spiral. Flames glow beneath its skin and spout from its sides where streams of oxygen escape from gouges in its hull.

My breath stops.

"I'm sorry, *ma chère.*" The ship twists abruptly, as if someone has yanked up on the thrust bars in desperation.

My mind moves too slowly. *That's the same make as Cassia's old ship,* I think dully. I stand paralyzed as the burning vessel crosses our vector and swings toward the

Mendicant, head-on. One heartbeat, two . . .

The ship's warning system springs to life, flashing red and shaking me from my stupor with a series of high, urgent beeps. I lunge for the controls and push us into a dive. But it's not enough. Our velocities are too great, the seconds to impact too short. The other ship fills our viewports, spinning out of control.

"Manman!" I scream, and throw my hands out before me to fend off the blow. The coms screech with feedback and I squeeze my eyes shut.

CHAPTER 14

I wake in the big bed, the one my *manman* and I share. The flock of scrap-metal birds I made for her dangle overhead, chiming softly against one another in the morning breeze. I made them for her birthday, I think. Yes, for her birthday, even though it wasn't really her birthday. She told me no one in the Gyre had one, but I had found my own marked down in a journal she kept—April 14—and I wanted her to have one, too.

Salt air and music from our neighbor's staticky radio drift through the open window. Dogs bay, roosters call from rooftop to rooftop, and hammers knock against wood and tin in the distance. I know without looking that this is the Gyre.

"Miyole!" My mother calls, singsong. The scent and sizzle of frying fish reaches my nose, and I sit up.

I pad into the main room. My mother stands at our portable gas stove, a cast-iron pan of fish and sugared plantains browning in the oil.

"You're home!" I say.

She looks up and smiles, almost hiding the weariness in her eyes. "There you are, lazybones. I thought you would sleep all morning."

I climb onto a stool across from her. "I thought you had a run today."

"I did it early." She lifts a cut of fish from the oil and gently turns it. "I thought we could spend the day together."

My heart becomes the lightest element. "Really?"

"*Wi, ma chère.*" She laughs. "Really. Now go get dressed. The day is wasting."

I look down. I'm wearing my pressure suit. Its airtight quilting is far too hot for a day out under the Pacific sun. I scurry off to our bedroom and lift the lid of our heavy old steamer trunk to pull out my best dress—noon-blue cotton with a white diamond pattern around the neck. Maybe we'll walk to the fish market or take one of the penny ferries around to South Gyre, where our neighbor Mrs. Acosta said she heard they had a flower market. But as I lower the lid, the light from the window changes. A rosy, end-of-day glow bathes the room, and the last bronze rays of the setting sun glints on my birds' wings.

"Miyole?" My mother sounds worried.

"In here, Manman," I call.

She arrives at the door, dressed in her flight clothes—boots, red-belted trousers, and a weather-beaten leather jacket. "I have to go now, *ma chère*. It's late."

I look out the window at the sun melting into the water and then back to her. "But you said we could spend the day together."

"I know." She strokes my hair. "Our hours are too short. Your food has gone cold."

"I don't want you to go." My eyes prickle. Something wet rolls down my hand, and when I look, my scars have opened up again and my hands are red with my own blood.

"Don't worry." My mother smiles sadly and looks over my shoulder. "Ava will take care of you."

I follow her gaze and find Ava sleeping in the bed my mother and I share. Her face and arms have a gray pallor to them, and I can't hear her breathe.

"She's not well. Manman, I don't think you should . . ." I turn back to find my mother gone. I'm speaking to an empty room.

Outside, the sun has set, and the waves crash and roll. The sea smells sick. I race down the steps clinging to the side of our house and out onto the pontoon that supports it.

"*Manman*!" I shout. Eerie, gray-green clouds thicken in the sky, and rain stings my face.

"Miyole!" The wind nearly drowns out my name.

I look up in the direction of the voice. A small dark-haired boy stands atop the widow's walk of a neighboring pontoon house. My friend, Kai. He points down the string of refitted boats and floating houses to the behemoth of our neighborhood—an old Icelandic research vessel that towers above the rest of the masts and rooftops. People pack the upper decks, peering out the glass into the storm.

"No." I step back. This is too familiar. I've seen it before. I know what happens to them, and then to Kai and Manman.

As I watch, the ocean's surface drops out from beneath the ship, and a swell as high as her receiving towers looms up in its place. The wave thrusts the ship on her side. The wind and rushing water fill the air, but I can still hear the passengers screaming. The wave crests. For a moment, I think the ship's bow will break over the top of the wall of water, but it hangs a moment too long, fighting gravity, and the wave tips them over.

I haven't moved, but now I'm atop the widow's walk, holding Kai's hand tight as the ocean foams around the capsized ship. I want to tell him I'm sorry, because even though he hasn't said it, I know his family was aboard the vessel—his father and mother, and all his brothers and sisters. But this is something too big even for sorrow, so I squeeze his hand tighter.

And then my mother's sloop is above us, battling the winds to stay aloft.

"Miyole! Kai!" Manman dangles from an emergency ladder spilling from her sloop's hatch. She holds out her hand. "Reach up to me!"

I am first on the ladder. Manman helps me up halfway, and then goes back for Kai. But he is shorter than I am, and the winds twist the ladder like a strip of tinfoil, so she jumps down to help him.

I pause near the top and look down at them. Manman lifts Kai up high enough so he can plant his feet on the bottom rung. He slips on the wet metal and freezes, terrified, clinging to the braided metal ropes.

"It's all right, *ma chère*!" My mother's voice carries over the wind.

He starts his climb again, slow and trembling, as if he didn't spend his days skipping from rigging to mast to rooftop like a cat.

My mother catches the ladder's tail and looks up at me.

Water swirls around her feet from the waves swamping our neighbor's house. I've never seen her afraid. She has always been fearless, one step ahead and ready to fight, but the look on her face as the widow's walk pitches is solid terror.

An ominous pause interrupts the storm, and then, suddenly, the sea sucks the platform down and out from beneath my mother's feet. Her knee catches the railing as the building drops, and she dangles like a marionette in the wind. A deeper shadow rises against the bruised sky. I stare in awe and terror at the wall of dark water rolling toward us. It reaches above the rooftops, snapping masts and footbridges as it bears down on our small sloop and its lifeline. For a moment the wave freezes, perfect and darkly lustrous, as if the sea has turned to jade, and then a ripple of white forms across its crest, and it curls its massive weight over us.

"Miyole, climb!" Manman screams. It is the voice that warned me against open flames and sharks in the water, amplified. It touches the center of my brain, and I obey.

Hand over hand, I race up the slick rungs. A shudder runs down the ladder as the ship strains to rise through the winds. Two steps from the top, my foot slips. Red flashes before my eyes—I'm falling—and then my hand finds the steel cable, the side of the ladder, and I jerk to a halt, dangling far above the churning gray sea.

Lightning flashes, illuminating the black wall of water, and for a moment, I see everything as if it's been cast in icy stone—the scraps of wood and the prow of a rowboat caught in the wave's face and my mother and Kai far below. Too far below. And then the rushing sound. I look up as the wave begins collapsing on itself.

One heartbeat.

I scramble back onto the ladder and climb. My hands don't hurt at all, and the rain washes away the blood before I have a chance to think of where it could be coming from.

Two.

The hatch hangs open above me. The rushing builds to a roar. *Up*, my body screams. *Climb!*

Three.

I reach the hatch and start to push myself up into the darkened berth. But a roaring force shoves at my back, and suddenly I am underwater, tumbling and turning in the dark. My shoulder slams against a wall. My eyes and throat burn. *I'm drowning.* And then the current reverses course. It gushes away, pulling me with it. I reach out, all instinct now, and catch something—one of the straps my manman used to tie down larger packages. I latch on to it with all the strength terror has lent me, until the water finishes emptying back into the sea.

The floor levels beneath me. I choke out a lungful of brine and take a wet, shuddering breath. All around me, the remnants of the packages my mother meant to deliver on her last run lie scattered on their sides in a shallow pool covering the length of the berth. The sloop's engines drop their pitch, and suddenly perfect sunlight floods in.

We've flown above the hurricane.

I unwind my arm from the packing strap and crawl to the edge of the hatch. The cloud tops against the blue sky look like paintings of heaven my manman showed me once, the hurricane a vast pinwheel beneath us. And there, the frayed metal ends of a severed emergency ladder whip in the high, empty winds of the stratosphere.

Static hissing . . .

Monsoon on the school roof. The canal by Ava and Rushil's lot at flood stage. An arc of water spraying from a burst valve in one of the city's bilge pipes. Patter, patter down, and we ran through the salt rain, shrieking. . . .

I open my eyes. No rain, no floods. I am on the floor of the *Mendicant's* cockpit, the low, empty rush of the open coms channel filling the room. I check my hands. No blood. The viewport before me shows nothing but clean, deep black, powdered with stars. My last moments of consciousness come back to me in pieces—the distress call, my mother's voice, the burning, spinning ship. . . .

I pick myself up, head pounding, and skim over the controls. Telemetry shows nothing moving outside, not even a debris field's scattered drift. The warning system lights stay dark, as if they've lost power. What the hell? The last time I looked, they were flashing imminent collision. I saw it with my own eyes.

I push back from the controls and stumble to the unruly forest of wires I half-finished repairing before the distress call came through. I rummage through the tangle until I find the warning system wires, thick, with light green-and-orange-striped insulation. I hold both ends of the connection in disbelief. I never repaired it. The warning system wasn't on, because I hadn't finished reuniting both sides of the snapped wire.

It can't be. I hurry back to the cockpit displays. My fingers tremble as I scroll through the coms controls and select playback.

Shock, I remind myself numbly. *You're in shock, that's all.*

Unidentified vessel, this is the Mendicant . . . My voice

sounds shell-hard, all business. I listen to myself ask for their coordinates, then pause and ask again, only to stop midsentence.

An eerie silence where my mother's voice should be stretches out on the recording.

I lean closer. Where is it? Where is she?

"Manman?" My own voice whispers back at me in hushed awe.

Still nothing in answer.

"Manman, how . . . Where are you?"

A long pause. The recording plays back my breath, harsh and elevated. *She's going to hyperventilate*, I think, forgetting for a moment that's it's me. And then my own scream. My voice carries the unmistakable stamp of terror. Another clammy wave ripples over my skin, and I ball my hands into fists to keep them from shaking.

I cut off the recording and lean against the controls, my head buried in my hands. No responses from the other ship, no warning alarms, only my own words spoken into the stillness.

I'm going mental. That's the only explanation. Rubio has his birds, and I have my mother's ghost.

I look out at the vast, empty expanse. We're still twelve days out from Enceladus, running on limited telemetry functions, with who knows how many other technical problems waiting to spring themselves, and the last functioning crew member has officially gone mad.

We limp into orbit around the closest station I've been able to find in the ship's databases, Outpost 247.281.5M. No one answers my calls for an approach vector, so I guide us in blind, using only the telemetry readouts, until the outline of the station appears against the stars. With its docking arms extended, the outpost spins like a windmill in the darkness—smoky-gray shielding nearly disappearing into the black.

No signal lights outline the station's extremities. Either we've just happened to show up in the middle of a power outage, or the station is abandoned. My fantasies about finding a doctor or a neural scan operator shrivel and shrink back into my chest. I might not even find air or gravity on the other side of our hull.

The docking bay doors sense us and slide open. *A good sign*, I think, until I realize that means the station power isn't out—someone turned off the signal lights on purpose, or at least didn't bother to fix them when they burned out.

We should go back. Find another outpost, an inhabited one.

But what guarantee do I have that the next station

won't be abandoned, too? Or worse yet, full of the same kind of traffickers who took Cassia's brother?

Ma chère, you didn't finish your rice, my mother's voice echoes down from the other end of the ship. I whip my head toward the sound before I can stop myself.

It isn't real. She's not there, I remind myself.

But the thing is, it was real once. I can't filter out the memories anymore. They sneak up on me, but jumbled, out of order. Sometimes my palms will bleed, but when I reach for the bandages, my wounds will close again. My mother's voice will startle me out of sleep, or scenes from the Gyre will superimpose themselves over my vision while I'm lying on my back, completing a repair—paint peeling from white iron railing, the smell of fish frying and the scrabbling of chickens on the roof, leaping the gaps between pontoons with Kai, handing him the string to a danger-red kite, fishing a strand of plastic pearls from the bleached, floating refuse of the Gyre plain and looping them around my neck. Whatever happened to that necklace? Or the red kite? Are they sunk to the ocean floor, along with my mother's bones?

The necklace becomes my *manman*'s bones, becomes my *manman*. My *manman* sitting with me over an enormous old paper book full of maps spread out on our kitchen table. Its pages are wrinkled and warped with age and water damage.

My *manman* smooths it with her hands and taps a small island in a field of faded blue. "That was our homeland, *ma chère*. Before the water rose."

"But we're not from there." I wrinkle my nose at the old book's smell. "We're Gyre people."

"Yes," my mother agrees. "But we're Haitian, too. Everyone from the Gyre is more than one thing. We all came here from somewhere else. You see?"

I shake my head, my braided pigtails hitting the sides of my face. I like the way they swing, so I keep doing it until my mother puts a hand on my arm.

"Answer me, Miyole. You see?"

I scrunch up my face. "But Haiti's not there anymore. We can't be from a place that isn't."

"The land is gone," my mother says. "But the rest of it we brought with us. So long as you and I and all the other Gyre folk from Haiti remember it, it still exists. The same as all the other lands our neighbors are from. As long as we exist, those places still exist, too."

Guilt fills up my pounding head. *I let myself forget. No, I made myself forget.* Not only Haiti, but the Gyre, too. Everyone else died in that storm, and I made myself forget.

I know what Ava and Soraya would say—that I had to forget to stay sane and keep functioning—but that doesn't dispel the cold, queasy feeling in my stomach or the prickles of shame traveling through my nervous system. Did the Gyre stop existing when I forgot it?

The stations' walls fill up the viewport, dark and silent, its outer air locks hanging open like slack mouths. I manage to maneuver the ship onto the magnetic docking track and let the station glide us forward. I listen for the reverberation of the air lock sealing around us, change into my pressure suit, and check on Cassia and Rubio before I hurry down to the hatch. They're both well under—sleeping the sleep of the drugged. Tibbet lies curled at his mistress's feet, either guarding her or taking advantage of her body heat. It's hard to tell with him. He's gotten weirder since Cassia stopped getting out of bed. When he isn't sleeping, his eyes stay dilated, and he stalks around the ship crashing into things and making lonely noises. He runs away whenever he sees me, even though I'm the one setting out softened, mashed protein bars for him each day.

"Take care of them, okay?" I whisper, and thank my stars Dr. Osmani isn't here to see me talking to a cat. If I don't get help soon, Tibbet is going to be the one most qualified to fly this ship. Leaving Cassia and Rubio alone while they're sedated sets off all the alarms from my medic training, but I don't have much choice. The only time Cassia stops vomiting is when she's unconscious, and Rubio will burrow through the walls if I leave him awake.

Down at the hatch, all the door's air-quality indicators show green. There's atmosphere on the other side, or at least the *Mendicant* thinks there is. I cross my fingers that the ship's exterior sensors haven't started malfunctioning, too, and reach up to double-check my pressure helmet. I press the hatch seal release.

The door opens onto a dark hangar, illuminated only by the light streaming from our ship's interior. My suit's readouts show breathable air. Score one for the *Mendicant's* systems. I retract my faceplate.

"Hello?" I call as I step down onto the dock and lift an LED torch over my head. My footsteps echo back to me in the empty space. This place was definitely a functioning dock once. The scuffed markings on the floor and the seams around the repair lifts leave no doubt. But our ship is the only one in the room, and the walls are bare, the typical accordion hoses and robotic arms that line most ship hangars stripped away. On the far side of the hangar, something skitters in the shadows.

"Hello?" I call again. A ripe, mildewed smell permeates

the air. I force myself forward, away from the ship. Midway across the hangar, a black, open corridor looms out of the darkness. I stop short, my heart pumping hard.

Stay calm, I remind myself, and swallow my panic. *Even if there's no one here, you could still find something to help. Supplies, or even a sunlight simulation chamber.*

Unless there is *someone here . . .* My blood pressure shoots up a notch. I shiver. Not for the first time, I miss the *Ranganathan*'s sprawling recreation gardens and its sunlamps. If I were there now, I would submerge myself in a bath of orange-gold vitamins and electrolytes.

The open corridor swallows me. I keep my torch raised and creep forward, hugging the wall. My footsteps patter down into the darkness and bound back. Ahead, the hallway splits. I shine my torch in both directions. To the right, a wheel-locked door; to the left, more darkness.

I choose the door. The wheel sticks at first, but eventually it gives, and I'm able to shoulder it open. Plastic tubs of flame-retardant powder line metal shelves, along with bins of re-breather masks and dusty water bottles. I pick a mask out of the pile and blow the dust from its mouthpiece. Its indicator lights blink on—four green, one orange. I try it on and inhale. Instantly, the air tastes fresher, like a cool drink of filtered water.

I find two other masks that still seem to be working and hook all three to my belt, then stuff my parka's pockets full of bottled water. The labels look at least five years out of date, but I'm willing to chance it. Anything is better than what comes out of the *Mendicant*'s moisture recycling system.

I backtrack and make my way down the hall in the opposite direction. What I really need is a station schematic. Clearly the outpost's solar arrays are still drawing enough power to keep the air filtration and artificial gravity systems working, so why not lights, too?

I pass a bank of lifts at what I think must be the center of the station and find an access shaft with a spiral staircase coiling up and down into the darkness like a single strand of DNA. I glance back at the lifts and then down into the narrow abyss.

It's only darkness. It can't hurt you, I tell myself. *Be smart. It's better than risking getting trapped in a lift shaft if the power really goes out.*

But that doesn't stop my knees from shaking as I shuffle out onto the landing.

"Stop it," I mutter, and slap my legs to bring the feeling back. I grip my torch and peer over the railing again. If this outpost is designed anything like the *Ranganathan*, its control center and life support system will be at its core, protected from a full-on assault or an accidental collision. That means down.

I take the stairs one at a time, one hand clamped around the handrail, the other clutching my torch. The steps round down and down, split occasionally by landings leading into other levels. After a while, I notice the wall shrinking away from me. Either I'm hallucinating again, or the staircase is broadening. I shine my torch on the riveted metal wall and stretch my hand out to it. One step, two, and then my fingers meet the cold surface.

Definitely broadening, I think, but then another sensation hits me. *And wet.*

I pull my hand back. A dilute red stain covers my glove and a metal tang finds its way to the back of my tongue. *Blood?* I dart my torch beam around, half certain I'll come face-to-face with some needle-fingered monster from the horror stories the girls at Revati used to trade. But I'm alone. I hold the torch above my hand and make myself look again. Not blood, rust.

I laugh, nervously. The sound echoes up the access shaft and rains back down on me. A memory races by—Kai and me, scaling the upper decks of an old research ship. I stepped on a corroded patch, and my foot broke through, letting loose a downpour of oxidized red flakes on the deck below. Manman had to fly all the way to West Gyre to buy tetanus vaccine.

I aim my LED torch up into the shadows of the access shaft. Somewhere in the darkness, an ominous metal groan sounds.

"*Chaila*," I whisper. Has the stair been making that noise the whole time? Who knows how long this station has before the rust eats all the way through it? One major jolt and the whole thing could crumble.

Get out, I think. But I've come this far. A station this size has to have a clinic, and that means medical supplies. I can't go back empty-handed. Not now.

The stairwell bottoms out on a level closed off by a reinforced wheel-locked door. I stow my torch in my belt and wipe my damp gloves on my legs. The hatch opens with a shriek. I poke my head inside and let my light play over the walls. A broad hallway lined with load-bearing buttresses opens up before me, and then disappears into darkness. Through the gloom, I make out a sign hanging from the ceiling—ENVIRONMENTALS. So I'm going in the right direction, at least.

I sidle through and let the door fall closed behind me. Immediately, my boot slips in something fine and powdery.

I drop my beam to the concrete floor. A thick layer of white, talc-like powder covers it in drifts, and a cold, chemical burn runs up my sinuses and down my throat. Flame retardant, maybe? Like the tubs upstairs? But how did it end up scattered all around the floor?

I take another step and stop. A few meters in front of me, a set of tracks cross through the powder. I'm hardly Wilderness Girl, but even I can tell they're human footprints. I've seen the same imprint on the sand at the Malabar Hill beaches. Cold prickles the back of my neck.

I swallow, but my throat still feels tight. "Hello?"

No one answers. Somewhere deep in the darkness, something scuffles across the floor. A whiff of rot mingles with the chemical burn in the air.

Supplies. I push myself forward, torch held high. Adrenaline surges in my bloodstream, and my breath comes harsh and fast in my own ears. I've never had a panic attack before, but I've read about them, and I'm pretty sure I'm on the verge of one now. The floor slopes down almost imperceptibly. I shine my light at the walls. Moisture sweats from the pores in the concrete and weeps down the uneven surface. Damp, sticky patches form on the floor, where runoff has seeped into the layer of powder.

Something crunches underfoot. I stop and lift my boot.

A small, yellowed skeleton lies crushed in the sticky mass of powder, tufts of gray fur still adhered to bones. It might have been a rat once, but it's hard to tell now. At least that explains the smell.

I keep walking. The odor of decay thickens, overtaking the chemical scent. Bits of trash—protein bar packages, broken glass, plastic insulation, and other flotsam—begin to pile up along the walls. It rises in drifts and spreads until I'm forced to pick my way down a narrow path at the center of the corridor.

Autolysis initiates the process of decomposition, the rate of which is dependent upon the concentration of enzymes in the material.

I step over an aluminum wrapper smeared with what looks like feces and look up. An orange glow lights the far end of the hallway, bright enough that I can make out the contours of the trash dunes ahead. I switch off my torch. I count out thirty seconds, waiting for my retinas to adjust, and then creep forward, careful to avoid the loose, rolling bottles and cardboard packing tubes littering the floor.

The hallway ends in a landing overlooking a deep, circular room lit by an emergency lantern balanced on the floor. More trash litters the stairs leading down to the bottom and then tapers away, replaced by a jumble of water barrels, gutted electronics, and stacked cots surrounding a cluster of terminals. A soft lapping sound echoes off the bare walls.

"Hello?" I call again. My voice almost fails me.

The lapping pauses, and then resumes. Whoever—or whatever—is down below has to know I'm here. I briefly think of turning on my heel and retreating back down the refuse-packed corridor, but the idea of someone following me through the dark makes me pause.

"*Vaat,*" I whisper, and lower my foot onto the first stair. The whole construction creaks under my weight, a deafening shriek that fills the room and puts my teeth on edge. I flinch and hurry down the rest of the way, images of the stairwell crumbling beneath me flashing through my head.

The structure shudders into silence. An eerie quiet fills the room.

The lapping sound starts again.

"Hello?" I round the water barrels. "Please . . . we need a doctor. Or the med bay, or . . ." I turn.

A figure crouches in the shadow of the stairs, its hands splayed against the wall. Bits of string, metal, and fur hang in its long, tangled black hair. I watch, paralyzed, as it opens its mouth against the concrete and catches a trickle of water with its swollen tongue.

I step back, banging into the barrels.

The creature beneath the stairs looks up. It pushes its hair from its eyes, wipes its mouth with the back of a pale hand, and locks eyes with me.

"You're younger than I thought." The voice is a harsh, tracheal croak.

Younger? I squeeze my eyes shut. Maybe this is another hallucination. I open them again. It still stands there, its head cocked to the side quizzically.

"Who . . ." I swallow and try to make my voice stop shaking. "Who are you?"

"I used to think I was Kaede-san." It's voice is thoughtful, almost sad. "But I know better now."

We stand in silence a moment. What is there to say after that?

"We heard you coming."

"We?" I repeat, my throat dry.

It waves its hands in the air, as if gesturing at a cloud of gnats. "Yes. We."

I decide not to press the issue.

"You need help." It scuffles closer, out into the lantern light. Its baggy clothes obscure its shape, but I start to think it might be a woman.

"I . . . I need supplies," I say, though my words sound as if they're echoing from someone else's mouth. "Or access to a medical bay. My friends, they're sick."

The woman smiles, displaying a red-stained mouth. "We can help."

Somehow, this isn't entirely comforting. I back around the water barrels, putting another meter of space between us. "You know where the med bay is?"

She shakes her head. "That place is no good, not anymore. But we can help."

My stomach sinks. "How?"

The woman draws herself up and shakes out her filthy robes. "We are *isha*. We are a doctor."

I follow her back through the refuse. I could run, but Kaede-san or Isha or whoever she is clearly knows this station better than I do, and that means she might lead me to the medical bay if I play along. She keeps one hand on her head, steadying a makeshift headlamp, and swats at the garbage with a plastic stick she holds in the other.

"They like to bite," she explains. "Rats."

I shudder and thank the stars for my pressure suit's boots.

"What should I call you?" I ask.

"You can call us doctor." She lets out a harsh wheezing sound I take to be a laugh. "Incorruptible Jewel of the Heavens, Lady of the Phoenix, High Priestess of the Winding Cloth—"

I interrupt. "I don't think I'm going to be calling you any of those things."

She frowns back at me. "Fine. Call us Isha."

We arrive at a service lift I missed on my way in. A metal bar sticks out of the seam where the double doors meet. Isha leans her weight against it, and the doors roll back, revealing a car with a thick carpet of damp debris and spattered stains on the walls. A single emergency light strip fills the carriage with a dull blue glow.

"This thing still runs?" I ask, incredulous.

Isha bobs her head. "Everything runs." She looks at me and waggles a finger. "Everything runs, except when we don't want it to run."

Fantastic. I make a mental note not to piss off Isha any more than I already have.

She smiles and holds out a hand, inviting me into the lift. "After you."

The car shrieks as it jolts into motion. I brace myself against the corner to keep from falling, but Isha barely moves.

"What happened here?" I lift my foot to examine something sticky on the bottom of my boot.

"Hubris," Isha says. "Sloth."

I frown. "I mean, did everyone leave you behind, or . . . ?"

"Not all of them." The lift picks up speed as it rises, its indicator lights strobing across Isha's face. "Would you want to see the bodies?"

My heart stops. "What?"

"The bodies," she repeats matter-of-factly. "The ones that stayed."

A chill runs through the pit of my stomach. "I . . . I don't know . . ." Did she kill them? Is that what she wants to show me? And if I answer wrong, will she add me to their number? I swallow. "Do you . . . do you want to show them to me?"

"Oh, they would like that." Isha reaches for the lift's controls. "They're so lonely. No one to mourn for them except us."

"What about my friends?" I ask.

Isha cocks her head to the side. "Do they want to stay here, too?"

"No," I say quickly. If I run, will she chase me? "No, we're expected on Enceladus. We . . . we only stopped because they're sick. Once we have some meds, we'll be out of your hair."

She shrugs. "Suit yourselves." The lift slows and then jerks to a stop. "Here we are."

I follow Isha down another dim corridor. A square of light shines at the far end, brilliantly sharp after all this darkness. As we approach, I glimpse the outline of bare trees through the fogged glass.

"Are those your gardens?" They must be, except most larger ships and stations keep tropical plants or evergreens aboard, not deciduous trees. How are the gardens supposed to keep your spirits up with no green?

Isha pauses with her hand on the latch and nods. "But you have to be very quiet." She drops her voice to a whisper. "They're sleeping."

"Who?" I ask, but she's already pulled the release and pushed the door back into its pocket.

Sunlight rolls over us. My skin turns to gooseflesh at its touch, and for a moment, I forget everything but the warmth of it. I close my eyes against the silvery glare. The vitamin D tablets I've kept us on throughout the flight are fine for staving off illness, but they're nothing like sunlight, even simulated sunlight. Never mind the madwoman who led me here, or the fact that I'm not one hundred percent sure she won't murder me. I feel fully alive for the first time in weeks.

"We tend them when we can," Isha says, close to my ear.

I open my eyes to a squint. A good-sized garden spreads out before us, with naked trees stretched thin along the perimeter and brown patches of what once must have been flower beds spotting the dead grass. I don't understand what I'm seeing on the ground at first. Logs, maybe, or the foundations of a crumbled wall? I step into the garden.

"What . . . ?" I start to say, but then my brain catches up. *Bodies*. The shapes laid out so neatly on the grass are bodies.

Isha passes me and circles a group laid around a tree like wagon spokes. Each rests its head over the roots and points its toes at the sky. Someone has arranged their limbs so their hands rest folded over their rib cages. The only smell is the subtle mineral odor of water and dirt. They've been out here long enough for the environs to soak up the smell of rot.

"What happened? Did you do this?"

"Yes, yes." Isha murmurs, bending over one corpse with

long blond hair and picking a fallen leaf from the remnants of a shirt. "They were sick. We brought them here to rest."

"You killed them?" My throat closes on itself.

Isha looks up sharply. "No. They're not dead. They're resting." She looks down at the blond woman again and smiles. "We take good care of them. Soon they'll be well again. Soon they'll wake up."

I back away. "I should go. My friends need me."

"Yes." Isha stares off at the tree-cloaked far wall, deep in thought, and then snaps her attention back to me. "Yes, your friends. We should see to them."

I hold up a hand. "I don't think you should . . . I mean, I don't know if they need a doctor after all. I think I can take care of it."

Isha's look darkens. "You think we're not a good doctor, because we let them fall ill." She sweeps a hand across the tableau behind her. "We did everything we could to keep it from spreading. Some diseases, you don't see them coming. Too late to stop them. You can treat them and pray. And we were only Kaede-san then."

"No." I swallow and open my eyes too wide, like Ava says I always do when I'm lying. Maybe she didn't kill these people, but whatever did has obviously driven her stark raving mad. "It's just . . . you're busy here with so many patients. I'm sure I can sort it myself."

"Nonsense." Isha scoffs. "They're sleeping. And your friends' illnesses are more acute, are they not?"

"Yes," I admit, against my better judgment.

She nods. "Then we'll go to them. She took an oath. Geneva. Kaede swore."

"Fine." I don't want to push her. She was a doctor once. Maybe there's enough knowledge left tucked up in the corners of her memory that she could help. And besides, she knows the way back to the dock better than I do. If she really wanted, she could find the *Mendicant* herself and leave me to find my own way through the station's lightless halls.

I roll back the door to the sleeping berth and peer into the darkness. "Cass?"

"Miyole?" Her voice croaks from disuse.

I move aside to let Isha in. "I brought help."

Cassia's eyes roll and widen. "What . . . what is that?"

"We are Isha." The old woman draws close to the bed, the soiled, tattered ends of her cloak trailing after her. She sits at Cassia's side. "And you are the sick."

Cassia looks to me, her face full of barely lucid horror.

"It's all right." I try to sound confident. "She's a doctor."

"She's a witch," Cassia whispers as Isha reaches out and gently presses the lymph nodes beneath her jaw.

"Yes," Isha agrees, taking Cassia's limp arm. "That, too." She lays two filth-stained fingers against the inside of Cassia's elbow, feeling for a pulse.

I chew my lip. "She has a concussion," I say. "She was on the mend at first, but now . . ." I trail off as Cassia's eyes flutter closed.

Isha inspects Cassia's bandage. "Hmm."

I pace to the opposite side of the bed. Maybe I should have taken her to Rubio first. It's hard to tell which of them is worse. I turn. "Do you think . . ."

Something catches the yellow light creeping in from the hall and flashes in the corner of my eye.

I whirl around. "What—"

Isha has a knife in her hand, an ugly, narrow thing like the kind used to debone chickens. In one swift movement, she draws the blade down the soft flesh of Cassia's inner arm and ducks to lick up the beads of blood that rise in its wake. Cassia groans in pain.

"*Kat le!*" I scramble across the bed. "Get away from her, you bloody *jholar*!"

Isha jumps up and backs into the corner, quick as a

lizard scaling a drainpipe, and points the knife at me. "Stay away. You asked us. You asked us to."

I skid to a stop well short of the knife. "I never asked you to cut her open!"

I glance back at Cassia. Blood spills onto the bed. I hurry to her side, rip loose one of the sheets, and bunch it up over her arm. *Direct pressure. Elevation,* the part of me that remembers my medic training recites, while the rest of me screams a string of obscenities. I hold the sheet tight against Cassia's wound and raise her arm above her heart.

I never should have brought a madwoman back to our ship, even a madwoman who claimed to be a doctor. Scratch that. *Especially* a madwoman who claimed to be a doctor.

"We were helping." Isha sounds hurt.

"Screw your bloody help!" I shout, and burst into tears.

Three weeks ago, my worst problem was a crabby Dr. Osmani, and now I'm stranded on a derelict station with two incapacitated crewmates, a knife-wielding witch doctor, a useless cat, and my own fraying line to reality. We're not going to make it. Never mind bringing Nethanel back from the deep; we're going to die here ourselves.

Isha lays a filthy hand on my shoulder. "It's not her head."

I shrug her away. "Don't touch me."

"Look, girl." Isha kneels beside the bed and begins unwinding Cassia's bandage. "It's not her head."

"Don't touch her," I spit.

"We can help, see?" Isha smiles at me, tentative. "The sickness, it's not in her head. It's in her blood."

"What do you mean?" I grip Cassia's arm tighter.

Isha raises her head and breathes in deep. "It's in the air. Poison in the air, poison in her blood." She cocks her head at me. "Maybe in your blood, too."

"My blood?" I echo, and shake my head. All Cassia's symptoms point to a concussion. "That doesn't make sense. I'm not sick."

"Aren't you?" Isha's stare drills into me, and I remember the constant headaches and my mother's voice as her phantom ship bore down on us.

"No," I say too quickly. "I mean, not like her."

Isha thumbs the knife. "If you let us taste . . ."

"No. You're not touching anyone else with that thing."

Isha glowers at me. "You have to let us help. You have to let us taste."

"*Chup kar, krūra vyakti,*" I growl back.

"You want her to die?" Isha nods at Cassia's gray-pale face. "We can find the poison. We can make her better."

I look from Cassia to the witch doctor and her knife. All

I have are bad choices. "Do you have to use that?" I look pointedly at the knife.

Isha frowns. "No," she says, but she sounds disappointed.

"Fine," I say. "Hand me that bandage."

I draw the needle from my arm and hold the syringe up to the light. "Is that enough?"

"Maybe," Isha says.

I glare at her and roll down my sleeve. I can't believe I'm doing this.

"Probably." She nods.

"Good." I deposit the blood into a narrow vial and hold it out to her. "Bottoms up."

Isha sips from the vial, pinkie out, as if she's having high tea. She smacks her lips, and then nods. "Poison."

My stomach twists. "What kind?" Who knows if there's any truth to what she says, or if I'm only feeding her delusion.

Isha closes her eyes and rotates a wrist above her head like a weather vane. "From the air. Carboxyhemoglobin."

I search my memory. I know I've heard that word before, but where? Then it comes to me, and my eyes fly wide. "Carbon monoxide poisoning? Is that what you mean?"

Isha nods furiously and points at me. "That's the one. That's the one."

I press the heels of my palms to my forehead. Of course. Cassia's headaches, Rubio's hallucinations. They all make sense now. We covered carbon monoxide poisoning briefly in my medic training, but we never spent much time on it. Early explorers used to come down with it all the time when their air cycling systems failed or their secondary fuel shrouds ended up perforated, but you hardly heard of it happening anymore, especially since ship makers dropped biological fuels altogether. But the *Mendicant* is old enough to be a hybrid.

"Yes," Isha agrees. "Carbon monoxide. Sometimes we forget the words."

I look at Rubio asleep on the couch, his face slack and sedated. "That's what's wrong with him, too, then?"

Isha raises the empty blood vial. "We can find out."

I make a face. "I don't think so." I start for the door, then think better of it and point at Isha. "You stay here. Don't touch him."

Cassia's eyes flutter open and struggle to focus on me.

"Hey."

She tries to answer and fumbles with the oxygen mask

covering her mouth. I catch her hand before she can pull it away.

"You're okay." I squeeze her palm. "You have to leave that on. You've been sick."

She winces and lifts her injured arm so she can see it above the oxygen canister and mask. We were out of skinknit bandages when I patched her up, so I had to give her old-fashioned sutures and wrap her forearm in clean strips of cloth. She'll heal, but she's going to have a very nasty scar. Cassia raises her eyebrows. *What happened?*

"Long story." I scowl, thinking of Isha. She could be up to all kinds of mischief out there in the ship, especially with Rubio still too weak to stop her. Hopefully she hasn't turned him into a shish kebab by now.

I pull my own mask up over my nose and mouth and rise to go, but Cassia tightens her grip.

"I'll be right back," I say. "I have to check on Rubio."

I find Isha in the common room. She stands facing the wall, smearing something red over its blank surface in the outline of a circle. A moment passes before I realize what it must be. *Blood.*

"What are you doing?" I stride over and make a grab for the small bowl of thick red liquid she holds.

Isha backs away, hissing, and hugs the bowl to her chest with red-stained fingers. Tibbet, watching us from beneath one of the torn lounges, flattens his ears against his head. I tried holding an oxygen mask over his face, too, but he scratched me.

"I'm sorry." I hold up my hands. "Sorry."

Isha eyes me suspiciously. Her breather hangs loose around her neck. "We're finishing the treatment." She dips her two forefingers into the bowl and gives me a warning look before placing them on the wall. "Preventative measures."

"Right." I nod as if this was not completely mental. "Just out of curiosity, where did you get that?" I point at the bowl.

"It's our own." She smiles and paints another swoop of the arc. "Only the best."

I glance at Rubio, propped up on the sofa in a cocoon of thermal blankets. He blinks at me groggily and takes a deep draw on his oxygen canister. At least he doesn't look like he's been bled in service of Isha's art project.

Isha completes the large circle and adds a smaller one at its center.

"What is it you're drawing?" I step forward to inspect her work.

"This ship is sick." Isha collects another daub and adds a line radiating out from the center circle to the larger one. She shakes her head. "Flying without a Wheel."

"A wheel?" An image flashes through my head—the wheel behind the soot on the wall of the burned-out Rover ship. "The Wheel of Heaven?"

Isha nods. "This station had no Wheel, and look what happened. We fixed it, though, didn't we? All better now." She shakes a finger at me. "We thought Rovers would know better."

"Us?" I laugh, and then bite my tongue. The more people think we're simple Rovers, the better. Even deranged hermits with dissociative identity disorder.

Isha frowns at me, thinking. "Maybe not you and the boy," she says at last. "But that girl is, certain. You should listen to her."

I shake my head. "I don't think she believes in your Wheel anymore."

"Believe in the Wheel." Isha snorts as if I've suggested milking dogs, and adds another spoke.

"Don't you?" I glance up at the immense red design forming on the wall.

"You think magic is real?" Isha pauses with her hand in the blood bowl and arches an eyebrow at me.

"No," I say cautiously. What is the protocol when a self-proclaimed witch asks you if you believe in magic?

"Neither do we." Isha looks over her work. "The Wheel gives us strength here." She touches her forehead. "And here." She touches her heart.

"So it's like a psychological trick?" I say. "If you think you're safe, you'll fly like you're safe?"

"Not a trick," she says. "A balm."

"A balm?" I wrinkle my nose.

Isha grunts in exasperation. "How many ways can you die out here? Radiation poisoning, decompression exposure, hypothermia, suffocation, immolation."

I shrug. Any Deep Sound applicant can recite the dangers in her sleep. "Your point is?"

"Would anyone venture off her sad, safe world if she didn't have some hope to cling to?"

"My world's not sad," I shoot back. It's hardly safe, either, but that doesn't seem like the best argument to make right now.

Isha looks at me with an expression I can't quite read—compassion, maybe. It doesn't fit her face. "Then you're a lucky one, aren't you?" she says.

I don't answer. That cold, sick guilt rolls over me again. I know I'm lucky. I could have died many times over between the day the hurricane hit and now. I've had more education than I ever could have dreamed of if I'd lived out my life in the Gyre. But now that I remember my mother and the home I lost, I know that luck didn't come cheap.

"No," Cassia says. "Absolutely not." She clutches Tibbet to her chest and strokes his fur.

"It's only a little thing," Isha says. "Fair payment for saving three lives."

"Cass—" I start to say.

"No," she interrupts, and glares from me to Isha. "You can have anything else you want, but you're not taking my cat."

Isha snorts. "What do we want with some gunk in a barrel? Blankets? Boots? Not enough. We want the cat."

"Cass." I lean toward her. "He might be safer here. Who knows what we're flying into?"

Cassia clutches Tibbet tighter. He squirms in her arms and jumps to the floor with a soft thump, then looks at all of us as if we've offended him. I'm not sure if he was hallucinating like we were, but his pupils are smaller and he's only vomited once since Cassia managed to get his nose into one of the oxygen canister face masks for a few minutes.

"Now look what you've done," Rubio jokes. "Maybe you should have asked him."

"Maybe you should shut up and put your mask back on," Cassia snaps.

I've found the crack in the secondary fuel shroud that's leaking poison into our air supply, but it's not an easy fix. We're still carrying around our oxygen canisters and breathers, only taking them off to speak.

"We would like a companion." Isha licks her lips. "Especially one that catches rats."

"I said *no*!" Cassia shouts, and bursts into tears. She throws off the blanket covering her legs, scoops up Tibbet, and runs from the room.

Rubio and I stare at each other for a moment, too shocked to move.

"Better go after her," he says at last.

I sigh and nod. I get that Cassia loves that *chirkut* cat, but why can't she see this is best for everyone? What good is Tibbet going to be when it comes to rescuing her brother?

I find the two of them in the cockpit, Cassia in the copilot's chair feeding Tibbet a pat of bean paste from her fingers. She looks up with me at red eyes as I enter.

"Hey," I say softly.

"Hey." She rubs the back of her hand over her eyes.

"I'm sorry," I say. "I didn't know what else to do but bring her here."

"I know." She scratches at her bandaged arm absentmindedly. "It's just . . ." Her eyes well with tears.

"Oh, Cass." As unreasonable as she's being, I can't stand to see her sad.

"He's the only family I have left," she says. "I know it's stupid. I know he's only a cat, but . . ."

I wince at the way my own thoughts sound coming from her mouth.

"I've never been away from them before. I didn't know it would be like this. I didn't know *this* part would be hard."

I don't know what to say, so I hug her instead. My whole life, I've floated at a distance from everyone else. I love Soraya and Ava, no question, but I've kept my tethers loose. Everyone leaves someday. Everyone dies. And isn't it easier if you leave first? Isn't it easier to hide away inside equations and term papers or ship yourself off to the far side of the Deep when you feel those tethers start to anchor you? Why be there when the inevitable happens?

"It's not stupid." I kneel beside her. I want to tell her it's beautiful, and I wish I could feel the same way, only there's something wrong with me. But the words stick inside, so I repeat. "It's not stupid at all."

"I know it would be better for him to stay here," she says. "Even if we never get him back. You're right."

"No—" An alarm interrupts me.

It echoes in from the station itself, long whooping waves of sound, and then a voice, polite and civilized as Advani-ji. "Caution. Vessel approaching. Please clear docking bay for landing. Caution. Vessel approaching . . ."

"What's that?" I sit up straight.

Cassia hits our telemetry display and links with the station's external eyes. An image appears—an angular gray ship with a full tail of engines and artillery batteries spiking from every surface, like a particularly nasty durian fruit, glides into view.

"*Chaila,*" I curse, because I've seen the ship before.

I look at Cassia. Her face has gone still and pale, and I know why. She's seen it before, too, the night she lost her brother and her ship, the night we pulled her from the burning wreckage. The *dakait* are here, and this time, there's no one to save us.

CHAPTER 16

Bootfalls on the floor overhead. We hold our breath, crammed together in the access vent—Cassia, Rubio, Isha, me, and Tibbet. I squeeze my eyes shut and listen closely. The *dakait* who left me cowering in the *Ranganathan*'s utility passage, the one I let get away, is he one of them?

". . . can't have been here long." A woman's voice. The floor buckles lightly under her step as she passes over us. "No dust, and the secondary power's still working. They must have seen us coming."

"They won't get far," a man answers. Not him. "There's no way off this station except through us."

A whoop echoes from deeper inside the ship. "*Förbannat!*" A younger man this time, his reedy voice full of unchecked excitement. Not him, either. "You're never gonna believe this."

"You found something?" The older man's words recede with his footsteps, followed by the woman's.

I frown up at the underside of the floor. What could the *Mendicant* possibly have aboard that—and then it hits me. *Chaila*. I share a glance with Rubio. *Sweetie's cryatine.*

The woman lets out a long, low whistle above us. "I got to give it to you, Warume. I never thought you'd suss out something good here."

"It's the pearl in the clam," he says proudly.

"Oysters," the older man says. "It's oysters have pearls."

"Oysters are high-class." Their voices move back toward us. "This here's plain clam."

"Will you two *manuke* shut up about sea meat?" the woman snaps. "The sooner we find the ones that brought this hulk here, the sooner we can leave this shithole of a station."

Isha jerks up and hisses.

"Hush." Rubio wraps a hand over her mouth, and she bites him.

He chokes down a cry and somehow manages to leave his hand where it is, with Isha's teeth stuck in him and a thin line of blood running down his palm. We all freeze, acutely aware of every small sound we've made.

"Did you hear that?" the young *dakait* asks.

"Probably just gas in the pipes. These old hybrid ships are noisy," the older man says.

I let out the breath I've been holding. And at that moment, Tibbet begins to growl. It starts low in his throat, an uneasy animal noise that raises the hair on the back of my neck. I glance over at him, crouched on Cassia's shoulder. His pupils dilate to full, death-dealing black, his hackles rise, and his ears fold flat against his head.

I shoot a worried look at Cassia.

"It's okay, little guy. Shhh," Cassia whispers, stroking the back of his neck, but the rumbling sound in him only grows.

"There," the woman says, directly above us.

The access panel shrieks open. The *dakait* stare down at us, all three of them holding slug guns, the younger man wearing an expression as stunned as our own. Tibbet leaps as if he's spring-loaded, launching himself at the older man's face. The gun discharges as the man falls back, punching an ugly hole in the floor and filling the hall with its deafening report.

The woman fires at Tibbet, misses, and then hits the floor as Isha leaps on her with a wild scream. Her gun goes spinning and crashes into the access shaft beside me. The youngest *dakait* stumbles back a step, looking for all the world like a little boy despite the web of tattoos covering the left side of his face.

Rubio vaults out and charges him, and suddenly I remember that he's a soldier. The *dakait* boy takes one look at Rubio and bolts for the open door leading to the dock. Rubio barrels after him.

The oldest *dakait* rips Tibbet from his face and throws him across the room. The cat's body hits the wall with a heavy thump.

Cassia screams, and she's on the man, clawing at his already-bleeding face and cursing. From the corner of my eye, I see Tibbet skitter to his feet, shake off the blow, and flee. The *dakait* flips Cassia off him and gropes for his gun through the veil of blood dripping over his right eye.

I lunge for the woman's gun and bring it up exactly as the oldest *dakait* wheels his own on Cassia.

"Don't," I say.

He freezes, the muzzle of his slug gun trained on Cassia, who lies furious and panting on the floor, propped up on one elbow. Blood flushes her cheeks and her eyes are bright.

The *dakait* chuckles. "You're going to use that thing on me, are you, *lillflicka*?"

"Not if you let her go." I try to sound menacing, but my voice cracks on the last word.

His shoulders relax like a snake uncoiling. He chambers a round and turns slowly, a grin playing over his lips. "Nah, you're not going to use it. You know why?" His gaze skips over to Isha and the *dakait* woman, still scuffling on the floor. He doesn't wait for me to answer.

"You're too civilized. Not enough wild left in you." He nods over his shoulder at Cassia. "Now that one, she's got fire still. Lot of men would pay a good price for some of that."

I raise the gun. *"Chup kar, jaan var fattu."*

His smile widens. "An educated miss. Maybe I was wrong. Maybe I'll double my sale. Or maybe I'll keep you for myself." He reaches for my gun.

A film passes before my eyes—memory overlaid with the present. *My mother is crouched beside me, wrapping my small hands around a pistol's grip, guiding my movements as I cock back the hammer* . . . and the *dakait* is reaching for me, a cruel smile on his lips . . . *I'm in a dark room, crouched behind the old sea chest where my mother kept our clothes, the pistol in my hand. A man is hurting my* manman . . . the *dakait's* hand closes over mine . . . *I struggle with the hammer—I'm so clumsy, and the gun was made for hands much bigger than mine—and in the struggle I forget what my* manman *said about not touching the trigger unless I mean to shoot, and when the hammer finally comes back, the air cracks open, an explosion of light and sound in my hand, and the force of it nearly kicks the gun from my grip* . . . and my finger moves beneath the *dakait's* grip.

The sound breaks through from that past, that dark room with the man hurting my *manman*, and echoes down the *Mendicant's* halls. The *dakait* collapses on the floor. His hand is a bloody mess and he's clutching his shin, but all I can see is that other man long ago.

He lay at the foot of my manman's *bed, wheezing in pain as a dark stain spread across his belly. Manman hit the light and his eyes went wild. His skin was a lighter brown than mine and my mother's, but those eyes of his, they were the same deep amber I saw when I looked at myself in my* manman's *hand mirror.*

My mother hobbled to me, her whole leg wet and red with blood, and took the gun from my hands. "Well done, ma chère." *She kissed the top of my head softly, then pulled back the hammer to chamber another round.*

"Don't look now," she said, and I hid my face against her side as she turned on the man.

"You bitch," the *dakait* howls, rocking in pain.

I blink and flinch as someone touches my trigger hand.

Cassia stands beside me, holding the older *dakait*'s gun. Behind us, Isha has finally wrestled the woman's hands behind her back and holds a knife at her throat.

"I didn't mean to," I half-whisper. There's so much blood.

Cassia looks at me as if I'm mental. "I'm glad you did."

She steps up to the *dakait* and kicks him. "Hey!" she shouts over his moans. "Dog face. Remember me?"

Pain glazes his eyes, but he looks her over without any spark of recognition. He shakes his head.

Her mouth narrows to a line. "Three weeks ago you took a Rover ship outside Ceres. You remember?"

He closes his eyes, cradles his ruined hand, and keeps rocking. *"Fitta,"* he mutters. "Heartless bitches."

Cassia kicks his leg again. "Do you remember?"

He gasps. "Rover ship. Yes, a Rover ship."

"My brother." Cassia's eyes water, but she blinks furiously. "Nethanel Kaldero. You took him from that ship. Where is he now?"

The *dakait* shakes his head.

"Answer me." Cassia levels the gun at him.

"How should I know?" Spit flies from the *dakait*'s mouth. His eyes are wide with shock and he begins to shake. "You think I care about some *koitsu*?"

"Cassia." He's going to black out if he keeps losing blood.

"You know who I'm talking about." Cassia says. "Look at me."

"*Shinjimae, fitta.*"

"Look at me!" she screams. "You know where he is. He looks just like me."

A half-hysterical laugh escapes the older man. "Maybe."

She raises the gun. "Son of a—"

I catch Cassia's arm. "Let me try," I murmur.

Our eyes lock for a moment. I wrinkle my brow. *Trust me.*

Cassia huffs and steps back. "Fine."

"Listen." I crouch down eye level with the *dakait*. "You're bleeding out. You can feel it, right? You're cold all over?"

A small edge of fear creeps into his scowl.

"I'm a medic," I say. "I can fix you up, stop the bleeding. All you have to do is answer her questions." I nod up at Cassia.

"Don't do it, Kol," the *dakait* woman bursts out. "Don't give that *yariman* the satisfaction."

"Hush," Isha hisses, and presses her knife closer to the woman's throat.

"You're going to shoot me either way." Kol looks from me to Cassia. "Why drag it out?"

"Maybe I will." Cassia's eyes are cold. "But like you said, my girl here is the civilized one. Maybe she won't let me."

"Right." I swallow. "So tell us what we want to know. Where's her brother?"

His eyes dart between us and he wets his lips nervously. "He looked like you, right?" He looks at Cassia. "Curly hair? Speckles on the face? Kilt wearers?"

Cassia nods once.

He closes his eyes. "He was in the parcel we dropped on Enceladus."

The *dakait* woman moans in defeat.

"Parcel?" I frown.

He nods. "Five hundred kilos of salt, couple hundred of taurine, five females, two males, and five barrels of cryatine."

"Who did you sell him to?" Cassia's voice is cold as the air around us.

The *dakait* shrugs. "Highest bidder."

Cassia's jaw tightens. "A name, *rövhål*."

He laughs, a short, nervous bark. "It don't work that way, *lillflicka*. It was a blind bid. We did it from orbit."

Cassia makes a show of turning to me. "I guess we won't need your services after all, Miyole."

"*Herregud.* Wait," the *dakait* cuts in. His eyes have begun to glaze over. "I can tell you the port where we dropped him. I can tell you that."

"Cassia," I mutter, my eyes on the growing pool of blood. The *dakait* blinks. We're losing him.

But we don't even need him to tell us, I realize. His ship's log will have the coordinates. "Cass—"

She follows my gaze to the blood. "Not yet."

"Ny Karlskrona," the *dakait* says. He glares from Cassia to his hand and shakes his head in disbelief. *"Fitta."*

"Ny Karlskrona." Cassia smiles sweetly. "Thank you."

And she pulls the trigger.

CHAPTER 17

The *dakait* woman utters a scream of rage that dissolves into a wet gurgle. I turn in time to see Isha draw her knife across the struggling woman's throat. Her eyes roll black with a mix of terror, fury, and confusion. A second later, they dull, and Isha lets her drop.

I blink from Isha to Cassia in disbelief. "What did you do?" My own voice rings high in my ears. I can understand Isha—she's plain mad—but Cassia?

"What did you do?" I say again.

Cassia crouches down over the first *dakait*'s body. She doesn't look at me as she speaks. "What I had to," she says. "For Nethanel."

"*Carajo.*"

I turn. Rubio holds the youngest *dakait* by his collar. The boy's eyes go wide, taking in the corpses, and then he doubles over and vomits. Rubio lets go of his shirt and backs against the bulkhead.

The solid *click* of another slug chambering brings me wheeling back around.

Cassia stands looking at me. "What should we do with him?"

A sick feeling creeps over me. "What do you mean?"

"Not many options." Cassia examines the gun in her hands.

"No." My mouth is dry. "No. Look at him, Cassia. He's not any older than we are."

Cassia regards him coldly. "So?"

"I . . . we . . . ," I stammer. What did I expect? To turn the *dakait* over to the DSRI or the Satellite Authority? I haven't been thinking beyond each crisis as it unfolds— steal the shuttle, deal with Sweetie, keep Cassia alive, keep the ship running, keep all of us alive.

"No one is coming to help us out here, Miyole," Cassia says. "We're the only justice there is."

"This isn't justice." I glance at the boy. *Warume,* I remember. That's what the woman called him. "It's vengeance."

Cassia scowls. "Splitting hairs."

"How much blood do you want on your hands?" I plant

myself between her and the boy. "Nethanel could still be alive. Killing a bunch of *dakait* isn't going to keep him that way."

Cassia waves the gun in the boy's direction. "We can't take him with us."

"So the only other choice is to kill him?"

Cassia turns up her hands. "What do you suggest?"

I look from her to Rubio, who has gone as green as I feel, and then to Isha, cleaning her knife with the hem of her skirt. A profoundly bad idea comes to me.

"Maybe . . ." I try to swallow. "Isha, you want company, right?"

"Company." She repeats the word as if it's foreign to her. "Yes. The cat. Good company."

"What if you could have something better than a cat?"

Isha cricks her head to the side, listening.

"What if you could have someone to talk to?" I spare a glance at Cassia. "What if you had someone who could talk back?"

Cassia and Isha look at the *dakait* boy. He stares back at them, face slick with sweat.

"What do you say?" My heart pounds. I don't know if this is justice, but it's better than murder. "Wouldn't you rather have him than Tibbet?"

The witch sniffs the *dakait* boy. "Will he catch rats?"

"Sure." Rubio steps in. "He's great at catching rats. All the rats you want."

I send him a warning glare. *Don't oversell it.* "What do you think, Cass?"

If only there was time to show her Isha's patients and the filthy warrens in the depths of the station. Then she would know my plan isn't as merciful as it seems.

"Wait." The *dakait* boy whimpers. "Don't I get a say?"

"Sure." Cassia gives him a cold smile. "Why not? Let's hear your plan."

He swallows. "Let me go. I didn't take your brother or anybody. All I did was work the door saw."

Cassia laughs. "Try again."

The *dakait* boy looks from Isha to his crewmates' bodies. "Do me like them, then." He lifts his chin, but for all his bravado, he's shaking. "I'm not staying here with that wrecked old witch." He spits at Isha's feet.

Cassia's eyes light up, but there's something wrong with them. One time when I was visiting Ava and Rushil, their neighbor had to put down a rabid dog. Her eyes are like that—glassy—seeing, but not seeing. This isn't the girl I know. This is a stranger.

"Perfect." She smiles to herself and then at Isha. "He's all yours."

Nutrition bar wrappers and cellophane crinkle under my boots as I duck into the *dakait* ship. I inch down the narrow corridors, trying not to touch the walls. The whole place stinks of piss and alcohol. Even the corner of the *Mendicant* where Tibbet has chosen to do his business doesn't smell this bad.

I reach the cockpit and squint into the harsh blue-white light bleeding up from behind the wall panels. More wrappers and bottles litter the controls, and a tiny hologram of a naked woman gyrates over the coms station. Charming. I pick up a flak jacket slung across one of the seats and sit down. There's information here. Coordinates for where the *dakait* have been. Docking codes. Maybe even names.

The litter rustles behind me, and I spin around.

Rubio stands in the doorway, looking as skeevy as I feel. "Find anything?"

"Not yet." I bring up the docking log. Something yellow and tacky is spattered across the screen. "I'm thinking we should bring in a decontamination crew."

"Heh." Rubio shoves his hands in his pockets and gazes up at a yellow-brown stain on the wall.

We both stay silent, me flipping through the logs,

Rubio nodding his head and taking in the room. Finally I can't take it anymore.

"Is she coming?"

Rubio freezes and then shakes his head. "She said she didn't want to see where they kept him."

I turn back to the controls. "I guess that's for the best."

"Miyole . . . ," Rubio starts.

"I don't want to talk about it."

"I'm as freaked out as you." Rubio takes a seat next to me and runs a hand through his hair. "I've never seen anyone . . . kill before."

I raise an eyebrow at him. "You never shot anyone down?"

He laughs. "*Vaya*, Mi. I've only been on security detail for a year. They teach you to shoot across the bow. Warning shots."

I don't say anything.

"I mean, all that blood . . ."

Blood—the dakait, *my mother, the man on our bedroom floor with my eyes.*

"Rubio." I raise my voice. "I said I don't want to talk about it. I want to find what we need and get out of here, okay?" I don't want to think the thoughts tapping at the back of my mind. *Should I ever have trusted Cassia? How much do I know her, even now? Is this whole rescue mission a mistake?*

"Fine." He raises his hands and stands up. "I get it."

I sigh. "Look, I'm sorry. Can you go back to fixing the air scrubbers and let me finish up with this?" I wave at the screen. "I just can't right now. This place is creeping me out."

"Yeah." Rubio shrugs. "All I'm saying is, we should keep a close eye on Cassia. I don't know what she's going to do when we get down on the surface, and I'd like to come out of this alive."

I hole up in the cockpit while Cassia and Rubio sleep, trying to concentrate on the information from the *dakait* ship's log. It's no use. I can't unsee the blood or the look on Cassia's face. I can't force that other memory—the man with my eyes, my *manman* taking the gun from me—back to the depths where it belongs. I can't look at Cassia without it all refreshing before me. I've been sleeping beneath a pile of coats on one of the common room couches or scrunched sideways in the pilot's chair since we left Isha's station. That is, when I sleep.

I rub my eyes and try to focus. The *dakait* made a host of port calls on Enceladus.

Dock Roppyaku, East Block Subport, Ny Kyoto: 36.637864, 155.522461

Aoki Diagnostik, Shio Subport, Ny Kyoto: 36.637865, 155.522460

Rangnvaldsson Keramik, Ny Karlskrona, Kyushu Province: 36.375480, 127.441406

Cryatics Wholesale, Kazan Spindle, Zaius Shelf Port: -76.052861, -89.472656

Norling Buki-ko, Jämtlands län, Ny Skaderna: -74.00182, -63.942321

A-1 Suchiru, Hiroi Glaciär Spindle, Ny Skaderna: -70.81924, -64.11021

Enceladus was supposed to be one of the *Ranganathan*'s ports of call, too—there was some talk about taking shore leave if we were on schedule—but I only remember the very basics about it. I should have paid more attention to the docking briefs in my preflight packet. I trail a finger over the names and pull up Ny Kyoto from the Mendicant's data banks.

Founded by Japanese and Swedish refugees fleeing rising tides, Ny Kyoto was the first colony established on Enceladus. Research indicates great potential for bioengineering ship components in the moon's subterranean oceans. . . .

I close the screen and groan. Clearly no one has

updated the *Mendicant*'s data banks in at least fifty years. Enceladus has been growing ship parts for decades. The skeletons of the *Ranganathan* and her sisters were born in the Enceladan ocean yards.

I scroll back up to the port call roster and press my fingertips against my temples, as if that will help me remember. Ny Kyoto, that's one of the biggest population centers. And the one with the Swedish name—if the coordinates are right, it's not too far from the city. That puts the others near the southern pole. Something itches in the back of my mind. Wasn't there something dangerous at the south pole? Riptides, maybe? There was some reason no major cities formed there.

What were you doing? Where did you leave him? I don't know any Swedish and my Japanese is terrible, but some of the locations look like businesses of some kind— *Cryatics Wholesale, Aoki Diagnostik.* And *buki-ko*, that has something to do with weapons, but I can't remember what.

I lean back in my chair and grind the heels of my hands into my eyes. We have the coordinates, but they could mean anything. And then there's Sweetie's delivery. Hopefully we haven't missed his message telling us the location of our drop point by diverting course to Isha's station. There's nothing to do but wait until we reach Enceladus and see for ourselves.

I turn off the cockpit's overhead lights and try to sleep, but my mind keeps turning over. Vishva and I always used to play If I Had a Time Machine back when we were at Revati together.

If I had a time machine, I'd go back and tell myself not to come to school the day Sanjita read my note about Roshan to the whole class.

I'd go back and tell the engineers about how the levee was going to breach.

I'd tell Mummy not give my stepfather a second chance.

I'd warn my mother about the hurricane.

If I had one now, how far would I go back and do things differently? Back to the moment I told Cassia I'd fly for her? To my missed chance to stop the *dakait*? To the moment I asked Rushil to fix my records for me? Or maybe even farther—back to save my mother, back to before the sea swallowed Earth's islands so we could have ridden out any storm on land and I would have a place to call my home. I lean forward and pull up the *Mendicant*'s data-bank entry on Haiti. The ship's records may be woefully out-of-date, but Haiti drowned hundreds of years before this ship was built, and as far as I can tell, its entry is more or less right. Or at least, it matches my memories from world history class.

The former slaves of Haiti won their years-long battle for independence from the French in 1804, under the command of Toussaint L'Overture.

It always felt so distant back then. My books weren't talking about anything to do with me. Now my mother's words run through my head as I read, like two streams weaving and curving together. *We were the first in the age of slavery to strike off our chains. Be proud of that,* ma chère. *Your people saw the chance for freedom and took it, no matter what the rest of the world said.*

I read on, words sparking memories, memories sparking memories, until I fall into a fitful sleep.

I am in my manman's *bedroom. I am playing with my doll. She has a long, dark braid, almost as long as her whole body, and I like to hold her by the tip of it and spin us both around and around.*

Heavy footsteps mount the stairs outside, a measure too slow to be my manman's. *Fear sinks into my chest like a spider. The front door unlocks, and the steps are in the house. I dive under the bed. Too late, I look back. My doll is all alone in the center of the bedroom floor. I wriggle forward to grab her, but the footsteps turn my way. I pull my arm back under the bed just in time.*

Two scuffed, pointy boots stop in the doorway. I want to squeeze my eyes shut, but I know if I do, I'll open them again and he'll be bending down, looking under the bed.

"Miyole!" he shouts, hitting the last syllable of my name hard.

I don't move. I am boneless, trembling.

He reaches down and snatches my doll. I stifle a little exhalation—oh. Where is he taking her? What is he going to do with her?

His footsteps retreat into the kitchen. I listen to him taking things off the shelf, making food, talking to someone on his satellite phone. Eventually I fall asleep beneath the mattress.

I wake to the sound of my manman's *sloop roaring overhead. The spider lets go of my chest. She's home. I crawl out from beneath the bed and peek around the corner into the living room. He sits in his big yellow chair, clipping his fingernails. No sign of my doll. I sneak into the hallway, where he can't see me, to wait for my* manman *and throw my arms around her legs as soon as she comes in the door.*

"Hello, ma chère. *Did you miss me?" she says.*

His voice cuts between us. "Where have you been?"

I look over my shoulder. He is staring straight at me, but it's my manman *who answers.*

"I have that new haul route to Mirny. I told you last week, remember?"

I freeze, watching him. Maybe he will rise up out of his chair and come at her. Maybe he will scream and curse. Maybe he will break something or take away something we need. Maybe he will say we all have to stay home with him.

Instead, we are lucky. He grunts and turns his attention back to his sat phone.

We eat dinner. He still says nothing about my doll. I want to ask him if I can have it back, but then I would have to admit I saw him take it. I would have to admit I was hiding from him, and that will make him angry like nothing else.

After dinner, I brush my teeth and hug my manman *good-night. She is in the kitchen, washing up the dishes. I try to slip away to my cot without him noticing, but this time I am not so lucky.*

"Miyole." He crooks a finger at me and beckons me over to his chair.

I stand beside his chair, enough distance that we aren't touching, but not so much that he can say I'm trying to stay away from him.

"Are you forgetting something?" He raises an eyebrow.

I hug him quickly, mechanically. "Good night, Papa."

"Good night," he says.

I turn to go.

"Miyole."

I stop and turn back around. I am too young to know the word dread, *but I feel it filling me up all the same.*

"I found that doll of yours," he says. "On the floor."

"What doll?" I say, even though I know exactly what he means. It is not a good lie. I don't have many toys. I am already shaking.

His eyes go wide. "What doll?" he repeats. "What doll?"

My manman *turns around, her hands still dripping soapy water. "Janjak, please."*

His eyes flash. "Don't you Janjak me. This girl is a liar. And how do you think she got that way?"

I back away one step.

"Don't you go anywhere." He points at me and pulls the doll out from behind his back. He's been sitting with it wedged between the cushions of his chair. "You don't appreciate what we give you. You're going to take this down to the brink and throw it in the water."

"No!" My eyes fill with tears. "Papa, please. I'm sorry. . . ."

"Pe dan w la!" He stands suddenly, towering over me. "Stop crying."

"Janjak." My mother steps between us, her voice calm.

His hand flies up and strikes her across the cheek and then he's hitting her and hitting her.

I run to the storage closet beside the washroom and close myself inside. It's my fault. If I hadn't made him mad, he wouldn't hit her. If I hadn't dropped my doll. If I had said I was sorry sooner. I should go tell him to stop, to hit me instead, but the shameful, cringing part of me is stronger. The truth is, I'm glad it's not me.

I wake in the pilot's chair and rub the sleep from my eyes. The giant gas planet that Enceladus orbits glows in the dark before us—a pale orange smear only now visible with the naked eye. Three days, and we'll be in its orbit, too. Three days, and we'll touch down on the moon's icy crust. I shiver.

I climb down to the storage room to find the body armor Rubio "reappropriated" from the *dakait* ship. If Sweetie's contacts on Enceladus are anything like Sweetie himself, I'm going to want all the protection I can get. I pick up an armored shirt—a black, beaded thing, thin but strong, perfect for dispersing the energy behind a fired slug. I've seen feeds of soldiers and rescue workers in armor like this, but I've never had to wear it myself. It moves like water, like snakeskin. I pause, weighing the shirt with my hand, then grab two more and head off to find Rubio.

I stop short in the doorway to the common room. Cassia sits on the couch with her back to me, stroking Tibbet's head and staring at the design Isha drew on the far wall. For half a moment, I think about turning around and locking myself in the cockpit, but I can't avoid her forever. I steel myself, walk past her, and dump the armor on a table. I cross my arms and stare down at it, not moving, but not looking at her, either.

I feel her eyes on me. She clears her throat. "I know you think it was wrong, what I did."

I turn around. "You killed him." Something sticks in my throat. "You killed him even after you told him we were going to spare him."

"So did Isha," Cassia points out.

"Do you really want to compare yourself to Isha?"

Cassia hugs Tibbet tight. "They were selling people, Miyole. *Selling people.* You heard what he said—what he would have done with us."

I shake my head, not because I don't believe her, but because I don't want the images cycling around in my mind. What could have happened to us. What has already happened to others. They were us, minus some luck.

"The Deep's better off without them." Cassia leans forward, and Tibbet leaps from her lap. "You know I'm right."

I look at the armor. "Right," I say. "But I don't want to be the one to decide those things." In Mumbai, even murderers receive trials, and on the *Ranganathan*, they have correctional hearings. A lone person doesn't hand down a death sentence.

"Lucky you weren't, then." Cassia's voice hardens.

It would be easy to believe that, nicer to think I had no choice in the matter. But I could have gone to that *dakait* at any time and stopped his bleeding.

The old memory plays again—the kick of the gun in my hands, the shock, my *manman*'s eyes so sad, and then her standing over the man. The gun's report, deafening in our tiny bedroom. I look at Cassia. Her hair hangs lank under the bandage, and the skin beneath her eyes is bruised. Was killing the *dakait* really so different from what my mother did? She was only protecting herself. And Cassia's right, the Deep is better off without people like that. So why does it feel different?

I take a step toward Cassia. I don't know what I mean to do. To speak? To throw my arms around her? To shove her away?

Rubio appears in the door, out of breath. "Telemetry's going crazy," he says. "There's something outside."

CHAPTER • 18

The three of us crowd into the cockpit and lean over the displays. Beyond the viewport, something small and white floats against the darkness, too perfectly round to be debris. I cut the engines and fire the fore thrusters to slow our approach.

"Anybody want to guess what the hell that is?" Rubio says.

"It's a drop." Cassia's voice is almost a whisper. "Our delivery coordinates."

I frown and toggle our coms. "It's just sitting there. Why isn't it streaming?"

"Some things are too . . . sensitive for streaming." Cassia nods at the screen. "We've picked those up before, on runs for Sweetie."

"You're sure?" I lean in closer.

Cassia nods. "The buyer usually launches a blind drop once Sweetie confirms the cargo is under way." She stands straight. "Let's bring it in and see what it says."

Rubio snaps to attention. "Whoa, wait. Bring it in?"

Cassia narrows her eyes. "How else are we going to figure out where we're going?"

"Okay, that's a terrible idea," Rubio says. "Even if it is for us—which, why should we assume it is?—how do you know it's not a pulse bomb or something?"

Cassia makes a face. "Why would Sweetie's buyer leave a bomb for us?"

"Why do you keep saying it's from Sweetie's buyer?"

Cassia throws up her hands. "Who else knows our specific trajectory coordinates?"

Rubio runs a hand through his hair. "Listen. I'm the only one with security experience here and—"

"Well, I'm the only one with smuggling experience," Cassia interrupts. "And I say we bring it in."

"Okay." Rubio shrugs. "You go get it, then."

"Gladly," Cassia says.

"Hold on." I step in. "Cass, your head—"

"I'm fine." She scowls over my shoulder at Rubio. "I'm not afraid like some people."

"You're still getting over a concussion and carbon

monoxide poisoning. The last thing you should do is try to walk outside."

"I can do it," she insists.

"No," I say, and I hear my *manman*'s voice in my own, firm, in control. "You can't." I glance at Rubio. "But I can."

The first time I did a spacewalk sim, I barely made it out of the antigravity chamber before I threw up. Second time: same. Third time: same. Luckily for me, the DSRI doesn't expect its scientists to be experts at zero G, so three successful sim runs were all I needed, and throwing up *outside* the sim chamber was still considered a success.

I stand in the *Mendicant*'s cramped air lock, waiting for the air pressure to bottom out so the ship doesn't eject me like a projectile as soon as Cassia and Rubio pop the lock. We're stopped several dozen meters from the drop sphere. I reach behind my back to double-check the tether hooked to my pressure suit. *I will not hyperventilate. I've done this before.* Well, more or less.

"Are you sure you want to do this?" Rubio calls over the coms.

"Yes." *No.*

"Because I could try to fit in your suit. We could rig it—"

I roll my eyes, even though Rubio can't see me. "Please. You're half a head taller than me."

The atmospheric indicator lights around my helmet's faceplate change from blue to yellow to red. We found a set of five bulky pressure suits in one of the *Mendicant*'s storage lockers, but something had chewed holes big enough to poke a finger through the outer insulating layers. My suit is it.

"Enough." Cassia's voice relays into my ear. "Ready, Miyole?"

Outside the small viewport, the Deep is thick with stars, like sugar spilled over a black tablecloth. It's gorgeous. It's majestic. But I prefer looking at it from behind dozens of layers of self-healing nacre and radiation shields.

I take a steadying breath. "Ready."

The air lock door winds open. I step up to the black.

Imagine throwing yourself from Mumbai's tallest skyscraper. Imagine drifting alone in an endless blank sea. Imagine being sealed, awake, in a light-tight coffin. Now combine those things, and add a dose of vertigo.

I make my way along the *Mendicant*'s side, one hand on its fuselage, until I reach its farthest spar. The drop sphere hangs some twenty meters in front of me, like a tiny, pale moon. I brace my feet against the ship, ready to kick off and launch myself out to grab it. My blood pressure rises, thumping beneath my collarbone. I look down at the endless kilometers of nothing below me. If my tether snaps, if I fly too far . . .

A memory engulfs me.

I am a little girl. I am up to my neck in water, treading, a trace of salt on my lips.

A boy—Kai, my friend Kai—splashes me. "Can't catch me, slow dough!"

I growl and show my teeth—my best shark impression. "Huh-uh. I'm going to eat you up!"

And then I'm flying, arms churning the water, as I race after him. I am fast and powerful in the ocean, like the dolphins we sometimes see at sunset. I'm gaining, and then I'm level with him. We swim far, as far out from the docks as we've ever gone, and then far as the older boys and girls. In a burst of speed, I overtake him. The rush of it carries me on, giddy glee flooding my arms with strength. I am made for this. I could swim forever.

"Miyole!" Kai's cry is far behind me.

I slow and kick myself around to look back. His head is a tiny dark shape bobbing in the water. The docks and pontoons of East Gyre rock gently behind him, stretched as far as I can see. From here, my home looks like a collection of little play ships and houses, small enough I could pick them up in my hand. I've never swum out so far before.

"Miyole!" Kai's voice barely carries to me. "Come back!"

I look from him to the open sea at my back. A stocky boat chugs along the horizon, as far from me as I am from the docks. Suddenly, the adrenaline drains out of me. I'm no longer powerful, no longer made for the sea. I'm a small thing with aching arms, too far from the Gyre's steady ships and footbridges. The blue beneath me is too blue, the depths too deep, and I am alone.

"Mi? Miyole?"

I blink.

"Mi?" Cassia's voice is back in my ear. "Can you hear me? Are you okay?"

I hear my own breathing before I can register what it is—harsh, quick gasps filling my helmet.

I gulp them down. "I'm okay," I say. "I'm okay. Just out of practice."

Rubio's voice now. "You've got to breathe slow so you don't burn all your oxygen too fast."

"Okay." I know that, but I'm too short of breath to argue with him.

I close my eyes, concentrate on the simple physics of what I'm about to do. Push off from the ship's side, but not too hard. *Force divided by mass equals acceleration.* Grab

the sphere. *Mass times velocity equals a change in momentum.*
Wait for Cassia and Rubio to winch my tether back in. *Time
equals distance divided by rate.*

I steady myself, open my eyes, and jump.

The sphere comes up fast, smacking me in the chest
so hard I barely remember to wrap my arms around it.
The impact spins me around, and I find myself facing the
Mendicant, my tether trailing loose behind me like a ghostly
umbilical cord. The ship's wedge-shaped face stares
blankly back. Vertigo starts to overtake me, but I squeeze
my eyes shut.

"Got it!" I say.

I try to keep my eyes closed tight as Cassia and Rubio
reel me back in, but every few minutes, the not knowing
is worse than the knowing, and I have to peek out from
beneath my eyelashes. The *Mendicant* grows before me,
dirty white against the darkness, like an unbleached
clamshell. And then I'm touching down in the air lock,
the ship's gravity steady under my feet, and the door seals
behind me.

Rubio's face appears in the inner air lock window. "You
okay?" he mouths.

I give him a thumbs-up and sink down against the wall,
clutching the drop sphere to my chest as the air pressure

gradually climbs back to normal. The lights around my faceplate fade from red to yellow to blue—safe atmosphere and pressure—and I pull off my helmet.

Cassia rushes in and takes the drop sphere, while Rubio holds out a hand to help me up. I look from him to Cassia, ignore Rubio's hand, and push myself upright. I'm sure I would forget about her if it was my family we were hunting for. I would snatch up that sphere first, too.

We follow Cassia into the common room, where she kneels on the floor and places the sphere in front of her. Rubio backs up against the wall, as far from the device as he can go. Cassia rolls her eyes at him and touches a finger to the sensor on the sphere's top. Its upper half splits and retracts, revealing a small metal tube cushioned inside.

Cassia picks it up. It fits easily inside her palm.

I lean in. "It looks like . . . lipstick?"

Cassia holds the tube up to the light, examining the hairline seam around its circumference. She raises an eyebrow at Rubio. "Still think it's a bomb?"

He looks at his feet and shrugs.

Cassia twists the tube. It pops open with a quick hiss of depressurizing air, depositing a heavy-gauge needle jack into her hand.

I take a sharp breath. I've seen one of those before—a

box of them, actually—in Ava and Rushil's house, of all places.

What's that?

Something for my friend Soli. You remember I told you about her?

But why does she need so many?

She gives them away. Presents. For crewe girls, like I was. So they can find their way here, if they want.

"Okay . . ." Rubio squints at the jack. "That's for . . . ?"

Cassia holds it up to the light. "It's some kind of manual line-in, I think."

Rubio pushes away from the wall and leans over us. "To what?"

Cassia shakes her head. "I don't know. I didn't think anyone was still using these. I'm not even sure the ship has a connector for it."

I clear my throat. "It's a directional."

"A directional?" Rubio says.

"Sure. It hooks in to your ship's navigation system." I reach for the jack. "It stores a preprogrammed set of coordinates. Ava, my sister—she hides them inside fans."

Cassia and Rubio both stare at me.

"It's a long story." I clear my throat. "We should plug it in, see where it wants us to go."

We make our way to the cockpit.

"What if it doesn't fit?" Cassia asks.

"It's an old ship. It's bound to have a line-in port." I drop down in the captain's seat and scan the controls. There. A port the size of a hypodermic needle. It all makes sense now. Newer ships wouldn't have a directional port, wouldn't be able to read the coordinates. This was left especially for us.

"See?" I push the directional home with a *click*.

A tooth-rending screech blares through the *Mendicant*'s coms system, followed by a babble of digital static. I clap my hands over my ears. Cassia jumps back, and Rubio slaps a hand down on the controls to silence the ship's internal coms.

"*Vaya.*" He rubs his ears. "What was that?"

"New coordinates." I point to the navigation readout: *-84.0219, -23.9082, a-18*. "That must be our drop point."

I expect the gas giant to take my breath away, but when I finally see it up close, I feel nothing. It looks so perfectly geometric, like a child's rendering; it doesn't seem real. Even its shadows are too neat and sharp. Telemetry lights up as we pass the nitrogen farming operations on Titan, Enceladus's sister moon, and then runs wild as we follow the coordinates to our destination. Ice crystals from the planet's outer ring fizzle against our shields. And then there it is—Enceladus—a ghostly mirror of ice reflecting light from the planet and its other nearby moons.

Once, when I was little, Ava and Rushil took me to a Diwali festival down in the Salt, and Rushil bought a sugar rock for me. It was the size of a cricket ball and so hard I couldn't bite it. Enceladus looks exactly like it. Like I could put it in my mouth. Like I could hold it on my tongue until the enzymes in my saliva begin to dissolve it.

We fall into orbit with the other ships waiting for entry clearance. From just above the moon's atmosphere, its imperfections come into relief—craters, canyons, ridges, and boreholes leading down to the liquid ocean beneath its icy crust.

"What's that?" Rubio points to a dazzling white flume rising from the moon's southern pole.

"An austral geyser." I lean toward the viewport, my voice rising in excitement. That's what I couldn't remember. "Enceladus is cryovolcanic. It has such a high degree of orbital eccentricity that it's subject to tidal heating, but the atmosphere is so cold, the erupting liquid freezes on contact."

Rubio raises both eyebrows. "Um . . . English?"

"It's an ice volcano," Cassia says.

Rubio's eyes widen. "Please tell me we're giving that a wide berth."

Cassia laughs. "Only crazy people fly near volcanos."

"Actually . . ." I glance at the coordinates we skimmed off the *Dakait* log.

Rubio groans. "You're kidding."

"It's one of the places they set down," I hurry to say. "But only if we don't find anything at the coordinates in Ny Karlskrona. We should check there first."

"And Sweetie's delivery," Cassia puts in. "I want that done with so we're free and clear to look for Nethanel."

Rubio glances over at me. "Where's that take us?"

"The drop sphere coordinates?" I bring up the navigation screen. "It looks like they're in Ny Kyoto."

Rubio grunts. "Sounds like a party."

We come in above Ny Kyoto. Nothing moves on the surface but gusts of powdered snow. It snakes between the spindle towers that mark each building's anchor point below the ice. From above, the city looks like a forest of needles—silver gray and glistening. We touch down on Onsen Subport, at the marker for pad 134. For a moment, we stare out at the whipping snow. Then a high-pitched squeal rises from somewhere outside, and the ship drops beneath us.

"Caray!" Rubio braces himself against the controls.

We stop short, a meter lower than we were on touchdown.

"Sorry," Cassia says. "I should have warned you. They get air pockets between the ice and the landing plates sometimes. Makes it a little bumpy."

Something thumps below us, and the landing plate begins to descend with a muffled hum. A chasm of ice rises around us, until the sky and blinding snow are only a bright, distant circle. The tenor of the hum changes. Dark water creeps up over the front viewport.

Something deep in my brain moves. All that water, covering us, bearing down on us . . . My nightmares always end like this. The Great Levee around Mumbai has broken and the hurricane has come again. I am trapped inside—sometimes at home, sometimes at Revati or the university—and the water is rising against my window, sealing me under the sea. I back against the bulkhead, breathing hard.

"Mi?" Cassia frowns at me. "What's the matter?"

I shake my head. My heart beats so hard I'm afraid I'm going to throw it up.

I squeeze my eyes closed. I'm not drowning. This isn't the hurricane. This is Enceladus, and this is how they live here, beneath the ocean. It keeps them warm, keeps them alive. *Average water temperature of -6 degrees Celsius near the ice, warming as the depth increases and in proximity to the poles,* I recite to myself.

Rubio lets out a low whistle. *"Vaya."*

I open my eyes. The water is aglow. All around us are structures like I've never seen before, enormous veins of lights, thicker around than Mumbai's biggest skyscrapers. Maybe bigger than a dozen city blocks. They reach down from their anchor points in the permanent layer of ice to the murky depths kilometers below. Dozens of them. Hundreds. A whole inverted city.

I gape. "What is this?"

"Ny Kyoto," Cassia says.

Other ships scud by, smaller ones more suited for the water. As the landing pad moves us closer to one of the structures, I make out segments in its length, like cells along a bamboo shoot. The scientist in me stirs. "What are those buildings made of?"

"Spindles," Cassia corrects. "I don't know. Something flexible. They have to be able to move a little when the current changes."

A porthole opens in the side of the nearest spindle, scattering more light through the water. The landing plate deposits us inside. Behind us, a muffled *thump* sounds, and the water drains from the dock. For a moment, everything is silent.

Our coms crackle on. "Mighty slow *skepp* you've got there," a man's voice croaks. "You're late."

I raise my eyebrows at Cassia. These are our buyers? The man's accent sounds so much like the *dakait*, his words coming from the back of his throat, like theirs did. I have to remind myself it only means he's Enceladan, too. We knew this. It shouldn't be a surprise. It shouldn't be setting off alarms in my head, but it is.

Cassia flicks the transmitter. "We're here, aren't we?"

"Hmph," he grunts. "And the cargo?"

"All ready for you," Cassia answers.

My eyes skip over the empty dock. *Something's wrong. Where is everyone?*

Cassia gives me a sideways glance. A small furrow forms in the center of her brow. "Why don't you show yourself so we can bring the cargo out to you?"

A long pause. Then: "You know your call signature isn't transmitting. Some warning you were coming before you tried to dock would have been polite. Makes everyone think something's off. Makes everyone a little gun-shy."

Cassia looks at me and raises her eyebrows.

Chaila. In all the chaos, I forgot about the signal dampener Rubio and I installed. It must be affecting our long-range coms, too.

"Sorry," I mouth.

"We . . . had a few mechanical problems," Cassia says. "But we're here. Nothing's wrong."

Someone mutters indistinctly on the other end. A pause, and then the bay doors on the far side of the dock unbolt and begin to roll open. Figures in faded brown-and-gray jumpsuits and knee-high wading boots file in, rifles slung across their backs.

"In that case," the man on the coms says, "welcome to Enceladus."

CHAPTER 19

The hatch opens on a small army of people with drawn guns. Okay, maybe not an army, but definitely a regiment. Or a contingent. Rubio would probably know the right word, but this doesn't seem like the best time to start discussing semantics with him. They aren't exactly pointing their weapons at us, but they aren't holstered, either. The air smells like saline and iron.

We file out onto the dock. We're wearing the body armor we scavenged, but it covers us only from shoulder to hip. Cassia scowls at the first person we pass, a tall, thin man in coveralls and a knit cap with a scuffed-up rifle he needs two hands to support.

They won't shoot us. I try to focus on the stained yellow walls behind our welcoming party. Faded words in kanji and what I think is Swedish cover the surface. *They aren't* dakait. *They're businesspeople, Sweetie's contacts. A few words and this will all be cleared—*

A phlegmy cough from the back of the room interrupts my thoughts. The crowd parts, and a squat man in a floor-length coat shuffles forward. His hair is white around the temples and at the tip of his short, bristly beard.

"Herr Tsukino," Cassia says, so quietly only I can hear.

"*Välkomna!*" I recognize the voice from our coms, the throaty rasp. "It's been a long time since we've had some of our friend Sweetie's associates as guests."

"Tsukino-sama." Cassia steps forward, hands held open. "Don't you remember me?"

Herr Tsukino looks her over. "Should I?"

"My family, we shipped for yours before. It was a few years ago, but—"

He holds up a hand. "*Mat.* I'm not so old and rot brained you can make up a history between us. All I care about is what's in your cargo hold."

Cassia crosses her arms. "You do this song and dance for all your deliveries, or just Sweetie's?"

"We've dealt with Sweetie plenty." Herr Tsukino pulls a rag from his pocket and blows his nose into it. "That's why you're going to stay right there until we're sure you brought what we were promised." He grins and stuffs the snot rag back in his pocket.

Rubio starts forward, hands raised. "Listen—"

The man in the knit cap cocks his rifle and levels it at Rubio's head. *"Rör dig inte."*

"Wait!" A girl with straight black hair pulled back in a ponytail elbows her way through the crowd and shoves the mouth of his rifle down. She wears a frayed blue cardigan over her charcoal jumpsuit. "What are you doing, *toroi?*"

She turns to the older man in the floor-length coat. "Jiiji, that's Cassia Kaldero. Ezar's daughter. Don't you recognize her?"

Cassia's eyes go wide. "Freja?" She runs down the ramp, heedless of the drawn guns, and throws herself into the other girl's arms.

For one tense moment, I'm convinced we're going to die. Then the old man laughs, and somehow that breaks the fear in the air.

"Kaldero." He laughs and waves a hand. Everyone lowers their guns. *"Wari wari.* I didn't recognize you in all that raider armor, tinker girl. I thought your father had learned his lesson about shipping for Sweetie."

But Cassia doesn't answer. She and Freja cling to each other, oblivious to everyone else around them.

"What are you doing here? I thought your family was out on the circuit for another year." Freja pulls back and holds Cassia at arm's length. She glances at Rubio and me, still standing at the top of the ramp, and screws up her heart-shaped face in a frown. "This isn't your ship. Where're your mother and father? Where're your brothers? And little Milah?"

"They . . . we . . ." Cassia chokes on her words. She swallows and tries again. "We were in past the belt and . . ." She stops.

"*Dakait.*" I step in. What did Sweetie call them? "The . . . the Söner Neitibu? They attacked the ship."

Cassia collects herself. "The ship's lost. Everyone survived, but they took Nethanel."

A sharp intake of breath traverses the room.

"The Söner?" Herr Tsukino's face goes green. "Little tinker, are you sure?"

Cassia nods.

Freja makes a sour face at me. "Who are you two, then? Sweetie's crew?"

"They're DSRI." Cassia wipes her eyes briskly and nods at us. "That's Miyole and that's Rubio."

"Bureaubrats?" Freja blinks at us. "*Iiya.* How did you end up with them?"

"Freja." The old man frowns. "Mind your tongue. They're guests."

Freja sighs heavily. "Sorry, Jiiji."

Jiiji again. I shuffle through my brain, trying to remember the bits of Japanese I learned at Revati. *That's* grandfather, I think, though the way they say the words is nothing like the way our instructor spoke.

"Ungdom-sa," the old man interrupts. "We can talk later, but for now, we have cargo to unload. Freja, why don't you take our guests out to get some tea? Something to eat." He looks at each of us in turn. "You'll need something to keep your strength up if it's the Söner you mean to face."

Freja leads us out onto a broad, dark metal stair that switchbacks down the inside of the spindle. Graffiti and scraps of pasteboard cover the inner wall, but the other side hangs open all the way to the bottom of the spindle, several hundred stories below. Footbridges and scaffolding jut across the empty space, linking platforms jammed with lighted storefronts. The air is wet. A light fog hangs over everything, slicking the handrails and causing the glowing signs and windows to bleed around the edges. A bustle of old women crowds by under umbrellas, speaking something that sounds not quite like Japanese. I stare after them, confused.

"What's the matter, bureaubrat? Your schools didn't teach you any Nihongska?" Freja smirks back at me.

"No." I flinch as a drop of water hits my forehead.

She laughs and grabs Cassia's arm. "Honestly, Cass. Where did you find these two?"

"At least my school taught me how not to be such a bloody *kuttiya*," I say under my breath.

Beside me, Rubio snorts.

We pass an umbrella and dried-seaweed snack stand hooked on to the outer side of the stair, and then another a few landings down selling everything from goggles to powdered tea and live fish in tanks.

"This way." Freja waves us out onto a narrow bridge, and then up three steps to a bright, narrow shop. The smell of warm broth and fry oil billows out, sweeping away the hints of wet iron and mildew in the air. My stomach gurgles. I decide to put my dislike for Freja on hold.

We cram into a booth and lose ourselves in fish-ball soup and spicy noodles. Between the buzz of conversation from the other tables and the steady *thwap* of a man pulling noodles in the back room, we can barely hear one another.

At last Rubio pushes away his bowl. "Are we going to talk about this?"

Cassia shrugs and stares down at her tea.

"Okay, then. Here's what I think." Rubio leans forward so we can hear him over the restaurant's din. "We can't fight them. That was lucky back on the outpost. We can't assume things will go like that again."

Cassia stays quiet. The lamp above our table casts deep shadows under her eyes. In the back room, the cook laughs and calls out something to the girl behind the counter. Ceramic cups and spoons clink.

I clear my throat. "So . . . what? Do we try to bribe them? Get them to sell Nethanel back to us?" I make a face at the tea Freja ordered. It has all the flavor of a boiled salt marsh, but my own question leaves an even worse taste in my mouth.

"With what?" Rubio says.

I grimace. "The ship?"

"But that means we'd be stuck here," Rubio says.

Freja lifts an eyebrow. "There *are* worse things."

I ignore her. "So we're stuck for a little bit, but at least Nethanel's free. Sweetie has the DSRI shuttle for collateral, so he won't come after us. We can work until we have enough for passage back to—"

"No." Cassia's voice cracks.

We all turn to her.

"We're not playing nice." She leans over the table. "If we pay them, they'll only do it again to someone else. We have to make them regret what they did to us. They're the ones who have to pay."

"Cass," I say gently. "What do you want—revenge? Or your brother back?"

She scowls at me. "Both."

Frustration flares in my chest. "And if you can only have one?"

Cassia pushes herself back against her seat, her eyes bright with tears. "*Shinjame*, Miyole."

"You're right, you know." Freja sits sideways in her chair, her back leaned against the wall.

"Who?" I say.

"Both of you." She points at Cassia. "You can't bargain with them, or they'll do it again. But the bureaubrats've got a point. You need a soft touch if you want your brother back. First Nethanel, then revenge."

Cassia hunches her shoulders and frowns. She won't look at any of us. I pull out my crow and open up the list of coordinates we took from the *dakait* ship.

"Have you heard of that third one?" I hand the crow to Freja. "The *dakait* said they dropped him in Ny Karlskrona."

"Rangnvaldsson Keramik," she says. "Yeah, I have."

I peer over her shoulder. "What is that place?"

She shrugs. "Rangnvaldsson's deals in ship upgrades and parts. We trade with them sometimes. In fact . . ." Freja's face lights up. "I bet my grandfather is planning to sell them some of that cryatine you brought us."

Cassia finally looks up. She, Rubio, and I exchange a look.

"Do you think he'd let us ride along?" she asks.

Freja shrugs again. "No harm in asking."

"Thank you. Tell him thank you."

"He hasn't said yes yet," Freja says, but she grins at Cassia and slides out of the booth. "You three stay here, finish your tea. I'll see what I can do."

We stare after Freja as she tromps out of the room, ponytail swaying, rubber boots squeaking on the restaurant floor.

Rubio clears his throat and points after her. "How do you know her, again?"

I turn to Cassia. I was wondering the exact same thing.

"My family traded here. Before . . ." Cassia shakes her head as though she's throwing off a bad memory. "Freja's grandfather was the one who introduced my father to Sweetie."

"Seems like they're not too friendly with him now," Rubio mutters.

Cassia ignores him. A smile starts at the corners of her mouth. "This one time, Freja and I took the pressure drop down to the seabed observation deck, and we walked in on this old man and a lady kissing. They gave us some visitor passes to the casinos on Dock Ornata so we'd keep quiet." She laughs. "There were these piles of pistachio mocha, and we ate so much we made ourselves sick."

"Did you . . . I mean, were you two . . ." I don't mean to sound jealous, but a sour note creeps in on the last word.

Cassia makes a face at me.

I hurry on. "I mean, you two seem so close. I only wondered . . ."

"No," she says shortly. "Just friends."

A heavy, awkward silence hangs in the air.

"Right. Well." Rubio slaps his hands on his knees and stands. "I don't know about you two, but this is getting weird and I haven't slept well in three weeks. I'm going back up to the ship to catch some shut-eye." He disappears out the door after Freja, leaving Cassia and me alone.

We sit in silence for several minutes, not looking at each other.

"I should go, too," I mutter into my tea. "I should

update the *Mendicant*'s data banks while we have the chance."

"Fine," Cassia says. She doesn't look at me.

I sigh. "Cass, I—"

"Don't."

"I'm sorry," I say. "It was stupid of me to ask."

Cassia looks my way. "Yeah, it was."

"*Chaila*, Cass, I'm trying to apologize."

A short laugh escapes her. "That's really what's worrying you now, whether Freja and I—"

"No!"

Tears brim in Cassia's eyes. "Freja's right," she says quietly. "You bureaubrats have it so easy, you just don't get it."

"Get what?" I say, exasperated. "Cass, I gave up everything to come out here with you." My anger hardens around me as I say it. It's true. No more DSRI. No more research. My whole barren life is stretched out in front of me, and the person I gave it up for is yelling at me in the middle of a strange noodle shop on an iced-in moon.

"Oh, you're so noble, aren't you?" Cassia shakes her head. Her eyes are red and bitter. "You, you, you. It's all about you."

I lean back in the booth, stung. "What?"

Cassia shakes her head. "I should never have brought you into this. I should never have kissed you."

Blood rushes to my face. "That had nothing to do with me wanting to help."

"Right." Cassia raises her eyes to the ceiling, tears streaking gossamer lines down her cheeks.

I lean forward to answer, but a shuffling sound stops me.

Freja stands a few paces from the table, looking back and forth between the two of us. "Bad time?"

"No." Cassia sniffs and clenches her jaw.

"You sure?" Freja glares knives at me.

I goggle back at her. *Me?* I'm not the one picking a fight here.

"Of course." Cassia lifts her chin and smiles at Freja. "What'd Herr Tsukino say?"

Freja breaks her death glare and looks at Cassia. "He said yes. As long as you don't break up the sale, you can come to Ny Karlskrona with us. We'll see if we can find your brother."

CHAPTER .20

The waters outside Ny Kyoto are murky with sediment and light from the spindles. I watch through the back viewport of the Tsukinos' submersible as the ocean closes over the city like so many scarves layered one on top of the other. The light fades. I look away. The water feels heavier in the dark, somehow.

I close my eyes and lean back against the bulkhead. *Pressure on a submerged object is equal to fluid density times gravity acceleration times the height of any fluid above—*

Rubio nudges me. "What are you whispering about?"

My eyes fly open. "Nothing." My face flames. Was I saying that out loud?

Rubio gives me a look that says he's pretty sure I'm going mental, but before he can say anything, a massive shadow flickers across the viewport.

I yelp. "What was that?"

Freja peers out the window. "A harrow, probably. Don't worry, they won't attack anything with lights on it."

I glance nervously at the window. "You're sure?"

One of Freja's comrades snickers, and the rest of them exchange grins.

Freja smirks. "I think I know more about my own moon than you, bureaubrat."

Before I can respond, Freja's grandfather ducks in.

"All right, *besättning*, we're under way." He looks over the twelve of us in the passenger hold—Freja, Cassia, Rubio, eight of his people who met us on the dock, and me—then wipes his nose and stuffs the rag in his back pocket. "Another few hours, and we'll be at Rangnvaldsson's gates. I want a quick, clean handoff. No friendly-making with their crew, but no brawling, either. We help them unload, chop, chop—we're back on our way with full pockets."

His crew shifts in their seats, murmur their assent.

"You three." He points at Cassia, Rubio, and me. "A word up front." He jerks his head at the cockpit.

We follow him to the darkened front of the submersible. The ceiling hangs so low Rubio has to duck to fit in.

Herr Tsukino drops himself into the pilot's seat with a small grunt. The control panel lights his face, giving him a bluish pallor. Beyond the viewport, nothing shows but thick darkness and the occasional flicker of debris caught in the ship's perimeter lights.

He clears his throat. "I'm letting you come along on account of the good trade we've done with the Kalderos over the years." He shifts his eyes to Rubio and me. "But you two don't know me, so it's only fair warning: you ruin my trade, you're out on the ice." He extends a finger up, toward the surface.

Rubio and I exchange a look. The Enceladan surface is hundreds of degrees below zero. Even with a suit, out on the ice means dead in a matter of hours. A weak, nervous laugh escapes me.

"I'm not joking, girl." Herr Tsukino frowns. "I don't play games with my livelihood. Understand?"

"Right." I nod. "Sorry. Of course. Got it."

Herr Tsukino bobs his head at the door. "Go on, then. Rest up. We've got another six hours before we reach Rangnvaldsson's."

We shuffle out of the cockpit and start making our way back to the hold.

"Cassia," Herr Tsukino calls after her.

She follows him back to the darkened room. I pause, listening outside in the narrow corridor.

"About your brother . . . I'm sorry," he says gently. "It shouldn't happen. Not to anybody, but especially not after his wife—"

"Thank you." Cassia's voice is hard. "I appreciate all you've done for us."

"Have you thought . . ." Herr Tsukino pauses. "I know you don't want to hear this, but Enceladus is a big moon, and even if Rangnvaldsson did buy him, he might not be there still. Maybe it's better if there's someone around to take good care of that little girl of his. Might be what he'd want."

"What he'd want is to see her again."

Herr Tsukino's voice is quiet. "Even if it costs his sister's life?"

Silence. The back of my neck prickles and my palms itch.

Finally Cassia speaks. "Thank you again, Herr Tsukino." Her voice comes near to breaking.

I turn as she stalks out of the cockpit. "Cass—"

But she brushes by me and hurries away as if I haven't been standing there waiting for her.

The smell of fresh-cut flowers and lemongrass pervades the dock at Rangnvaldsson's. Everything is bright white, as blinding as snow. Even Rangnvaldsson's heavy machinery operators wear white. The Tsukino crew's worn brown jumpsuits and stained boots stand out like smudges against the pristine dock.

A woman with butter-yellow hair and a crisp sky-blue kimono patterned with lingonberries strides to Freja's grandfather, arms open wide. A cluster of attendants in the palest pastels shadow her.

"Tsukino-san. It's been too long."

"Fru Rangnvaldsson." Herr Tsukino inclines his head in a slight bow. "What do they say? 'Absence makes the heart grow fonder.'"

"And pockets lighter." Fru Rangnvaldsson offers her hand to Herr Tsukino. "Please, Tsukino-san, you're always so formal. You must call me Nanami."

So this is the woman who might have Nethanel. I glance at Cassia. She looks like she wants to tackle Fru Rangnvaldsson to the deck and knock out all of her perfectly bleached teeth.

Herr Tsukino grunts in what might be agreement and delivers a perfunctory kiss to the back of her hand. "The pockets we can fix. You want the cryatine here, or are we taking it to storage for you?"

Fru Rangnvaldsson smiles wide, but it doesn't reach

her eyes. "But, please, your crew must be famished. We have a dinner laid out for you. *Dozo*, come and eat. We can worry about cargo after."

"*Domo tack gozaimasu,*" Herr Tsukino answers. "How can we refuse such a generous offer?"

"You'll want to leave guards, of course." Fru Rangnvaldsson tilts her head at the submersible. "We'll bring a nice little something out to them."

"How kind." Herr Tsukino gives a stiff nod and locks eyes with two of his crew. "Shun. Alvar. You have the watch. Everyone else with me."

"This way." Fru Rangnvaldsson beckons us, kimono sleeves billowing.

I fall in close behind Freja and Herr Tsukino as we make our way down the hall, Cassia, Rubio, and the others following after. The walls glister like mother-of-pearl, and glowing nests of lights hang from the high ceiling.

"I can't tell you how delighted we are to renew trade with you, Tsukino-san," Fru Rangnvaldsson calls over her shoulder as she walks. "It's been so long since you had such interesting cargo."

A tinge of purple-red flares along Herr Tsukino's jawline. "Hmn," he grunts.

Freja doubles her steps to keep up with her grandfather.

"Shun and Alvar?" she hisses under her breath. "You shouldn't have split us up, Jiiji."

He slows his pace ever so slightly, lengthening their distance from Fru Rangnvaldsson, and speaks low. "Steady, Freja-chan. If things go badly, you make for the sub, understand?"

"Yes, Jiiji," she mutters, then glances back at me and scowls. I concentrate on the floor and try to keep up the polite fiction that I'm not listening.

"Take the tinker girl and her friends, too," Herr Tsukino says. "No one's going to say I let Rangnvaldsson or anyone else do harm to my guests."

Freja nods stiffly.

Ahead, the hallway opens onto a vast dining room with vaulted ceilings rising some twenty meters above our heads, a long table draped in snowy linen, and Lucite chairs lined up for the meal. More light nests shine above us, and glowing panels line the walls, chasing away any hint of shadow.

"Forgive the formality." Rangnvaldsson places a hand to her chest and waits as one of her attendants draws out the chair at the head of the table for her. "We were so thrilled to hear from you again, Tsukino-san. Perhaps we have gone too far?"

Herr Tsukino clears the phlegm from his throat.

"Not at all. We all love a good fish, don't we?" He glances down the table at the rest of us, a warning in his eye.

"Of course," Freja says a bit too loud. The rest of us nod along together.

We take our seats. A young woman in a powder-blue *yukata* circles the table, pouring a sour-smelling liquid the color of skimmed milk into each of our glasses. Circular panels at the center of the table slide back, and silver platters loaded with buttered turnips and what look like enormous rings of pale calamari rise into place. A pungent vinegar smell rolls off the plates.

"Please, help yourselves." Fru Rangnvaldsson smiles at us.

I slide a ring of fish onto my plate. To my right, Rubio attempts a bite and gags. Cassia and Freja glare at him.

"This one must be new to your crew." Fru Rangnvaldsson smiles. "Offworlders often tell me whiteroot is an acquired taste."

"Yes," Herr Tsukino agrees. Beads of sweat dot his hairline, even in the cool air of the dining room. "I have several new indentures I'm training."

"You'll come to like it, young man." Fru Rangnvaldsson nods knowingly at Rubio. "Your body needs the protein."

I lean close to Cassia and eye the not-calamari. "What's whiteroot?"

"It's a tuber worm that grows on the seafloor," she whispers back. "They harvest them when the summer currents come through and preserve them for later in the year."

"A tuber worm?"

"Don't be such a snob." Cassia takes a bite of her whiteroot and makes a face. "It's much better fresh."

"How is your daughter, Fru Rangnvaldsson?" Herr Tsukino asks. "Still seeing that luxuries trader in Ny Kyoto?"

Fru Rangnvaldsson smiles down at her drink. "Engaged."

"Congratulations," he says.

An awkward silence falls, full of the clink and scrape of forks. Freja nudges her grandfather. Cassia and I exchange a glance, and I bite the inside of my lip. Will he do what we've agreed?

Herr Tsukino scowls at her but turns to our host. "I wondered, Fru Rangnvaldsson . . . we're finding ourselves short on the labor end of things." He throws a meaningful look at the servant hovering behind her. "We thought you might have contacts that could help us turn up some extra warm bodies."

Fru Rangnvaldsson places her fork gently beside her plate, folds her fingers, and stares over them at him. "You're interested in sponsoring more indentures?"

Herr Tsukino's face darkens. He shifts his eyes to Cassia. "I was looking for something more . . . permanent."

The clinking of cutlery stops short.

Fru Rangnvaldsson raises an eyebrow. "Tsukino-san, I'm surprised at you." She wags a finger. "I thought you were against such practices. If I remember correctly, you called them *barbaric*, no?"

Herr Tsukino clears his throat and shoots a look at his granddaughter. I've seen Soraya give me that look before. *I'm doing this because I love you very much, but I also want to kill you a little bit.* "We've found it's . . . an unpleasant necessity."

"Yes, well, I can see that." Fru Rangnvaldsson nods slowly, as if she's considering Enceladan economics for the first time. "You spend time and money training indentures, and then you have them for, what? Three years? Five? That's quite a hit for small traders such as yourselves."

"That's . . . the whole of it." Herr Tsukino's face has turned a dangerous shade of purple red. He balls his dinner napkin in his fist.

Fru Rangnvaldsson picks up her fork and toys with

it, studying Herr Tsukino. I try to focus on my plate and pretend not to be interested, like the rest of the Tsukino crew. Everyone is studiously chewing their food, except Cassia. She stares at Fru Rangnvaldsson, nearly vibrating. I find her hand beneath the table. It's cold and clammy, as if she has a fever. *Please give us something, some small clue. . . .*

"I'm sorry to say, Tsukino-san, but I can't help you. We only deal in indentures here." Fru Rangnvaldsson spears another ring of whiteroot. "Small dealers can fly beneath Earth's notice, but we have contracts to keep. The International Orbital Patrol Authority, the Obremski Group, DSRI—"

My head snaps up. "DSRI?"

Rubio kicks me beneath the table, and Freja and her grandfather give me a death glare. Fru Rangnvaldsson looks at me as if I've merely lost my mind.

"You see what I have to work with." Herr Tsukino waves a hand at me. "Indentures!"

"I truly wish I could help you," Fru Rangnvaldsson says. "But the flesh trade isn't in our line."

Cassia pulls her hand from mine and wipes it furiously with her napkin. *Vaat.* Even if our hostess knows where Nethanel is, she's never going to admit it.

"In fact," Fru Rangnvaldsson says, "I had to turn away

a group of gentlemen selling exactly what you're talking about not three weeks ago."

Beside me, Cassia stiffens.

"Did you?" Herr Tsukino leans forward and attacks his turnips. "Any idea where they were bound, these gentlemen?"

"Someplace to the south." Fru Rangnvaldsson waves her hands vaguely. "Ny Skaderna, I think. But that's too far to be worth your while."

Ny Skaderna. That was on the *dakait*'s list. I force myself not to look at Cassia or Rubio, not to betray anything. *Ny Skaderna, Ny Skaderna. Don't forget.*

Herr Tsukino shoots a look at Cassia and grunts. "*Hai.* Too far."

Fru Rangnvaldsson picks up her cloudy white drink and examines it. "If you're short on funds, though, I have a proposition that might interest you." She takes a delicate sip and smiles at Freja's grandfather.

Herr Tsukino and Freja exchange a look. "What's that?"

"Yes, well . . ." Fru Rangnvaldsson pushes away her plate. "We're having a bit of a problem with harrows, you see."

"Harrows?" His eyebrows shoot up.

"One in particular. He's a big one. Smart. Not afraid of our perimeter lights."

"And you want us to . . ." Herr Tsukino trails off.

"I'm afraid we've reached the point where he needs to be destroyed." Fru Rangnvaldsson locks eyes with Freja's grandfather. "We're prepared to offer you a contract. Eleven hundred upfront, plus a twenty-five percent share in the profits from the rendered carcass."

"That's illegal, isn't it?" Herr Tsukino frowns. "Hunting harrows?"

"I have a special permit, of course." Fru Rangnvaldsson's smile is tight. "As I said, everything here has to be aboveboard."

Herr Tsukino kneads one hand into the other and looks down the table at his crew. "Fifteen hundred and a fifty percent share."

Fru Rangnvaldsson smiles. "We both know that's not fair market. What do you say to twelve hundred and a thirty-five percent share? More of my people will be in the water than yours."

Herr Tsukino works his jaw as if he's grinding something between his teeth. "Done." He sticks out a hand, and Fru Rangnvaldsson shakes it.

Too late, I realize Herr Tsukino's crew includes me. Which means I'm going harrow hunting.

CHAPTER .21

"I don't think I can do this." I stare down at the armored board I'm supposed to pilot through the water.

"It's not like you're out there without a shell," Freja says. She taps the controls on her own board, and a clear aerodynamic dome slides into place, enclosing her inside it. She trails her hand across the surface again, and it retracts. "See?"

"It's not that. I . . ."

"What, are you afraid?" Freja stares at me, half disbelieving, half delighted.

"Come on, cut it out," Rubio says. "Miyole's a scientist, not a big-game hunter. She's not used to this kind of thing."

I grit my teeth. "Thanks, Rubio."

"What?" He blinks at me.

"If you don't want to help, you can stay here," Cassia mutters.

Freja looks up. "No, she can't."

"No," I agree, gripping the board. "I can't."

I lie down on the board, seal the dome over me, and try to breathe deep. I will not hyperventilate. I will not throw up. I will not cry.

We exit Rangnvaldsson's spindle and glide through the warm-water docks. My hands won't stop sweating. The perimeter lights illuminate the skeletons of ships growing in the ocean's natural nutrient bath, the new ones no more than a spiderweb-thin scaffolding, the older ones beginning to develop the sheen of mature nacre. They'll be sold as modular replacement grafts. Some of them are probably even marked for the DSRI already.

"Five hundred meters west, twenty fathoms down," Herr Tsukino's voice crackles across our open coms. "Big bioelectric signature."

I glance back. Rangnvaldsson's people make up the left flank, with Cassia, Rubio, me, Freja, and the rest of the Tsukino crew on the right, all of us on boards. Freja's grandfather follows behind us in the submersible.

"I want a net formation," he says. "We come in quiet, surround it on all sides, and close in slow. No one fires until it notices us."

We pass over tube-worm groves blanketing the ocean

floor. Their bodies flare white in the beams from our boards, with a bloodred portion protruding at the tip, like an engorged tongue. I shudder and concentrate on the water before us. It makes it easier to pretend it's the familiar darkness of space, not an icebound sea.

"Coming up ahead," Herr Tsukino says. "Be ready to cut your lights and go to heat vision on my signal."

The seabed drops down, and the pressure inside my dome increases, like a blood pressure cuff squeezing my entire body. Jagged rock formations appear in the periphery of our lights, venting a great dark flume into the water above.

"What is that?" Rubio's voice comes in at a whisper. "Smoke?"

"It's blackwater," Freja answers. "It's full of minerals."

"That's what keeps everything down here alive without any sunlight, right?" I say. "The water gets superheated by the geothermal vents and the sea stays warm." I know I'm babbling, but I'm too nervous to stop.

"A-plus, bureaubrat," Freja says, but I hear a note of surprise in her voice.

"Too much chatter," Herr Tsukino's voice breaks in. "Heat vision, everyone."

I toggle the controls like Freja showed us. At once, the world is a deep black blue, with white-hot streams shooting up where the blackwater vents were before. The other boarders are a dimmer red, silently angling through the water like Humboldt squid. And then, beyond another cluster of vents, we see it—a thick, sinuous body laid across the abyssal plain, lit up in cold, spectral blue.

"Chaila," I whisper. The harrow could easily swallow the submersible, to say nothing of the forty or so of us in the water. It lies between a series of smaller vents, warming itself against them. It might be asleep, but the heat vision makes it impossible to tell whether or not its eyes are closed. *If it has eyes.* I wipe my hands on my sleeves.

"Fan out," Herr Tsukino says quietly.

I guide my board up into position. We form a sort of domed net around the harrow. No matter which way it swims, one of us will be there to fire on it. The beast lifts its head, maybe sensing the subtle vibrations in the water, and opens its mouth as if tasting the current. I kill my board's propulsion power. Maybe I'm not in exactly the position Herr Tsukino wanted, but it's close enough.

"Now," he says.

Our rough noose of red stars begins to close on the harrow. Fifty meters. Forty. Thirty.

The harrow lifts its head again.

Twenty-five. Twenty. Fifteen.

The harrow whips to the left, then up at the divers above it. It opens its mouth. A deep wave of sound I more feel than hear shudders through my chest. I release the board's throttle without meaning to.

In one fluid movement, the harrow rises from the ocean floor and lunges at one of the divers. The coms erupt in noise.

". . . ten degrees—"

"Watch it, Sila—"

"Pull in!"

"Firing!"

A bright flash erupts at my left, and something yellow-warm spills from the harrow's side. The beast screams—a ripple of sound I feel through my body—and jerks away. Another flash. Another spill of heat that dissipates into the cold water.

Blood, I realize. *It's blood.*

To my right, Freja surges forward, followed by Cassia and Rubio.

"Bureaubrat." Freja's voice fills my ears. "Keep up. You're leaving a hole in the net."

I fumble at my controls. Below me, the harrow writhes, spouting streams of blood. It rolls left, impossibly fast for something so large, crushing against a low rocky ridge.

"Watch out!"

"On your ten!"

"Up!"

Quick, too quick, one of the boards disappears beneath the harrow's body. My coms fill with an animal scream.

"Cass!" I shout. *Please don't let it be her. Please don't let it be her.* I push my board into a dive. It can't be her. She can't die like this, not when we're so close to finding her brother. It's impossible to tell which red smudge is who, and the coms are a chaos of shrieks and screams, the harrow's subaudible howls shaking through everything.

"Miyole!" Rubio's voice reaches me through the clamor. "She's . . ." But then the shouts and static drown him out again.

I reach for the throttle, but my hand slips on the controls. Heat vision drops away, and my board's lights flicker on. The beam falls on the horror below me. A great, pale, eel-like creature with blank white eyes writhes against the seabed, stirring up clouds of gray-black silt and trailing plumes of blood. It flinches from the light, then whips around and surges toward me, bellowing.

"Lights, Miyole! Lights!" Rubio shouts.

I turn my board and push the throttle, the harrow following mere meters behind me. *Turn the lights off, turn the lights off.* But how? I start to hyperventilate. Fear has wiped my mind clean. The harrow bears down on me like a lev train.

"Top right screen, bureaubrat. Externals." Freja's voice is firm over the coms. It's what I need. "The yellow circle. See it?"

Externals. I see it. I tap the controls and the lights extinguish. Back to heat vision. The water in front of me is a flat, dark blue mass punctuated by the bright, condensed burn of the blackwater vents. The board's protective dome vibrates as the harrow bellows again, closer than ever. I glance back. Its mouth gapes open, revealing a second set of jaws inside.

A hot spike of fear shoots through me. I push the board as fast as I can, mind racing. The harrow's screaming—could that be some form of echolocation? Sound waves rebounding off objects, creating a rough map for the creature. The frequency and intensity of the echoes differentiating me from the vents or the water around me. I look down. If I'm right, I could flatten out the sound waves reflecting back to the harrow by dropping close to the seabed.

I dive. The harrow snaps at me, the tip of its snout jostling my board. I drop low over the barren floor, but still it follows. *Not enough.* I maneuver lower, letting my board skim the rocks and silt and sending up cloudy furrows behind me. The drag slows me, but the harrow pulls back, too. I can lose it. If I keep going, I can lose it.

"Miyole, what are you doing?" Cassia's voice breaks in on the coms.

"Cass!" She's okay. She's alive.

"Bring it back around," Cassia barks. "You're leading it away from us."

"It's too fast." My voice pitches high. "It's going to kill me."

"Turn around," Cassia says. "We can't help you if you're moving away from us."

My hands are wet on the board's controls. I pull up, leaving the safety of the silt cloud. The harrow barrels after me. Cassia and the rest of the divers hover several hundred meters away, dim red dots in the distance.

"Faster, Miyole!" It's Rubio.

"I'm not going to make it!" I shout.

"We're coming to meet you." Freja's voice. "Just keep moving."

The harrow jostles me again. I cut right and dive low, sending up another cloud of grit. *Variances in interaural time difference indicate location. . . .*

A huge blackwater vent rises before me, jetting its

superheated current into the frigid ocean. Wait . . . a jet. Yes.

I pull away from the floor and power on the board's lights.

"What are you doing?" Freja shouts. "You're making it mad."

I cut off my coms. I know what an incredibly terrible idea this is, and I need all my concentration to pull it off without getting myself killed.

The harrow howls and snakes after me. I glide low, the nose of my board pointed at the blackwater vent. I've eaten plenty of eel in my life. I only hope this one cooks like all the others. Out of the corner of my eye, I see the creature closing on me, but then I'm at the base of the vent and it's time. I jerk up on the controls, taking my board nearly vertical against its side. Blackwater billows above us, hot enough to sear flesh and boil me alive if I get too close. The harrow surges after me.

I tug the controls left at the last second, skirting the vent's mouth. The harrow plunges straight through the simmering jet. Its scream reverberates through my bones and fills my ears like water. The board's dome rattles around me. My lights flicker and the primary power dies, sending me spiraling headfirst into the rough seabed. I brace myself as the board hits, bounces, rolls. I land upside down, tipped against a rocky mound, my board's lights strobing.

The world swims, a kaleidoscope of alarms and half-frozen glimpses of the harrow writhing in the flickering lights. Darkness. Teeth. Its great blind eyes rolling. And then the shapes of boards above me, descending on the harrow. They swarm around the monster. It thrashes beneath them, its blood filling the ocean, until at last it shudders and lies still.

CHAPTER .22

The sound of my own panting fills my ears. I reach out and flip the coms back on. "Hello?"

"There she is." I hear Rubio's voice, full of relief. "She made it."

"Tell her she's as lucky as she is stupid," Freja says.

The blood in my face might be from hanging upside down, or it might not. "I . . . um . . . lost propulsion," I say. "What do I do?"

"Stay there," Freja says. "We're coming for you."

One of Rangnvaldsson's crew hitches my board to the back of his own, while Freja does the same for the diver injured when the harrow first rolled. The rest of the divers drive massive hooks into the harrow and attach lines to the back of Herr Tsukino's submersible. We drag the harrow's corpse behind us, all the way back to Rangnvaldsson's headquarters.

We're met on the dock with congratulatory applause and medics for the injured.

"Beautifully done." Fru Rangnvaldsson clasps Herr Tsukino's hands. "Congratulations on a clean hunt."

"It wasn't entirely clean." He glances at the injured diver being hurried away on a stretcher.

Fru Rangnvaldsson waves a hand. "The cost of doing business."

I catch Freja's eye. Would she be saying that if she had been in the water with us, listening to the woman's screams?

"You're welcome to warm yourselves in the salt baths," Fru Rangnvaldsson says. "We wouldn't want our guests catching a chill."

The baths are a series of honeycombed rooms, each one with a deep oval basin and walls carved out of pale pink salt. I sink up to my neck in the steaming bath, close my eyes, and try not to see the harrow chasing me through the icy darkness. The warm salt water buoys me and eases the cramps in my muscles. I drop my head below the water and massage my scalp. This is a million times better than the best hot shower I've ever taken back in Mumbai, and a million squared compared to the cold rag baths we got by with on the *Mendicant*. It's like sitting in my own private stretch of shallow, sun-warmed ocean.

I finally step out of the bath, rub my hair with a towel, and wrap myself in one of the fluffy blue robes hanging on the inside of the chamber door. I pad down the steamy halls, finally feeling warm for the first time in over a month. And weirdly hungry. Now if I could have a nice bowl of udon and sleep for a week . . .

A small laugh from somewhere ahead interrupts my napping fantasy.

A girl's voice. "Here?"

I round the corner. "Cass?"

In the steaming mist, I make out two figures in robes, one with sleek black hair in a ponytail and one with her wet curly hair hanging in hanks around her shoulders. Time slows. Freja and Cassia. They pull apart, but it's too late. I can't unsee Cassia's lips on Freja's, Freja's hand threaded into Cassia's hair.

Cassia's face drops. "Mi . . ."

All the warmth drains from my chest. I am the harrow, speared through its heart. I don't wait to hear what she has to say. I run.

I grab my freshly washed clothes from a cubby near the salt baths' entrance and dress hurriedly in the changing room. My vision blurs as I bend to tie my boots. I'm not going to think about it.

I stand, my chest heaving against the unbearable pressure. It hurts. Not only my heart, my whole body. I kick the pink salt wall. *Vaat.* Moving makes the pressure more bearable, so I do it again and again and again. Screw Cassia and that *kuttiya.* I rub the wet blur from my eyes. I should have known.

"Miss?" A woman with a soft voice knocks on the door. "Are you well, miss?"

I stop, suddenly conscious of the small animal sounds escaping me with each kick. "I'm fine," I call back, but my voice wavers.

A pause. And then, "Forgive me, miss. I'm coming in."

I quickly straighten out my shirt, suddenly aware that my hair is a half-dried mess and my eyes are puffy.

A young woman in the pale blue *yukata* of Rangnvaldsson's servants slips inside and closes the door behind her. I've seen her before. She was in the dining room, standing behind Fru Rangnvaldsson as we ate. She takes in my bloodshot eyes and wild hair.

"I heard about what happened with the harrow," she says quietly. "Anyone would be shaken, miss."

"It's not that. . . ." I look away and stop.

"I can fetch a cooling soak for your eyes if you like, miss."

"No, that's okay. And you don't need to call me *miss*." It's too much like Rubio's old *memsahib*.

She falls silent for a moment. "May I ask you something, miss?"

I sigh and sit heavily on the dressing room's padded bench. "Sure."

"You came with Herr Tsukino, yes?"

I nod. "That's right."

She glances over her shoulder and lowers her voice almost to a whisper. "He was asking about slaves."

The word hits me like a wall. *Slaves.* No one else has said it plainly. The pit of my stomach drops, and I swallow. What am I doing wallowing in self-pity when there are other human beings enslaved around me? "Look . . . we're not really trying to—"

"I know," she interrupts softly.

I look up. "You do?"

She sits next to me on the bench. "I was brought here on a slaver seven months ago. But they tried to sell me in Ny Kyoto first. Herr Tsukino was one of the few who didn't even want to listen to my captors' pitch." Her voice is no more than a murmur. She smiles to herself. "He even spit on their captain. I like to think he did that for me."

"But . . . I thought Rangnvaldsson only kept indentured servants." I stare at her. She can't be much older than I am.

She shrugs. "That's what my paperwork says. That Rangnvaldsson sponsored the cost of my transport here, and I'm to compensate them with seven years of service. But they'll only draw up new documents when those years are up. Some of the other servants and laborers have been here twenty, thirty years."

I lean over and rest my head on my knees, the pieces of her story clicking together. Rangnvaldsson keeps slaves. The DSRI buys from her. The *Ranganathan* might have even have grown in the warm-water docks we passed on our way to hunt the harrow. All those pleasant gardens, the galleys and living quarters, my own odd little lab where I gazed out at the stars—they were built on this, the very thing my mother's people fought and died to end hundreds and hundreds of years ago. This thing that is supposed to be a dark chapter in Earth's history, not something that has traveled with us out into the stars. I feel sick.

I sit up. "What can I do?"

"Nothing," she says. "Not for me. Not right now, anyway."

Despair sucks at me. "What, then?"

"There was a boy. A young man," she says. "He had the same marks on his face as that girl has. What do you call them?" She gestures over the bridge of her nose, where Cassia's freckles are the densest.

"Freckles." My head feels light.

She nods. "Yes, that."

"Was he deaf? He couldn't hear?"

She frowns. "Maybe." Her eyes widen as if she's just solved an equation. "Yes. He never spoke. They said his brain was stunted, but he was always watching everything. Sharp eyes."

I stand. "That's her brother. Did you . . . is he here?"

She shakes her head. "He's not here. They took him south with all the rest Fru Rangnvaldsson didn't want. I can give you the name."

Dye mon, gen mon, my mother would say. Beyond the mountain, another mountain.

"Please," I say. "Yes."

She hands me a scrap of paper.

Cryatics Wholesale, Zaius Shelf Port. One of the *dakait's* other stops.

I look up from the paper and frown. "Fru Rangnvaldsson said they went to Ny Skaderna after here."

The girl shakes her head. "They had already been to

Ny Skaderna when they stopped here. That's where they were going next." She points to the paper. "You hear bad things about Kazan Spindle. I was lucky to be sold here."

A chill runs up my spine, despite the humid air.

"Thank you." I tuck the paper inside my shirt. "Are you sure . . . I mean, isn't there anything we can do to help you?"

She looks uncertain. "You know people in the DSRI, don't you?"

"How . . ."

She purses her lips. "I saw your face when Fru Rangnvaldsson said it."

"I guess I do. I mean, I did."

"I hear they don't allow this sort of thing. What Rangnvaldsson and those slavers do." She fixes me with a meaningful look.

"They don't." The image of Commander Dhar at the head of the officers' table comes back to me. Her refusing to lift a finger to save Nethanel. "But I don't know if they'd do anything about it."

"But they might," she insists. "They're the closest thing to civilization that makes it out here into the reaches. How could they ignore a thing like this? If you told them . . ."

I look down at my hands. Even if the DSRI would do anything, I'm on the run from them.

"I'm sorry," I say, guilt crawling over me. "I don't know if I have a way of doing that anymore."

She looks crestfallen. "Then come back for us," she finally says. "After you find that boy, after you free him, come back and do the same for us."

"We . . ." I swallow. I don't want to promise something I can't deliver. "We might not even make it out alive."

"If you do, though," she says. "Promise."

"Okay," I say. "I promise . . ."

"Petya," she offers.

"Petya," I repeat. "I promise."

CHAPTER 23

Herr Tsukino's crew sings shanties all the way back to Ny Kyoto. They have their payment for the cryatine and an advance from Rangnvaldsson on the proceeds from the rendered harrow. I huddle at the back of the submersible and pretend to sleep so I won't be asked to join in.

Cassia catches my arm as we disembark. "Miyole, I . . ." She looks away, and then back at me. "Can we talk?"

I cast a weary glance at Freja, standing at the top of the submersible's loading ramp. "Not now, okay?"

"I just want to—"

"Not now." My eyes burn. I blink, trying to hold in the tears. The last thing I need is to break down crying in front of Cassia.

Freja hurries down the ramp to us. "It's not her fault." Her voice is a low growl.

"Chup kar, soover chod!" I spit. It doesn't matter that they can't understand my words. My tone is enough.

"Come on, Cass." Freja puts an arm around Cassia's shoulders and pulls her away, glaring at me.

More guilt joins the awful loneliness in my chest as I watch them hurry off. Everything Cassia has done since we pulled her from the wreck of her family's ship has been out of grief. Maybe this is the same. But then why was she laughing when she kissed Freja?

Rubio bumps my shoulder. "What was that about? Lovebird issues?"

I scowl at him.

"Whoa." He holds up his hands in surrender. "What's wrong, Sour Face? You killed that harrow almost all on your own. And none of us are dead. You should be celebrating."

My shoulders slump. "Cassia and Freja . . ."

Rubio cocks an eyebrow. "I never pegged you for the jealous girlfriend type."

"I walked in on them kissing."

"Oh." He looks deeply uncomfortable. "So, does that mean . . . I mean, are the two of you done, then?"

"I think so," I say miserably.

"I'm really sorry, Miyole." He puts an arm around my

shoulders and gives me an awkward shake that I think might be a hug. "Feelings are the worst."

"Yeah," I agree. "They're the worst."

"I'd offer to beat Freja up for you, but I think she might stab me."

I let out a short laugh. "She definitely would."

He gives me a look that's either sympathy or pity. Maybe both. "Well, if you want to come punch some more holes in the *Mendicant*'s siding with me . . ."

I look away. I'm rubbed too thin to keep this up. "Thanks."

"Okay, then." Rubio stuffs his hands in his pockets. We stand in awkward silence for a moment.

"If there's something I'm supposed to be doing, you have to tell me," he says. "I usually get my friends drunk when they break up, but, I don't know . . . is that a guy thing?"

"Probably not." I don't have any idea what I'm supposed to do, either. Does anyone have a frame of reference for a breakup in the middle of an extrajudicial rescue mission? I close my eyes. "I think I just want to be alone for a little bit."

"Yeah, sure." Rubio pats my arm and starts to walk away.

That's when I remember—*Petya. Cryatics Wholesale.*

I open my eyes. "Rubio! Wait."

He stops and turns back.

I shove the piece of paper into his hand. "There is something. Get back to the *Mendicant*. See if you can plot our route here."

I'm alone with a cup of tea when Cassia finds me in the Tsukinos' galley. I'm starting to get used to it without the usual milk, spice, and sweetness. At least it keeps me warm.

"Hey." She gestures to the bench across from me. "Can I sit?"

I nod.

She slides in but doesn't say anything. I sip my tea.

"Mi," she says quietly.

I look up. I still want to kick all the walls, but her face . . . the way she bites the corner of her lip . . .

"I should never have done it," she says.

I soften a fraction. "I'm not going to pretend I'm not mad—"

"No. I mean, I should never have started anything with you. Or Freja. With anyone." She looks up at me. "I'm a mess, Mi. I needed something to keep me from thinking about Nethanel every minute. About what they were doing to him."

"You were using me," I say flatly. *It's better when you're here. It's distracting.*

"It's more than that." She reaches across the table. "I needed you."

I pull my hands away and wrap them tight around my mug. "But not anymore?"

She looks away. "I can't keep manipulating people like this. It's not fair."

"You didn't manipulate me." I shake my head, frustrated. "I wanted to make sure Milah got her father back even before I . . ."

. . . fell in love with you, I don't finish.

She stares down at the table. "You should leave. You should go find your research ship. Tell them I kidnapped you or blackmailed you or something. Same as Rubio."

I think about it. Go back to my comfortable life aboard the *Ranganathan*, where the worst thing that can happen is that I don't get my own lab. Make notes on pollinator mutations and follow a regimen of carefully calibrated exercise and nutrition. Keep my life going along the trajectory I set when I was still in pigtails. How can I do that now, when I know other people are being bought and sold out here in the Deep? When I've seen the brutality it brings out? When I know how the DSRI fits in to it all? How can I turn my back on Nethanel and Petya and everyone like them?

I shake my head. "I'm not leaving."

Cassia looks at me like I'm stark raving mad.

"I'm not joking, Cass." I see my *manman* looking up at me through the storm. My *manman* putting down the man who hurt her, the man with my eyes. I know what she would do in my place. I stand. "Come on."

She looks up in surprise. "Where are we going?"

"To Kazan Spindle," I say. "To find your brother."

The *Mendicant* rises back to the surface. Rubio flies, with me in the copilot's seat, while Cassia stays in the common room. We've left Tibbet with Freja and her grandfather. There's no place for him where we're going.

The moon's surface is pristine, broken only by the clusters of spindle towers that mark the location of each settlement beneath the ice. Most of the air traffic peters out south of Ny Kyoto, and then drops and drops as we near the south pole, until we are alone in the air.

"You don't have to come with us, you know," I say to Rubio. "You didn't sign up for this."

"I know." He shifts in the pilot's seat and frowns out the front viewport.

"You could still go back. Stay with the Tsukinos and signal the *Ranganathan*."

He raises an eyebrow. "Me and Tibbet?"

I roll my eyes at him. "You know what I mean."

Rubio stays quiet a moment. He checks the altimeter and fuel readouts. "You know I have a little sister back at Apex?" he says finally.

"No," I say. "I didn't."

"I do," he says. "Two sisters, actually, but the younger one's fifteen. She wants to be a biochemist."

"Yeah?" I try to imagine Rubio's sister, a younger version of him, maybe a little more awkward, a little less cocksure. Future biochemist. I smile.

"She's my kid sister, you know?" He takes his eyes off the viewport and looks at me. "I'd do anything to protect her."

"Yeah." I think I know what he means. "It's funny Cass feels that way about Nethanel when he's the older—"

"No," Rubio says. "I'm not talking about Nethanel."

I frown at him. Who is he talking about, then?

"You have a sister, too, right?" Rubio says. "And a mom? Or is it a foster mother?"

"Ava and Soraya." I look at my palms, at the scars.

"So you don't think they want to protect you as much

as Cassia wants to protect Nethanel?" Rubio looks almost angry, gripping the push bars and grinding his jaw. I've never seen him like this before.

"Rubio—"

"Don't you think they need you to come back as much as Cassia and Milah need Nethanel?" Rubio's face has gone red. "Don't you think they care just as much?"

"I . . ." I haven't really thought about that. "I guess they do. But I don't have a kid. I don't have anyone depending on me like Nethanel does."

"You sure about that?" Rubio asks.

I shrug. Ava and Soraya love me, but they don't depend on me. The only things that have ever truly depended on me were the butterflies, and someone else could care for them as easily as I could. There's nothing unique about me, nothing irreplaceable. So doesn't my life have more worth if I'm using it to save other people?

We fly in on in silence. The cryovolcano appears on the horizon, its peak disappearing in the swirl of snow and ice erupting from its top. Rubio keeps our altitude low, beneath the stratum of ice fanning out into the upper atmosphere, but even so, the air currents jostle us wildly. Cassia climbs out of the berth and straps herself into one of the passenger chairs at the back of the cockpit. We touch down beside the lone tower that marks Kazan Spindle, near blind from the haze of falling snow.

Rubio stares out at the storm. "Well, at least we'll die in an interesting way."

I think it's more likely we'll die under the surface than out in the cold, but I won't say that aloud. The plan is that we'll present ourselves as itinerant workers in search of a quick job that will give us money for ship repairs. We look the part, anyway. And if what we've heard is right and we're lucky, we'll find Nethanel down there.

I turn from the viewport. "Are you both okay with this?"

"Of course not," Rubio says. "But I haven't had a better idea."

"You could have stayed in Ny Kyoto with Tibbet," Cassia mutters.

"Nah." Rubio throws an arm around her. "I'm the one with security experience, right? I can't let you two wander off and get killed."

I lean over the controls and peer out the viewport. We're well inside the landing pad, but we haven't moved since we set down. "Shouldn't they have read us by now? Why aren't they bringing us down?"

We exchange worried glances.

"It's a small station." Cassia chews on her lip. "Maybe they don't man it unless they're expecting someone."

"Too bad our long-range coms are shot." Rubio kicks at the wall. "We could send out a call and check."

Cassia scowls. "It's not my fault they burned out. I'm not the one that installed a damper and then shoved in the directional."

Rubio sighs. "I'm not blaming you. All I'm saying is your man Sweetie saddled us with the worst ship imaginable."

"*My man* Sweetie—"

A soft beep sounds from the instrument panel.

"Hey, cut it out." I point to the telemetry readout. "Listen."

Cassia and Rubio fall silent. A small beep sounds, and a light pulses on the screen.

Rubio's head snaps up to the viewport. "Something's out there?"

I squint outside. Nothing but white, nothing but blinding, driving snow, the base of the tower barely visible through it.

The beep and pulse come through again, faster this time, closer.

I lean over the controls and peer out the viewport.

"What is it?" Cassia asks behind me.

"Dunno," Rubio answers. "It's alive, but other than that, I can't tell."

Pulse . . . beep. Closer.

A small dark shape resolves against the white, walking toward us. I suck in a breath. "Look." I nudge Rubio's arm.

The figure draws nearer. A person, out in the storm.

"Someone from the spindle?" he says.

"Must be," I agree. "But why only one of them?"

"We should suit up," Rubio says. "Go out there and meet them."

"We can't," Cassia says.

"Why not?"

"Because it's -261 degrees outside," Cassia says. "You need a full suit out there and all of ours are full of rat holes."

"Cryonecrosis," I mutter, staring at the tiny figure in the snowstorm.

Cassia and Rubio turn to me in tandem and give me a strange look.

I clear my throat. "Frostbite," I explain. "Instant frostbite." Apparently, my brain is still spotty on the first seven years of my life, but it's plenty good at trivia.

"Why can't we use the deep suits?" Rubio says. "I mean, we don't need them to hold pressure, only to keep out the cold, so the rat holes shouldn't matter."

I shake my head. "You'd end up looking like that cheese—the one with the holes."

"Swiss?" Rubio says.

"Can we please stop talking about cheese?" Cassia raises her voice.

She points to the viewport, where the figure has stopped several dozen meters from our ship. It lifts an arm and gives an exaggerated wave.

"They're waiting for us," she says.

My body goes cold. The *dakait* are waiting for us. They're all there, underneath our feet.

"Someone has to go." Cassia gives me a meaningful look.

"What?"

"Someone has to meet them." She tilts her head and widens her eyes at me.

"Vaat," I curse. Because we do have one working deep suit. Mine.

CHAPTER · 24

Out on the surface, everything is silent and gloom-blue. The wind skitters across the ground, sending eddies of snow snaking over the plain. I walk stiffly, layered in my pressure suit, then the body armor, then a long coat lined with synthesized fur that the Tsukinos gave us. I wipe the powder from my faceplate and struggle to the figure waiting among the drifts.

My welcoming party wears a long, hooded coat like mine, mirrored goggles, and some sort of device that looks like a re-breather covering the lower half of its face. She— or he?—taps the side of her head, signaling to me to turn on my short-range coms.

I switch them on and give a thumbs-up.

A man's voice fills my headset. "Your ship's com receiver's off-line." He sounds scratchy, like a toad with a sore throat, but I'm not sure how much of that is his transmitter.

"I know. We found a . . . I mean, it shorted."

He cocks his head to the side. "You lost?"

"This is Kazan Spindle, right?" I say cautiously. "We're looking for Cryatics Wholesale."

He nods. "One and the same. What do you want?"

"My friends and I . . ." I wave back at the *Mendicant*. "We're looking for work. Our ship's in bad repair."

"*Sasuga.*" He snorts and stares over the whipping snow at the spot where we landed. "How many?"

"Three," I say. "Just the three of us."

"We'll have to see what our recruiter says." He nods at the ship. "Tell them they should come out."

"They can't," I say. My coms whine with feedback, and I raise my voice over the noise. "We don't have enough pressure suits. Like I said, we need some repairs—"

"They'll have to ride down in the ship, then," he says.

"No problem," I say. "Let me just—"

"Transit," he interrupts. "Bring her under."

A hum builds under the ice, almost imperceptible at first, but rising until I feel it in my chest. A crack reverberates across the snow. A neat circle of ice around the *Mendicant* drops half a meter, taking the ship with it.

"What are you doing?" I yelp. If these people are the ones who have Nethanel, the last thing we want is to be split up. "Shouldn't I go with them?"

"No need." Our envoy sounds bored. "You can ride down the spindle with me. It's much more comfortable."

"But—" I glance back at the *Mendicant*, slowly sinking on its plate of ice. *Vaat.*

"You'll see your shipmates on the other side." The man trudges a few paces, then turns back for me. "Come on. It's *förkylning* out here. You want to freeze to death?"

I hesitate for a moment, staring into the storm. I don't really have a choice. The *Mendicant* is gone. There's nothing else but the spindle for thousands of kilometers around. It's follow him or take my chances with hypothermia and oxygen deprivation, so I hurry after him through the snow.

"You can take off your mask now," says the man once we're aboard the spindle's creaking lift. He does the same, revealing a flushed round face and tousled red hair pulled up in the same topknot every *dakait* I've met has worn. His beard brushes his chest. "So hot, these things." He still sounds like a frog.

I unseal my helmet and tuck it under my arm. My hair is probably as wild as his. I try to comb it down with my fingers and then give up. Why should I care about impressing a bunch of *jhaant ke pissu* who buy and sell their fellow human beings?

The redheaded man stares at me.

"What?" I look down at my suit. Melting snow clings to my coat and boots, but his clothes are no different. Unease creeps in at the base of my stomach.

"Nothing." He grins. "It's been awhile since we've seen a *kurai tös* around here, that's all. The boys will eat you up with a spoon."

I don't know what he's called me, but the way he says it makes my skin crawl. *Careful, Miyole.* If we were anywhere but here, I'd come back at him with something smart. But we are here, and I'm alone, so I set my jaw and stay quiet.

"That's a right pretty suit for someone whose ship needs repairing." The man raises an eyebrow at me.

I glare back. "It belonged to the last person who asked me too many questions." It's a line I picked up watching talkies with Rushil, and it sounds significantly less tough coming out of my mouth than from an ancient screen cowboy.

He laughs. "Okay, *lillflicka*. Fits you nice, though."

"Miyole," I say.

"Miyole," he repeats with a smile. "You can call me Rött."

The smell of mildew grows as the lift carries us down. Through the carriage's open frame, rusted metal sheets bolted onto the spindle's nacre glide into view. Images from my History of Medicine course skip through my head—metal pins and plates holding together bone. A shiver travels down from my occipital lobe to the back of my neck. I concentrate on the clack and squeak of the lift, and the ever-deepening shaft growing above me.

Rött leans against the side of the carriage. "What kind of work are you looking for?"

"Whatever's needed." It's what Cassia told us to say, what her parents always said when they wanted a job. "What is it you do here?"

"You have any experience diving?" he asks.

I think of the harrow. "A little."

"Maybe we can use you, then." The lift jolts, and he rocks with it. "How long are you wanting to sign on?"

I swallow, trying to force down the feeling that my stomach wants to climb up out of my throat. I look him in the eye. "As long as it takes."

He laughs. "Don't you have someone waiting for you back wherever you're from?"

"Doesn't everybody?" I say.

Rött frowns out of the side of the lift, looking at

something I can't see. "You'd be surprised." He turns back to me, smile in place again. "Where'd you say you're from?"

I look up. I can't see the top of the shaft anymore. "Does it matter?"

He shrugs. "It's all the same to me."

The lift slows to a stop with a shriek. The doors roll open exactly as the *Mendicant* rises, dripping, from an air lock built into the floor. I start toward it, but Rött pulls me back.

"Not so fast, *lillflicka*."

"Let go." I try to shrug out of his grip, but his fingers dig into my shoulder where the armor doesn't cover it.

"You're hurting me." Fear edges into my voice.

Rött laughs. "Believe me, *tös*, when I'm hurting you, you'll know."

I swallow. My palms are clammy inside my gloves. Do they suspect us? I've never seen Rött before, so how could they? Did my DSRI suit give us away? Rött walks me forward until we're within sight of the *Mendicant*. The mirroring on the front viewport makes it impossible to see in, but I know Rubio and Cassia are watching from inside. Something clicks and whines behind me, and then rises and rests cold against my temple.

Rött releases my shoulder. He raises his free hand to

the *Mendicant*, makes a sharp, beckoning motion with it, and then presses the gun harder against my head. I close my eyes. *Pressure is equal to force divided by area. Force equals mass times acceleration.*

The ship's doors open, and Cassia and Rubio walk down the ramp, hands up. A group of men with slug guns across their shoulders file out from behind the *Mendicant* and surround them.

"Don't be shy, little children." Rött smiles. "Come out, come out."

"What are you doing?" My voice shakes. "We just came looking for work."

"Did you now?" Rött circles around to face me. "Take off your coat."

"What?"

"Take off your coat." Rött gestures with the gun. His smile is gone.

Vaat. I fumble with the zipper, pull one arm out, then the other. The coat falls in a pile at my feet, exposing the body armor I'm wearing over my pressure suit.

"Where did you get this?" Rött taps the plating over my abdomen with his gun.

"We bought it." I shoot a look at Cassia and Rubio. "From a junker in Ny Kyoto."

"Interesting." He raises his eyebrows. "Some tinkers who are only looking for a job spent enough for three sets of armor, and yet they say they don't have the money to fix their ship."

I stay silent.

"We lost a ship a few weeks back," Rött says. "And three good crewmen, kitted out with armor a lot like what you have here. You wouldn't happen to have seen them, would you?"

I glare at him, gritting my teeth. I will not look at Cassia. I will not give anything else away.

Rött signals to one of his crew. "Juna."

A woman with broad shoulders and her hair in the same topknot as the men steps forward.

"Take these three down to confinement. We'll see if they're feeling more talkative after some time in the dark."

Juna pins my arms behind me in one swift movement.

I struggle against her. "You're making a mistake. We're DSRI. They'll come looking for us."

Rött laughs. "Who do you think our best buyer is?"

"You're lying," I say. Maybe the DSRI would buy from Rangnvaldsson, but not here. Not from outright slavers.

Rött shrugs. "One thing I know for sure, that's no

government ship you flew in on. I'm willing to bet a pretty penny no one knows you're here."

My heart sinks. I said too much. *Just the three of us. Our ship's in bad repair. We don't have enough pressure suits.* He knows we're trapped.

"Now then," Rött says. "Let's discuss the terms of your employment."

An iron-plated door slams closed behind us. I blink into the darkness and start as Cassia's cold hand grabs mine. Wherever we are, the air is thick with the stench of waste—feces, urine, and sweat. Rött and his men have taken my coat, the body armor, and my helmet, leaving me with only my pressure suit and boots. I squeeze back.

A shuffling scrape sounds in front of us. A dim yellow glow radiates from several slots in the wall on the far side of the room, sketching the outline of figures moving. I back into the door. I can feel them more than hear them—the heat and stench of unwashed bodies, the stuffy, twice-breathed air.

More shuffling. A cough. And then a voice from the darkness. *"Bienvenidos al infierno, niños."*

Rubio stiffens. *"Quien habla?"* He steps forward. "Show yourself."

"Ay, que es la voz de mi juventud." Something rough and greasy brushes the back of my hand and the voice speaks at my elbow. *"La hora viena. Ki ki ri ki! Ki ki ri ki!"*

"Papá." A woman's this time. "Stop with that rooster nonsense. Leave them alone."

"Déjenles." His voice turns sad. *"Déjenles solo. Solo. Solos. Solitos."*

"Who's there?" Rubio moves another step into the room. *"Quienes son?"*

"We're no one." A different man's voice. He coughs wetly. "And neither are you."

Cassia tugs at the sleeve of my deep suit. "We need a light."

"I don't—" Cassia tugs at my sleeve again, and I remember. My suit has tracking lights so I can be found if my tether should snap in space.

"Shield your eyes," I call out into the dark.

"Cobren sus ojos," Rubio repeats.

Two stark blue-white rods light up at my wrists, illuminating a mob of thirty or so people in a room far too small for them. They flinch away from the light, a gnarl of dirty limbs and matted hair. An old man steps into the circle of light, and I swallow a scream. Where his nose should be, there are only two holes, like a skull.

"Bienvenidos." He grips my hand, then Cassia's, then Rubio's. *"Bienvenidos."*

"G . . . gracias." Rubio's voice falters.

I look closer at the crowd. Some of them are missing ears, fingers. Some of them have burns and knife marks across their faces. Metal benches line the wall, and the floor slopes down to what looks like a drain in one corner.

Cassia peers into the faces. Suddenly, her hand tightens on my arm and a small noise escapes her throat.

"Nethanel." She rushes forward and falls to her knees beside one of the men. "Nethanel, it's me."

He looks up. Shock and recognition flit across his face. He throws his arms around her, and they rock together on the floor.

A murmur runs through the room. I step closer to Rubio. The ghost of my mother's hands are on my back, smoothing my hair, and my homesickness for her hits me like it never has before.

Finally Cassia and her brother draw apart, and then they are a flurry of hands, signing rapidly and silently. I pick out a few words—the symbols for *daughter* and *sick* and *ice*. Then Cassia waves a hand at Rubio and me and makes the sign for *friend*. Nethanel catches first my eyes, then Rubio's, and nods his thanks.

"That's the sister?" says the same woman who spoke to us in the dark.

I turn to her. Her dark hair is pulled back with a piece of string, her cheekbones hollow. Her skin was probably olive once, but has gone sallow, and dark circles droop beneath her eyes. She's thin—too thin—everywhere except for the odd bulge at her waist. It takes me a moment to piece together. She's pregnant.

Nethanel stands and waves her over, gathers her in with one arm, and signs to Cassia with his free hand.

Cassia turns back to Rubio and me, a half smile on her face.

I eye her. "What?"

"My brother says thank you for helping me find him. He and Aneley have been figuring out a plan to escape, but most of the people here are too weak." Her smile widens. "He wants to know if we can help."

We sit in a circle, those of us who are well enough to plan, while everyone else huddles against the wall, out of my lights' reach. There are ten of us: Nethanel, Aneley, Cassia, Rubio, me, and five other captives. The youngest is a skinny boy of twelve or thirteen who calls himself Pulga. The oldest is a woman around Soraya's age, Lisbeth. Aneley's father sits with us, too, but all he can do is rock back and forth and chant, *"La hora viene, la hora viene, la hora viene."*

Cassia translates for her brother, and Aneley repeats the words in Spanish for her father.

"Nethanel has the security codes for the control room. One of the guards thought he wouldn't understand and typed it in right in front of him." Cassia smiles conspiratorially at her brother. "Sometime in the next day or so, they'll come to take us to the diving transport, right at the entrance to the bay. There are never more than two guards, one at the front of the line, and one at the back. That's when we act."

"Put me at the front." Rubio scowls. "I'd like some quality time with these *putamadres.*"

Cassia looks at her brother. He nods and signs something to her.

"Good," she tells Rubio. "Nethanel wants to know if you can show everyone some basic defense moves. Ways to incapacitate someone."

"I can do that." Rubio nods. "But it would be better if we can get our hands on some weapons, too. Anything, a knife or even a rock . . ."

Aneley signals to Nethanel. He lifts the foot of one of the benches while she reaches down and pulls a handful of round, palm-sized shells with serrated edges from a hole in the floor.

I squint in the low light. "Are those . . ."

"Limpet shells." Aneley holds one up. "They grow on the sides of the ships. We've been collecting them whenever we're sent on a dive."

"Are those all you have?" Rubio nods at the stack in her hand.

"For now," Aneley says. "We've been sneaking them back a few at a time. If we carry too many, they'll notice." She glances nervously at the ceiling.

Nethanel signs to her, a swimming motion with his hand.

"We can get more, though," Aneley says. "The next time they take us out."

Rubio swallows. "If that's the best we have." I don't think I've ever seen him look scared before, not when we fought the *Dakait*, not when we faced down the harrow, not even when Rött captured us. He glances at me. "Kind of makes you wish we'd brought the cat along, huh?"

Nethanel signs to Cassia again. She looks down, silent for a moment, and then nods. My stomach tightens.

"There's one more thing." Her mouth wavers. "We aren't all going to make it. Someone has to stay behind and barricade themselves in the control room to open the air locks. The rest will run for diving transports. We'll need two to fit everyone, which means two pilots—"

"What about the *Mendicant*?" I interrupt. "Everyone could fit in there. And we'd only need one pilot, so if one of us who can fly didn't . . ." I stop and swallow the lump rising in my throat.

Cassia nods. "That would be less risky. But we still need someone for the control room."

"I'll do it." Lisbeth looks up from her lap, her face a map of pain.

The room falls silent.

"Are you sure?" I ask.

She looks at me. "How old are you, *mija*?"

"Sixteen," I say quietly.

She pats my knee. "My boy, he would be one year older than you if his oxygen line hadn't split down in the warmwater." She lifts her chin and surveys the rest of the circle. "I'm sure."

"If we make it, we fly back to the Tsukinos in Ny Kyoto." Cassia signs to her brother as she speaks. "From there, we figure out how to get you back to Milah."

I lean close to Aneley. "How did you two manage to figure out as much as you did?" I glance at Nethanel. "I mean, when you couldn't talk."

"We found a way." Aneley holds out her hand and traces an *S* on her palm. "I saw him the first time they took us all out to work. They thought he was simple, but I knew better. I could see it in his eyes."

She looks at him. "One of them kept . . . he was trying to touch me, and Nethanel . . . he let the winch he was turning slip. He looked right at me and let it go, even though he knew what they would do to him."

"They make you work?" I glance at her stomach and frown. "Even with . . ." I've taken only one reproductive biology course, but she must be at least five months along.

A mix of fear and fury crosses her face. She looks away from me, at the bolted door. Her jaw tightens. "Yes."

Pulga whips his head toward the door. *"Ya vienen."* He looks at me, panic all over his face. "The light."

No. Not yet. We need more time. Everyone scurries for the corners, a whisper of bare feet and ragged clothes. I reach for my sleeves and slap off the lights just in time. Our prison door swings open.

CHAPTER .25

They sort us into two lines, shouting and sparking the electric prods they carry. *They're only men*, I try to remind myself, but it's all I can do to stand my ground and not back against the wall.

"You." Juna, the lone female guard in the group, points at me. "You can swim?"

My stomach sinks, but I nod.

"Good. Fall in." She jerks her thumb to where Aneley and her father stand and turns to Cassia. "What about you, *tös*? Can you swim?"

"Of course I can." Cassia sounds brave enough, but underneath, I hear something that might be fear.

They march us down the corridor to the lift in two lines, Rubio and Nethanel in one, Cassia and me in the other. I catch Rubio's eye, and he shakes his head ever so slightly. *Not yet.* We need more time to go over the plan, and he needs time to teach us to fight. Whatever is at the end of this long walk, we have to live through it.

I clench my fists. I killed a harrow. I fought off a band of *dakait*. I walked into a witch's lair and saved us from poisoning. I survived a typhoon. These pieces of *tatti* aren't going to be the end of me.

Behind me, Cassia chokes down a whimper. I glance back, quick. Her face is green.

"What's wrong?" I whisper.

She shakes her head.

They herd us onto the lift, the same one Rött used to bring me down from the surface. I push us near the back, away from the guards, and bend my head toward hers. "What is it?"

"I lied." She looks at me, and her eyes are too big. "I don't know how to swim."

I swallow and wrap my hand around hers. "Stay close to me, okay? Don't let them split us up."

Then the doors are opening, and we're back on the main deck. Several guards watch us from the glassed-in control room overlooking the open hangar. My pulse jumps at the sight of the *Mendicant*. It's still there, its loading ramp open. But then we're shuffled past. The *dakait* push us onto different windowless shuttles, separating Cassia and me from Rubio and Nethanel. Low metal benches stretch along the walls of the shuttle's hold. The floor is an open sluice. I grip Cassia's hand harder as the loading door seals shut behind us.

"Maybe they have boards," she murmurs, eyes fixed on the floor.

I glance at the man standing guard. His eyes are flat and disinterested. I don't see any boards.

"Maybe." Even I don't think I sound convincing.

A grind and thump sound outside the hull, and we jostle into each other. The hum of the ship's engines deepens.

"She's away!" the pilot shouts back to our guard.

The guard grunts and pulls a bin from a compartment in the bulkhead, then hands it down to Aneley's father, sitting on the floor by his feet. The old man lifts out a pair of goggles, a headlamp, and a worn plastic sack with shaking hands, then passes the bin to the woman next to him. I take my own set and examine them. The goggles' elastic is frayed and a whorl of scratches clouds the lenses. Definitely no diving boards. I wrack my brain, trying to remember what I read about the Enceladan oceans. What is the water like? Freezing, like it was outside Ny Kyoto? Or boiling from the cryovolcano? Are there harrows here, too? I should have spent less time feeling sorry for myself and more time with the *Mendicant*'s data banks after we got back to the Tsukinos' spindle.

The shuttle engine slows.

"All up!" the guard barks.

We climb to our feet, and I catch Aneley's eye. "They have suits for us, right?"

She flicks a fearful look at the guard and shakes her head.

Of course they don't. They're about to send pregnant women and old men out into the dark sea to do . . . what?

I don't have time to ask. The guard passes around another container, this one full of unrendered cryatine. One by one, the captives dip into the bucket and coat their exposed hands and feet in the mixture. This is how they're going to send us out, then.

"Grove five. In position," the pilot shouts.

The guard opens a compartment built into the bulkhead, revealing several reels of clear plastic tubing, each the width of a garden hose and dozens of times as long. He pulls the end of one and passes it to Aneley's father. The old man fits it in his mouth.

I look at Lisbeth. *If his oxygen line hadn't split* . . . She nods.

Chaila. My hands start to sweat.

The guard taps a command into a keypad on the wall, and then pulls back a lever built into the floor plating. The cabin fills with a sucking, rushing sound. A whirling vortex of water and pressurized air appears where there was a section of floor a moment before. An air lock.

One by one, the others strap on their goggles and headlamps and line up. Cassia and I file in behind them. The guard hands each person a tube and hand chisel. And then they jump. The whirlpool spits as they disappear through it, spattering water across the walls. When my turn comes, I stop short, staring down past the vortex and into the darkness beyond. I can hear Cassia breathing fast and sharp behind me.

I can't do this. I can't do this.

The guard shoves an air hose at me. "You want air or not?"

I take the hose and a chisel, numb, and step up to the edge. I don't have a choice. *It's okay. Hydrostatic pressure is equal to gravitational pull times liquid density times depth times. Hydrostatic pressure . . .* But I can't seem to make my feet move any farther. I take a tiny step back.

Behind me, the guard sighs. He shoves me, and I fall.

Spray whips at my cheeks and hair. I nearly lose my

goggles but press them fast against my face and hold on to the air tube. The water hits me. Darkness and pressure. Cold. Cold, but not freezing. I take a deep, gasping breath through the hose and inhale a lungful of stale, mildewed air. I force myself not to cough and draw away. *Don't panic. Don't panic.* I have to get my bearings.

I fumble at the headlamp and switch it on. The beam doesn't penetrate far through the murk and debris, but several meters below me, I catch sight of the other divers' above the bubbling blackwater vents. Their air hoses trail behind them, leading back to the shuttle. It hovers above us, lights glowing in the salt water. For some reason, I think of angler fish.

Cassia plunges in behind me, thrashing and flailing. She screams—a long trail of bubbles streaming out of her mouth as she begins to sink under the weight of her own clothes. I kick hard and catch her breathing line before it can whip away. I grab her, thrust the tube back into her hands, and link her arm through mine. She coughs into the hose. I point at my feet, and she twitches her legs in a rough imitation of mine. We're still sinking, but it's slowly now, more controlled. I nod and flip on her headlamp.

We follow the others down to a flat space between the vents, the pressure tightening around us. I grip my air hose and glance back as we touch down on the shale seabed. There are dozens more blackwater vents here than in the waters outside Fru Rangnvaldsson's spindle. Salt and minerals thicken the water, making it difficult to see anything more than the lights on our fellow divers.

We push forward, our headlamps tracing out the few meters before us. It's all I can do to get enough air and keep us moving through the water. *Step, breathe, step, breathe.* The lights ahead of us stop. Suddenly my beam sweeps across something immense and white. *Harrow. Get back!*

But it doesn't move. I reach out and brush the whiteness with my fingertips. Hard and smooth, like a wall. I look up. The structure curves up as far as my beam can reach, stippled with dark spots.

No, not spots. Portholes.

A ship.

I look at Cassia, the words bursting in my throat. *A ship.* But then the full meaning of it descends on me. A ship like the *Ranganathan*, grown here. *Who do you think our best buyer is?*

Cassia tugs at me. I blink and tear my gaze away from the ship. Aneley stands a few meters away in the murk, waving us forward. We follow her around the ship's prow and climb through one of the lower portholes into a stripped-down version of one of the *Ranganathan*'s corridors. The walls to either side of us are thick and smooth, but the ceiling has yet to finish growing. I stare up into the ship's delicate inner scaffolding—translucent chains of nutrients that will grow into floors, service shafts, dining halls. For a moment, I forget why we're here. A wave of wonder rushes over me. Living on one of these ships, it's easy to forget what an elegant work of bioengineering they are—cascading chemical reactions between a keratin-compound base and the mineral-rich Enceladan seas. How many people have the chance to stand inside one while it's still growing, see it being born around them? But then reality comes rushing back, like all the weight of the sea above me. I'm not a scientist surveying the triumph of human endeavor. I'm trapped here, along with everyone else.

Aneley hands me a chisel and points to the others, chipping away at barnacles and limpets stuck to the ship's inner walls. Rage sucks away the last of my wonder.

We join them, prying the barnacles loose and shoving them into sacks. The limpets turn out to be the real challenge. Something about them feels more alive than the barnacles, and if we're not fast enough, they suction themselves to the wall with an unbreakable seal. I finally free one and toss it in the bag, but Aneley fishes it out and shakes her head at me. She slides the limpet in her pocket.

ALEXANDRA DUNCAN

Right. Weapons, or the closest thing we have to them. I can see how Nethanel's deafness wouldn't matter down here. His way of talking with his hands might even be a benefit.

I lose my grasp on time. Barnacles, bag. Limpets, Aneley. When her pockets are full, she points to Cassia. I try counting out minutes—*one one thousand, two one thousand*—but the numbers slip and jumble and my head feels heavy. I can't be getting enough oxygen.

A muffled shout breaks through my fog. I turn and see Lisbeth holding her hand, spotlighted by her headlamp. A bright red cloud billows from it. Everyone near her recoils. Aneley catches Lisbeth's breathing tube before it can snake away and pushes it back into the other woman's mouth. Lisbeth wheezes into it, her eyes popped wide with pain. A deep gash runs across her palm. Her chisel lies at her feet.

I swim to her and turn her hand so I can look more closely. A loose flap of skin lies over the laceration, gushing blood. It's cut all the way down to the bone. We need to staunch the bleeding and dress it before she loses too much blood. No one besides Aneley moves to help. Some of them are even wrapping up their chisels in their sacks and making for the porthole where we came in.

Aneley clenches her air hose in her teeth and rips off a piece of her shirt. We wrap it around Lisbeth's hand and tie it in place with the string from her hair, but a thin trace of blood still seeps out into the water. Lisbeth blinks slowly and leans against the wall. Aneley looks around and points up. *The shuttle.*

Her father shakes his head, but Aneley makes her hand into a claw and mimes it crawling, then points at Lisbeth's hand. The blood. Something in the water will come after the blood.

Aneley's father and the last of the others swim for the porthole where we entered. Aneley shakes Lisbeth's arm, but the older woman doesn't move. I shine my headlamp in her eyes. Her pupils don't shrink like they should. She's still breathing, but we don't have much time. Aneley slings one of Lisbeth's arms over her shoulders and gestures frantically for me to do the same.

We carry her through the porthole. The shuttle blinks, several dozen meters above us. Some of the other divers are no more than lights in the distance, already swimming for the air lock. Lisbeth's head droops, and I catch her air tube again, push it back into her mouth. What could be coming? Something worse than the tiger sharks that lurked beneath the Gyre's waste plain? Something worse than the harrow?

Someone tugs at the back of my suit. I whirl around. Cassia stares at me, eyes wide, and I remember. She can't swim. If I help carry Lisbeth up, who will help Cassia? How will she make it up to the shuttle?

Aneley looks back and forth between the two of us, anxiety written on her face. She jerks her head up at the distant lights. *Hurry.* I hold out a hand to Cassia. *Stay here.* Then I point to myself, up to the shuttle, and back to her. *I'll come back for you.* She nods and backs against the ship's hull.

Aneley and I push off, Lisbeth hanging between us. My leg muscles burn. The water feels thicker, somehow, and I take great gulps of sour air from the hose. I don't look up, just push and push and pray for buoyancy, and then we're there. The air lock swirls above our heads. Aneley and I shove Lisbeth into the vortex. Someone on the other side grabs her by the arms and pulls her through. Aneley ducks in after her.

For a moment, I'm alone, and the sea closes on my chest like a vise. I kick off into a dive. There's blood in the water, and something is coming.

This time there are no guiding lights to show me the ocean floor. Only darkness and cold all around. A shadow flickers on the edge of my headlamp's beam. My heart beats faster, and I don't fight it. I need all the adrenaline my body can make. Then the ship resolves into view, and there is Cassia, clinging to the porthole.

As I reach her, something moves along the seabed. Or rather, the seabed itself moves. I watch as an iridescent gray, crab-like creature scuttles into my headlamp's beam, followed by another, then another, then a tide of them rolling toward us. I bite back a scream. I grab Cassia's hand and launch myself back up. Cassia kicks, too, and we rise through the water. This time, I do look up at the ship's lights. We're still so slow, and I'm beginning to flag. Something flickers in the periphery of my vision. Cassia stops kicking. I look back. The creatures are piling on top of one another, rising up after us, impossibly fast. *Vaat.* The sound of hundreds of claws clicking over exoskeletons reaches through the water. I yank on Cassia's arm—*keep going*—and swim harder.

We're almost there. Twelve meters . . . nine . . . seven . . . five . . . Without warning, the air hose whips out of my mouth and retracts up into the shuttle, Cassia's flying after it. Cassia jerks and flails, and it is all I can do to hold on to her while my lungs tighten around the last thin breath I took from the tube. Black spots spackle my vision. We're lost. They've given us up for lost. I look down. The creatures rise below us, sharp-beaked mouths snapping as they climb on one another's backs.

Keep moving. My mother's voice reaches out of the

darkness to me. We are on the seaward side of the Gyre in a netted area cordoned off from passing sharks and flesh-eating squid. *One arm over the other.* She is in the water with me, only a few strokes away, but it feels so far. *I know you're tired, but you're almost to me,* ma chère. *Keep swimming.*

Light opens above me, and the sucking sound of the air lock. Cassia has stopped struggling. I wrap one hand around her wrist and thrust the other up into the vortex. Dry, rough fingers close around mine and haul both of us up and into the shuttle.

CHAPTER .26

When we return to the dock, the shuttle that took Rubio and Nethanel is nowhere to be seen. We're back early, and Lisbeth sports a newly split lip because of it.

"*Aho.*" Our guard spits into the drainage grates and glares at us. "You can all thank this useless *fitta* here for a longer dive tomorrow."

Lisbeth doesn't look up. She leans heavily on Aneley, clutching her shoulder with her good hand. Her makeshift bandage is soaked through, and her face has a gray pallor. She's lost a lot of blood.

The guards march us past the *Mendicant.* Cassia sinks her nails into my arm.

"What?" I whisper.

She nods at the *Mendicant.* Two men descend the loading ramp, deep in conversation. One of them leans against the door's pneumatic risers and points back into the ship's belly.

"Hurry up." Our guard shoves me from behind with his prod. "You want to go back in the water? You want me to throw you back to the *rovdjur* crabs?"

The electric shock sends a wave of cold fire through my body. I round on him, scowling, my hands clenched into fists.

"Whoa-ho!" He laughs. "Still feisty, are we, *lillflicka*?" He pulls a knife from his belt and slashes me across the cheekbone in one fluid movement.

My eyes water, and blood dribbles down my chin, but it's the shock and humiliation of it that stings the worst. I am a child again, hiding in the storage closet, choking on shame and rage.

"Up for some more fun?" He grins at me as if he hopes I'll say yes.

I wipe blood from my face and dart a look at the *Mendicant*. It's so close, mere meters away. But the shuttle carrying Nethanel and Rubio is nowhere in sight. I grit my teeth. Our freedom is a stone's throw away and a million light years at the same time.

"Come on, Mi." Cassia pulls me back into the line.

"Another time, then!" he calls after me, sliding the knife back into his belt. "I have my eye on you."

I walk with my head down, shaking, all the way back to the cell.

We wait in the darkness for the others to return. Lisbeth sleeps on one of the benches while Cassia, Aneley, and I huddle in a circle on the other side of the room, trying to stay warm. Cassia presses up next to me, shivering. I hesitate for a moment, and then lift my arm around her. At least I have the benefit of my pressure suit, even if my hair is damp. Everyone else is soaked through.

"How long until she's better?" Cassia whispers.

"I don't know." I touch my cheek gingerly. My own cut was shallow. It's already begun to crust over, but if I don't treat it, I'll have another scar for my collection. "She'll be weak for a day or two from the blood loss, but a wound that deep is going to take weeks to heal fully. If it doesn't get infected."

I look toward the open sewer drain. I can't make it out in the dark, but the smell is impossible to ignore. It will be a miracle if we manage to keep Lisbeth's cut clean.

Chaila. We have to get her out of here. All of us have to get out of here.

Aneley shifts in the darkness. "She won't be able to manage the security controls fast enough with only one hand." She keeps her voice low. It's what we've all been thinking, but Lisbeth doesn't need to hear it.

"I could do it," Aneley says.

"Aneley, no!" I say at the same moment Cassia utters a wordless cry. That's a death sentence. Or worse.

"Shhh." Aneley hushes us. "You'll wake her."

"But your baby . . . ," I whisper.

"My baby's good as dead already." Aneley's voice is thick. "I'm not going to let it grow up here."

"So it won't," Cassia says. "It can grow up out there." I can't see, but she must be gesturing at the far-off sky.

"Even then . . . who else would do it?" Aneley sounds tired.

Silence falls over us. A drop of water pats against the floor somewhere in the darkness. I know what I should say. I know what my mother would say if she were here. But I'm not my mother, and I can't make myself form the words. I want to get out of here. I want to stay alive.

"I will," Cassia says into the stillness.

"Cass . . ."

"No." Her voice wavers, but she pulls it under control. "Think about it. You, Rubio, and Nethanel are the only ones who can fly a ship, so we can't risk any of you. Lisbeth's hurt. Aneley's pregnant. Pulga's too young. I came out here to make sure Milah gets her father back, and that's what I'm going to do."

I feel as though the gravity has been yanked out from under me.

"You know that's not what Nethanel would want."

"That's why you're not going to tell him." A hard edge creeps into Cassia's tone. "Either of you."

I want to scream and cry and throw up all at the same time. How can Cassia do this? If she dies or, worse, stays trapped here . . . I can't think about it. Doesn't she know her life is worth as much as Nethanel's? Doesn't she know there's no trade, no finite price? That everyone loses if either of them is left here to die?

"Promise," Cassia says.

A thump sounds in the hallway. The door lock shrieks. We scatter and scuttle against the walls. Lisbeth raises her head and blinks into the sudden stab of light from the hallway.

Nethanel, Rubio, and the others from the second shuttle file in, damp and shivering. Cassia runs to Nethanel and throws her arms around him, followed close by Aneley.

He signs something quick before the door slams, taking the light with it.

I sink down against the wall. It doesn't do me any credit to admit it, but I'm glad Cassia argued against me being the one to stay behind. No one wants to be raped, beaten, killed—whatever is in store for those of us who don't make it onto the *Mendicant* and out of this spindle—and I'm no different. I'm not brave. I'm no hero. I press the heels of my hands into my eyes and try not to imagine those things happening to Cassia. What Rubio said about Ava and Soraya on the flight to Kazan Spindle bobs up in my mind. *Don't you think they need you to come back as much as Cassia and Milah need Nethanel? Don't you think they care just as much?* I think I see what he means now. My life or Cassia's, neither one gains more meaning if we give it up. A life—any life, every life—has value all on its own. We can't give up Cassia. I won't give up myself, not without a fight. There has to be another way.

The ship. The memory of those two men standing on the loading ramp flares up before me. Were they doing something to it? Fitting it with a tracking device or disabling it? If Rött believed me about the DSRI after all, if he thinks the ship could be used to trace us in any way, he'll want to dispose of it as soon as possible. Chop it up or sink the whole thing to the bottom of the ocean.

I stand. "Aneley?"

"Yes?"

"Is there any other way out of here that isn't monitored? Up to the dock, I mean?"

"It's solid all the way around." She bangs her fist against the nearest wall. "If there was a way, we'd have tried it already. Why? What do you have in mind?"

"*Clínico,*" Aneley's father mutters, somewhere behind her.

"Did you see Rött's men near our ship?" I say. "They had the loading ramp open. We don't want to escape and then find it's disabled or—"

"*Clínico!*" Aneley's father says louder. "*Clínico! Clínico! Clínico!*"

"All right, Papá." Aneley turns to him. "*Què es eso del clínico? Què quieres decir?*"

"*Hay un conducto de aire en el techo del clínico.*" The old man's voice shakes with urgency. "*Lo he visto. Lo he visto.*"

Aneley's eyes widen. "He says there's an air duct in the clinic. It might connect to the dock."

"I have to get up there and check the ship," I say.

"How?" Aneley says. "They only ever take us up that high to clean."

But even as the words are leaving her mouth, it comes to me. I turn to where Lisbeth lies in the darkness. If I can convince our captors she's worth saving, maybe I can save the rest of us, too.

○ ○ ○

We have been banging on the door for what feels like hours before the guards come.

One of them cracks open the door. "*Dou itta!* What in hell is all this racket?"

"Please." I do my best meek face and let all the fear building up in me flood my voice. "Lisbeth, she's worse. You have to do something for her."

He rolls his eyes, and I vow never to roll mine again. "No one's calling in a doctor. If she wanted to keep the hand, she shouldn't have been so careless." He shoves me back and starts to pull the door closed.

"Wait." I grab the door. "I'm a medic. I can take care of it myself, if you let me."

He pauses, considering.

"She's a good worker, isn't she?" I say. "Isn't she worth something to you?"

He raises an eyebrow and grunts. "Wait here."

The door slams. I pace, counting out the minutes. *Two, five, seven* . . . The lock slides back again, and Rött stands in the doorway, Juna and another guard a few paces behind him.

"A medic?" he says.

I nod.

"Come with me." He turns.

"But what about—"

"I said, *Come with me.*" I cast a helpless look at Lisbeth, and then hurry after him.

I try to memorize the twists and turns we take through the spindle. Up two levels by lift. A long hallway. Left turn. Short hallway. Right turn and then left again. We stop in front of a scuffed gray door. One of the guards punches a key code into the lock, and it slides open, revealing a jumble of boxes and vials on plain metal shelves and an exam table covered in cracked vinyl. The clinic? I glance around. There it is—a metal grate in the top left corner of the room.

Rött boosts himself up on the table, pulls his shirt over his head, and twists around. A huge, pus-filled cyst bubbles up on his back, purpling and swollen.

"You take care of this, you get some bandages for your careless friend," Rött says.

I glance at Juna. This could go wrong any number of ways. "I'll need some gloves."

She waves a hand at the chaos on the shelves. "Bound to be some in there."

I step around Rött and pick through the boxes. I find one latex glove, and then another. They're made for different-sized hands, but they'll have to do. There's no sink, so I scrub down my forearms with an ancient bottle of Betadine and snap on the gloves. I approach Rött's back.

"I'm going to touch it, okay?" Calm and confident. Like a doctor. No one wants to kill a doctor.

Rött grunts in agreement.

I press lightly against the lump, feeling its contours beneath the skin. "Does that hurt?"

"Of course it hurts," Rött snaps. "Dumb *fitta*."

I step back. "It looks like it's only a sebaceous cyst, but it's gotten infected. We'll have to excise it."

"What the hell does that mean?" Juna asks.

"I have to cut it open and drain it." I meet Rött's eye. "It's going to hurt, but afterward, it'll be a lot better."

"I got no problem with pain," Rött says. "Just get it out of me."

I nod. "Okay. I need some gauze, a scalpel, and a roll of skinknit."

The guards exchange looks. Juna lets out a humorless laugh. "A scalpel, huh? How stupid do you think we are?"

"Give it to her," Rött says through gritted teeth. He eyes me. "She knows what'll happen if she tries anything smart."

I nod. They find what I asked for, and I lay it out neatly on the exam table beside the Betadine. I wipe down Rött's back, then make a small X-shaped incision at the crown of the cyst. Blood and pus dribble out, along with a rank smell.

The male guard gags, and Rött glares at him.

"This is the part that's going to hurt," I say. I push against the base of the lump, and an oily, yellow-white curl of pus spouts from the incision. I wipe it away and bear down again.

"*Jävlar!*" Rött swallows a groan.

I press my lips together. *Good. I hope it hurts.*

I keep pushing until the pus turns pink with blood, and then runs red. I clean his back again, pack the wound, and tear off a strip of skinknit to cover the incision. When no one is looking, I pocket the rest of the roll.

Rött rolls his shoulder experimentally and pulls his shirt back on. "Good."

"You've got to keep it clean," I say. I try not to look at the duct. "It could come back, even if you're careful."

Rött scowls. "I'm not doing that again."

I pull off the gloves. "There's a steroid injection I could give you if it starts to come back, but . . ." I gesture at the mess on the shelves. *Who knows what's in here?*

"You'll clean it up, then. Find what you need." Rött slides off the table and works his shoulder again. "Juna, find her something to eat."

Juna raises her eyebrows.

"You heard me." Rött looks me over approvingly. "It's not often you catch something with an actual skill."

Juna glares at me but nods and leaves the room.

I swallow. "What about Lisbeth? I need to get back to her."

Rött snorts. "If you care so much, you can look in on her when you're done here."

He waves to the other guards, who file out after him, leaving me alone with a jumble of medical supplies, a wad of dirty gauze, and my passage to the *Mendicant*.

The air duct is barely wide enough for my shoulders, but I inch forward all the same. I had to wait for Juna to come back with a slice of dry white bread and an unidentifiable piece of smoked fish before I could risk the climb. I didn't want her to watch me eat, but she wouldn't leave unless I finished it, and besides, my stomach wouldn't stop groaning at me.

She leaned against the door as I chewed. "So you're Rött's pet now."

I didn't answer.

"Hmph." She narrowed her eyes and hit the door controls to let herself out. "Don't go thinking you're special, *tös*. Rött gets tired of all his pets eventually. What do you think happened with that Aneley girl?"

The horror on my face must have been enough to satisfy her, because she laughed and let the door slide shut behind her.

The duct branches in front of me, two equally dim paths. I close my eyes and try to remember as much of the spindle's layout as I can. The dock lies three levels above the cell where they keep all of us, with a direct entry from the lift. That means it should be one floor above me now, and somewhere to my left. I keep crawling, wincing every time a knee or elbow strikes the wall and sends a muted echo down the empty space before and behind me.

I come to a grate and peer through. Several of the guards lounge in chairs scattered around a table, tearing chunks from a loaf of bread and smearing it with some kind of green paste. A boxing dummy stands in the corner, my helmet shoved down over the stump where its head would be. Darts and knives protrude from its chest. *Chaila.* I move on, quiet as I can, until I reach a bend in the duct. It rises four meters straight up, and splits into two different passageways at the top.

"Vaat." When I was little, I used to brace my bare feet against the edges of the door frame in my bedroom and

scoot up to the top. Ava would tease me and say I must have gecko feet. But I'm heavier now, and I stopped climbing things for fun years ago.

I stand in the shaft, press my palms against the side of the duct, and hop up so I can plant my feet along the sides, too. The metal thunders as my feet crash into it. I stop dead. They must have heard that. I wait, but minutes pass and no one comes.

I inch up the shaft, bit by bit, my arms burning. Finally, I lever myself over the edge and slide into the next-level duct. I lie facedown, panting. I should never have stopped climbing doorways.

I pick myself up and continue crawling. The next grate reveals a room full of lockers, and then the control room overlooking the hangar, and finally, the dock, bright and buzzing with lights. Both shuttles sit dripping on their mooring pads, the *Mendicant* beside them, directly over one of the airlocks. Its loading ramp still hangs open. A small piece of luck in a gauntlet of terribleness. I'll have to dash across half the length of the fully lit hanger to reach our ship and pray no one is watching the entire time.

I hold my breath, listening. No sounds, no voices, only the buzz of the lights high above. I twist the tabs holding the grate in place and lower it to the floor as gently as I can. My hands are sweating, and I almost drop it. I peer out, left, then right. Still no one. I slither onto the bright, deserted dock and crouch by the wall. The lights are so loud. Everything is so loud. My heart. My breath. The rustle of my suit as I stand. *Now*, I tell myself. *It has to be now. Before someone comes.*

But my body won't move. I can't make myself start forward. I'm standing exposed in the midst of my enemy, and my blood is frozen. I'm in our storage closet at home in the Gyre, and I can't stop what's happening on the other side of the door. *They're watching you. They're waiting for you to move. They'll catch you.*

Go. You need to go. I hear my mother. *Climb, Miyole!*

I dash for the *Mendicant*.

One one thousand.

Two one thousand.

Three one thousand.

Four one thousand.

Five one thousand.

The loading ramp clatters under my feet and the dark, open berth swallows me up. I pause at the top, breathing hard. No one behind me. No one raising the alarm. I've made it, at least this far.

CHAPTER .27

The ship's auxiliary lights still glow along the floor, but I don't dare try to turn anything else on as I make my way to the cockpit. I keep one hand on the wall as I edge along. A strange feeling creeps over me, as if I've made this walk before, as if I know what I'm going to find.

I still let out a small gasp when I see it. The synaptic panels outside the cockpit itself have been gutted, fully and methodically. Where the wires and connectors once were, there are two empty, perfect squares cut into the wall. Someone has cracked open the casing over the control panel and left its mechanics exposed.

"No." The word comes out a whisper. I can't feel my feet, but somehow I'm moving forward into the cabin. I lay my hands over the exposed spacers and wires, as if that would somehow fix them. The jack that gave us the

Tsukinos' location lies in two pieces on the floor, next to a scattering of loose bolts. I know I told Aneley this is what I was afraid of, but I still can't believe I'm seeing it. They're breaking down the *Mendicant* for parts.

I sink down into the captain's chair and stare blindly out at the dock. I didn't think they would gut her so quickly. I thought . . . I don't know . . . that I could fix it, somehow. That I'd be able to reverse whatever they'd done. We were all supposed to leave together. No one stranded if one of the pilots was injured. I know we can fall back on the shuttles, but the risk doubles every time we split the group.

I tap the controls' tracking pad halfheartedly. Lights flicker on the right side of the console. I slide over to the copilot's chair and examine what we have left. Telemetry, pneumatics, and lighting. No connection to the engines. No air circulation. Nothing that will get us out of here.

A sudden movement catches my eye. Two men stride across the hangar, heading directly for the *Mendicant. Vaat.* I jump to my feet and shut down the controls. I turn to the holes gouged in the walls, and then back to the viewport. There's no time to make it out. I back against the bulkhead. I have to hide, but where?

The storage compartments. They'll have checked those for goods first thing, so maybe they won't go in there again.

Unless they've found the clinic empty and have come looking for me. There must be security eyes all throughout the spindle, but whether anyone has been watching their feeds is another question. I hurry down the corridor, swift and quiet, as footsteps thump the loading ramp.

". . . going to have to take a heat saw to the whole thing."

Chaila. I'm not going to make it to storage.

"At least we can use it for scrap. What's that saying about a gift horse? Never look it in the face, or something?"

I turn back. Not storage. Not the cockpit. Not the sleeping berth. The holes in the *Mendicant*'s walls are large enough for Tibbet to crawl inside, but not for a taller-than-average girl in a pressure suit.

One of the men laughs. "Your baba teach you that? I'll never figure out those old-world sayings."

A section of the floor buckles as I hurry past. Of course. The utility shaft where we hid from the *dakait*. If Rött's men are breaking down the ship, they're more likely to look in there, but they're almost on me. I'm out of other options.

I pull up the section of floor, jump down, and settle the panel back in place just as Rött's men enter the corridor. I press both hands over my mouth to muffle my breathing.

"I don't know why we can't get the hands up here to do it."

"*Che.* You really want them wielding heat saws?"

"Not the new ones. I mean the ones that are broke in already."

Hands . . . broke in . . . he must mean us. The people trapped in that lightless cell three levels below. Anger floods my bloodstream. I want to bash their heads against the wall. I want to watch them bleed out slowly.

"He won't want to risk letting them out until all that official traffic passes by. One of them gets loose and starts running its mouth, it makes it hard for those government types to turn a blind eye."

A snort. "I'd like to see them hack it here for a year. They'd do the same as us."

Government types? Official traffic? Someone important is in orbit above Enceladus. Someone who would look bad if they were seen to let slavers slide. *Shore leave,* I suddenly remember. The *Ranganathan.* Could it be them? I calculate the timing in my head. Four weeks in transit at the *Ranganathan*'s slower speed . . . it could be. They're due to stop here. It's possible. Probable, even. And if I can reach them . . . the *Ranganathan*'s brig is definitely preferable to this.

Doubt creeps into my chest. Even if it is them, the DSRI isn't interested in looking past the surface at Rangnvaldsson's. Why should they look here? They buy ships from Rött, or at least from the people Rött sells to. He said as much.

"*Jalvar.*" One of the guards spits. "Bunch of hypocrites don't want to hear about how their own sausage is made."

I look at the wires and ports all around me. The signal dampener Rubio and I put in place at the beginning of our journey is still there. I could remove it. Maybe that was part of what disrupted our long-range coms when we plugged in the jack from the drop sphere. If I pull out the dampener, I could repair them, given enough time. Maybe. If the dampener was the problem. If Rött's men leave me alone long enough. I wish Rubio were here. I may be able to fix people, but he's much better at machines.

"You still want those chairs?" one of the men above me asks.

"*Säkerligen*, I want 'em. Better than what we have up in the control room now." Their footsteps retreat in the direction of the cockpit.

I let out a breath. They can take anything from the cockpit they want, as long as it doesn't further disable the coms.

I lie on my back and work my fingernails under the plate that covers the signal controls. I always thought the nail-strengthening pastes the other girls at Revati painted on were vain, but now I wish I had some. Better yet, a knife. Or a magnetic lever. I move the plate enough to fit my fingers inside. One of my fingernails cracks, but I swallow my yelp of pain and suck the blood away. Almost there.

The plate falls loose on my chest, revealing the signal readout and the dampening frame, a white plastic square fitted in the place where the amplifier should go. Our signal is nothing but a blue line fizzling along the bottom of the readout's auditory range.

I hesitate. What if this is all for nothing? What if the *Ranganathan* isn't up there at all? What if I send out a distress pulse and they ignore it? They wouldn't send fighters after the *dakait* ship when Nethanel was kidnapped right before their eyes. Why should they send anyone to respond to an anonymous signal? It will only be a matter of time before Rött and his men figure out the *Mendicant* is transmitting. And even if I make it back through the ducts to the clinic before they figure out I'm missing, they'll have to blame someone. They'll lock us down even tighter, and we'll lose any chance we had to take the shuttles.

A screech tears through the quiet, followed by a clatter and thump of something falling over. *Chairs.* That must have been one of the seats in the cockpit being pulled from the floor.

Tears blur my eyes, but I wipe them away.

"Manman," I whisper. "What do I do?"

You don't have to make up your mind now, some deep, quiet part of my brain answers. *You don't even know if you can fix the long-range coms. Better to give yourself as many options as you can and then see what happens.*

I pull the dampening frame from its fittings. At once, the signal readout jumps—not the clean, pretty line we'd need to transmit words or data to the *Ranganathan,* but enough power to send out the distress pulse DSRI ships use when they're in danger. If I can get back to the cockpit to see if the long-range transmitter is working and program the pulse.

The screech of the other chair pulling loose echoes through the ship, followed by muted voices.

". . . heavier than it looks."

"You get this one and I'll take the other."

A long, sharp squeal resonates in my teeth—the chairs being dragged. They screech toward me, then over the utility shaft. I press my hands over my ears and clench my jaw. One passes, then the other. They rumble down the loading ramp and hit the dock with a metallic *clang*. I wait, listening. A high-pitched whine cuts under my hearing, but nothing else.

I sit up and push the floor panel away. The corridor is empty. I make my way to the cockpit, soft-footed as I can. It looks bigger without the pilot seats. The two guards have made it across the dock and are pulling the chairs up to the dock-side control room. I stand above the console, wavering. Maybe I should go back while I still can. Rött's men surely haven't figured out I'm missing from the clinic, or they wouldn't be wandering around talking about furnishings. Nethanel and Aneley's plan for the shuttles is a surer thing.

But it's also a sure thing that at least one of us will be left behind. If they aren't letting us out again until whoever is up there is gone, that means days, maybe a week, cramped in utter darkness. How long does Lisbeth have? How long until Rött's men get bored and beat one of us, or cut off a nose, or do to one of us what they've done to Aneley?

It's a risk either way. I wish Cassia and the others were here to tell me which way to go, but they aren't. I have to decide, here and now. If I'm wrong, if it isn't the *Ranganathan*, we'll pay when Rött and his men find out.

My stomach turns. Is this how my *manman* felt when she aimed that gun at the man on our floor? How my mother's and my people felt all those many years ago when they were deciding whether to fight for their freedom or bide their time? How does anyone ever know what's right? Or do they simply jump and pray it was the right decision?

I look down at the console and then back out through the viewport at Rött's men positioning the *Mendicant*'s seats in the control room. I imagine Rött's hands on Cassia, the look Aneley has in Cassia's eye. I can't know. I may never know.

I power up the controls.

CHAPTER .28

The coms readout springs to life. I turn down the receiver volume and open an outside channel. Nothing. I bump up the volume. A low, thin hum fills the air, but nothing else. None of the traffic chatter I should be hearing, no call signatures registering. Cold sweat prickles on my forehead. I look across the dock to the control room. One of the *Dakait* is laughing, reclining in his stolen chair. *It doesn't mean anything.* The transmitter could still work, even if the long-range receiver is out.

I duck under the console. Our captors haven't gutted the coms system, so at least there's that. I open the *Mendicant*'s ancient systems management interface and pull up communications diagnostics. The receiving line is red, but the transmitter's is green. It should work. I only have to program it to send the DSRI's unique distress sequence.

I pop my head up and check on the *dakait*. Still in the control room. No one new on the hangar floor. I change the coms to pulse mode and set the pitch and frequency, open it to all receivers. Rött's men might pick it up, too, but I don't know the *Ranganathan's* call signature by heart, so it's a risk I'll have to take. *Please be up there. Please hear us.*

I switch back to diagnostics and hold my breath. The transmitter line spikes. Spikes again. Green. It works. We can't receive anything in return, and I don't know how long it will hold out, but for the moment, it works. For few seconds, I let myself imagine escaping, what I would do if I got out. Hug Soraya again, the way I used to when I was a little girl, and Ava and Rushil, too. Go visit New Gyre, like Ava is always trying to get me to do. See if it's anything like my childhood home . . .

Enough. I can't let myself dive too deep into that fantasy. I program the distress burst to repeat and look in on the *dakait* again. One of them is drinking something. The other has his feet up. Time to go.

I kneel in the shadow of the *Mendicant's* loading ramp. It's only a matter of time now, whether the *Ranganathan* sends someone for us, or Rött and his men discover the transmission. I have to get back to the others and tell them. We have to be ready.

Twenty-odd meters of well-lit open space lie between me and the duct. How long will it take to run that far and pull the grate back into place? Ten seconds? Fifteen? The men up in the control room could look out at any time. Even if they don't catch me, they could still raise the alarm. But the longer I wait, the more I risk Juna or Rött noticing I'm gone. My chances for making it back to the others decrease exponentially with every minute.

I run full tilt for the open duct—*Don't look. Don't look. Don't look.* I stop short at the wall and spend a few precious seconds maneuvering myself into the duct feetfirst. My knee thuds against the side as I wiggle backward on my stomach. I freeze. *Vaat.*

The electronic hush of the control-room door opening fills the silence.

"What was that? Did you hear knocking?"

I pick up the grate with shaking fingers and fit it into the opening. The tabs lock back in place with a whisper of a scrape. I wince. *Not here, not here. Don't look here.*

"I don't hear anything. Maybe the lift?"

"No, it was over this way." Footsteps on the stairs, moving closer.

"You hearing ghosts now?" The other man follows him. "You shouldn't listen to Njord. His head's up his ass."

"*Skit på dig.* I thought . . ." One of the men's legs comes into view through the grate. I squeeze my eyes shut.

"There's nothing here." The second man.

"Yeah . . ." Doubt still hangs on the first man's voice.

I open my eyes.

"I'm telling you, it's the lift."

"Yeah, the lift. Or we've got rats again, maybe."

The first man laughs. "You know what that means. Rat fricassee time."

The other joins in. "Rat sausage."

"Rat pie."

I crawl backward, shaking. The sound of their laughter fades as I go. The way back is easier than the way up, especially dropping down the shaft between floors. I brace my hands and feet against the sides again and use them to slow my descent so I don't crash into the bottom. I move silently past the room with the lockers and the one with the dummy wearing my helmet.

At last I reach the clinic and peer out through the grate. The room looks exactly as I left it. A few bread crumbs on the exam table, and disorder reigning on the shelves.

I land on the floor, reattach the grate, and then bend over and let out a deep breath. It feels so good, the breath turns into a laugh, and then I'm laughing so hard I can barely breathe. It bubbles out of me—all the tension and silence—coming and coming until it hurts so much my eyes water. Nothing is funny and I ache down to the center of my breastbone, but I can't stop. One time when I was little, I ate some spoiled butter and couldn't stop throwing up until it was all out of me. This feels the same. As if my body won't stop until everything is gone.

I put the loose gloves and rolls of skinknit away, and organize the bottles of pills and serums. Where is Juna? Is she watching me, waiting for me to finish? But she can't be, or else she would have seen the empty room and sent everyone in the spindle looking for me. I find boxes of sutures, another of swabs. More Betadine and, better still, antibacterial skin glue. I pocket a tube of it and wipe down the shelves.

Are they coming back for me? Rött said they would. He said I could tend to Lisbeth when I was done. *He also kidnapped everyone down in the cell and held a gun to your temple,* my own voice answers. *Why would he tell the truth about anything?*

I rub my scars. They can't leave me here alone in the clinic indefinitely. Can they? The image of Rött meeting Commander Dhar, claiming nothing is wrong and the *Mendicant* is only a malfunctioning piece of scrap, plays behind my eyes. All of us left here. Living under Rött's hand. Dying here.

My throat closes. I was willing to give up my lab, my spot in the DSRI, but my whole life? I never truly thought before now that we might fail. I knew we could, in theory, but I never believed it was a real possibility until this moment. In my mind, we rescued Nethanel and I found another way to live, another way to use my skills. I got the chance to show Cassia Mumbai's beaches and gardens. I got the chance to know what she's really like, not the frightened, vengeful side of her. I got to tell her all my hopes and memories. My eyes burn. Who will remember my mother when I'm gone? Who will remember the Gyre, or the stories my mother told me about Haiti? They'll die with me in a dingy clinic on an ice moon.

I bang my fist on the door. "Juna!"

No one answers.

I bang again, harder. "Juna, please!"

Still silence.

I hit the door with both fists. "Please, let me out!" My vision blurs and I pound faster. "Juna, anyone, please!"

Juna bursts into the room. "What's going on in here?" She takes in the shelves and my tear-streaked face. "What in *helvete* is wrong with you?"

I drive my fingernails into my palms. I need to stop crying, but I can't.

Juna slaps me, then grabs me by the back of the neck and shakes me. "Shut up! I said *shut up!*"

"I thought you were leaving me here," I choke out.

Juna's face reads half disgust, half alarm. I've clearly gone mad. "You want to go back to your hole? Is that what you want?"

I don't dare nod. No one in her right mind would ask to leave the relative comfort of the clinic for our dank, cold cell.

"Lisbeth . . . ," I say through dry lips. Surely she remembers.

Juna rolls her eyes. "Still on about her?"

I say nothing.

She presses her lips into a line. "Fine." She keeps her grip firm on my neck and pushes me out of the room, down the lift, and back to the cell where the other captives wait. *Thank you, thank you,* I think, even though her hand is hurting me. She pulls open the door and shoves me in, then quickly pushes it shut behind me. I land on my knees, winded and bruised, but back where I need to be.

"Mi?" Cassia runs to my side. "What happened? Are you all right?"

"I'm okay." I wave her away and turn on my suit's lights. "I'm fine. No one hurt me."

Rubio hurries to us, Aneley and Nethanel crowding in behind him. "What happened? Did you make it to the ship? Is it still fit to fly?"

I stop laughing and swallow hard. "Yes, I made it. And no. They've started scrapping the ship. The only things that were working were the lights and our long-range—"

Rubio groans.

Nethanel taps Cassia's shoulder and signs to her. "It's okay," she translates for the rest of us. "We still have the shuttles to fall back on, right?"

"We do . . ."

"See?" Cassia says. "It's back to the old plan, that's all. It can still work."

"The thing is . . ." I hesitate.

The others turn to me.

"I heard them talking. I think there's a chance the *Ranganathan*'s in orbit above us."

"What's that?" Aneley looks from me to Nethanel.

"It's our DSRI ship," Rubio says. "The one that tried to chase those *dakait* away." He looks at Nethanel. "I'm sorry we didn't get there in time."

Nethanel shakes his head.

I clear my throat. "You should know . . . I . . . um . . . I did something."

Silence seizes the room. The others exchange tense looks.

"I would have asked you, but there wasn't time. I thought . . ."

"What did you do?" Aneley asks.

"I got the *Mendicant*'s coms working," I say. "Not completely, but a little bit. Enough to send a distress pulse."

Silence stretches out between us, until it's nearly too taut to bear.

Rubio stares at me, disbelief on his face. "Are you saying . . . the *Ranganathan*'s coming for us?"

Cassia and Nethanel begin signing furiously to each other.

"Maybe," I say.

"What do you mean, *maybe*?" Cassia says.

"I don't know for certain it's them. And even if it is, I don't know if they'll come." I look at Nethanel. "They wouldn't authorize us to come after your brother."

"But they might?" Aneley's voice rises with excitement. She turns to me. "Rött wouldn't fight a government ship."

Rubio shakes his head. "One distress pulse. They might miss it altogether."

"That's why I programmed it to transmit on a loop," I say.

Silence again. Rubio points up. "You mean it's still going?"

I nod.

Rubio pushes away from the floor. *"Maldito sea."*

"What?" Aneley asks. "What is it?"

"They're going to find it, that's what." Rubio scowls. "Rött and his boys. They're still taking apart the ship. Don't you think they'll notice?"

"What?" Aneley sounds as if the breath has been knocked out of her.

"Miyole, why?" Cassia looks stricken.

"I had to risk it." I look at Cassia, willing her to understand. *I did it for you. I didn't want you left here alone. I didn't want you to sacrifice yourself.*

"Oh, god." Aneley stands. "They're going to kill us. They're going to kill us before anyone finds us."

Nethanel jumps up and pulls her close, shaking his head.

"You don't know." She looks at me, eyes wild. "You don't know what they're capable of."

"But we can fight them." The certainty I had standing over the *Mendicant*'s console falters. "We just have to hold them off long enough—"

"You said yourself they might not come," Cassia says.

"They wouldn't send anyone after the *dakait*. Why would they come now? If it's even them!"

Rubio frowns at her. "We chased them away when your ship was under attack. You keep forgetting."

"If it's right in front of them," I say. "If they can't ignore it—"

Aneley's father cuts me off with a cry. *"Ki ki ri ki! Ki ki ri ki!"*

A moment of silence follows his outburst, and in it, I hear something that turns my blood cold. The rumble of boots approaching.

Rubio motions for us to back away from the door and throws himself flat against the wall beside it. I kill my suit's lights. Being accustomed to the darkness might be our only advantage.

The door bursts open. Rubio hooks his foot around the first guard's ankle and sends him sprawling. The guard's electric prod skitters across the wet floor. Cassia scoops it up and runs at the next man through the door, screaming. Nethanel follows her, and then Aneley, wielding limpet-shell shards in each hand. One of the guards swings his prod at Nethanel, who dodges and elbows the man in the ribs. Aneley stabs wildly at the same guard's shoulders, misses, and sinks one shell into his neck. He cries out—a wet sound—and clamps a hand to his neck, dropping his prod.

I dive for it, but Pulga reaches it first. He snatches it and stabs it into the next guard's foot. Electricity runs up his leg, snapping and arcing across the metal findings in his boots. The man convulses, eyes rolled back in his head, and collapses just inside the door. A claxon blares from the hallway, so deafening I can feel it pulsing through my eyes. Nethanel doesn't falter, though. He delivers a solid hit across one guard's jaw and barrels into another, knocking both of them into the hall. One of the guards in the hallway raises his prod to slam Nethanel, but Cassia is there with her own. She catches the guard in the chest.

"Come on!" Rubio screams.

I run for the door, but then I remember—*Lisbeth*. The older woman has pushed herself off the bench and is working her way to the door with one hand out against the wall to steady her steps.

"Go on," she says. Her face is drawn with pain. "I'll catch up."

"No, you won't." I grip her around the ribs and drape her injured arm over my shoulders. Blood has soaked all the way through her makeshift bandage. I remember the roll of skinknit in my pocket, but there's no time now.

We hurry to the hallway with the others. The guards litter our path. Some of them are bloody. Some of them are dead. Maybe this should bother me, but it doesn't. I don't have time to feel anything, especially for them. I grab a discarded prod and step over one last body.

Rubio, Cassia, Nethanel, and Aneley lead us down the corridor. We should be running, but the most some of the captives can manage is a quick, shuffling walk. Lisbeth and I draw closer to the front. We stop in front of the lifts. Cassia reaches for the call button, but Rubio catches her hand.

"Not that way. We'll be trapped."

"There's no other way up to the dock," Cassia argues. "How else are we going to get out?"

Nethanel tugs at her sleeve. He points down the corridor that branches off to the right and makes a stair-climbing motion with his forefingers.

"An access stair?" She raises her eyebrows.

He nods.

We hurry down the corridor, passing empty rooms with no doors. What was this place built to be? The beginnings of a city like Ny Kyoto? A research outpost? Whatever it was, I doubt it was this. We come to the stair.

"Access code?" Cassia whispers, signing to Nethanel as she speaks.

Nine three two four, he responds, and I realize what she's doing. Getting the keypad lock codes, preparing to stay behind, without him ever knowing.

Cassia activates the door, and we file in, Rubio in the lead. Lisbeth looks up at the flights rising above us and knits her brows.

"I've got you." I tighten my grip on her. "We'll make it, okay?"

Rubio reaches the first landing. He stops, a hand held out to the rest of us, his head cocked, listening. He jerks as if he's been shocked.

"Back!" he says in a hoarse whisper, waving his arms at us and hurrying down the steps. "Go back!"

A murmur of fear runs through the group. Some freeze in place, while others try to jumble through the narrow doorway.

Aneley wades in. "One at a time," she murmurs, touching people's shoulders, steering them to the door. "Keep moving. One at a time."

But now I hear what Rubio heard. Footsteps pounding down the stairs.

I look around, heart battering at my chest. We had surprise on our side before, but now our captors know we're loose, and only a few of us are fit to run, much less fight. I pull Lisbeth down into the wedge of darkness beneath the stairs. Pulga crawls in after us.

Aneley has shepherded almost everyone through the door, leaving Cassia, Rubio, and a few stragglers, when the first pair of boots hits the landing above us. Rubio whirls around and pushes Cassia behind him.

"Stop right there!" Juna's voice rings through the stairwell.

I crawl forward and peek out between the railing. Juna descends the stairs one step at a time, five other guards close behind her. Each of them carries a slug rifle. I pull my head back into the shadows and try not to breathe too loudly.

"You little *skitstövels* are going to pay for this." Juna steps down from the last stair. "You think you've seen blood, but you haven't seen nothing."

Rubio's eyes flicker to me and then back to Juna. I feel the weight of the prod in my hand. I know what he wants me to do.

Rubio raises his hands, buying time. "We only did what you would have done."

"We fed you, gave you a place to live." Juna takes another step. "This is how you repay us?"

My *manman*'s voice runs through my head. *Your people saw the chance for freedom and took it.* Sweat slicks my hand.

I wipe it on my suit, grip the prod, and slide out from beneath the stairs.

Juna starts to turn. I jab the prod up, through the stair rails, into the hollow at the back of her knee. She cries out and drops, her body jerking. The other guards open fire. Rubio falls back on Cassia, and screaming fills the hall outside the stairwell.

I pull the prod from Juna's body. One of the other guards wheels on me and fires just as something wrenches me back beneath the stairs. I scramble against the wall next to Lisbeth, breathing hard. Pulga. He looks at me, pupils wide, and then darts out into the fray.

"No!" I scramble after him and try to snatch the edge of his shirt, but he's gone.

Rubio has crawled forward and found Juna's gun. He fires up the stairs, knocking one of the guards back against the wall. Pulga rushes another, screaming, and plunges his weapon into the man's sternum. The remaining guards return fire. Pulga's body spasms. He tips backward and his head hits the bottom step with a sickening *crack*.

The air sucks from the stairwell. I stumble to my feet, ears ringing.

A primal sound rises from the survivors, something between a scream and a moan. Unearthly, anguished. It is in my mouth and my blood and bones. I am that sound and everyone making it.

Cassia charges forward, shouting, wordless. We surge after her, mounting the stairs, engulfing the last three guards in a wave. I strike out with the prod, and one of them drops. Fists clutching limpet shells rise and fall and screams of pain and rage twist together until all that's left is the smell of blood and my own breath, harsh and fast in my ears.

I patch up the wounded as quickly as I can. Tourniquets for the worst wounds, skinknit for the lesser ones. For the dead, there's nothing we can do but to leave them where they fell. More guards could be on us any minute.

Eighteen of us continue up. Thirteen lie on the stairs. I've bound Lisbeth's hand properly, but she's still shaky from blood loss. The others support the wounded as we make our slow, painful way up the spindle. Cassia and Rubio head the group, while Nethanel and Aneley bring up the rear. The alarm still bleats overhead, but my brain has stopped processing the sound.

We stop inside the door that leads to the dock.

"Everyone with a weapon to the front," Rubio says. "There's no telling how many of them are on the other side."

I hand Lisbeth to another woman, Belen, and make my way to the front.

Rubio gives me a crooked grin. "You want to go first, Miyole? You're pretty badass with that prod."

Rubio. Trying to joke, even now. But the smile doesn't reach his eyes, and something about it breaks my heart. I swallow the lump in my throat. "After you."

He presses his back against the door and nods. I push down on the activation pad. The door slides away and Rubio enters firing. Cassia, Nethanel, Aneley, and I charge in after him, our weapons held high.

We've run several meters before I realize no one is trying to stop us. No one is fighting back. The last of Rubio's shots trails off in an echo. The dock is empty, except for the shuttles and the *Mendicant*'s shell.

"Where are they?" I say, breathless. We've killed a few of the guards, but some of the others were only injured, and we haven't seen Rött at all. Something isn't right.

"Does it matter?" Cassia says. "They're not here."

"Everyone keep sharp." Rubio backs toward the shuttles, scanning the room. "Be ready."

Cassia catches my arm. "Make sure he stays on the shuttle, okay?" Her eyes go to Nethanel, walking quickly, hand in hand with Aneley. "Try to keep him distracted."

I stop. "What?" And then I see the control room, and I remember. I failed. The *Ranganathan* hasn't sent anyone, if they were ever there in the first place. And now Cassia is going to give herself up.

"You shouldn't have to do this," I say.

Cassia looks tired. "Who else is going to do it?"

"I don't know, maybe . . ." I look around at the knot of survivors making their way to the shuttles. But this isn't the kind of thing you make someone else do. Someone has to volunteer.

"This is how it has to be, Mi," she says. "Trust me. Remember?"

A knot forms in my throat. I do remember. *Don't stay here*, I still want to say. *Don't give yourself up.* But my lungs have a choke hold on themselves.

"Right," I manage.

"Go on." She lifts her chin at the waiting shuttles. "They need you. Steer them out of here."

I turn away, eyes burning. Cassia's right. They need me. And if I get out, I can find someone who cares about what's happening at Kazan Spindle and all the other dirty corners beneath Enceladus's ice. Someone will come for her. If she's still alive. If she isn't broken like Aneley's father.

I fight the urge to look back as I walk toward the others.

Nethanel hasn't noticed yet, but Aneley gives me a sad nod. *This is how it has to be.*

Behind her, Rubio tries to activate his shuttle's door. It doesn't open. He catches my eye, frowns, and tries again.

A flash of orange flares across the dock. The sound hits me—a squeal and bang like trains colliding. Something shoves me. I don't remember falling, but I'm on my back staring up at the tracks of lights in the rafters and I taste blood. I raise my hand—it's streaming from my nose. *What happened?* I push myself up. My ears whine, and a cloud of black smoke spreads over the remains of the shuttle Rubio was standing beside. Time slows and tunnels.

"No!" I feel the words in my throat, but all I can hear is the buzz in my ears.

Nethanel, Aneley, and the rest of their group crouch near the second shuttle, their eyes wide with shock. Aneley raises a hand to cover her mouth. There are bodies on the floor next to the wreckage of the first shuttle.

Behind them, the door to the remaining shuttle opens. Rött and seven of his men step out into the clearing smoke, smiling at the destruction.

CHAPTER .29

Someone seizes my arm. I wrench free and turn to fight, but it's only Cassia. Her mouth forms words I can't hear.

I shake my head. "Rubio!" I try to say, but she pulls me up the steps to the control room.

Something whiffs by my shoulder. I look up. Rött and four of his guards stand on the dock, pointing slug rifles at Nethanel, Aneley, and the other survivors. Another kneels beside them, his weapon trained on Cassia and me.

Cassia says something. I can hear the urgency in her voice, but her words come to me muffled, as if I'm underwater. She bends close to the keypad lock.

A bullet embeds itself in the wall behind us. Cassia flinches, but the door slides open at last. We tumble inside as shots ricochet off the control room's protective glass. Cassia throws herself into one of the *Mendicant*'s chairs and starts tapping at the control panels.

I lie on the floor, dazed. Rubio's body floats before my eyes. Is he alive? If I could have checked his vitals . . . But he was too close to the blast. If he did survive, there's no way he has long to live. My chest tightens, and tears well in my eyes. If we were aboard the *Ranganathan*, maybe they could fix him. If we were anywhere else, we could at least try.

I pull myself to my feet and stare out at the dock through the glass walls. One of the bullets has left a cloudy spiderweb pattern where it struck. Rött and his remaining men have what's left of our group kneeling on the floor beside the remaining shuttle, hands folded behind their heads. He points his gun at the closest woman's head— Belen—and shouts something. I scan the controls and flip the intercom on.

Rött's voice fills the small room. I can barely make out the words through the buzzing in my ears. "I'm giving you thirty seconds to come out."

I wet my lips. They taste like blood. "You'll kill us."

"Not if you come out now," he says. "But if you decide to stay in there, I'm going to have to take it out on your friends here."

I glance at Cassia. She shakes her head and looks deliberately at the controls. What is she trying to tell me? I move closer to look over her shoulder.

"Time's up." Rött looks down at Belen kneeling beside him, smiles at her, and pulls the trigger.

My hands fly up over my eyes and I scream. When I pull my fingers away, Belen lies slumped on the floor at his feet.

Rött holds my eyes and walks to the next person in line. Aneley.

"Wait . . ."

Aneley turns to me and shakes her head slowly. *Don't come out.*

But what else are we going to do? We can stay in here until we starve to death and all our friends are dead, or we can go out now and take our one chance to save them.

"Miyole," Cassia whispers. She points to the spindle's telemetry readout. Someone is landing far above us on the ice, their signal strong and clear. A DSRI signature.

"We . . . we're coming." I tell Rött. "Please, don't shoot her. We're coming, okay?"

I look at Cassia and nod ever so slightly. She taps a command into the system, freeing access to the spindle's lift.

"Now," Rött says, raising his rifle to Aneley's head.

"Yes." I raise my hands and walk to the door, one foot in front of another.

"The other girl, too."

Cassia rises slowly from the controls and raises her hands as well. She casts one look back at the telemetry readout and moves to my side. Time. We need time. Only a few minutes for whoever the *Ranganathan* has sent to reach the lift and make it down to us.

I open the door. One foot in front of the other. *Time.* Rött's guards grab us at the bottom of the stairs and march us across the hangar. I glance at Rubio, but I can't tell if his chest is rising and falling ever so slightly or if it's only my brain trying to deny his utter stillness.

The guards shove us down beside the others kneeling on the floor.

Rött paces in front of us. "I thought we had an understanding." He stops and holds a hand out to the bodies lying next to the ruined shuttle. "You see what happens when you try to go against me?"

I look away.

"Now the question is, why would you do such a thing?" Rött slings his rifle back over his shoulder. "Some of you have never given me any problems before. You don't want to cause trouble. You know what kind of lesson I'd have to teach you then. Someone's been putting ideas in your head."

Rött's gaze pauses on me for a second before landing on Cassia. He steps closer to her. "Someone new. Someone who hasn't been properly broken in."

I glance at the lift doors. *Please, hurry.*

Rött stands in front of her. "Now the question is, do I try to break her in right, or is it more trouble than it's worth?"

Cassia glares at him silently.

Rött flexes his fingers around the rifle barrel. "My uncle always said you don't keep a rabid animal in the pack. It'll infect the others." He swings the rifle down so it points at Cassia's head and fingers the trigger. "I'm thinking maybe that's good advice here."

Nethanel tries to lunge for Cassia, but Aneley wraps her arms around him and holds him back.

"Stop!" I jump up. I don't know what I mean to do. All I know is we need a few more minutes. Only a little more time.

A hand lands on my shoulder, and one of the guards behind me shoves me back down.

Rött smirks. "Do we have an objection, *kurai tös?*"

"It . . . it wasn't her," I say.

"Oh?" Rött raises an eyebrow and sweeps a hand at Belen's body. "What, are you going to tell me it was her idea, then?"

"No." My mind scrambles for anything that will buy us more time. "It was me," I say. I'm valuable. I'm a medic. I have to hope that means enough to keep everyone alive a few more minutes. "I'm the one who put them up to it."

"No!" Cassia shoots a fierce glare at me. "Shut up, Mi."

"Enough!" Rött shouts. "You both want to die? Is that it?"

I stare at Cassia, willing her to back down. *Let me take the blame. They won't kill me. Let me buy us the time we need.* I glance at the lift door again, doubt swimming in my stomach. Where are they? They should be here by now.

"Fine," Rött says. "Let's see who'll go first."

He points a finger at Cassia, then me, and alternates between us with each syllable, taking his time. "*Chu, chu, ta, ka . . .*" He lands on her and smiles, cold as the ice above us. "*Nochu.* You first, *lillflicka.*"

"Wait!" I scream, but one of the guards is dragging me forward by the hair.

Rött pulls Cassia out of the line and shoves her down beside me. We kneel, facing the others. Cassia and

Nethanel stare at each other. His neck is taut and his eyes glimmer with tears. Aneley holds him tighter, her eyes squeezed shut, mouth moving silently.

"I want all of you to see this," Rött tells them. "And be grateful it isn't you."

I look at the lift doors again. Doubt gives way to dread. They need to come now.

Cassia looks at me. *I'm sorry*, she signs.

"Don't—" I start to say, but my voice gives out. Instead, I make a sign she taught me all those weeks ago under our cocoon of blankets: *I love you.*

Rött cocks his rifle and levels it at Cassia's head.

I reach for her hand.

Metal scrapes behind me, and something thunks and rolls across the dock. Rött's eyes go wide.

A metal canister rolls to a stop between us and the bombed-out shuttle. For a moment, it lies silent, and then it clicks and spews white smoke into the air.

"*Kör!*" Rött shouts. "We're breached! Get down!"

He and the other guards bolt for the control room, but the smoke spreads too fast. It engulfs them in white mist. Rött staggers in the center of it, and the guards begin to drop, first one, then another, barely visible through the fog. A chemical taste spreads on my tongue. Bitter. My head swims.

Someone pushes me flat on the floor. I twist around, trying to summon the will to keep fighting, but then I recognize Nethanel. He pushes Cassia to the floor, too, and lies down next to us. The smoke is thinner here. I make out Rött's boots through the fog as he stumbles and then falls. The soles of his shoes are black like a fish eye and the smoke rolls like waves—cold, bitter water lapping over me.

"Stay awake, Mi." Cassia shakes me. "Breathe through your clothes." She stretches the neck of her shirt up over her nose.

But my suit doesn't give that way. The smoke thickens around us. The last things I see before the darkness closes in on me are a bright blue pinpoint of light floating in the fog and a shadow bending over me.

CHAPTER .30

I'm cold. I am falling through the sea, down and down. Down to my mother's bones. I don't dare breathe, because my lungs will fill with salt water and I'll sink faster. But it's too hard. I can't fight forever. I take a shallow breath, expecting the burn and the panic, expecting to drown. Instead my lungs fill with sweet, soft air.

My eyes flutter open. Everything around me is a gentle blue, not the wild dark of an icy sea. Something covers my mouth and nose. An oxygen mask. I try to pull it away and realize someone has my hand. I blink through the blurs in my vision. Cassia.

"You're awake." Relief floods her voice.

I tug down the mask. "What happened?" But even as I say the words, my memory clicks together. The smoke. The light bobbing toward me. We aren't dead, which can only mean one thing. Someone must have come for us after all.

Cassia places the oxygen mask gently back over my face. "They said you have to keep that on. Your people pulled us out. We're back on your ship. In the medical deck."

The light keeps changing, and I realize it's the far wall, playing images of flowers on a loop—frangipani, ginger lily, larkspur, jasmine.

"Nethanel says thank you. He's with Milah." Cassia smiles at me.

I breathe deep. I'm so tired. Maybe I could close my eyes again, only for a little while.

I come awake sharply. "Rubio?"

"He . . ." Her face is unreadable. "They have him down the hall."

I stare at her, uncomprehending, and then the words begin to sink in. "He's okay? He's not dead?"

She presses her lips together. "They're still working on him."

"But he's alive?" I try to sit up, and a sharp pain in my arm lets me know I'm hooked up to an IV. "Can I see him?"

Cassia eases me back onto the bed. "We'll know more in a few hours. Just rest for now, okay?"

I drop my head against the pillows. "You have to tell me, all right? As soon as you hear something?"

"I promise," she says. "If you promise to sleep."

I close my eyes. *Sweet juice by the levee, bare feet on the sand, swinging hands . . .*

The last thing I feel before I lose consciousness is Cassia's soft hand on my forehead.

When I wake again, I'm alone in the blue room. And thirsty. So thirsty. I pull off the oxygen mask, withdraw my own IV, and ease my bare feet onto the floor. A carafe of water sits on the small table at the foot of my bed. I drink the whole thing straight from the jar as I watch the wall cycle through its flowers, and then hug myself, suddenly cold. Where is everyone? Where is Cassia?

I tug on a blue robe hanging next to my bed and pad down the corridor, checking the data sheets on each door for Rubio's name. I find him twelve rooms down from my own.

Name: Hayden Rubio

Age: 19

Condition: Critical but stable

I sigh in relief and scan the rest of the sheet, stopping on the procedural codes. They had to replace his kidneys, and he's scheduled for surgery again next week for . . .

I scroll down and cover my mouth. Guilt over-whelms me.

. . . skin grafts and bionic replacement of his left arm and both legs below the knee. I place the data sheet back in its slot and close my eyes. *This is my fault. If I had tried harder to keep Cassia from dragging him aboard when we escaped. If I had let him get away on Ceres or convinced him to stay behind with the Tsukinos. If he didn't care about me at all* . . .

I flee back to my room, climb into bed, and pull the thin blanket over my head. I thought I was doing the right thing. Or maybe not the right thing, but the best thing I could. I thought I was only risking myself, but it was more than that. I was risking Rubio. I was risking what's left of Haiti and the Gyre, stored away in my memory. I was risking all the people whose history would be lost if I died without passing their stories on. I used to think my life only mattered for what it might become someday, for how I could use it, trade it, not for what it has been all along. I was wrong.

"Specialist Guiteau?"

I sit up in bed. Commander Dhar stands in the doorway, shoulders squared and her hands clasped behind her back.

"Commander." I hug my robe tight around me, not sure what else to say.

"I've been told you asked to see Mr. Rubio."

My throat is dry. "I . . ." I swallow. "If I can. Yes."

"Follow me." She turns on her heel without waiting to see if I'll move from the bed.

As I trail her down the hall, I catch a glimpse of myself in the mirrored glass outside one of the exam rooms and realize what a wreck I am. Red eyes underlined with bags. Uncombed hair. Ashen skin.

Commander Dhar stops in front of Rubio's room and swipes her thumb across the door's controls. I follow her in. Rubio lies on the bed, deep asleep, his head slightly elevated. An intubation line sprouts from the side of his mouth. His eyelids look thin and purple. From where I stand, I can't see his left arm, but the bedcovers lie flat where his legs should be.

I step closer. A tingling sensation runs over my skin—sanitizing nanobots scrubbing away any bacteria I carry. I want to reach out, take his hand, but he's so deep under I don't think he would feel it. It would make only me feel better, and I don't think I deserve to feel better.

"Rubio." I choke. "I didn't mean for . . ."

Commander Dhar's hand closes on my shoulder.

I look at her. "Is he going to be all right? Can he . . . Will he be able to fly again?"

"Maybe. We'll have to wait and see. The doctors say he'll need six months or so for his body to adapt to his new limbs."

I bite my lip. "And after that?"

Commander Dhar shakes her head. "It depends on how strong his neural connections are. If they don't atrophy, then maybe, after a while. He might regain enough fine motor control."

I turn away. I don't want to look at Rubio's broken body. I knew I would have to face the consequences of running off with Cassia eventually. I just didn't know they were going to be this.

"He'll be taken care of, naturally," Commander Dhar says. "Full DSRI pension. A lifetime of medical care, if he needs it."

I shake my head. That's not what he wanted. He wanted to fly.

A moment of silence passes. We both stare at Rubio, watching his chest rise and fall as the ventilator pumps air into his lungs in waves.

"This is my fault," I say.

"Why would you say that?" Commander Dhar sounds genuinely curious.

"I helped Cassia. I went along with it. I should have found a way to get him back—"

"I've seen the feed records," Commander Dhar interrupts. "It's the correction board's view that you weren't the instigator. Mr. Rubio had multiple opportunities to return to us in the interim."

I wince. *Correction board.* "It doesn't matter," I say. "If I had been next to that shuttle instead of him—"

"Don't say that."

I look away.

"Specialist." Commander Dhar's voice sharpens. "You're not to say that. It was the *dakait* who did this to him. Not you."

I watch Rubio's chest rise and fall with the compression of the ventilator pump.

"There are honorable things other than sacrifice," the commander says quietly. "Surviving. Living. Those are honorable, too. Sometimes that's the harder path."

Climb, Miyole! My *manman* stands at the bottom of the ladder. Her ship fights through the wind and slanting rain, its lights piercing the gray. To find me.

"Come with me," Commander Dhar says suddenly.

I follow her down the corridor to a small, windowless lift I never knew existed.

She swipes her thumb across the keypad, and for an instant, her face cracks into a small smile. "Senior officers' lift."

We ride down to the commander's office, a small, valve-shaped room filled with a broad bronze desk and white chairs. Antique compasses and telescopes line the natural ridge that slopes up the wall. I eye the ridge uneasily. It reminds me too much that this ship was grown and not built. And of where I now know it was grown.

"Please, sit." Commander Dhar holds out a hand to one of the chairs.

I do.

The commander takes a chair across from me, on the other side of the desk. We stare at each other. Half of me wants to apologize for what I did, to ask about the correctional hearing and beg for clemency. But in the other half, my blood is rising. Commander Dhar is right. It was the *dakait* who caused all of this, but who let the *dakait* run free? Who bought ships from them and helped them prosper? Who was willing to turn a blind eye as long as it wasn't one of their own suffering?

"We've debriefed Ms. Kaldero." Commander Dhar breaks the silence. "Is there anything you want to say for yourself?"

I squirm in my chair. There is something I want to say, but not for myself.

"Did you know?" I ask finally.

Commander Dhar blinks. "Know?"

"Where the ships come from," I say.

Commander Dhar pauses before she answers, and then laces her fingers together, leans forward, and looks me in the eye. "We had every assurance from our distributor that our ships were sourced from fair-wage and indenture facilities."

I frown. "But didn't anyone check? Didn't anyone want to make sure?"

Commander Dhar looks away and presses her lips together, as if considering the chart on her wall showing the *Ranganathan*'s progress through the system. So many moons and planets. So many colonies and outposts. What else does the DSRI not want to know?

"Specialist, you can rest assured that the DSRI will rigorously investigate any future ship purchases," she finally says.

"That's brilliant," I say, not really meaning it. "But what about the people being held captive? What about the false indentures at Rangnvaldsson's? There have to be hundreds more places like the ones we found."

"Yes." Commander Dhar clears her throat. Her eyes stray to an old star chart hanging on the wall in a gilded frame. "You'll be happy to hear Rangnvaldsson Keramik has been ordered to turn over its records for a full audit."

"So Petya and all of them, they're free now?"

Commander Dhar nods. "Yes."

"And you'll help root out the others? You'll send in rescue teams like you did for us?"

Commander Dhar hesitates. "We can only be responsible for our own actions, Specialist." She gives me a tired look. "The DSRI isn't a police force. And the politics of this situation are complicated."

"How is it complicated?" My voice rises. "Is it legal to own slaves on Enceladus?"

"No, but—"

"Then why can't you do something?" Tears of frustration spring to my eyes. "Or tell someone who can do something?"

The commander furrows her brow. "I've read your record, Specialist Guiteau. You're young. Maybe too young to understand. This isn't only about what the DSRI wants. It's about Enceladan sovereignty."

"It's about human beings," I shoot back. "It's about human sovereignty."

Commander Dhar stares down at her desk. "You're tired, Specialist. You've been through quite an ordeal. I think perhaps some more rest might be in order." She taps her desk com. "Might we have an escort for Ms. Guiteau?"

Two wellness orderlies appear at the door. I glare back at Commander Dhar as they lead me away. There's nothing more to say.

CHAPTER .31

My door opens only from the outside. Once a day, the orderlies escort me down the hall to David and his origami cranes, and then let me stop to look in on Rubio on my way back. His color looks better and he's off the ventilator, but still too drugged to hear me say *I'm sorry*. I ask for Cassia, but she doesn't come. Or maybe my messages never reach her.

They bring me meals. I eat them but don't taste them. I watch the flowers fading in and out on my wall until I've memorized the order of their rotation. I sleep. I sleep more.

And then one night I wake to the soft *bong* and hush of air as my door slides open.

I roll over. Commander Dhar stands in the entryway, holding a book.

"What do you want?" I sit up.

"Just to talk." She gestures to the foot of the bed. "May I?"

I swallow. "Okay."

"You know." She lays the book down on the bed, next to me. "I read your notes on the pollinator project."

"Oh?" I glance down. Is that what she brought me?

"You were right about the solution being a genetic one." She nods at the book. "I think you'll be glad to hear your subjects are thriving now."

"Oh." I don't know what else to say. I'm glad the pollinators are doing well, but being right about them doesn't matter now. All of that feels like another life.

"You're a good scientist, Ms. Guiteau." Commander Dhar smiles at me. "No matter what else might be said about you."

I stare at her. "Is that what you came to tell me? In the middle of the night?"

"No." The commander meets my eye. "I want your opinion on a delicate matter."

"My opinion?" I raise an eyebrow.

"What if—" She stops.

I look at her sharply. "What if what?"

"There are people on Enceladus who hate what's happening as much as you and I do, correct?" She folds her hands and examines them.

I eye her. "Yes . . ."

She looks up at me. "What if I were to tell you the DSRI allocates a certain amount of disposable income for each mission to be dispensed at the commander's discretion?"

I frown and clear my throat. "How much are we talking about?"

"Enough to fund a freelance team of Enceladans interested in shutting down slavers and investigating indenture fraud."

I don't say anything, so she goes on. "It wouldn't fix everything, but it would be a start."

"Are you asking me to be part of that team?" I say.

"Oh, no!" She laughs, sudden and sharp. "I'm afraid your recent misadventure makes that impossible."

"Am I going to be taken to the correctional board?"

"You would be." She picks up the book and taps it to life. "Only it seems the DSRI made quite the mistake allowing you on board in the first place."

"Oh?" My stomach flutters.

Commander Dhar pins me with a look. "How old are you, Specialist?"

"Eight—" I catch the quirk at the corner of her mouth and stop. What's the use in lying at this point? "Sixteen."

The commander nods. "We can't subject a minor to a correctional hearing, can we?"

"No?" I say.

"No," she agrees. "But we do have a duty to send her home."

"Home?" A lump rises in my throat.

"We've already sent word to your guardian and arranged for your transport," Commander Dhar says.

"When . . . when do I leave?" I ask.

"As soon as our orbital positioning window is open," Commander Dhar says. "Two days."

"Two days?" I repeat. "Will Rubio . . . I mean . . ."

"We don't know yet." Commander Dhar gives me a sympathetic frown. "We'll see."

The flowers fade in and out—daylily, blue vanda, tea rose, champa.

Commander Dhar clears her throat. "In another five years, the DSRI will be preparing for another mission. You'll be, what? Twenty-one?"

I nod. I can't really imagine myself that age. It doesn't feel possible, even if the math says so. Twenty-one sounds so grown up.

"Well," Commander Dhar says. "I, for one, would be glad to see you reapply for another DSRI mission when that time comes. Under my command, of course. And with the understanding that you don't steal any more shuttles."

I look at her, cautious. "Really?"

"Really." The commander stands. "You don't give up, Specialist Guiteau. And even if I can't say so in my official report, I admire that."

They finally let Cassia visit me the next morning. She comes bringing news of Rubio, and also bringing Tibbet.

"They stopped to meet with the Tsukinos after they raided Rangnvaldsson's," she says as she drops the cat on the bed next to me. "Commander Dhar wanted me along since I know them. Like an ambassador."

"Hello, Stink Beast," I say to Tibbet. He butts me with his head and rumbles deep in his throat.

"Rubio's awake," Cassia says. "He opened his eyes this morning. His body's accepting the limb grafts."

I look up from scratching Tibbet under his chin. "Have you been to see him?"

Cassia nods. "He asked about you."

"Yeah?"

"Yeah. He wanted me to tell you he always wanted a biomechanical skeleton anyway."

A short, shocked laugh bursts out of me, quickly replaced by a prickle in my eyes. I shake my head and wipe at them with the back of my hand. "Rubio."

Cassia traces a circle on the bed. "What are you going to do when you're back home?"

"I don't know. Be in trouble with Soraya forever?"

She laughs. "After that."

I hook my finger around hers. "I know I want to go back and see what's rebuilt in the Gyre. But the rest . . . I thought you might want to come with me."

"Mi . . ."

"I know you'd be away from your family, but it wouldn't be forever," I rush on. "Only until I'm eighteen, and then we can go wherever we want."

"Miyole."

"You said you shouldn't be with anyone while Nethanel was missing, but now that everything's going to be calm again—"

"Miyole." Cassia leans forward and clasps my arms. "I can't."

I stop. A small vacuum opens up inside me. "Why . . . why not?" I search her face.

Cassia pauses. She looks down and wets her lips. "Commander Dhar, she told me about her plan. She asked if I wanted to put together a liberation team on Enceladus."

"Oh," I say softly. The one thing I can't do. The one thing I can't ask her not to do.

"I just . . . I have to do this. I can't let them keep doing what they did to Nethanel and Aneley and all the rest."

"I want to go with you," I say. "We never got a chance—"

Her face crumples. "Don't, Mi. This is already too hard."

My mind whirrs, trying to figure out a loophole. Some way to stay together. Some way to get out of being sent away from her.

"I could break out of here. We could run away again."

Cassia and I stare at each other for a moment and then burst out laughing. I rock forward. In the history of spectacularly bad ideas, that has to be the worst.

Cassia sobers first. "But then how would there be a liberation team? Commander Dhar is the one paying for it."

My laughter dries up. I bury my head in my hands. She's right. I don't want her to be, but she is.

In the silence, she moves beside me on the hospital bed and wraps an arm around me. I lean my head against her shoulder. She leans her head against mine, and I close my eyes. I want to feel her skin, the warmth of her, the soft waves of her hair against my shoulder, for as long as I can. I want to kiss her and memorize the pattern of her freckles. I want more time to learn the real her.

"We'll find each other," she says quietly. "When all of this is done, we'll find each other again."

I pick up my head so I can look at her. "Promise?"

"I promise." She presses her forehead against mine.

Our lips come together. I kiss her and kiss her and hold back my tears because I don't want her last memory of me to taste like sadness. I kiss her because I don't know how long it will be before each of us finishes what she has to do. I kiss her because this is how it has to be.

EPILOGUE

"Steady," Ava says. "Stay low enough to keep out of the gusts."

"I'm on it." I sit in the pilot's seat of Ava's sloop, squinting against the harsh Pacific sunshine. A small flotilla appears on the horizon, ships and pontoons linked together in the beginnings of an enclave. Beyond them, acres of plastic and debris float on the ocean's surface.

"Is that it?" I glance at Ava, sitting in the copilot's seat. She nods. "That's New Gyre."

I turn back to the shimmering sun and watch the ships growing as we make our approach. A flock of gulls circles one of the masts. "Do you think it'll be anything like the old one?"

"Maybe yes, maybe no." Ava frowns. "Have you changed your mind?"

"No," I say. Our hold is full of medical supplies—vaccines, antibiotics, splints, painkillers, and skinknit. I'll set up shop here, and in a month's time, Ava will be back with more of what I need. I won't save the world, but I'll break off my own small piece. I'll see that cuts don't become gangrenous, that broken limbs can heal, that pain doesn't accompany the birth of a child or mar a man's last days. I'll do what I can.

I look up at the blue, blue sky through the viewport. Somewhere out there, Cassia is making people whole again, and here I'll do the same.

We land on the traders' docks. They aren't on the seaward-facing side, where they were so many years ago before the storm, but something about them tickles my memory. The air smells like salt and home. If I close my eyes, I can see my *manman* waving to me from the roof of our old house. I can see Kai racing over the footbridges and the boats going out at dawn. I will pay the price of living and remember. I will remember and I will heal.

I open my eyes. High above the rooftops and gently swaying masts, a red kite soars in the breeze.

ACKNOWLEDGMENTS

First and foremost, many thanks to my husband, Jeremy, for encouraging me, understanding when I was terrible about cleaning the cats' litter box while on deadline, and re-reading this manuscript more times than I thought was humanly possible You are my favorite human and my best friend.

Also, a huge thank-you goes to my editor, Virginia, and everyone at Greenwillow Books, including Preeti Chibber and Gina Rizzo. Thank you for continuing to push me and challenge me to be a better writer with every draft, and for all of your encouragement and support. Thanks as well to my agent, Kate Testerman, who confirmed my suspicion that Miyole needed her own story and who cheered me on, along the way.

My mother, Leslie Golden, consulted with me on medical aspects of the book, and for that, I am incredibly grateful. Any factual errors or liberties taken with medical science are my own. She is also the person who taught me to live with compassion and showed me how to stand up for what I believe in, even if I was afraid. Mom, you are an incredible woman.

The inimitable Stephanie Perkins, Megan Shepherd, and super-librarian Lauren Biehl have my thanks for serving as first readers and cheerleaders. There would be no book without you guys. Thanks as well to Nathan Ballingrud, Meagan Spooner, Beth Revis, Alan and Wendi Gratz, and all the writers at Bat Cave and the Chocolate Lounge. You are the reason I am still sane.

Finally, thank you to all my colleagues and to the patrons in the Buncombe County Public Library system. Your support along this crazy writing journey has meant the world to me, even if I can't help turning bright red and hiding behind the circulation desk when you talk to me about it. Just know that is my introverted way of saying thank you.